THE CITY
OF
EMBER
DELUXE EDITION

The Books of Ember

THE CITY OF EMBER
THE PEOPLE OF SPARKS
THE PROPHET OF YONWOOD
THE DIAMOND OF DARKHOLD

THE CITY

OF

EMBER

DELUXE EDITION

the first Book of Ember

JEANNE DuPRAU

RANDOM HOUSE 🏠 NEW YORK

The poster art consists of an image of the original cover of *The City of Ember*, designed by Chris Riely, and an image by Niklas Asker from *The City of Ember: The Graphic Novel*, copyright © 2012 by Niklas Asker. The image from *The City of Ember: The Graphic Novel* is used by permission of the illustrator.

Explore Ember at BooksofEmber.com!

Visit us on the Web! randomhouse.com/kids

Educators and librarians, for a variety of teaching tools, visit us at
RHTeachersLibrarians.com

The Library of Congress has cataloged the non-deluxe edition of this work as follows:
DuPrau, Jeanne.
The city of Ember / by Jeanne DuPrau.
p. cm.
Summary: In the year 241, twelve-year-old Lina trades jobs on Assignment Day
to be a messenger, to run to new places in her beloved but decaying city,
perhaps even to glimpse Unknown Regions.
[1. Fantasy.] I. Title. PZ7.D927 Ci 2003 [Fic]—dc21 2002010239

Deluxe edition ISBN 978-0-385-37135-3 (pbk.) — ISBN 978-0-385-37136-0 (ebook)

Cover design and map by Chris Riely

Printed in the United States of America   10 9 8
First Deluxe Edition 2013

Contents

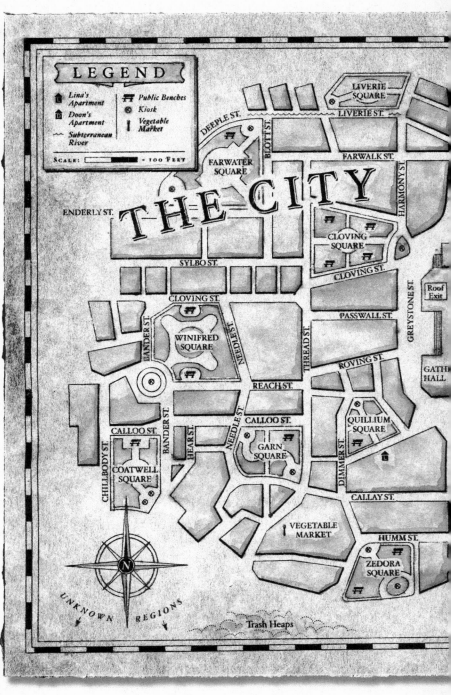

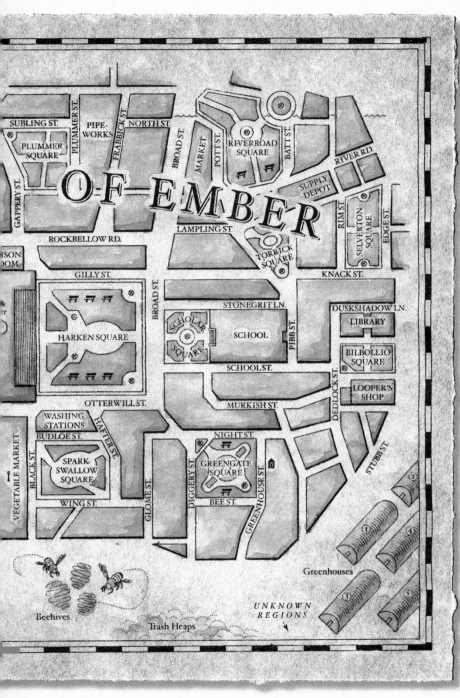

Introduction to the Deluxe Edition

Dear Readers,

Many years ago, the image of a city appeared in my mind—a city that was only a faltering spot of light in a vast darkness. I hadn't been thinking about cities, especially, or about darkness. This image, which felt intriguing and powerful, came as a surprise. As it turned out, it was the first in a long series of surprises that marked the story of *The City of Ember*—both the writing of the book and its progress in the world.

I was about halfway through the first draft of *The City of Ember* when I came across another surprise. I discovered to my chagrin that writing a novel was far harder than I'd expected it to be. Over the course of my life I'd read thousands of novels. Shouldn't I know how to write one? I wondered. But I struggled with *The City of Ember* for years before I finally got it right. I still have ancient drafts of it at the bottom of my closet. There's a version in which the mayor has a wife. There's one with a long section that takes place in the storerooms. Many of the characters have different names in these early versions. Doon, for instance, was once named Willet. Sometimes, as I wrote and crossed out what I'd written and rewrote time and again, I wasn't sure I'd ever make it to the end.

But I did, and then came the next surprise, which I liked much better than the previous one. I'd always known that it wasn't easy to get a book published. Even writers who had gone on to become famous often received piles of rejections before the acceptance finally came. But I had the great good fortune to find, almost right away, an agent who liked my book. Then she found an editor who liked it, too, and that agent and that editor have been a joy to work with ever since.

More surprises followed. There happened to be an artistic genius at Random House just at the time my book needed a cover. He designed the glowing light bulb with the wire that spelled out "ember." It is dark but still faintly glimmering, like the city itself.

The book came out in 2003, and it soon found an audience, one which was different in some ways from what I'd expected. When I'd imagined boys and girls reading *The City of Ember*, I'd pictured them sitting at home nestled in an armchair, with a lamp beaming down and rain falling in a cozy way outside. I certainly hope that happens. But—surprise!—kids also read *Ember* in schools. To this day I get letters from whole classes that have read it. I also hear from schools that stage an Ember Day, with a lottery and jobs and science projects in which kids make generators. Like Doon in *The City of Ember,* students are learning to find ingenious solutions to their world's problems; like Lina, they're exercising their imaginations and thinking about the future.

Then there was the movie. That was a *staggering* surprise. I got to see my city through someone else's eyes. While it wasn't my vision of Ember, it was a strange and fascinating vision of its own. Bill Murray made a delightfully sleazy mayor!

And of course there are the three other Ember books. You might not think they'd be a surprise— hadn't I had them in mind from the beginning? The answer is no. I hadn't planned on writing them at all. I was going to say goodbye to Lina and Doon and Poppy up there in the hills above Ember, by themselves, looking out on the beautiful world, and leave what happened next to the reader's imagination. But the story had an unexpected pull on me. Somehow, it demanded to keep going.

Now there's the graphic novel, drawn by an artist whose vision is so close to my own that he almost seems to have visited Ember and gotten to know its streets and buildings and people. How did he manage that? Once again—I'm astonished.

Best of all is that so many readers, of all ages and in all different countries, have loved the story of Ember. What more could a writer want? That has been a truly wonderful way to be surprised.

Most gratefully yours,
Jeanne DuPrau

THE CITY

OF

EMBER

DELUXE EDITION

The Instructions

When the city of Ember was just built and not yet inhabited, the chief builder and the assistant builder, both of them weary, sat down to speak of the future.

"They must not leave the city for at least two hundred years," said the chief builder. "Or perhaps two hundred and twenty."

"Is that long enough?" asked his assistant.

"It should be. We can't know for sure."

"And when the time comes," said the assistant, "how will they know what to do?"

"We'll provide them with instructions, of course," the chief builder replied.

"But who will keep the instructions? Who can we trust to keep them safe and secret all that time?"

"The mayor of the city will keep the instructions," said the chief builder. "We'll put them in a box with a timed lock, set to open on the proper date."

"And will we tell the mayor what's in the box?" the assistant asked.

"No, just that it's information they won't need and must not see until the box opens of its own accord."

"So the first mayor will pass the box to the next mayor, and that one to the next, and so on down through the years, all of them keeping it secret, all that time?"

"What else can we do?" asked the chief builder. "Nothing about this endeavor is certain. There may be no one left in the city by then or no safe place for them to come back to."

So the first mayor of Ember was given the box, told to guard it carefully, and solemnly sworn to secrecy. When she grew old, and her time as mayor was up, she explained about the box to her successor, who also kept the secret carefully, as did the next mayor. Things went as planned for many years. But the seventh mayor of Ember was less honorable than the ones who'd come before him, and more desperate. He was ill—he had the coughing sickness that was common in the city then—and he thought the box might hold a secret that would save his life. He took it from its hiding place in the basement of the Gathering Hall and brought it home with him, where he attacked it with a hammer.

But his strength was failing by then. All he managed to do was dent the lid a little. And before he could return the box to its official hiding place or tell his successor about it, he died. The box ended up at the back of a closet, shoved behind some old bags and bundles. There it sat, unnoticed, year after year, until its time arrived, and the lock quietly clicked open.

CHAPTER 1

Assignment Day

In the city of Ember, the sky was always dark. The only light came from great flood lamps mounted on the buildings and at the tops of poles in the middle of the larger squares. When the lights were on, they cast a yellowish glow over the streets; people walking by threw long shadows that shortened and then stretched out again. When the lights were off, as they were between nine at night and six in the morning, the city was so dark that people might as well have been wearing blindfolds.

Sometimes darkness fell in the middle of the day. The city of Ember was old, and everything in it, including the power lines, was in need of repair. So now and then the lights would flicker and go out. These were terrible moments for the people of Ember. As they came to a halt in the middle of the street or stood stock-still in their houses, afraid to move in the

4

utter blackness, they were reminded of something they preferred not to think about: that someday the lights of the city might go out and never come back on.

But most of the time life proceeded as it always had. Grown people did their work, and younger people, until they reached the age of twelve, went to school. On the last day of their final year, which was called Assignment Day, they were given jobs to do.

The graduating students occupied Room 8 of the Ember School. On Assignment Day of the year 241, this classroom, usually noisy first thing in the morning, was completely silent. All twenty-four students sat upright and still at the desks they had grown too big for. They were waiting.

The desks were arranged in four rows of six, one behind the other. In the last row sat a slender girl named Lina Mayfleet. She was winding a strand of her long, dark hair around her finger, winding and unwinding it again and again. Sometimes she plucked at a thread on her ragged cape or bent over to pull on her socks, which were loose and tended to slide down around her ankles. One of her feet tapped the floor softly.

In the second row was a boy named Doon Harrow. He sat with his shoulders hunched, his eyes squeezed shut in concentration, and his hands clasped tightly together. His hair looked rumpled, as if he hadn't combed it for a while. He had dark, thick eyebrows, which made him look serious at the best of times and, when he was anxious or angry, came together to form a straight line across his forehead. His brown corduroy jacket was so old that its ridges had flattened out.

Both the girl and the boy were making urgent wishes. Doon's wish was very specific. He repeated it over and over again, his lips moving slightly, as if he could make it come true by saying it a thousand times. Lina was making her wish in pictures rather than in words. In her mind's eye, she saw herself running through the streets of the city in a red jacket. She made this picture as bright and real as she could.

Lina looked up and gazed around the schoolroom. She said a silent goodbye to everything that had been familiar for so long. Goodbye to the map of the city of Ember in its scarred wooden frame and the cabinet whose shelves held *The Book of Numbers, The Book of Letters,* and *The Book of the City of Ember.* Goodbye to the cabinet drawers labeled "New Paper" and "Old Paper." Goodbye to the three electric lights in the ceiling that seemed always, no matter where you sat, to cast the shadow of your head over the page you were writing on. And goodbye to their teacher, Miss Thorn, who had finished her Last Day of School speech, wishing them luck in the lives they were about to begin. Now, having run out of things to say, she was standing at her desk with her frayed shawl clasped around her shoulders. And still the mayor, the guest of honor, had not arrived.

Someone's foot scraped back and forth on the floor. Miss Thorn sighed. Then the door rattled open, and the mayor walked in. He looked annoyed, as though *they* were the ones who were late.

"Welcome, Mayor Cole," said Miss Thorn. She held out her hand to him.

The mayor made his mouth into a smile. "Miss Thorn," he said, enfolding her hand. "Greetings. Another year." The mayor was a vast, heavy man, so big in the middle that his arms looked small and dangling. In one hand he held a little cloth bag.

He lumbered to the front of the room and faced the students. His gray, drooping face appeared to be made of something stiffer than ordinary skin; it rarely moved except for making the smile that was on it now.

"Young people of the Highest Class," the mayor began. He stopped and scanned the room for several moments; his eyes seemed to look out from far back inside his head. He nodded slowly. "Assignment Day now, isn't it? Yes. First we get our education. Then we serve our city." Again his eyes moved back and forth along the rows of students, and again he nodded, as if someone had confirmed what he'd said. He put the little bag on Miss Thorn's desk and rested his hand on it. "What will that service be, eh? Perhaps you're wondering." He did his smile again, and his heavy cheeks folded like drapes.

Lina's hands were cold. She wrapped her cape around her and pressed her hands between her knees. Please hurry, Mr. Mayor, she said silently. Please just let us choose and get it over with. Doon, in his mind, was saying the same thing, only he didn't say please.

"Something to remember," the mayor said, holding up one finger. "Job you draw today is for three years. Then, Evaluation. Are you good at your job? Fine. You may keep it. Are you unsatisfactory? Is there a greater need elsewhere? You will be re-assigned. It is *extremely important*," he said, jabbing his finger at the class, "for all . . . work . . . of Ember . . . to be done. To be *properly* done."

He picked up the bag and pulled open the drawstring. "So. Let us begin. Simple procedure. Come up one at a time. Reach into this bag. Take one slip of paper. Read it out loud." He smiled and nodded. The flesh under his chin bulged in and out. "Who cares to be first?"

No one moved. Lina stared down at the top of her desk. There was a long silence. Then Lizzie Bisco, one of Lina's best friends, sprang to her feet. "I would like to be first," she said in her breathless high voice.

"Good. Walk forward."

Lizzie went to stand before the mayor. Because of her orange hair, she looked like a bright spark next to him.

"Now choose." The mayor held out the bag with one hand and put the other behind his back, as if to show he would not interfere.

Lizzie reached into the bag and withdrew a tightly folded square of paper. She unfolded it carefully. Lina couldn't see the look on Lizzie's face, but she could hear the disappointment in her voice as she read out loud: "Supply Depot clerk."

"Very good," said the mayor. "A vital job."

Lizzie trudged back to her desk. Lina smiled at her, but Lizzie made a sour face. Supply Depot clerk wasn't a bad job, but it was a dull one. The Supply Depot clerks sat behind a long counter, took orders from the storekeepers of Ember, and sent the carriers down to bring up what was wanted from the vast network of storerooms beneath Ember's streets. The storerooms held supplies of every kind—canned food, clothes, furniture, blankets, light bulbs, medicine, pots and pans, reams of paper, soap, more light bulbs— everything the people of Ember could possibly need. The clerks sat at their ledger books all day, recording the orders that came in and the goods that went out. Lizzie didn't like to sit still; she would have been better suited to something else, Lina thought—messenger, maybe, the job Lina wanted for herself. Messengers ran through the city all day, going everywhere, seeing everything.

"Next," said the mayor.

This time two people stood up at once, Orly Gordon and Chet Noam. Orly quickly sat down again, and Chet approached the mayor.

"Choose, young man," the mayor said.

Chet chose. He unfolded his scrap of paper. "Electrician's helper," he read, and his wide face broke into a smile. Lina heard someone take a quick breath. She looked over to see Doon pressing a hand against his mouth.

You never knew, each year, exactly which jobs would be offered. Some years there were several good jobs, like greenhouse helper, timekeeper's assistant, or messenger, and no bad jobs at all. Other years, jobs like Pipeworks laborer, trash sifter, and mold scraper were mixed in. But there would always be at least one or two jobs for electrician's helper. Fixing the electricity was the most important job in Ember, and more people worked at it than at anything else.

Orly Gordon was next. She got the job of building repair assistant, which was a good job for Orly. She was a strong girl and liked hard work. Vindie Chance was made a greenhouse helper. She gave Lina a big grin as she went back to her seat. She'll get to work with Clary, Lina thought. Lucky. So far no one had picked a really bad job. Perhaps this time there would be no bad jobs at all.

The idea gave her courage. Besides, she had reached the point where the suspense was giving her a stomach ache. So as Vindie sat down—even before the mayor could say "Next"—she stood up and stepped forward.

The little bag was made of faded green material, gathered at the top with a black string. Lina hesitated a moment, then put her hand inside and fingered the bits of paper. Feeling as if she were stepping off a high building, she picked one.

She unfolded it. The words were written in black ink, in small careful printing. PIPEWORKS LABORER, they said. She stared at them.

"Out loud, please," the mayor said.

"Pipeworks laborer," Lina said in a choked whisper.

"Louder," said the mayor.

"Pipeworks laborer," Lina said again, her voice loud and cracked. There was a sigh of sympathy from the class. Keeping her eyes on the floor, Lina went back to her desk and sat down.

Pipeworks laborers worked below the storerooms in the deep labyrinth of tunnels that contained Ember's water and sewer pipes. They spent their days stopping up leaks and replacing pipe joints. It was wet, cold work; it could even be dangerous. A swift underground river ran through the Pipeworks, and every now and then someone fell into it and was lost. People were lost occasionally in the tunnels, too, if they strayed too far.

Lina stared miserably down at a letter B someone had scratched into her desktop long ago. Almost anything would have been better than Pipeworks laborer. Greenhouse helper had been her second choice. She imagined with longing the warm air and earthy smell of the greenhouse, where she could have worked with Clary, the greenhouse manager, someone she'd known all her life. She would have been content as a doctor's assistant, too, binding up cuts and bones. Even street-sweeper or cart-puller would have been better. At least then she could have stayed above ground, with space and people around her. She thought going down into the Pipeworks must be like being buried alive.

One by one, the other students chose their jobs. None of them got such a wretched job as hers. Finally the last person rose from his chair and walked forward.

It was Doon. His dark eyebrows were drawn together in a frown of concentration. His hands, Lina saw, were clenched into fists at his sides.

Doon reached into the bag and took out the last scrap of paper. He paused a minute, pressing it tightly in his hand.

"Go on," said the mayor. "Read."

Unfolding the paper, Doon read: "Messenger." He scowled, crumpled the paper, and dashed it to the floor.

Lina gasped; the whole class rustled in surprise. Why would anyone be angry to get the job of messenger?

"Bad behavior!" cried the mayor. His eyes bulged and his face darkened. "Go to your seat immediately."

Doon kicked the crumpled paper into a corner. Then he stalked back to his desk and flung himself down.

The mayor took a short breath and blinked furiously. "Disgraceful," he said, glaring at Doon. "A childish display of temper! Students should be *glad* to work for their city. Ember will prosper if all . . . citizens . . . do . . . their . . . best." He held up a stern finger as he said this and moved his eyes slowly from one face to the next.

Suddenly Doon spoke up. "But Ember is *not* prospering!" he cried. "Everything is getting worse and worse!"

"Silence!" cried the mayor.

"The blackouts!" cried Doon. He jumped from his seat. "The lights go out all the time now! And the shortages, there's shortages of everything! If no one does anything about it, something terrible is going to happen!"

Lina listened with a pounding heart. What was wrong with Doon? Why was he so upset? He was taking things too seriously, as he always did.

Miss Thorn strode to Doon and put a hand on his shoulder. "Sit down now," she said quietly. But Doon remained standing.

The mayor glared. For a few moments he said nothing. Then he smiled, showing a neat row of gray teeth. "Miss Thorn," he said. "Who might this young man be?"

"I am Doon Harrow," said Doon.

"I will remember you," said the mayor. He gave Doon a long look, then turned to the class and smiled his smile again.

"Congratulations to all," he said. "Welcome to Ember's work force. Miss Thorn. Class. Thank you."

The mayor shook hands with Miss Thorn and departed. The students gathered their coats and caps and filed out of the classroom. Lina walked down the Wide Hallway with Lizzie, who said, "Poor you! I thought *I* picked a bad one, but you got the worst. I feel lucky compared to you." Once they were out the door, Lizzie said goodbye and scurried away, as if Lina's bad luck were a disease she might catch.

Lina stood on the steps for a moment and gazed across Harken Square, where people walked briskly, bundled up cozily in their coats and scarves, or talked to one another in the pools of light beneath the great streetlamps. A boy in a red messenger's jacket ran toward the Gathering Hall. On Otterwill Street, a man pulled a cart filled with sacks of potatoes. And in the buildings all around the square, rows of lighted windows shone bright yellow and deep gold.

Lina sighed. *This* was where she wanted to be, up here where everything happened, not down underground.

Someone tapped her on the shoulder. Startled, she turned and saw Doon behind her. His thin face looked pale. "Will you trade with me?" he asked.

"Trade?"

"Trade jobs. I don't want to waste my time being a messenger. I want to help save the city, not run around carrying gossip."

Lina gaped at him. "You'd rather be in the *Pipeworks*?"

"Electrician's helper is what I wanted," Doon said. "But Chet won't trade, of course. Pipeworks is second best."

"But why?"

"Because the generator is in the Pipeworks," said Doon.

Lina knew about the generator, of course. In some mysterious way, it turned the running of the river into power for the city. You could feel its deep rumble when you stood in Plummer Square.

"I need to see the generator," Doon said. "I have . . . I have ideas about it." He thrust his hands into his pockets. "So," he said, "will you trade?"

"Yes!" cried Lina. "Messenger is the job I want

most!" And not a useless job at all, in her opinion. People couldn't be expected to trudge halfway across the city every time they wanted to communicate with someone. Messengers connected everyone to everyone else. Anyway, whether it was important or not, the job of messenger just happened to be perfect for Lina. She loved to run. She could run forever. And she loved exploring every nook and cranny of the city, which was what a messenger got to do.

"All right then," said Doon. He handed her his crumpled piece of paper, which he must have retrieved from the floor. Lina reached into her pocket, pulled out her slip of paper, and handed it to him.

"Thank you," he said.

"You're welcome," said Lina. Happiness sprang up in her, and happiness always made her want to run. She took the steps three at a time and sped down Broad Street toward home.

CHAPTER 2

A Message to the Mayor

Lina often took different routes between school and home. Sometimes, just for variety, she'd go all the way around Sparkswallow Square, or way up by the shoe repair shops on Liverie Street. But today she took the shortest route because she was eager to get home and tell her news.

She ran fast and easily through the streets of Ember. Every corner, every alley, every building was familiar to her. She always knew where she was, though most streets looked more or less the same. All of them were lined with old two-story stone buildings, the wood of their window frames and doors long unpainted. On the street level were shops; above the shops were the apartments where people lived. Every building, at the place where the wall met the roof, was equipped with a row of floodlights—big cone-shaped lamps that cast a strong yellow glare.

Stone walls, lighted windows, lumpy, muffled shapes of people—Lina flew by them. Her slender legs felt immensely strong, like the wood of a bow that flexes and springs. She darted around obstacles—broken furniture left for the trash heaps or for scavengers, stoves and refrigerators that were past repair, peddlers sitting on the pavement with their wares spread out around them. She leapt over cracks and potholes.

When she came to Hafter Street, she slowed a little. This street was deep in shadow. Four of its streetlamps were out and had not been fixed. For a second, Lina thought of the rumor she'd heard about light bulbs: that some kinds were completely gone. She was used to shortages of things—everyone was— but not of light bulbs! If the bulbs for the streetlamps ran out, the only lights would be inside the buildings. What would happen then? How could people find their way through the streets in the dark?

Somewhere inside her, a black worm of dread stirred. She thought about Doon's outburst in class. Could things really be as bad as he said? She didn't want to believe it. She pushed the thought away.

As she turned onto Budloe Street, she sped up again. She passed a line of customers waiting to get into the vegetable market, their shopping bags draped over their arms. At the corner of Oliver Street, she dodged a group of washers trudging along with bags of laundry, and some movers carrying away a broken table. She passed a street-sweeper shoving dust around with his broom. I am so lucky, she thought, to have the job I want. And because of Doon Harrow, of all people.

When they were younger, Lina and Doon had been friends. Together they had explored the back alleys and dimly lit edges of the city. But in their fourth year of school, they had begun to grow apart. It started one day during the hour of free time, when the children in their class were playing on the front steps of the school. "I can go down three steps at a time," someone would boast. "I can hop down on one foot!" someone else would say. The others would chime in. "I can do a handstand against the pillar!" "I can leapfrog over the trash can!" As soon as one child did something, all the rest would do it, too, to prove they could.

Lina could do it all, even when the dares got wilder. She yelled out the wildest one of all: "I can climb the light pole!" For a second everyone just stared at her. But Lina dashed across the street, took off her shoes and socks, and wrapped herself around the cold metal of the pole. Pushing with her bare feet, she inched upward. She didn't get very far before she lost her grip and fell back down. The children laughed, and so did she. "I didn't say I'd climb to the top," she explained. "I just said I'd climb it."

The others swarmed forward to try. Lizzie wouldn't take off her socks—her feet were too cold, she said—so she kept sliding back. Fordy Penn wasn't strong enough to get more than a foot off the ground. Next came Doon. He took his shoes and socks off and placed them neatly at the foot of the pole. Then he announced, in his serious way, "I'm going to the top." He clasped the pole and started upward, pushing with his feet, his knees sticking out to the sides. He pulled himself upward, pushed again—he was higher now than Lina had been—but suddenly his hands slid and he came plummeting down. He landed on his bottom with his legs poking up in the air. Lina laughed. She shouldn't have; he might have been hurt. But he looked so funny that she couldn't help it.

He wasn't hurt. He could have jumped up, grinned, and walked away. But Doon didn't take things lightly. When he heard Lina and the others laughing, his face darkened. His temper rose in him like hot water. "Don't you dare laugh at me," he said to Lina. "I did better than you did! That was a stupid idea anyway, a stupid, stupid idea to climb that pole. . . ." And as he was shouting, red in the face, their teacher, Mrs. Polster, came out onto the steps and saw him. She took him by the shirt collar to the school director's office, where he got a scolding he didn't think he deserved.

After that day, Lina and Doon barely looked at each other when they passed in the hallway. At first it was because they were fuming about what had happened. Doon didn't like being laughed at; Lina didn't like being shouted at. After a while the memory of the light-pole incident faded, but by then they had got out of the habit of friendship. By the time they were twelve, they knew each other only as classmates. Lina was friends with Vindie Chance, Orly Gordon, and most of all, red-haired Lizzie Bisco, who could run almost as fast as Lina and could talk three times faster.

Now, as Lina sped toward home, she felt immensely grateful to Doon and hoped he'd come to no harm in the Pipeworks. Maybe they'd be friends again. She'd like to ask him about the Pipeworks. She was curious about it.

When she got to Greystone Street, she passed Clary Laine, who was probably on her way to the greenhouses. Clary waved to her and called out, "What job?" and Lina called back, "Messenger!" and ran on.

Lina lived in Quillium Square, over the yarn shop run by her grandmother. When she got to the shop, she burst in the door and cried, "Granny! I'm a messenger!"

Granny's shop had once been a tidy place, where each ball of yarn and spool of thread had its spot in the cubbyholes that lined the walls. All the yarn and thread came from old clothes that had gotten too shabby to be worn. Granny unraveled sweaters and picked apart dresses and jackets and pants; she wound the yarn into balls and the thread onto spools, and people bought them to use in making new clothes.

These days, the shop was a mess. Long loops and strands of yarn dangled out of the cubbyholes, and the browns and grays and purples were mixed in with the ochres and olive greens and dark blues. Granny's customers often had to spend half an hour unsnarling the rust-red yarn from the mud-brown, or trying to fish out the end of a thread from a tangled wad. Granny wasn't much help. Most days she just dozed behind the counter in her rocking chair.

That's where she was when Lina burst in with her news. Lina saw that Granny had forgotten to knot up her hair that morning—it was standing out from her head in a wild white frizz.

Granny stood up, looking puzzled. "You aren't a messenger, dear, you're a schoolgirl," she said.

"But Granny, today was Assignment Day. I got my job. And I'm a messenger!"

Granny's eyes lit up, and she slapped her hand down on the counter. "I remember!" she cried. "Messenger, that's a grand job! You'll be good at it."

Lina's little sister toddled out from behind the counter on unsteady legs. She had a round face and round brown eyes. At the top of her head was a sprig of brown hair tied up with a scrap of red yarn. She grabbed on to Lina's knees. "Wy-na, Wy-na!" she said.

Lina bent over and took the child's hands. "Poppy! Your big sister got a good job! Are you happy, Poppy? Are you proud of me?"

Poppy said something that sounded like, "Hoppy-hoppyhoppy!" Lina laughed, hoisted her up, and danced with her around the shop.

Lina loved her little sister so much that it was like an ache under her ribs. The baby and Granny were all the family she had now. Two years ago, when the coughing sickness was raging through the city again, her father had died. Some months later, her mother, giving birth to Poppy, had died, too. Lina missed her parents with an ache that was as strong as what she felt for Poppy, only it was a hollow feeling instead of a full one.

"When do you start?" asked Granny.

"Tomorrow," said Lina. "I report to the messengers' station at eight o'clock."

"You'll be a famous messenger," said Granny. "Fast and famous."

Taking Poppy with her, Lina went out of the shop and climbed the stairs to their apartment. It was a small apartment, only four rooms, but there was enough stuff in it to fill twenty. There were things that had belonged to Lina's parents, her grandparents, and even *their* grandparents—old, broken, cracked, threadbare things that had been patched and repaired dozens or hundreds of times. People in Ember rarely threw anything away. They made the best possible use of what they had.

In Lina's apartment, layers of worn rugs and carpets covered the floor, making it soft but uneven underfoot. Against one wall squatted a sagging couch with round wooden balls for legs, and on the couch were blankets and pillows, so many that you had to toss some on the floor before you could sit down. Against the opposite wall stood two wobbly tables that held a clutter of plates and bottles, cups and bowls, unmatching forks and spoons, little piles of scrap paper, bits of string wound up in untidy wads, and a few stubby pencils. There were four lamps, two tall ones that stood on the floor and two short ones that stood on tables. And in uneven lines up near the ceiling were hooks that held coats and shawls and nightgowns and sweaters, shelves that held pots and pans, jars with unreadable labels, and boxes of buttons and pins and tacks.

Where there were no shelves, the walls had been decorated with things of beauty—a label from a can of peaches, a few dried yellow squash flowers, a strip of faded but still pretty purple cloth. There were drawings, too. Lina had done the drawings out of her imagination. They showed a city that looked somewhat like Ember, except that its buildings were lighter and taller and had more windows.

One of the drawings had fallen to the floor. Lina

retrieved it and pinned it back up. She stood for a minute and looked at the pictures. Over and over, she'd drawn the same city. Sometimes she drew it as seen from afar, sometimes she chose one of its buildings and drew it in detail. She put in stairways and street-lamps and carts. Sometimes she tried to draw the people who lived in the city, though she wasn't good at drawing people—their heads always came out too small, and their hands looked like spiders. One picture showed a scene in which the people of the city greeted her when she arrived—the first person they had ever seen to come from elsewhere. They argued with each other about who should be the first to invite her home.

Lina could see this city so clearly in her mind she almost believed it was real. She knew it couldn't be, though. *The Book of the City of Ember,* which all children studied in school, taught otherwise. "The city of Ember was made for us long ago by the Builders," the book said. "It is the only light in the dark world. Beyond Ember, the darkness goes on forever in all directions."

Lina had been to the outer border of Ember. She had stood at the edge of the trash heaps and gazed into the darkness beyond the city—the Unknown Regions. No one had ever gone far into the Unknown Regions—or at least no one had gone far and returned. And no one had ever arrived in Ember from the Unknown Regions, either. As far as anyone knew, the darkness *did* go on forever. Still, Lina wanted the other city to exist. In her imagination, it was so beautiful, and it seemed so real. Sometimes she longed to go there and take everyone in Ember with her.

But she wasn't thinking about the other city now. Today she was happy to be right where she was. She set Poppy on the couch. "Wait there," she said. She went into the kitchen, where there was an electric stove and a refrigerator that no longer worked and was used to store glasses and dishes so Poppy couldn't get at them. Above the refrigerator were shelves holding more pots and jars, more spoons and knives, a wind-up clock that Granny always forgot to wind, and a long row of cans. Lina tried to keep the cans in alphabetical order so she could find what she wanted quickly, but Granny always messed them up. Now, she saw, there were beans at the end of the row and tomatoes at the beginning. She picked out a can labeled Baby Drink and a jar of boiled carrots, opened them, poured the liquid into a cup and the carrots into a little dish, and took these back to the baby on the couch.

Poppy dribbled Baby Drink down her chin. She ate some of her carrots and poked others between the couch cushions. For the moment, Lina felt almost perfectly happy. There was no need to think about the fate of the city right now. Tomorrow, she'd be a messenger! She wiped the orange goop off Poppy's chin. "Don't worry," she said. "Everything will be all right."

* * *

The messengers' headquarters was on Cloving Street, not far from the back of the Gathering Hall. When Lina arrived the next morning, she was greeted by Messenger Captain Allis Fleery, a bony woman with pale eyes and hair the color of dust. "Our new girl," said Captain Fleery to the other messengers, a cluster of nine people who smiled and nodded at Lina. "I have your jacket right here," said the captain. She handed Lina a red jacket like the one all messengers wore. It was only a little too large.

From the clock tower of the Gathering Hall came a deep reverberating bong. "Eight o'clock!" cried Captain Fleery. She waved a long arm. "Take your stations!" As the clock sounded seven more times, the messengers scattered in all directions. The captain turned to Lina. "Your station," she said, "is Garn Square."

Lina nodded and started off, but the captain caught her by the collar. "I haven't told you the rules," she said. She held up a knobby finger. "One: When a customer gives you a message, repeat it back to make sure you have it right. Two: Always wear your red jacket so people can identify you. Three: Go as fast as possible. Your customers pay twenty cents for every message, no matter how far you have to take it."

Lina nodded. "I always go fast," she said.

"Four," the captain went on. "Deliver a message

only to the person it's meant for, no one else."

Lina nodded again. She bounced a little on her toes, eager to get going.

Captain Fleery smiled. "Go," she said, and Lina was off.

She felt strong and speedy and surefooted. She glanced at her reflection as she ran past the window of a furniture repair shop. She liked the look of her long dark hair flying out behind her, her long legs in their black socks, and her flapping red jacket. Her face, which had never seemed especially remarkable, looked almost beautiful, because she looked so happy.

As soon as she came into Garn Square, a voice cried, "Messenger!" Her first customer! It was old Natty Prine, calling to her from the bench where he always sat. "This goes to Ravenet Parsons, 18 Selverton Square," he said. "Bend down."

She bent down so that her ear was close to his whiskery mouth.

The old man said in a slow, hoarse voice, "My stove is broke, don't come for dinner. Repeat."

Lina repeated the message.

"Good," said Natty Prine. He gave Lina twenty cents, and she ran across the city to Selverton Square. There she found Ravenet Parsons also sitting on a bench. She recited the message to him.

"Old turniphead," he growled. "Lazy old fleaface. He just doesn't feel like cooking. No reply."

Lina ran back to Garn Square, passing a group of Believers on the way. They were standing in a circle, holding hands, singing one of their cheerful songs. It seemed to Lina there were more Believers than ever these days. What they believed in she didn't know, but it must make them happy—they were always smiling.

Her next customer turned out to be Mrs. Polster, the teacher of the fourth-year class. In Mrs. Polster's class, they memorized passages from *The Book of the City of Ember* every week. Mrs. Polster had charts on the walls for everything, with everyone's name listed. If you did something right, she made a green dot by your name. If you did something wrong, she made a red dot. "What you need to learn, children," she always said, in her resonant, precise voice, "is the difference between right and wrong in every area of life. And once you learn the difference—" Here she would stop and point to the class, and the class would finish the sentence: "You must always choose the right." In every situation, Mrs. Polster knew what the right choice was.

Now here was Mrs. Polster again, looming over Lina and pronouncing her message. "To Annisette Lafrond, 39 Humm Street, as follows," she said. "My confidence in you has been seriously diminished since I heard about the disreputable activities in which you engaged on Thursday last. Please repeat."

It took Lina three tries to get this right. "Uh-oh, a

red dot for me," she said. Mrs. Polster did not seem to find this amusing.

Lina had nineteen customers that first morning. Some of them had ordinary messages: "I can't come on Tuesday." "Buy a pound of potatoes on your way home." "Please come and fix my front door." Others had messages that made no sense to her at all, like Mrs. Polster's. But it didn't matter. The wonderful part about being a messenger was not the messages but the places she got to go. She could go into the houses of people she didn't know and hidden alleyways and little rooms in the backs of stores. In just a few hours, she discovered all kinds of strange and interesting things.

For instance: Mrs. Sample, the mender, had to sleep on her couch because her entire bedroom, almost up to the ceiling, was crammed with clothes to be mended. Dr. Felinia Tower had the skeleton of a person hanging against her living room wall, its bones all held in place with black strings. "I study it," she said when she saw Lina staring. "I have to know how people are put together." At a house on Calloo Street, Lina delivered a message to a worried-looking man whose living room was completely dark. "I'm saving on light bulbs," the man said. And when Lina took a message to the Can Café, she learned that on certain days the back room was used as a meeting place for people who liked to converse about Great Subjects. "Do you think an Invisible Being is watching over us all the time?" she heard someone ask. "Perhaps," answered someone else. There was a long silence. "And then again, perhaps not."

All of it was interesting. She loved finding things out, and she loved running. And even by the end of the day, she wasn't tired. Running made her feel strong and big-hearted, it made her love the places she ran through and the people whose messages she delivered. She wished she could bring all of them the good news they so desperately wanted to hear.

Late in the afternoon, a young man came up to her, walking with a sort of sideways lurch. He was an odd-looking person—he had a very long neck with a bump in the middle and teeth so big they looked as if they were trying to escape from his mouth. His black, bushy hair stuck out from his head in untidy tufts. "I have a message for the mayor, at the Gathering Hall," he said. He paused to let the importance of this be understood. "The mayor," he said. "Did you get that?"

"I got it," said Lina.

"All right. Listen carefully. Tell him: Delivery at eight. From Looper. Repeat it back."

"Delivery at eight. From Looper," Lina repeated. It was an easy message.

"All right. No answer required." He handed her twenty cents, and she sprinted away.

The Gathering Hall occupied one entire side of Harken Square, which was the city's central plaza. The square was paved with stone. It had a few benches bolted to the ground here and there, as well as a couple of kiosks for notices. Wide steps led up to the Gathering Hall, and fat columns framed its big door. The mayor's office was in the Gathering Hall. So were the offices of the clerks who kept track of which buildings had broken windows, what streetlamps needed repair, and the number of people in the city. There was the office of the timekeeper, who was in charge of the town clock. And there were offices for the guards who enforced the laws of Ember, now and then putting pickpockets or people who got in fights into the Prison Room, a small one-story structure with a sloping roof that jutted out from one side of the building.

Lina ran up the steps and through the door into a broad hallway. On the left was a desk, and at the desk sat a guard: "Barton Snode, Assistant Guard," said a badge on his chest. He was a big man, with wide shoulders, brawny arms, and a thick neck. But his head looked as if it didn't belong to his body—it was small and round and topped with a fuzz of extremely short hair. His lower jaw jutted out and moved a little from side to side, as if he were chewing on something.

When he saw Lina, his jaw stopped moving for a moment and his lips curled upward in a very small smile. "Good day," he said. "What business brings you here today?"

"I have a message for the mayor."

"Very good, very good." Barton Snode heaved himself to his feet. "Step this way."

He led Lina down the corridor and opened a door marked "Reception Room."

"Wait here, please," he said. "The mayor is in his basement office on private business, but he will be up shortly."

Lina went inside.

"I'll notify the mayor," said Barton Snode. "Please have a seat. The mayor will be right with you. Or pretty soon." He left, closing the door behind him. A second later, the door opened again, and the guard's small fuzzy head re-appeared. "What *is* the message?" he asked.

"I have to give it to the mayor in person," said Lina.

"Of course, of course," said the guard. The door closed again. He doesn't seem very sure about things, Lina thought. Maybe he's new at his job.

The Reception Room was shabby, but Lina could tell that it had once been impressive. The walls were dark red, with brownish patches where the paint was peeling away. In the right-hand wall was a closed door. An ugly brown carpet lay on the floor, and on it stood a large armchair covered in itchy-looking red material, and several smaller chairs. A small table held a teapot and some cups, and a larger table in the middle of the room displayed a copy of *The Book of the City of*

Ember, lying open as if someone were going to read from it. Portraits of all the mayors of the city since the beginning of time hung on the walls, staring solemnly from behind pieces of old window glass.

Lina sat in the big armchair and waited. No one came. She got up and wandered around the room. She bent over *The Book of the City of Ember* and read a few sentences: "The citizens of Ember may not have luxuries, but the foresight of the Builders, who filled the storerooms at the beginning of time, has ensured that they will always have enough, and enough is all that a person of wisdom needs."

She flipped a few pages. "The Gathering Hall clock," she read, "measures the hours of night and day. It must never be allowed to run down. Without it, how would we know when to go to work and when to go to school? How would the light director know when to turn the lights on and when to turn them off again? It is the job of the timekeeper to wind the clock every week and to place the date sign in Harken Square every day. The timekeeper must perform these duties faithfully."

Lina knew that not all timekeepers were as faithful as they should be. She'd heard of one, some years ago, who often forgot to change the date sign, so that it might say, "Wednesday, Week 38, Year 227" for several days in a row. There had even been timekeepers who forgot to wind the clock, so that it might stand at noon or at midnight for hours at a time, causing a very long day or a very long night. The result was that no one really knew anymore exactly what day of the week it was, or exactly how many years it had been since the building of the city—they called this the year 241, but it might have been 245 or 239 or 250. As long as the clock's deep boom rang out every hour, and the lights went on and off more or less regularly, it didn't seem to matter.

Lina left the book and examined the pictures of the mayors. The seventh mayor, Podd Morethwart, was her great-great—she didn't know how many greats—grandfather. He looked quite dreary, Lina thought. His cheeks were long and hollow, his mouth turned down at the corners, and there was a lost look in his eyes. The picture she liked best was of the fourth mayor, Jane Larket, who had a serene smile and fuzzy black hair.

Still no one came. She heard no sounds from the hallway. Maybe they'd forgotten her.

Lina went over to the closed door in the right-hand wall. She pulled it open and saw stairs going up. Maybe, while she waited, she'd just see where they went. She started upward. At the top of the first flight was a closed door. Carefully, she opened it. She saw another hallway and more closed doors. She shut the door and kept going. Her footsteps sounded loud on the wood, and she was afraid someone would hear her and come and scold her. No doubt she was not supposed to be here. But no one came, and she climbed on, passing another closed door.

The Gathering Hall was the only building in Ember with three stories. She had always wanted to stand on its roof and look out at the city. Maybe from there it would be possible to see beyond the city, into the Unknown Regions. If the bright city of her drawings really did exist, it would be out there somewhere.

At the top of the stairs, she came to a door marked "Roof," and she pushed it open. Chilly air brushed against her skin. She was outside. Ahead of her was a flat gravel surface, and about ten paces away she could see the high wall of the clock tower.

She went to the edge of the roof. From there she could see the whole of Ember. Directly below was Harken Square, where people were moving this way and that, all of them appearing, from this top-down view, more round than tall. Beyond Harken Square, the lighted windows of the buildings made checkered lines, yellow and black, row after row, in all directions. She tried to see farther, across the Unknown Regions, but she couldn't. At the edges of the city, the lights were so far away that they made a kind of haze. She could see nothing beyond them but blackness.

She heard a shout from the square below. "Look!" came a small but piercing voice. "Someone on the roof!" She saw a few people stop and look up. "Who is it? What's she doing up there?" someone cried. More people gathered, until a crowd was standing on the steps of the Gathering Hall. They see me! Lina thought, and it made her laugh. She waved at the crowd and did a few steps from the Bugfoot Scurry Dance, which she'd learned on Cloving Square Dance Day, and they laughed and shouted some more.

Then the door behind her burst open, and a huge guard with a bushy black beard was suddenly running toward her. "Halt!" he shouted, though she wasn't going anywhere. He grabbed her by the arm. "What are you doing here?"

"I was just curious," said Lina, in her most innocent voice. "I wanted to see the city from the roof." She read the guard's name badge. It said, "Redge Stabmark, Chief Guard."

"Curiosity leads to trouble," said Redge Stabmark. He peered down at the crowd. "You have caused a commotion." He pulled her toward the door and hustled her down all three flights of stairs. When they came out into the waiting room, Barton Snode was standing there looking flustered, his jaw twitching from side to side. Next to him was the mayor.

"A child causing trouble, Mayor Cole," said the chief guard.

The mayor glared at her. "I recall your face. From Assignment Day. Shame! Disgracing yourself in your new job."

"I didn't mean to cause trouble," said Lina. "I was

looking for you so I could deliver a message."

"Shall we put her in the Prison Room for a day or two?" asked the chief guard.

The mayor frowned. He pondered a moment. "What is the message?" he said. He bent down so that Lina could speak into his ear. She noticed that he smelled a little like overcooked turnips.

"Delivery at eight," Lina whispered. "From Looper."

The mayor smiled a tight little smile. He turned to the guard. "Just a child's antics," he said. "We will let it go this time. From now on," he said to Lina, "behave yourself."

"Yes, Mr. Mayor," said Lina.

"And you," said the mayor, turning to the assistant guard and shaking a thick finger at him, "watch visitors much . . . more . . . carefully."

Barton Snode blinked and nodded.

Lina ran for the door. Outside, the small crowd was still standing by the steps. A few of them cheered as Lina came out. Others frowned at her and muttered words like "mischief" and "silliness" and "show-off." Lina felt embarrassed suddenly. She hadn't meant to show off. She hurried past, out into Otterwill Street, and started to run.

She didn't see Doon, who was among those watching her. He had been on his way home from his first day in the Pipeworks when he'd come across the cluster of people gazing up at the roof of the Gathering Hall and laughing. He was tired and chilly. The bottoms of his pants legs were wet, and mud clung to his shoes and smeared his hands. When he raised his eyes and saw the small figure next to the clock tower, he realized right away that it was Lina. He saw her raise her arm and wave and hop about, and for a second he wondered what it would be like to be up there, looking out over the whole city, laughing and waving. When Lina came down, he wanted to speak to her. But he knew he was filthy-looking and that she would ask him questions he didn't want to answer. So he turned away. Walking fast, he headed for home.

CHAPTER 3

Under Ember

That morning, Doon had arrived at the Pipeworks full of anticipation. This was the world of serious work at last, where he would get a chance to do something useful. What he'd learned in school, and from his father, and from his own investigations—he could put it all to good purpose now.

He pushed open the heavy Pipeworks door and stepped inside. The air smelled strongly of dampness and moldy rubber, which seemed to him a pleasant, interesting smell. He strode up a hallway where yellow slickers hung from pegs on the walls. At the end of the hallway was a room full of people, some of them sitting on benches and pulling on knee-high rubber boots, some struggling into their slickers, some buckling on tool belts. A raucous clamor filled the room. Doon watched from the doorway, eager to join in but not sure what to do.

After a moment a man emerged from the throng. He thrust out a hand. "Lister Munk, Pipeworks director," he said. "You're the new boy, right? What size feet do you have—large, medium, or small?"

"Medium," said Doon, and Lister found him a slicker and a pair of boots. The boots were so ancient that their green rubber was cracked all over, as if covered with spiderwebs. He gave Doon a tool belt, too, in which were wrenches and hammers, spools of wire and tape, and tubes of some sort of black goop.

"You'll be in Tunnel 97 today," Lister said. "Arlin Froll will go down with you and show you what to do." He pointed at a short, delicate-looking girl with a white-blond braid down her back. "She may not look like an expert, but she is."

Doon buckled his tool belt around his waist and put on his slicker, which, for some reason, smelled like sweaty feet. "This way," said Arlin, without saying hello or smiling. She wove through the crowd of workers to a door marked "Stairway" and opened it.

Stone steps led so far down that Doon couldn't see the end of them. On either side was a sheer wall of dark reddish stone, glistening with dampness. There was no railing. Along the ceiling ran a single wire from which a light bulb hung every few yards. Water stood in shallow pools on each stair, in the hollow worn into the stones by years of footsteps.

They started down. Doon concentrated on his

feet—the clumsy boots made it hard not to stumble. As they went deeper, he began to hear a low roar, so low he seemed to hear it more with his stomach than his ears. It grew louder and louder—was it a machine of some kind? Maybe the generator?

The stairway came to an end at a door marked "Main Tunnel." Arlin opened it, and as they stepped through, Doon realized that the sound he had been hearing wasn't a machine. It was the river.

He stood still, staring. Like most people, he had never been really sure what a river was—just that it was water that somehow flowed on its own. He'd imagined it would be like the clear, narrow stream that came out of the kitchen faucet, only bigger, and horizontal instead of vertical. But this was something entirely different—not a stream of water, but endless tons of it pouring by. Wide as the widest street in Ember, churning and dipping and swirling, the river roared past, its turbulent surface like black, liquid glass scattered with flecks of light. Doon had never seen anything that moved so fast, and he had never heard such a thunderous, heart-stopping roar.

The path they stood on was about six feet wide and ran parallel to the river for farther than Doon could see in both directions. In the wall along the path were openings that must lead, Doon thought, to the tunnels that branched everywhere below the city. A string of lights like the one in the stairway hung high up against the arched ceiling.

Doon knew he was standing beneath the north edge of Ember. In school, you were taught to remember the directions this way: north was the direction of the river; south was the direction of the greenhouses; east was the direction of the school; and west was the direction left over, having nothing in particular to mark it. All the Pipeworks tunnels branched off from the main tunnel to the south, toward the city.

Arlin leaned toward Doon and shouted into his ear. "First we'll go to the beginning of the river," she said. She led him up the main tunnel for a long way. They passed other people in yellow slickers, who greeted Arlin with a nod and glanced curiously at Doon. After fifteen minutes or so, they came to the east edge of the Pipeworks, where the river surged up from a deep chasm in the ground, churning so violently that its dark water turned white and filled the air with a spray that wet Doon's face.

In the wall to their right was a wide double door. "See that door right there?" Arlin shouted, pointing.

"Yes," Doon shouted back.

"That's the generator room."

"Can we go in?"

"Of course not!" said Arlin. "You have to have special permission." She pointed back down the main tunnel. "Now we'll go to the end of the river," she said.

She led him back, past the stairway door, all the way to the west edge of the Pipeworks. There the river flowed into a huge opening in the wall and vanished into darkness.

"Where does it go?" Doon asked.

Arlin just shrugged. "Back into the ground, I guess. Now let's find Tunnel 97 and get to work." She pulled a folded piece of paper from her pocket. "This is the map," she said. "You have one in your pocket, too. You have to use the map to find your way around in here." The map looked to Doon like an immense centipede—the river arched across the top of the page like the centipede's body, and the tunnels dangled down from it like hundreds of long, long legs all tangled up with each other.

To get to Tunnel 97, they followed a complicated route through passageways lined with crusty, rusted pipes that carried water to all the buildings of Ember. Puddles stood on the floor of the tunnel, and water dripped in brown rivulets down the walls. Just as in the main tunnel, there was a string of bulbs along the ceiling that provided dim light. Doon occupied his mind by calculating how far underground he was. From the river to the ceiling of the main tunnel must be thirty feet or so, he thought. Above that were the storerooms, which occupied a layer at least twenty feet high. So that meant he was fifty feet underground, with tons of earth and rock and buildings above him. The thought made him tense up his shoulders. He cast a quick glance upward, as if all that weight might collapse onto his head.

"Here we are," said Arlin. She was standing next to a leak that spurted a stream of water straight out from the wall. "We have to turn the shut-off valve, take the pipe apart, put on a new connector, and stick it back together again."

With wrenches, hammers, washers, and black goop, they did this, getting soaked in the process. It took them most of the morning and proved to Doon that the city was in even worse shape than he'd suspected. Not only were the lights about to fail and the supplies about to run out, but the water system was breaking down. The whole city was crumbling, and what was anyone doing about it?

When the lunch break came, Arlin took her lunch sack from a pocket in her tool belt and went off to meet some friends a few tunnels away. "You stay right here and wait until I get back," she said as she left. "If you wander around, you'll get lost."

But Doon set out as soon as she disappeared. Using his map, he found his way back to the main tunnel, then hurried to the east end. He wasn't going to wait for special permission to see the generator. He was pretty sure he could find a way to get in on his own, and he did. He simply stood by the door and waited for someone to come out. Quite soon, a stout woman carrying a lunch sack pushed open the door and walked away. She didn't notice him. Before the door could close again, Doon slipped inside.

Such a horrendous noise met him that he staggered backward a few steps. It was an earsplitting, growling, grinding, screaming noise, shot through with a hoarse *rackety-rackety* sound and underscored with a deep *chugga-chugga-chugga*. Doon clapped his hands over his ears and stepped forward. In front of him was a gigantic black machine, two stories high. It was vibrating so hard it looked as if it might explode any second. Several people wearing earmuffs were busy around it. None of them noticed him come in.

He tapped one of them on the shoulder, and the person jumped and whirled around. He was an old man, Doon saw, with a deeply lined brown face.

"I want to learn about the generator!" Doon screamed, but he might as well have saved his breath. No one could be heard in the uproar. The old man glared at him, made a shooing motion with his hand, and turned back to work.

Doon stood and watched for a while. Beside the huge machine were ladders on wheels that the workers pushed back and forth and climbed up on to reach the high parts. All over the room, greasy-looking cans and tools littered the floor. Against the walls stood big bins holding every kind of bolt and screw and gear and lever and rod and tube, all of them black with age and jumbled together. The workers scurried between the bins and the generator or simply stood and watched the thing shake.

After a few minutes, Doon left. He was horrified. All his life he had studied how things worked—it was one of his favorite things to do. He could take apart an old watch and put it back together exactly as it had been. He understood how the faucets in the sink worked. He'd fixed the toilet many times. He'd made a wheeled cart out of the parts of an old armchair. He even had a hazy idea of what was going on in the refrigerator. He was proud of his mechanical talent. There was only one thing he didn't understand at all, and that was electricity. What was the power that ran through the wires and into the light bulbs? Where did it come from? He had thought that if he could just get a look at the generator, he would have the clue he needed. From there, he could begin to work on a solution that would keep the lights of Ember burning.

But one glimpse of the generator showed him how foolish he was. He'd expected to see something whose workings he could understand—a wheel turning, a spark being struck, some wires that led from one point to another. But this monstrous roaring thing—he wondered if *anyone* understood how it worked. It looked as if all they were doing was trying to keep it from flying apart.

As it turned out, he was right. When the day was over and he was upstairs taking off his boots and slicker, he saw the old man from the generator room and went to talk to him. "Can you explain to me about the generator?" he asked. "Can you tell me how it works?"

The old man just sighed. "All I know is, the river makes it go."

"But how?"

The man shrugged. "Who knows? Our job is just to keep it from breaking down. If a part breaks, we got to put on a new one. If a part freezes up, we got to oil it." He wiped his hand wearily across his forehead, leaving a streak of black grease. "I been working on the generator for twenty years. It's always managed to chug along, but this year . . . I don't know. The thing seems to break down every couple minutes." He cracked a wry smile. "Of course, I hear we might run out of light bulbs before that, and then it won't matter if the generator works or not."

Running out of light bulbs, running out of power, running out of time—disaster was right around the corner. That's what Doon was thinking about when he stopped outside the Gathering Hall on his way home and saw Lina on the roof. She looked so free and happy up there. He didn't know why she was on the roof, but he wasn't surprised. It was the kind of thing she did, turning up in unexpected places, and now that she was a messenger, she could go just about anywhere. But how could she be so lighthearted when everything was falling apart?

He headed for home. He lived with his father in a two-bedroom apartment over his father's shop in Greengate Square—the Small Items shop, which sold things like nails, pins, tacks, clips, springs, jar lids, doorknobs, bits of wire, shards of glass, chunks of wood, and other small things that might be useful in some way. The Small Items shop had overflowed somewhat into their apartment above. In their front room, where other people might display a nice teapot on a tabletop or a few attractive squashes or tomatoes on a shelf, they had buckets and boxes and baskets full of spare items for the shop, things Doon's father had collected but not yet organized for selling. Often these items spilled over onto the floor. It was easy to trip over things in this apartment, and not a good idea to go barefoot.

Today Doon didn't stop in at the shop to see his father before going upstairs. He wasn't in the mood for conversation. He removed two buckets of stuff from the couch—it looked like mostly shoe heels—and flopped down on the cushions. He'd been stupid to think he could understand the generator just by look-ing at it, when other people had been working on it their entire lives. The thing was, he had to admit, he'd always thought he was smarter than other people. He'd been sure he could learn about electricity and help save the city. He wanted to be the one to do it. He had imagined many times a ceremony in Harken Square, organized to thank him for saving Ember, with the entire population in attendance and his father beaming from the front row. All Doon's life, his father had been saying to him, "You're a good boy and a smart boy. You'll do grand things someday, I know you will." But Doon hadn't done much that was grand so far. He ached to do something truly important, like finding the secret of electricity, and, as his father watched, be rewarded for his achievement. The size of the reward didn't matter. A small certificate would do, or maybe a badge to sew on his jacket.

Now he was stuck in the muck of the Pipeworks, patching up pipes that would leak and break again in a matter of days. It was even more useless and boring than being a messenger. The thought made him suddenly furious. He sat up, grabbed a shoe heel out of the bucket at his feet, and hurled it with all his might. It arrived at the front door just as the door opened. Doon heard a hard *thwack* and a loud "Ouch!" at the same moment. Then he saw the long, lean, tired-looking face of his father in the doorway.

Doon's anger drained away. "Oh, I hit you, Father. I'm sorry."

Doon's father rubbed the side of his head. He was a tall man, bald as a peeled potato, with a high forehead and a long chin. He had kind, slightly puzzled gray eyes.

"Got me in the ear," he said. "What *was* that?"

"I got angry for a second," said Doon. "I threw one of these old heels."

"I see," said his father. He brushed some bottle tops off a chair and sat down. "Does it have to do with your first day at work, son?"

"Yes," said Doon.

His father nodded. "Why don't you tell me about it," he said.

Doon told him. When he was finished, his father ran a hand across his bald head as if smoothing down the hair that wasn't there. He sighed. "Well," he said, "it sounds unpleasant, I have to admit. About the generator, especially—that's bad news. But the Pipeworks is your assignment, no way around it. What you get is what you get. What you *do* with what you get, though . . . that's more the point, wouldn't you say?" He looked at Doon and smiled, a bit sadly.

"I guess so," Doon said. "But what can I do?"

"I don't know," said his father. "You'll think of something. You're a clever boy. The main thing is to pay attention. Pay close attention to everything, notice what no one else notices. Then you'll know what no one else knows, and that's always useful." He took off his coat and hung it from a peg on the wall. "How's the worm?" he asked.

"I haven't looked at it yet," said Doon. He went into his room and came out with a small wooden box covered with an old scarf. He set the box on the table and took the scarf off, and he and his father both bent over to look inside.

A couple of limp cabbage leaves lay on the bottom of the box. On one of the leaves was a worm about an inch long. A few days before school ended, Doon had found the worm on the underside of a cabbage leaf he was slicing up for dinner. It was a pale soft green, velvety smooth all over, with tiny, stubby legs.

Doon had always been fascinated by bugs. He wrote down his observations about them in a book he had titled *Crawling and Flying Things*. Each page of the book was divided lengthwise down the center. On the left he drew his pictures, with a pencil sharpened to a needle-like point: moth wings with their branching patterns of veins; spider legs, which had minute hairs and tiny feet like claws; beetles, with their feelers and their glossy armor. On the right, he wrote what he observed about each creature. He noted what it ate, where it slept, where it laid its eggs, and—if he knew—how long it lived.

This was difficult with fast-moving creatures like moths and spiders. To learn anything about them, he had to catch what glimpses he could as they lived their lives out in the open. If he put them in a box, they scrambled around for a few days and then died.

This worm, though, was different. It seemed perfectly happy to live in the box Doon had made for it. So far, it did only three things: eat, sleep (it looked like sleeping, though Doon couldn't tell if the worm closed its eyes—or even if it had eyes), and expel tiny black poop balls. That was it.

"I've had it for five days now," said Doon. "It's twice as big as it was when I got it. It's eaten two square inches of cabbage leaf."

"You're writing all this down?"

Doon nodded.

"Maybe," said his father, "you'll find some interesting new bugs in the Pipeworks."

"Maybe," said Doon. But to himself he said, No, that's not enough. I can't go plodding around the Pipeworks, stopping up leaks, looking for bugs, and pretending there's no emergency. I have to find something important down there, something that's going to help. I have to. I just *have* to.

CHAPTER 4

Something Lost, Nothing Found

One day when Lina had been a messenger for several weeks, she came home to find that Granny had thrown all the cushions from the couch onto the floor, ripped up a corner of the couch's lining, and was pulling out wads of stuffing.

"What are you doing?" Lina cried.

Granny looked up. Wisps of sofa stuffing stuck to the front of her dress and clung to her hair. "Something is lost," she said. "I think it might be in here."

"What's lost, Granny?"

"I don't quite recall," said the old woman. "Something important."

"But Granny, you're ruining the couch. What will we sit on?"

Granny tore a bit more of the covering off the couch and yanked out another puff of stuffing. "It doesn't matter," she said. "I'll put it back together later."

"Let's put it back now," Lina said. "I don't think what's lost is in there."

"You don't know," said Granny darkly. But she sat back on her heels, looking tired.

Lina began cleaning up the mess. "Where's the baby?" she asked.

Granny gazed at Lina blankly. "The baby?"

"You haven't forgotten the baby?"

"Oh, yes. She's . . . I think she's down in the shop."

"By herself?" Lina stood up and ran down the stairs. She found Poppy sitting on the floor of the shop, enmeshed in a tangle of yellow yarn. As soon as she saw Lina, Poppy began to howl.

Lina picked her up and unwound the yarn, talking soothingly, though she was so upset that her fingers trembled. For Granny to forget the baby was danger-ous. Poppy could fall downstairs and hurt herself. She could wander out into the street and get lost. Granny had been forgetful lately, but this was the first time she'd completely forgotten about Poppy.

When they got upstairs, Granny was kneeling on the floor gathering up the white tufts of stuffing and jamming them back into the hole she'd made in the couch. "It wasn't in there," she said sadly.

"*What* wasn't?"

"It was lost a long time ago," said Granny. "My father told me about it."

Lina sighed impatiently. More and more, her grandmother's mind seemed caught in the past. She could explain the rules of pebblejacks, which she'd last played when she was eight, or tell you what happened at the Singing when she was twelve, or who she'd danced with at the Cloving Square Dance when she was sixteen, but she would forget what had happened the day before yesterday.

"They heard him talking about it when he died," she said to Lina.

"They heard who talking?"

"My grandfather. The seventh mayor."

"And what did they hear him say?"

"Ah," said her grandmother with a faraway look. "That's the mystery. He said he couldn't get at it. 'Now it is lost,' he said."

"But what *was* it?"

"He didn't say."

Lina gave up. It didn't matter anyway. Probably the lost thing was the old man's left sock, or his hairbrush. But for some reason, the story had taken root in Granny's mind.

The next morning on her way to work, Lina stopped in at the house of their neighbor, Evaleen Murdo. Mrs. Murdo was brisk in her manner, and in her person thin and straight as a nail, but she was kind in her unsmiling way. Until a few years ago, she'd run a shop that sold paper and pencils. But when paper and pencils became scarce, her shop closed. Now she spent her days sitting by her upstairs window, watching people in the street with her sharp eyes. Lina told Mrs. Murdo about her grandmother's forgetfulness. "Will you look in on her sometimes and make sure things are all right?" she asked.

"I will, certainly," said Mrs. Murdo, nodding twice, firmly. Lina went away feeling better.

That day Lina was given a message by Arbin Swinn, who ran the Callay Street Vegetable Market, to be delivered to Lina's friend Clary, the greenhouse manager. Lina was glad to carry this message, though her gladness was mixed a little with sadness. Her father had worked in the greenhouses. It still felt strange not to see him there.

The five greenhouses produced all of Ember's fresh food. They were out past Greengate Square, at the farthest edge of the city. Nothing else was out there but the trash heaps, great moldering, stinking hills that stood on rocky ground and were lit by a few floodlights high up on poles.

It used to be that no one went to the trash heaps but the trash collectors, who dumped the trash and left it. Now and then a couple of children might go there to play, scrambling up the side of the heaps and tumbling down. Lina and Lizzie used to go when they were younger. They'd pull out the occasional treasure—some empty cans, maybe an old hat or a cracked plate. But not anymore. Now there were guards posted at the trash heaps to make sure no one poked around. Just recently, an official job called trash sifter had been created. Every day a team of people methodically sorted through the trash heaps in search of anything that might be at all useful. They'd come back with broken chair legs that could be used for repairing window frames, bent nails that could become hooks for clothes, even filthy rags, stiff with dirt, that could be washed out and used to patch holes in window blinds or mattress covers. Lina hadn't thought about it before, but now she wondered about the trash sifters. Were they there because Ember really was running out of everything?

Beyond the trash heaps there was nothing at all— that is, only the vast Unknown Regions, where the darkness was absolute.

From the end of Diggery Street, Lina could see the long, low greenhouses. They looked like big tin cans that had been cut in half and laid on their sides. Her breath came a little faster. The greenhouses were a home to her, in a way.

She knew that she was most likely to find Clary somewhere around Greenhouse 1, where the office was, so that was where she headed first. A small toolshed stood beside the door to Greenhouse 1; Lina peeked into it but saw only rakes and shovels. So she opened the greenhouse door. Warm, furry-smelling air washed over her, and all her love for this place came rushing back. Out of habit, she gazed up toward the ceiling, as if she might see her father there on his ladder, tinkering with the sprinkler system, the temperature gauges, and the lights.

The greenhouse light was whiter than the yellowish light of the Ember streetlamps. It came from long tubes that ran the length of the ceiling. In this light, the leaves of the plants shone so green they almost hurt Lina's eyes. On the days when she'd come here with her father, Lina had spent hours wandering along the gravel paths that ran between the vegetable beds, sniffing the leaves, poking her fingers into the dirt, and learning to tell the plants apart by their look and smell. There were the beans and peas with their curly tendrils, the dark green spinach, the ruffled lettuce, and the hard, pale green cabbages, some of them as big as a newborn baby's head. What she loved best was to rub the leaves of the tomato plant between her fingers and breathe in their pungent, powdery smell.

A long, straight path led from one end of the building to the other. About halfway down the path, Clary was crouching by a bed of carrots. Lina ran toward her, and Clary smiled, brushed the dirt from her hands, and stood up.

Clary was tall and solid, with big hands and knobby knuckles. She had a square jaw and square shoulders, and brown hair cut in a short, squarish way. You might have thought from looking at her that she was a gruff, unfriendly person—but her nature was just the opposite. She was more comfortable with plants than with people, Lina's father had always said. She was strong but shy, a person of much knowledge but few words. Lina had always liked her. Even when she was little, Clary did not treat her like a baby but gave her jobs to do—pulling up carrots, picking bugs off cabbages. Since her parents had died, Lina had come many times to talk to Clary, or just to work silently beside her. Clary was always kind to her, and working with the plants took Lina's mind off her grief.

"Well," said Clary. She smiled at Lina, wiped her hands on her already grimy pants, and smiled some more. Finally she said, "You're a messenger."

"Yes," said Lina, "and I have a message for you. It's from Arbin Swinn. 'Please add four extra crates to my order, two of potatoes and two of cabbages.'"

Clary frowned. "I can't do that," she said. "At least, I can send him the cabbages, but only one small crate of potatoes."

"Why?" asked Lina.

"Well, we have a sort of problem with the potatoes."

"What is it?" asked Lina. Clary had a habit of answering questions in the briefest possible way. You had to keep asking and asking before she would believe you really wanted to know and weren't just being polite. Then she would explain, and you could see how much she knew, and how much she loved her work.

"I'll show you," she said. She led the way to a bed where the green leaves were spotted with black. "A new disease. I haven't seen it before. When you dig up the potatoes, they're runny inside instead of hard, and they stink. I'm going to have to throw out all the ones in this bed. There are only a few beds left that aren't infected."

Most people in Ember had potatoes at every meal—mashed, boiled, stewed, roasted. They'd had fried potatoes, too, in the days before the cooking oil ran out.

"I'd hate it if we couldn't have potatoes anymore," Lina said.

"I would, too," said Clary.

They sat on the edge of the potato bed and talked for a while, about Lina's grandmother and the baby, about the trouble Clary was having with the beehives, and about the greenhouse sprinkler system. "It hasn't worked right since . . ." Clary hesitated and glanced sideways at Lina. "For a long time," she said. She didn't want to say "since your father died." Lina understood that.

She stood up. "I should go," she said. "I have to

take Arbin Swinn the answer to his message."

"I hope you'll come again," said Clary. "You can come whenever . . . you can come any time." Lina said thank you and turned to go.

But just outside the greenhouse door, she heard running footsteps and a strange, high, sobbing sound. Or rather, she heard sobs and then a wail, sobs and then a shout, and then more sobs, getting louder. She looked back toward the rear of the greenhouses, toward the trash heaps. "Clary," she called. "There's something . . ."

Clary came out and listened, too.

"Do you hear it?"

"Yes," said Clary. She frowned. "I'm afraid it's . . . it's someone who . . ." She peered toward the cry-ing noise. "Yes . . . here he comes." Her strong hand gripped Lina's shoulder for a moment. "You'd better go," she said. "I'll take care of this."

"But what is it?"

"Never mind. Just go on."

But Lina wanted to see. Once Clary had walked away, she ducked behind the toolshed. From there she watched.

The noise came closer. Out beyond the trash heaps, a figure appeared. It was a man, running and stumbling, his arms flopping. He looked as if he was about to fall over, as if he could hardly pick up his feet. In fact, as he came closer he *did* fall. He tripped over a hose and crumpled to the ground as if his bones had dissolved.

Clary stooped down and said something to him in a voice too low for Lina to hear.

The man was panting. When he turned over and sat up, Lina saw that his face was scratched and his eyes wide open in fright. His sobs had turned into hiccups. She recognized him. It was Sadge Merrall, one of the clerks in the Supply Depot. He was a quiet, long-faced man who always looked worried.

Clary helped him to his feet. The two of them came slowly toward the greenhouse, and as they got closer Lina could hear what the man was saying. He spoke very fast in a weak, trembly voice, hardly stopping for breath. ". . . was sure I could do it. I said to myself, Just one step after another, that's all, one step after another. I knew it would be dark. Who doesn't know that? But I thought, Well, dark can't hurt you. I'll just keep going, I thought. . . ."

He stumbled and sagged against Clary. "Careful," Clary said. They reached the door of the greenhouse, and Clary struggled to open it. Without thinking, Lina darted out from behind the toolshed and opened it for her. Clary shot her a quick frown but said nothing.

Sadge didn't stop talking. ". . . But then the farther I went the darker it was, and you can't just keep walking into black dark, can you? It's like a wall in front of you. I kept turning around to look at the lights of the city, because that's all there was to see, and then I'd say to myself, Don't look back, keep moving. But I kept tripping and falling. . . . The ground is rough out there, I scraped my hands." He held up one hand and stared at the red scratches on it, which oozed drops of blood.

They got him into Clary's office and sat him down in her chair. He rambled on.

"Be brave, I said to myself. I kept going and going, but then all of a sudden I thought, Anything could be out here! There could be a pit a thousand feet deep right in front of me. There could be . . . something that bites. I've heard stories . . . rats as big as garbage bins . . . And I had to get out of there. So I turned around and I ran."

"Never mind," said Clary. "You're all right now. Lina, get him some water."

Lina found a cup and filled it from the sink in the corner. Sadge took it with a shaking hand and drank it down.

"What were you looking for?" Lina asked. She knew what *she* would have been looking for if she'd gone out there. She'd thought about it countless times.

Sadge stared at her. He seemed to have to puzzle over her question. Finally he said, "I was looking for something that could help us."

"What would it be?"

"I don't know. Like a stairway that leads somewhere, maybe. Or a building full of . . . I don't know, useful things."

"But you didn't find anything? Or see anything?" Lina asked, disappointed.

"Nothing! Nothing! There is nothing out there!" His voice became a shout and his eyes looked wild again. "Or if there is, we can never get to it. Never! Not without a light." He took a long, shaky breath. For a while he stared at the floor. Then he stood up. "I think I'm all right now. I'll be going."

With uncertain steps, he went down the path and out the door.

"Well," said Clary. "I'm sorry that happened while you were here. I was afraid you might be scared, that's why I told you to go."

But Lina was full of questions, not fear. She had heard tales of people who tried to go out into the Unknown Regions. She had thought about it herself— in fact, she'd wondered the same things as Sadge. She had imagined making her way out into the dark and coming to a wall in which she would find the door to a tunnel, and at the end of the tunnel would be the other city, the city of light that she had dreamed about. All it would take was the courage to walk away from Ember and into the darkness, and then to keep going.

It might have been possible if you could carry a light to show the way. But in Ember, there was no such thing as a light you could carry with you. Outside lights were fixed to their poles, or to the roofs of houses; inside lights were set into the ceiling or had cords that had to be plugged in. Over the course of Ember's history, various clever people had tried to invent a movable light, but all of them had failed. One man had managed to ignite the end of a stick of wood by holding it against the electric burner on his stove. He'd run across the city with the flaming stick, planning to use it to light his journey. But by the time he got to the trash heaps, his torch had gone out. Other people latched on to his idea—one woman who lived on Dedlock Street, very near the edge of the city, managed to get into the Unknown Regions with her flaming stick. But the stick burned quickly, and before she could go far, the flame singed her hands and she threw it down. Everyone who had tried to penetrate the Unknown Regions had come back within a few hours, their enterprise a failure.

Lina and Clary stood by the open door of the greenhouse and watched Sadge shuffle toward the city. As he neared the trash heaps, two guards who had been sitting on the ground got to their feet. They walked over to Sadge, and each of them took hold of one of his arms.

"Uh-oh," said Clary. "Those guards are always looking for trouble."

"But Sadge hasn't broken any law," said Lina.

"Doesn't matter. They need something to do. They'll get some fun out of scaring him." One of the guards was shaking his finger at Sadge and saying something in a voice almost loud enough for Lina to hear. "Poor man," said Clary with a sigh. "He's the fourth one this year."

The guards were marching Sadge away now, one on either side of him. Sadge looked limp and small between them.

"What do you think is out in the Unknown Regions, Clary?"

Clary stared down at the ground, where the light from the greenhouse was casting long, thin shadows of them both. "I don't know. Nothing, I guess."

"And do you think Ember is the only light in the dark world?"

Clary sighed. "I don't know," she said. She gave Lina a long look. Her eyes, Lina thought, looked a little sad. They were a deep brown, almost the color of the earth in the garden bed.

Clary put a hand in her pocket and drew something out. "Look," she said. In the palm of her hand was a white bean. "Something in this seed knows how to make a bean plant. How does it know that?"

"I don't know," said Lina, staring at the hard, flat bean.

"It knows because it has life in it," said Clary. "But where does life come from? What *is* life?"

Lina could see that words were welling up in Clary now; her eyes were bright, her cheeks were rosy.

"Take a lamp, for instance. When you plug it in, it comes alive, in a way. It lights up. That's because it's connected to a wire that's connected to the generator, which is making electricity, though don't ask me how. But a bean seed isn't connected to anything. Neither are people. We don't have plugs and wires that connect us to generators. What makes living things go is *inside* them somehow." Her dark eyebrows drew together over her eyes. "What I mean is," she said finally, "something is going on that we don't understand. They say the Builders made the city. But who made the Builders? Who made *us*? I think the answer must be somewhere outside of Ember."

"In the Unknown Regions?"

"Maybe. Maybe not. I don't know." She brushed her hands together in a time-to-get-back-to-work way.

"Clary," said Lina quickly, "here's what I think." Her heart sped up. She hadn't told this to anyone before. "In my mind, I see another city." Lina watched to see if Clary was going to laugh at her, or smile in that overly kind way. She didn't, so Lina went on. "It isn't like Ember; it's white and gleaming. The buildings are tall and sort of sparkle. Everything is bright, not just inside the buildings but all around them, too, even up in the sky. I know it's just my imagination, but it feels real. I think it *is* real."

Clary said, "Hmmm," and then she said, "Where would such a city be?"

"That's what I don't know. Or how to get to it. I keep thinking there's a door somewhere, maybe out in the Unknown Regions—a door that leads out of Ember, and then behind the door a road."

Clary just shrugged her shoulders. "I don't know," she said. "I have to get back to work. But here—take this." She handed Lina the bean seed, took a little pot from a shelf, scooped some dirt into it, and handed the pot to Lina, too. "Stick the bean in here and water it every day," she said. "It looks like nothing, like a little white stone, but inside it there's life. That must be a sort of clue, don't you think? If we could just figure it out."

Lina took the seed and the pot. "Thank you," she said. She wanted to give Clary a hug but didn't, in case it would embarrass her. Instead, she just said goodbye and raced back toward the city.

CHAPTER 5

On Night Street

Granny's mind was getting more and more muddled. Lina would come home in the evenings and find her rifling through the kitchen cupboards, surrounded by cans and jars with their lids off, or tearing the covers off her bed and trying to lift up the mattress with her skinny arms. "It was an important thing," she would say, "the thing that was lost."

"But if you don't know what it was," said Lina, "how will you know when you've found it?"

Granny didn't try to answer this question. She just flapped her hands at Lina and said, "Never mind, never mind, never mind," and kept on searching.

These days, Mrs. Murdo spent a great deal of time sitting by their window rather than her own. She would tell Granny she was just coming to keep her company. "I don't want her to keep me company,"

Granny complained to Lina, and Lina said, "Maybe she's lonely, Granny. Let her come."

Lina rather liked having Mrs. Murdo around—it was a bit like having a mother there. She wasn't anything like Lina's own mother, who had been a dreamy, absent-minded sort of person. Mrs. Murdo was mother-like in quite a different way. She made sure they all ate a good breakfast in the morning—usually potatoes with mushroom gravy and beet tea. She lined up the vitamin pills by each person's plate and made sure they were swallowed. When Mrs. Murdo was there, shoes got picked up and put away, spills were wiped off the furniture, and Poppy always had on clean clothes. Lina could relax when Mrs. Murdo was around. She knew things were taken care of.

Every week, Lina—like all workers between age twelve and age fifteen—had Thursday off. One Thursday, as she was standing in line at the Garn Square market, hoping to get a bag of turnips for stew that night, she overheard a startling conversation between two people standing behind her.

"What I wanted," said one voice, "was some paint for my front door. It hasn't been painted for years. It's gray and peeling, horrible. I heard a store over on Night Street had some. I was hoping for blue."

"Blue would be nice," said the other voice wistfully.

"But when I got there," the first voice continued, "the man said he had no paint, never had. Disagreeable man. All he had were a few colored pencils."

Colored pencils! Lina had not seen colored pencils in any store for ages. Once she'd had two red ones, a blue one, and a brown one. She'd used these for her drawing until they were stubs too small to hold. Now she had only one plain pencil left, and it was rapidly growing shorter.

She longed to have colored pencils for her pictures of the imaginary city. She had a feeling it was a color-ful place, though she didn't know what its colors might be. There were other things, of course, on which her money would be better spent. Granny's only coat was full of holes and coming apart at the seams. But Granny rarely went out, Lina told herself. She was either at home or in her yarn shop. She didn't really need a new coat, did she? Besides, how much could a few pencils cost? She could probably get a coat for Granny *and* some pencils.

So that afternoon she set out for Night Street. She took Poppy with her. Poppy had learned how to ride piggyback—she wrapped her legs around Lina's waist and gripped Lina's throat with her small, strong fingers.

On Budloe Street, people were standing in long lines with their bundles of laundry at the washing stations. The washers stirred the clothes in the washing machines with long poles. In days past, the machines themselves had whirled the clothes around, but not one of them worked anymore.

Lina turned up Hafter Street, where the four streetlamps were still out and a building crew was repairing a partly collapsed roof. Orly Gordon called out to her from high on a ladder, and Lina looked up and waved. Farther on, she passed a woman with bits of rope and string for sale and a man pulling a cart full of carrots and beets to the grocery stores. At the corner, a cluster of little children played catch with a rag ball. The streets were alive with people today. Moving fast, Lina threaded her way among them.

But as she went into Otterwill Street, she saw something that made her slow down. A man was standing on the steps of the Gathering Hall, shouting and howling, and a crowd of people had gathered around him. Lina went closer, and when she saw who it was, her insides gave a lurch. It was Sadge Merrall. His arms flailed wildly, and his eyes were stretched wide open. In a high, rapid voice, he wailed out a stream of words: "I have been to the Unknown Regions!" he cried. "There is nothing, nothing, nothing there! Did you think something out there might save us? Ha! There's only darkness and monsters, darkness and terrible deep holes, darkness forever! The rats are the size of houses! The rocks are sharp as knives! The darkness sucks your breath out! No hope for us out there, oh no! No hope, no hope!" He went on like this for a few minutes and then crumpled to the ground. The people watching him looked at each other and shook their heads.

"Gone mad," Lina heard someone say.

"Yes, completely," said someone else.

Suddenly Sadge sprang up again and resumed his terrible shouting. The crowd stepped back. Some of them hurried away. A few of them approached Sadge, speaking in calming voices. They took him by the arms and led him, still shouting, down the steps.

"Who dat? Who dat?" said Poppy in her small, piercing voice. Lina turned away from the miserable spectacle. "Hush, Poppy," she said. "It's a poor, sad man. He doesn't feel good. We mustn't stare."

She headed toward Night Street, which ran along Greengate Square. There a stringy-haired man sat cross-legged on the ground playing a flute made out of a drainpipe, and five or six Believers circled him, clapping and singing. "Soon, soon, coming soon," they sang. What's coming soon? Lina wondered, but she didn't stop to ask.

Two blocks beyond, she came to a store that had no sign in its window. This must be the one, she thought.

At first it looked closed. Its window was dark. But the door opened when she pushed on it, and a bell attached to its doorknob clanked. From the back room came a black-haired man with big teeth and a long neck. "Yes?" he said.

Lina recognized him. He was the one who'd given her the message for the mayor on her very first day of work. His name was Hooper—no, Looper, that was it.

"Do you have pencils for sale?" she asked. It seemed doubtful. The shop's shelves were empty except for a few stacks of used paper.

Poppy squirmed on Lina's back and whimpered a little.

"Sometimes," said Looper.

Poppy's whimper became a wail.

"All right, you can get down," Lina said to her. She set her on the floor, where she tottered about unsteadily.

"What I'd like to see," said Lina, "are your colored pencils. If you have any."

"We have a few," said Looper. "They are somewhat expensive." He smiled, showing his pushy teeth.

"Could I see them?" said Lina.

He went into the back room and returned a moment later, carrying a small box, which he set down on the counter. He took the lid off. Lina bent forward to look.

Inside the box were at least a dozen colored pencils—red, green, blue, yellow, purple, orange. They had never even been sharpened; their ends were flat. They had erasers. Lina's heart gave a few fast beats.

"How much are they?" she said.

"Probably too much for you," the man said.

"Probably *not*," said Lina. "I have a job."

"Good, good," the man said, smiling again. "No need to take offense." He picked up the yellow pencil and twirled it between his fingers. "Each pencil," he said, "five dollars."

Five dollars! For seven, you could buy a coat—it would be an old, patched coat, but still warm. "That's too much," Lina said.

He shrugged and began to put the lid back on the box.

"But maybe . . ." Lina's thoughts raced. "Let me look at them again."

Once more the man lifted the lid and Lina bent over the pencils. She picked one up. It was painted a deep clear blue, and on its flat top was the blue dot of the lead. The pink eraser was held on by a shiny metal collar. So beautiful! I could buy just one, Lina thought. Then I could save a little more and buy a coat for Granny *next* month.

"Make up your mind," said the man. "I have other customers who are interested, if you aren't."

"All right. I'll take one. No, wait." It was like hunger, what she felt. It was the same as when her hand sometimes seemed to reach out by itself to grab a piece of food. It was too strong to resist. "I'll take two," she said, and a faint, dazzly feeling came over her at the thought of what she was doing.

"Which two?" the man said.

There were more colors in that box of pencils than in all of Ember. Ember's colors were all so much the same—gray buildings, gray streets, black sky; even the colors of people's clothes were faded from long use into mud green, and rust red, and gray-blue. But these colors—they were as bright as the leaves and flowers in the greenhouse.

Lina's hand hovered over the pencils. "The blue one," she said. "And . . . the yellow one—no, the . . . the . . ."

The man made an impatient noise in the back of his throat.

"The green one," said Lina. "I'll take the blue and the green." She lifted them out of the box. She took the money from the pocket of her coat and handed it to the man, and she put the pencils in her pocket. They were hers now; she felt a fierce, defiant joy. She turned to go, and that was when she saw that the baby was no longer in the store.

"Poppy!" she cried. She whirled around. "Did you see my little sister go out?" she asked the man. "Did you see which way she went?"

He shrugged. "Didn't notice," he said.

Lina darted into the street and looked in both

directions. She saw lots of people, some children, but no Poppy. She stopped an old woman. "Have you seen a little girl, a baby, walking by herself? In a green jacket, with a hood?" The old woman just stared at her with dull eyes and shook her head.

"Poppy!" Lina called. "Poppy!" Her voice rose to a shout. Such a little baby couldn't have gone far, she thought. Maybe down toward Greengate Square, where there were more people walking around. She began to run.

And then the lights flickered, and flickered again, and went out. Darkness slammed up in front of her like a wall. She stumbled, caught herself, and stood still. She could see absolutely nothing.

Shouts of alarm came from up and down the street, and then silence. Lina stretched her arms out. Was she facing the street or a building? Terror swept through her. I must just stand still, she thought. The lights will come on again in a few seconds, they always do. But she thought of Poppy alone in the blackness, and her legs went weak. *I must find her.*

She took a step. When she didn't bump into anything, she took another step, and the fingers of her right hand crumpled against something hard. The wall of a building, she thought. Keeping her hand against it, she turned left a little and took another step forward. Then suddenly her hand touched empty air. This would be Dedlock Street. Or had she passed Dedlock Street already? She couldn't keep the picture of the streets clear in her mind. The darkness seemed to fill not just the city around her but the inside of her head as well.

Heart pounding, she waited. Come back, lights, she pleaded. Please come back. She wanted to call out to Poppy, to tell her to stand still, not to be afraid, she would come for her soon. But the darkness pressed against her and she couldn't summon her voice. She could hardly breathe. She wanted to claw the darkness away from her eyes, as if it were someone's hands.

Small sounds came from here and there around her—a whimpering, a shuffling. In the distance someone called out incoherently. How many minutes had gone by? The longest blackout ever had been three minutes and fourteen seconds. Surely this was longer.

She could have endured it if she'd been on her own. It was the thought of Poppy, lost, that she couldn't stand—and lost because she had been paying more attention to a box of pencils. Oh, she'd been selfish and greedy, and now she was so, so sorry! She made herself take another step forward. But then she thought, What if I'm going *away* from Poppy? She began to tremble, and she felt the sinking and dissolving inside her that meant she was going to cry. Her legs gave way like wet paper and she slid down until she was sitting on the street, with her head on her knees. Trembling, her mind a wordless whirl of dread, she waited.

An endless time went by. A moan came from somewhere to the left. A door slammed closed. Footsteps started, then stopped. Into Lina's mind floated the beginning of the worst question: What if the lights never . . . ? She squeezed her arms around her knees and made the question stop. Lights come back, she said to herself. Lights come back, come back.

And suddenly they did.

Lina sprang up. There was the street again, and people looking upward with their mouths hanging open. All around, people started crying or wailing or grinning in relief. Then all at once everyone started to hurry, moving fast toward the safety of home in case it should happen again.

Lina ran toward Greengate Square, stopping everyone she passed. "Did you see a little girl walking by herself just before the lights went out?" she asked. "Green jacket with a hood?" But no one wanted to listen to her.

On the Bee Street side of the square stood a few people all talking at once and waving their arms. Lina ran up to them and asked her question.

They stopped talking and stared at her. "How could we have seen anyone? The lights were out," said Nammy Proggs, a tiny old woman whose back was so bent that she had to twist her head sideways to look up.

Lina said, "No, she wandered away *before* the lights went out. She got away from me. She may have come this direction."

"You have to keep your eye on a baby," Nammy Proggs scolded.

"Babies need watching," said one of the women who'd been singing with the Believers.

But someone else said, "Oh, a toddler? Green jacket?" and he walked over to an open shop door and called, "You have that baby in there?" and through the door came someone leading Poppy by the hand.

Lina dashed to her and lifted her up. Poppy broke into loud wails. "You're all right now," said Lina, holding her tightly. "Don't worry, sweetie. You were just lost a moment, now you're all right. I've got you, don't worry." When she looked up to thank the person who'd found her, she saw a face she recognized. It was Doon. He looked the same as when she'd last seen him, except that his hair was shaggier. He had on the same baggy brown jacket he always wore.

"She was marching up the street by herself," he said. "No one knew who she belonged to, so I took her into my father's shop."

"She belongs to me," Lina said. "She's my sister. I was so afraid when she was lost. I thought she might fall and hurt herself, or be knocked over, or . . . Anyway, thank you *so much* for rescuing her."

"Anyone would have," said Doon. He frowned and looked down at the pavement.

Poppy had calmed down and was curled up against Lina's chest with her thumb in her mouth. "And your job—how is it?" Lina asked. "The Pipeworks?"

Doon shrugged his shoulders. "All right," he said. "Interesting, anyway."

She waited, but it seemed that was all he was going to say. "Well, thank you again," she said. She hoisted Poppy around to her back.

"Lucky for you Doon Harrow was around," said Nammy Proggs, who'd been watching them with her sideways glare. "He's a good-hearted boy. Anything breaks at my house, he fixes it." She hobbled after Lina, shaking a finger at her. "You'd better watch that baby more carefully," she called.

"You shouldn't leave her alone," the flute player added.

"I know," said Lina. "You're right."

When she got home, she put the tired baby to bed in the bedroom they shared. Granny had been taking an afternoon nap in the front room and hadn't noticed the blackout at all. Lina told her that the lights had gone out for a few minutes, but she didn't mention anything about Poppy getting lost.

Later, in her bedroom, with Poppy asleep, she took

the two colored pencils from her pocket. They were not quite as beautiful as they had been. When she held them, she remembered the powerful wanting she had felt in that dusty store, and the feeling of it was mixed up with fear and shame and darkness.

CHAPTER 6

The Box in the Closet

It was strange how people didn't talk much about the blackout. Power failures usually aroused lively discussion, with clumps of people collecting on corners and saying to each other, "Where were you when it happened?" and "What's the matter with the electricians, we should kick them out and get new ones," and that sort of thing. This time, it was just the opposite. When Lina went to work the next morning, the street was oddly silent. People walked quickly, their eyes on the ground. Those who did stop to talk spoke in low voices, then hurried on their way.

That day, Lina carried the same message twelve times. All the messengers were carrying it. It was simply this, being passed from one person to another: Seven minutes. The power failure had been more than twice as long as any other so far.

Fear had settled over the city. Lina felt it like a cold chill. She understood now that Doon had been speaking the truth on Assignment Day. Ember was in grave danger.

The next day a notice appeared on all the city's kiosks:

TOWN MEETING

ALL CITIZENS ARE REQUESTED TO ASSEMBLE

IN HARKEN SQUARE AT 6 P.M. TOMORROW

TO RECEIVE IMPORTANT INFORMATION.

MAYOR LEMANDER COLE

What kind of important information? Lina wondered. Good news or bad? She was impatient to hear it.

The next day, people streamed into Harken Square from all four directions, crowding together so close that each person hardly had room to move. Children sat on the shoulders of fathers. Short people tried to push toward the front. Lina spotted Lizzie and called a greeting to her. She saw Vindie Chance, too, who had brought her little brother. Lina had decided to leave Poppy at home with Granny. There was too much danger of losing her in a crowd like this.

The town clock began to strike. Six vibrating bongs rang out, and a murmur of anticipation swept through the crowd. People stood on tiptoe, craning to see. The door of the Gathering Hall opened, and the mayor came out, flanked by two guards. One of the guards handed the mayor a megaphone, and the mayor began to speak. His voice came through the megaphone both blurry and crackly.

"People of Ember," he said. He waited. The crowd fell silent, straining to hear.

"People of Ember," the mayor said again. He looked from side to side. The light glinted off his bald head. "Our city has experienced some slight diff-cushlaylie. Times like this require gresh peshn frush all."

"What did he say?" people whispered urgently. "What did he say? I couldn't hear him."

"Slight difficulties," someone said. "Requires great patience from us all."

"But I stand here today," the mayor went on, "to reassure you. Difficult times will pass. We are mayg effn effuff."

"What?" came the sharp whisper. "What did he say?"

Those near the front passed word back. "Making every effort," they said. "Every effort."

"Louder!" someone shouted.

The mayor's voice blared through the megaphone louder but even less clear. "Wursh poshuling!" he said. "Pank. Mushen pank. No rrrshen pank."

"We can't hear you!" someone else yelled. Lina felt

a stirring around her, a muttering. Someone pushed against her back, forcing her forward.

"He said we mustn't panic," someone said. "He said panic is the worst possible thing. No reason to panic, he said."

On the steps of the Gathering Hall, the two guards moved a little closer to the mayor. He raised the megaphone and spoke again.

"*Slooshns!*" he bellowed. "*Arbingfoun!*"

"Solutions," the people in front called to the people in back. "Solutions are being found, he said."

"*What* solutions?" called a woman standing near Lina. People elsewhere in the crowd echoed what the woman had said. "What solutions? What solutions?" Their cry became a chorus, louder and louder.

Again Lina felt the pressure from behind as people moved forward toward the Gathering Hall. Jostling arms poked her, bulky bodies bumped her and crushed her. Her heart began to pound. I have to get out of here! she thought.

She started ducking beneath arms and darting into whatever space she could find, making her way toward the rear of the crowd. Noise was rising everywhere. The mayor's voice kept coming in blasts of incomprehensible sound, and the people in the crowd were either shouting angrily or yelping in fear of being squashed. Someone stepped on Lina's foot, and her scarf was half yanked off. For a few seconds she was afraid she was going to be trampled. But at last she struggled free and ran up onto the steps of the school. From there she saw that the two guards were hustling the mayor back through the door of the Gathering Hall. The crowd roared, and a few people started hurling whatever they could find—pebbles, garbage, crumpled paper, even their own hats.

At the other side of the square, Doon and his father battled their way down Gilly Street. "Move fast," his father said. "We don't want to be caught up in this crowd." They crossed Broad Street and took the long way home, through the narrow lanes behind the school.

"Father," said Doon as they hurried along, "the mayor is a fool, don't you think?"

For a moment his father didn't answer. Then he said, "He's in a tough spot, son. What would you have him do?"

"Not lie, at least," Doon said. "If he really has a solution, he should have told us. He shouldn't pretend he has solutions when he doesn't."

Doon's father smiled. "That would be a good start," he agreed.

"It makes me so angry, the way he talks to us," said Doon.

Doon's father put a hand on Doon's back and steered him toward the corner. "A great many things make you angry lately," he said.

"For good reason," said Doon.

"Maybe. The trouble with anger is, it gets hold of you. And then you aren't the master of yourself anymore. Anger is."

Doon walked on silently. Inwardly, he groaned. He knew what his father was going to say, and he didn't feel like hearing it.

"And when anger is the boss, you get—"

"I know," said Doon. "Unintended consequences."

"That's right. Like hitting your father in the ear with a shoe heel."

"I didn't mean to."

"That's exactly my point."

They walked on down Pibb Street. Doon shoved his hands into the pockets of his jacket and scowled at the sidewalk. Father doesn't even *have* a temper, he thought. He's as mild as a glass of water. He can't possibly understand.

Lina was running. She'd already dismissed the mayor's speech from her mind. She sped by people on Otterwill Street going back to open their stores and overheard snatches of conversation as she passed. "Expects us to believe . . . ," said one voice. "He's just trying to keep us quiet," said another. "Heading for disaster . . . ," said a third. All the voices shook with anger and fear.

Lina didn't want to think about it. Her feet

slapped the stones of the street, her hair flew out behind her. She would go home, she would make hot potato soup for the three of them, and then she would take out her new pencils and draw.

She climbed the stairs next to the yarn shop two at a time and burst through the door of the apartment. Something was on the floor just in front of her feet, and she tripped and fell down hard on her hands and knees. She stared. By the open closet door was a great pile of coats and boots and bags and boxes, their contents all spilled out and tangled up. A thumping and rattling came from inside the closet.

"Granny?"

More thumps. Granny's head poked around the edge of the closet door. "I should have looked in here a long time ago," she said. "This is where it would be, of course. You should *see* what's in here!"

Lina gazed around at the incredible mess. Into this closet had been packed the junk of decades, jammed into cardboard boxes, stuffed into old pillowcases and laundry bags, and heaped up in a pile so dense that you couldn't pull one thing out without pulling all the rest with it. The shelf above the coatrack was just as crammed as the space below, mostly with old clothes that were full of moth holes and eaten away by mildew. When she was younger, Lina had tried exploring in this closet, but she never got far. She'd pull out an old scarf that would fall to pieces in her hands, or open a box that proved to be full of bent carpet tacks. Soon she would shove everything back in and give up.

But Granny was really doing the job right. She grunted and panted as she wrenched free the closet's packed-in stuff and tossed it behind her. It was clear that she was having fun. As Lina watched, a bag of rags came tumbling out the door, and then an old brown shoe with no laces.

"Granny," said Lina, suddenly uneasy. "Where's the baby?"

"Oh, she's here!" came Granny's voice from the depths of the closet. "She's been helping me."

Lina got up from the floor and looked around. She soon spotted Poppy. She was sitting behind the couch, in the midst of the clutter. In front of her was a small box made of something dark and shiny. It had a hinged lid, and the lid was open, hanging backward.

"Poppy," said Lina, "let me see that." She stooped down. There was some sort of mechanism on the edge of the lid—a kind of lock, Lina thought. The box was beautifully made, but it had been damaged. There were dents and scratches in its hard, smooth surface. It looked as if it had been a container for something valuable. But the box was empty now. Lina picked it up and felt around in it to be sure. There was nothing inside at all.

"Was there something in this box, Poppy? Did you

find something in here?" But Poppy only chortled happily. She was chewing on some crumpled paper. She had paper in her hands, too, and was tearing it. Shreds of paper were strewn around her. Lina picked one up. It was covered with small, perfect printing.

CHAPTER 7

A Message Full of Holes

It was the printing that sparked Lina's curiosity. It was not handwriting, or if it was, it was the neatest, most regular handwriting she had ever seen. It was more like the letters printed on cans of food or along the sides of pencils. Something other than a hand had written those words. A machine of some kind. This was the writing of the Builders. And so this piece of paper must have come from the Builders, too.

Lina gathered up the scraps of paper from the floor and gently pried open Poppy's fists and mouth to extract the crumpled wads. She put all this into the dented box and carried it to her room.

That evening, Granny and the baby were both asleep by a little after eight. Lina had nearly an hour to examine her discovery. She took the scraps from the box and spread them out on the table in her bedroom. The paper was thick; at each torn edge was a fringe of tangled fibers. There were many little pieces and one big piece with so many holes that it was like lace. The chewed bits were beyond saving—they were almost a paste. But Lina spread out the big lacy piece and saw that on one edge of it, which was still intact, was a column of numbers. She collected all the dry scraps and puzzled over them for a long time, trying to figure out where they fit into the larger piece. When she had arranged them as well as she could, this was what she had:

Instru   r Egres

This offic   doc   in stric
secur   period of   ears.
        prepara   made for
inha   city.
as foll

1. Exp
    riv   ip   ork .
2.   ston   marked with E by r
        dge
3.   adde down iverb nk
            to edge appr   eight
        low.
4.   acks to the
    wat r,   find door of bo
        ker. Ke   hind small steel

pan   the right   . Rem
   ey, open do .

5.   oat,   stocked with
   nec   uip ent. Bac
   ont   s   eet.

6. Usi   opes, lowe
    ter. Head dow st   . Us pa
  av   cks and assist over rap .

7.   approx. 3 hours. Disem
     . Follow   pat .

Lina could make sense of only a few words here and there. Even so, something about this tattered document was exciting. It was not like anything Lina had ever seen. She stared at the very first word at the top of the page, "Instru," and she suddenly knew what it must be. She'd seen it often enough at school. It had to be the beginning of "Instructions."

Her heart began knocking at her chest like a fist at a door. She had found something. She had found something strange and important: instructions for something. But for what? And how terrible that Poppy had found it first and ruined it!

It occurred to Lina that this might be what her grandmother had been talking about for so long. Perhaps *this* was the thing that was lost. But of course not knowing what had been lost, Granny wouldn't have recognized the box when she saw it. She would have tossed it out of the closet just as carelessly as she tossed everything else. Anyhow, it didn't matter whether this was the thing or not the thing. It was a mystery in itself, whatever it was, and Lina was determined to solve it.

The first step was to stick the scraps of paper down. They were so light that a breath could scatter them. She had a little bit of glue left in an old bottle. Painstakingly, she put a dot of glue on each of the scraps and pressed each one into its place on one of her precious few remaining whole sheets of paper. She put another piece of paper on top of this and set the box on top to flatten everything down. Just as she finished, the lights went out—she'd forgotten to keep an eye on the clock on her windowsill. She had to undress and get in bed in the dark.

She was too excited to sleep much that night. Her mind whirled around, trying to think what the message she'd found might be. She felt sure it had something to do with saving the city. What if these instructions were for fixing the electricity? Or for making a movable light? That would change everything.

When the lights went on in the morning, she had a few minutes before Poppy wakened to work at the puzzle. But there were so many words missing! How could she ever make sense of such a jumble? As she pulled on her red jacket and tied the frayed and knotted laces of her shoes, she thought about it.

If the paper was important, she shouldn't keep it to herself. But who could she tell? Maybe the messenger captain. She would know about things like official documents.

"Captain Fleery," Lina said when she got to work, "would you have time to come home with me later on today? Just for a minute? I found something I'd like to show you."

"Found what?" asked Captain Fleery.

"Some paper with writing on it. I think it might be important."

Captain Fleery raised her skinny eyebrows. "What do you mean, important?"

"Well, I'm not sure. Maybe it isn't. But would you look at it anyway?"

So that evening Captain Fleery came home with Lina and peered at the bits of paper. She bent down and inspected the writing. "Foll?" she said. "Acks? Rem? Ont? What kind of words are those?"

"I don't know," said Lina. "The words are all broken up because Poppy chewed on them."

"I see," said Captain Fleery. She poked at the paper. "This looks like instructions for something," she said. "A recipe, I suppose. 'Small steel pan'—that would be what you use to cook it with."

"But who would have such small, perfect writing?"

"That's the way they wrote in the old days," said Captain Fleery. "It could be a very *old* recipe."

"But then why would it have been kept in this beautiful box?" She showed the box to Captain Fleery. "I think it was locked up in here for some reason, and you wouldn't lock up something unless it was important. . . ."

But Captain Fleery didn't seem to have heard her. "Or," she said, "it could be a school exercise. Someone's homework that never got turned in."

"But have you ever seen paper like this? Doesn't it look as if it came from someplace else—not here?"

Captain Fleery straightened up. A look of puzzlement came over her face. "There *is* nowhere but here," she said. She put both her hands on Lina's shoulders. "You, my dear, are letting your imagination run away with you. Are you overtired, Lina? Are you anxious? I could put you on short days for a while."

"No," said Lina, "I'm fine. I am. But I don't know what to do about . . ." She gestured toward the paper.

"Never mind," said Captain Fleery. "Don't think about it. Throw it away. You're worrying too much— I know, I know, we all are, there's so much to worry about, but we mustn't let it unsettle us." She gave Lina a long look. Her eyes were the color of dishwater. "Help is coming," she said.

"Help?"

"Yes. Coming to save us."

"Who is?"

Captain Fleery bent down and lowered her voice, as if telling a secret. "Who built our city, dear?"

"The Builders," said Lina.

"That's right. And the Builders will come again and show us the way."

"They will?"

"Very soon," said Captain Fleery.

"How do you know?"

Captain Fleery straightened up again and clapped a hand over her heart. "I know it here," she said. "And I have seen it in a dream. So have all of us, all the Believers."

So that's what they believe, Lina thought—and Captain Fleery is one of them. She wondered how the captain could feel so sure about it, just because she'd seen it in a dream. Maybe it was the same for her as the sparkling city was for Lina—she *wanted* it to be true.

The captain's face lit up. "I know what you must do, dear—come to one of our meetings. It would lift your heart. We sing."

"Oh," said Lina, "thank you, but I'm not sure I . . . maybe sometime . . ." She tried to be polite, but she knew she wouldn't go. She didn't want to stand around waiting for the Builders. She had other things to do.

Captain Fleery patted her arm. "No pressure, dear," she said. "If you change your mind, let me know.

But take my advice: forget about your little puzzle project. Lie down and take a nap. Clears the mind." Her narrow face beamed kindness down at Lina. "You take tomorrow off," she said. She raised a hand goodbye and went down the stairs.

Lina took advantage of her day off to go to the Supply Depot to see Lizzie Bisco. Lizzie was quick and smart. She might have some good ideas.

At the Supply Depot, crowds of shopkeepers stood in long, disorderly lines that stretched out the door. They pushed and jostled and snapped impatiently at each other. Lina joined them, but they seemed so frantic that they frightened her a little. They must be very sure now that the supplies are running out, she thought, and they're determined to get what they can before it's too late.

When she got close to the head of the line, she heard the same conversation several times. "Sorry," the clerk would say when a shopkeeper asked for ten packets of sewing needles, or a dozen drinking glasses, or twenty packages of light bulbs. "There's a severe shortage of that item. You can have only one." Or else the clerk would say, "Sorry. We're out of that entirely." "Forever?" "Forever."

Lina knew that it hadn't always been this way. When Ember was a young city, the storerooms were full. They held everything the citizens could want—so much it seemed the supplies would never run out.

Lina's grandmother had told her that schoolchildren were given a tour of the storerooms as part of their education. They took an elevator from the street level to a long, curving tunnel with doors on both sides and other tunnels branching off it. The guide led the tour down the long passages, opening one door after another. "This area," he would say, "is Canned Goods. Next we come to School Supplies. And around this bend we have Kitchenware. Next come Carpentry Tools." At each door, the children crowded against each other to see.

"Every room had something different," Granny told Lina. "Boxes of toothpaste in one room. Bottles of cooking oil. Bars of soap. Boxes of pills—there were twenty rooms just for vitamin pills. One room was stacked with hundreds of cans of fruit. There was something called pineapple, I remember that one especially."

"What was pineapple?" asked Lina.

"It was yellow and sweet," said Granny with a dreamy look in her eyes. "I had it four times before we ran out of it."

But these tours had been discontinued long before Lina was born. The storerooms, people said, were no longer a pleasure to look at. Their dusty shelves stood mostly empty now. It was rumored that in some rooms nothing was left at all. A child seeing the rooms where powdered milk had been stored, or the rooms that stored bandages or socks or pins or notebooks, or—most of all—the dozens of rooms that had once held thousands of light bulbs—would not feel, as earlier generations of children had, that Ember was endlessly rich. Today's children, if they were to tour the storerooms, would feel afraid.

Thinking about all this, Lina waited in the line of people at Lizzie's station. When she got to the front, she leaned forward with her elbows on the counter and whispered, "Lizzie, can you meet me after you're through with work? I'll wait for you right outside the door." Lizzie nodded eagerly.

At four o'clock, Lizzie came trotting out the office door. Lina said to her, "Will you come home with me for a minute? I want to show you something."

"Sure," said Lizzie, and as they walked, Lizzie talked. "My wrist is killing me from writing all day," she said. "You have to write in the tiniest letters to save paper, so I get a terrible *cramp* in my wrist and my fingers. And people are so *rude*. Today they were worse than ever. I said to some guy, 'You can't have fifteen cans of corn, you can only have three,' and he said, 'Look, don't tell me that, I saw plenty of cans in the Pott Street market just yesterday,' and I said, 'Well, that's why there aren't so many left today,' and he said, 'Don't be smart with me, carrot-head.' But what am I supposed to do? I can't *make* cans of corn out of thin air."

They passed through Harken Square, around the Gathering Hall, and down Roving Street, where three of the floodlights were out, making a cave of shadow.

"Lizzie," said Lina, interrupting the flow of talk. "Is it true about light bulbs?"

"Is what true?"

"That there aren't very many left?"

Lizzie shrugged. "I don't know. They hardly ever let us go downstairs into the storerooms. All we see are the reports the carriers turn in—how many forks in Room 1146, how many doorknobs in 3291, how many children's shoes in 2249 . . ."

"But when you see the report for the light bulb rooms, what does it say?"

"I never get to see that one," said Lizzie. "That one, and a few other ones like the vitamin report, only a few people can see."

"Who?"

"Oh, the mayor, and of course old Flab Face." Lina looked at her questioningly. "You know, Farlo Batten, the head of the storerooms. He is so *mean*, Lina, you would just hate him. He counts us late if we come in even two minutes after eight, and he looks over our shoulders as we're writing, which is awful because he has bad breath, and he runs his finger over what we've written and says, 'This word is illegible, that word is illegible, these numbers are illegible.' It's his favorite word, illegible."

When they came to Lina's street, Lina ducked her head in the door of the yarn shop and said hello to Granny, and then they climbed the stairs to the apartment. Lizzie was talking about how hard it was to stand up all day, how it made her knees ache, how her shoes pinched her feet. She stopped talking long enough to say hello to Evaleen Murdo, who was sitting by the window with Poppy on her lap, and then she began again as Lina led her into her bedroom.

"Lina, where were you when the big blackout came?" she asked, but she went right on without waiting for an answer. "I was at home, *luckily*. But it was scary, wasn't it?"

Lina nodded. She didn't want to talk about what had happened that day.

"I hate those blackouts," Lizzie went on. "People say there's going to be more and more of them, and that someday—" She stopped, frowned, and started again. "Anyway, nothing bad happened to me. After that, I got up and figured out a whole new way to do my hair."

It seemed to Lina that Lizzie was like a clock wound too tightly and running too fast. She'd always been a little this way, but today she was more so than ever. Her gaze skipped from one spot to another, her fingers twiddled with the edge of her shirt. She looked paler than usual, too. Her freckles stood out like little smudges of dirt on her nose.

"Lizzie," said Lina, beckoning toward the table in the corner of her room. "I want to show you—"

But Lizzie wasn't listening. "You're so lucky to be a messenger, Lina," she said. "Is it fun? I wish I could have been one. I would have been so good at it. My job is so boring."

Lina turned and looked at her. "Isn't there *anything* you like about it?"

Lizzie pursed her lips in a tiny smile and looked sideways at Lina. "There's one thing," she said.

"What?"

"I can't tell you. It's a secret."

"Oh," said Lina. Then you shouldn't have mentioned it at all, she thought.

"Maybe I'll tell you someday," said Lizzie. "I don't know."

"Well, I like *my* job," Lina said. "But what I wanted to talk to you about was what I found yesterday. It's this."

She lifted the box away and took up the piece of paper covering the patched-together document. Lizzie gave it a quick look. "Is it a message someone gave you? That got torn up?"

"No, it was in our closet. Poppy was chewing on it, that's why it's torn up. But look at the writing on it. Isn't it strange?"

"Uh-huh," said Lizzie. "You know who has beautiful handwriting? Myla Bone, who works with me.

You should see it, it's got curly tails on the y's and the g's, and fancy loops on the capital letters. Of course Flab Face hates it, he says it's illegible. . . ."

Lina slid the piece of paper back over the pasted-down scraps. She wondered why she had thought Lizzie would be interested in what she'd found. She'd always had fun with Lizzie. But their fun was usually with games—hide-and-seek, tag, the kinds of games where you run and climb. Lizzie never had been much interested in anything that was written on paper.

So Lina quietly put the document back in its place, and she sat down with Lizzie on the floor. She listened and listened until Lizzie's chatter ran down. "I'd better go," Lizzie said. "It was fun to see you, Lina. I miss you." She stood up. She fluffed her hair. "What was it you wanted to show me? Oh, yes—the fancy writing. Really nice. Lucky you to find it. Come and see me again soon, all right? I get so bored in that office."

Lina made beet soup for dinner that night, and Poppy spilled hers and made a red lake on the table. Granny stared into her bowl, stirring and stirring the soup with her spoon, but she didn't eat. She didn't feel quite right, she told Lina; after a while she wandered off to bed. Lina cleaned up the kitchen quickly. As soon as her chores were out of the way, she could get back to studying her document. She washed Poppy's clothes. She sewed on the buttons that had come off her messenger jacket. She picked up the rags and sacks and boxes and bags that Granny had tossed out of the closet. And by the time she had done all this and put Poppy to bed, she still had almost half an hour to study the fragments of paper.

She sat down at her desk and uncovered the document. With her elbows on either side of it and her chin resting in her hands, she pored over it. Though Lizzie and Captain Fleery had paid it no attention, Lina still thought this torn-up page must be important. Why else would it have been in such a cleverly fastened box? Maybe she should show it to the mayor, she thought reluctantly. She didn't like the mayor. She didn't trust him, either. But if this document was important to the future of the city, he was the one who should know about it. Of course, she couldn't ask the mayor to come to her house. She pictured him puffing up the stairs, squeezing through the door, looking disapprovingly at the clutter in their house, recoiling from Poppy's sticky hands—no, it wouldn't do.

But she didn't want to take her carefully patched-together document to the Gathering Hall, either. It was just too fragile. The best thing to do, she decided, was to write the mayor a note. She settled down to do this.

She found a fairly unspoiled half-piece of paper, and, using a plain pencil (she wasn't going to waste her colored ones on the mayor), she wrote:

Dear Mayor Cole,

    I have discovered a document that was in the closet. It is instructions for something. I believe it is important because it is written in very old printing. Unfortunately it got chewed up by my sister, so it is not all there. But you can still read some bits of it, such as:

      marked with E
      find door of bo
      small steel pan

    I will show you this document if you want to see it.

                Sincerely yours,
                Lina Mayfleet, Messenger
                34 Quillium Square

She folded the note in half and wrote "Mayor Cole" on the front. On her way to work the next morning, she took it to the Gathering Hall. No one was sitting at the guard's desk, so Lina left the note there, placed so that the guard would see it when he arrived. Then, feeling that she had done her duty, she went off to her station.

Several days went by. The messages Lina carried were full of worry and fear. "Do you have any extra Baby Drink? I can't find it at the store." "Have you heard what they're saying about the generator?" "We can't come tonight—Grandpa B. won't get out of bed."

Every day when she got home from work, Lina asked Granny, "Did a message come for me?" But there was nothing. Maybe the mayor hadn't gotten her note. Maybe he'd gotten it and paid no attention. After a week, Lina decided she was tired of waiting. If the mayor wasn't interested in what she'd found, too bad for him. *She* was interested. She would figure it out herself.

Twice during the week, when Poppy and Granny were both asleep, she'd had a little free time. She'd spent this time making a copy of the document, in case anything happened to the fragile original. It had taken her a long time. She used one of her few remaining pieces of paper—an old label, slightly torn, from a can of peas. The copy was as accurate as she could make it, with the missing bits between the letters carefully indicated as dashes. She had tucked it under the mattress of her bed for safekeeping.

Now she finally had a whole free evening. Poppy and Granny were both asleep, and the apartment was tidy. Lina sat down at her table and uncovered the patched-together document. She tied back her hair so it wouldn't keep falling in her face, and she put a piece of paper next to her—blank except for a little bit of Poppy's scribbling—to write down what she decoded.

She started with the title. The first word she'd already figured out. It had to be "Instructions." The next word could be "for." Then came "Egres"—she wasn't sure about that. Maybe it was someone's name. Egresman. Egreston. "Instructions for Egreston." She decided to call it "The Instructions" for short.

She went on to the first line. "This offic doc" probably meant "This official document." Maybe "secur" meant "secure." Or "security." Then there were the words "period" and "ears" and "city." But after that, so much was missing.

She studied the line next to the number 1. *Exp.* That could be *Expect* or *Expert* or so many things. She moved on to *riv.* That might be part of a word like "drive" or "strive." What could *ip* and *ork* possibly be? They were so close together, maybe they were part of one word. What ended with *-ip*? *Whip,* Lina thought. *Trip. Slip.* What ended with *-ork*? *Fork* came to mind immediately. *Tripfork. Slipfork.* Nothing she could think of made sense.

Maybe it wasn't *fork.* What else ended in *-ork*? Starting at the beginning of the alphabet, Lina went through all the words that rhymed with *fork.* Most of them were nonsense: *bork, dork, gork, hork, jork.* . . . This isn't going to work, she thought miserably. Oh . . . *work*! The word could be *work.*

Then what would the first part be? *Tripwork? Flipwork?* But maybe there was a letter between the p and the w. *Dipswork? Pipswork?*

Suddenly it came to her. Pipeworks. Pipeworks!

That had to be it. Something in this message was about the Pipeworks!

Lina looked back at *Exp* and *riv. Riv!* That could be *river!* Rapidly she ran her eyes down the page. In line 3, she saw *iverb nk*—that looked like *riverbank.* The word *door* jumped out at her from line 4, whole on its scrap of paper. Lina took a quick breath. A door! What if it was the one she'd wished for, the one that led to the other city? Maybe her city was real after all, and these were instructions for finding it!

She wanted to leap from her chair and shout. The message had something to do with the river, a door, and the Pipeworks. And who did she know who knew about the Pipeworks? Doon, of course.

She pictured his thin, serious face, and his eyes looking out searchingly from beneath his dark eyebrows. She pictured how he used to bend over his work at school, holding his pencil in a hard grip, and how, during free time, he was usually off by himself in a corner studying a moth or a worm or a taken-apart clock. That was one thing, at least, that she liked about Doon: he was curious. He paid attention to things.

And he cared about things, too. She remembered how he'd been on Assignment Day, so furious at the mayor, so eager to trade his good job for her bad one so he could help save the city. And he'd taken Poppy inside his father's shop on the day of the blackout so she wouldn't be afraid.

Why had she stopped being friends with Doon? She vaguely recalled the incident of the light pole. It seemed silly now, and long ago. The more she thought about Doon, the more it seemed he was the very person—the *only* person—who might be interested in what she had found.

She placed the plain sheet of paper over the Instructions and put the box on top. I'll go and find Doon, she thought. Tomorrow was Thursday—their day off. She would find him tomorrow and ask for his help.

CHAPTER 8

Explorations

Doon had taken to wandering the Pipeworks alone. He would go to his assigned tunnel and do his job quickly—once you got good at using your wrenches and brushes and tubes of glue, it wasn't hard. Most of the workers did their jobs quickly and then gathered in little groups to play cards or have salamander races or just talk and sleep.

But Doon didn't care about any of that. If he was going to be stuck in the Pipeworks, he would at least not waste the time he had. Since the long blackout, everything seemed more urgent than ever. Whenever the lights flickered, he was afraid the ancient generator might be shuddering to a permanent halt.

So while the others lounged around, he headed out toward the edges of the Pipeworks to see what he could see. "Pay attention," his father had said, and that's what he did. He followed his map when he could, but in some places the map was unclear. There were even tunnels that didn't show up on the map at all. To keep from getting lost, he dropped a trail of things as he walked—washers, bolts, pieces of wire, whatever he had in his tool belt—and then he picked them up on his way back.

His father had been at least a little bit right: there were interesting things in the Pipeworks if you paid attention. Already he had found three new crawling creatures: a black beetle the size of a pinhead, a moth with furry wings, and the best of all, a creature with a soft, shiny body and a small, spiral-patterned shell on its back. Just after he found this one, while he was sitting on the floor watching in fascination as the creature crept up his arm, a couple of workers came by and saw him. They burst into laughter. "It's bug-boy!" one of them said. "He's collecting bugs for his lunch!"

Enraged, Doon jumped up and shouted at them. His sudden motion made the creature fall off his arm to the ground, and Doon felt a crunch beneath his foot. The laughing workers didn't notice—they tossed a few more taunts at him and walked on—but Doon knew instantly what he'd done. He lifted his foot and looked at the squashed mess underneath.

Unintended consequences, he thought miserably. He was angry at his anger, the way it surged up and took over. He picked the bits of shell and goo off the sole of his boot and thought, I'm sorry. I didn't mean to hurt you.

In the days that followed, Doon went farther and farther into the Pipeworks, holding on to the hope that he might find something not only interesting but important. But what he found didn't seem important at all. Once he came upon an old pair of pliers that someone had dropped and left behind. Twice he found a coin. He discovered a supply closet that appeared to have been completely forgotten, but all it held were some boxes of plugs and washers and a rusty box containing shriveled bits of what must once have been someone's lunch.

He found another supply closet at the far south end of the Pipeworks—at least, he assumed that's what it was. It was at the end of a tunnel with a rope strung across it; a sign hanging from the rope said, "Caved In. No Entry." Doon entered anyway, ducking under the rope. He found no sign of a cave-in, but there were no lights. He groped his way forward for twenty steps or so, and there the tunnel ended in a securely locked door—he couldn't see it, but he felt it. He retraced his steps, ducked back under the rope again, and walked on. A short distance away, he found a hatch in the ceiling of the tunnel—a square wooden panel that must lead, he thought, up into the storerooms. If he'd had something to stand on, he could have reached it and tried to open it, but it was about a foot above his upstretched hand. Probably it was locked anyhow. He wondered if the Builders had used openings like this one during the construction of the city to get more easily from one place to another.

On days when his job was near the main tunnel, he sometimes walked along the river after he'd finished working. He stayed away from the east end, where the generator was; he didn't want to think about the generator. Instead, he went the other way, toward the place where the river rushed out of the Pipeworks. The path grew less level at this end, and less smooth. The river here was bordered with clumps of wrinkled rock that seemed to grow out of the ground like fungus. Doon liked to sit on these clumps, running his fingers along the strange creases and crevices that must have been carved somehow by running or dripping water. In some places there were grooves that looked almost like writing.

But as for things of importance, Doon found none. It seemed that the Pipeworks was no use after all to a person who wanted to save the city. The generator was hopeless. He would never understand electricity. He used to think he could use electricity to invent a movable light, if he studied hard enough. He took apart light bulbs; he took apart the electric outlets on the wall to see how the wires inside wound together and in the process, got a painful, vibrating jolt all through his body. But when he tried to wind wires of his own together in exactly the same way, nothing happened. It was what came *through* the wires that made the light, he finally understood, and he had no idea what that was.

Now he could see only two courses of action: he could give up and do nothing, or he could start to work on a different kind of movable light.

Doon didn't want to give up. So on his day off one Thursday, he went to the Ember Library to look up fire.

The library occupied an entire building on one side of Bilbollio Square. Its door was at the end of a short passage in the middle of the building. Doon went down the passage, pushed open the door, and walked in. No one was there except for the librarian, ancient Edward Pocket, who sat behind his desk writing something with a tiny pencil clutched in his gnarled hand. The library had two big rooms, one for fiction, which was stories people made up out of their imaginations, and the other for fact, which was information about the real world. The walls of both rooms were lined with shelves, and on most of the shelves were hundreds of packets of pages. Each packet was held together with stout loops of string. The packets leaned against each other at angles and lay in untidy stacks. Some were thick, and some were so slim that only a clip was needed to hold them together. The pages of the oldest packets were yellowed and warped, and their edges were uneven rows of ripples.

These were the books of Ember, written over the years by its citizens. They contained in their close-written pages much that was imagined and everything that was known.

Edward Pocket looked up and nodded briefly at Doon, one of his most frequent visitors. Doon nodded back. He went into the fact room, to the section of shelves labeled "F." The books were arranged by subject, but even so, it wasn't easy to find what you wanted. A book about moths, for instance, might be under "M" for moths, or "I" for insects, or "B" for bugs. It might even be under "F" for flying things. Usually you had to browse through the entire library to make sure you'd found all the books on one subject. But since he was looking for "fire," he thought he might as well start with "F."

Fire was rare in Ember. When there was a fire, it was because there had been an accident—someone had left a dishtowel too close to an electric burner on a stove, or a cord had frayed and a spark had flown out and ignited curtains. Then the citizens would rush in with buckets of water, and the fire was quickly drowned. But it was, of course, possible to start a fire on purpose. You could hold a sliver of wood to the stove burner until it burst into flame, and then for a moment it would flare brightly, giving off orange light.

The trick was to find a way to make the light last. If you had a light that would keep going, you could go out into the Unknown Regions and see what was there. Finding a way to explore the Unknown Regions was the only thing Doon could think of to do.

He took down a book from the "F" shelf. *Fungus,* it was called. He put it back. The next book was called *How to Repair Furniture.* He put that back, too. He went through *Foot Diseases, Fun with String, Coping with Failure,* and *Canned Fruit Recipes* before he finally found a book called *All About Fire.* He sat down at one of the library's square tables to read it.

But the person who had written the book knew no more about fire than Doon. Mostly the book described the dangers of fire. A long section of it was about a building in Winifred Square that had caught fire forty years ago, and how all its doors and all its furniture had burned up and smoke had filled the air for days. Another part was about what to do if your oven caught on fire.

Doon closed the book and sighed. It was useless. *He* could write a better book than that. He got up and wandered restlessly around the library. Sometimes you could find useful things just by choosing randomly from the shelves. He had done this many times—just reached out and grabbed something— in the hope that by accident he might come upon the very piece of information he needed. It would be something that another person had written down without understanding its significance, just a sentence or two that would be like a flash of light in Doon's mind, fitting together with things he already knew to make a solution to everything.

Although he'd often found something interesting in these searches, he'd never found anything *important.* Today was no different. He did come across a collection called *Mysterious Words from the Past,* which he read for a while. It was about words and phrases so old that their meanings had been forgotten. He read a few pages.

> Heavens above
> > Indicates surprise. What "heavens" means
> > is unclear. It might be another word for
> > "floodlight."
>
> Hogwash
> > Means "nonsense," though no one knows
> > what a "hog" is or why one would wash it.
>
> Batting a thousand
> > Indicates great success. This might possibly
> > refer to killing bugs.
>
> All in the same boat
> > Means "all in the same predicament."
> > The meaning of "boat" is unknown.

Interesting, but not useful. He put the book back on the shelf and was about to leave when the door of the library opened, and Lina Mayfleet came in.

CHAPTER 9

The Door in the Roped-Off Tunnel

Lina saw Doon immediately—he was reaching up to set a book back on its shelf. He saw her, too, when he turned around, and his dark eyebrows flew up in surprise as she hurried over to him.

"Your father told me you were here," she said. "Doon, I found something. I want to show it to you."

"To me? Why?"

"I think it's important. It has to do with the Pipeworks. Will you come to my house and see it?"

"Now?" Doon asked.

Lina nodded.

Doon grabbed his old brown jacket and followed Lina out of the library and across the city to Quillium Square.

Granny's shop was closed and dark when they arrived, and so Lina was surprised when they went upstairs and saw Evaleen Murdo sitting in her place by the window. "Your grandmother's in her bedroom," Mrs. Murdo said. "She didn't feel well, so she asked me to come."

Poppy was sitting on the floor, banging a spoon on the leg of a chair.

Lina introduced Doon, then led him into the room she shared with Poppy. He looked around, and Lina felt suddenly self-conscious, seeing her room through his eyes. It was a small room with a lot crammed into it. There were two narrow beds, a very small table that fit into a corner, and a four-legged stool to sit on. On the wall, clothes hung from hooks, and more clothes were strewn untidily on the floor. Beneath the window was a brown stain made by the bean seed in its pot on the windowsill. Lina had been watering it every night because she'd promised Clary she would, but it was still nothing but dirt, flat and unpromising.

A couple of shelves beside the window held Lina's important possessions: the pieces of paper she'd collected for drawing, her pencils, a scarf with a silver thread woven through it. On the parts of the wall that had no hooks and no shelves, she had pinned up some of her pictures.

"What are those?" Doon asked.

"They're from my imagination," Lina said, feeling slightly embarrassed. "They're pictures of . . . another city."

"Oh. You made it up."

"Sort of. Sometimes I dream of it."

"I draw, too," said Doon. "But I draw other kinds of things."

"Like what?"

"Mostly insects," said Doon. He told her about his collection of drawings and the worm he was currently observing.

To Lina, this sounded far less interesting than an undiscovered city, but she didn't say so. She led Doon over to the table. "Here's what I want to show you," she said. She lifted the metal box. Before she could reach for the papers underneath, Doon took the box and started examining it.

"Where did this come from?" he asked.

"It was in the closet," Lina said. She told him about Granny's wild search and about finding the box with its lid open and Poppy with paper in her mouth. As she talked, Doon turned the box over in his hands, opened and closed its lid, and peered at the latch.

"There's some sort of odd mechanism here," he said. He tapped at a small metal compartment at the front of the box. "I'd like to see inside this."

"Here's what was in the box," said Lina, lifting the covering paper from her patchwork of scraps. "At least, it's what's left of what was in there."

Doon bent over, his hands on either side of the paper.

Lina said, "It's called 'Instructions for Egreston.' Or maybe 'Egresman.' Someone's name, anyhow. Maybe a mayor, or a guard. I just call it 'The Instructions.' I told the mayor about it—I thought maybe it was important. I wrote him a note, but he hasn't answered. I don't think he's interested."

Doon said nothing.

"You don't have to hold your breath," said Lina. "I glued the pieces down. Look," she said, pointing. "This word must be *Pipeworks*. And this one *river*. And look at this one—*door*."

Doon didn't answer. His hair had fallen forward, so Lina couldn't see the expression on his face.

"I thought at first," Lina went on, "that it must be instructions for how to do something. How to fix the electricity, maybe. But then I thought, What if it's instructions for going to another place?" Doon said nothing, so Lina went on. "I mean someplace that isn't here, like another city. I think these instructions say, 'Go down into the Pipeworks and look for a door.'"

Doon brushed the hair back from his face, but he didn't straighten up. He gazed at the broken words and frowned. "Edge," he murmured. "Small steel pan. What would that mean?"

"A frying pan?" said Lina. "But I don't know why there'd be a frying pan in the Pipeworks."

But Doon didn't answer. He seemed to be talking

to himself. He kept reading, moving a finger along the lines of words. "Open," he whispered. "Follow."

Finally he turned to look at Lina. "I think you're right," he said. "I think this *is* important."

"Oh, I was sure you'd think so!" Lina cried. She was so relieved that her words poured out in a rush. "Because you take things seriously! You told the truth to the mayor on Assignment Day. I didn't want to believe it, but then came the long blackout, and I knew—I knew things were as bad as you said." She stopped, breathless. She pointed to a word on the document. "This door," she said. "It has to be a door that leads out of Ember."

"I don't know," said Doon. "Maybe. Or a door that leads to *something* important, even if it isn't that."

"But it *must* be that—what else could be important enough to lock up in a fancy box?"

"Well . . . I suppose it could be a storage room with some special tools in it or something—" A look of surprise came over his face. "Actually, I *saw* a door where I didn't expect to see one—out in Tunnel 351. It was locked. I thought it was an old supply closet. I wonder if that could be it."

"It must be!" cried Lina. Her heart sped up.

"It wasn't anywhere near the river," Doon said doubtfully.

"That doesn't matter!" Lina said. "The river goes

through the Pipeworks, that's all. It's probably something like, 'Go down by the river, then go this way, then that way . . .'"

"Maybe," said Doon.

"It *must* be!" Lina cried. "I *know* it is! It's the door that leads out of Ember."

"I don't know if that makes sense," said Doon. "A door in the Pipeworks could only lead to something underground, and how could that . . ."

Lina had no patience for Doon's reasoning. She wanted to dance around the room, she was so excited. "We have to find out," she said. "We have to find out right away!"

Doon looked startled. "Well, I can go and try the door again," he said. "It was locked before, but I suppose . . ."

"I want to go, too," said Lina.

"You want to come down into the Pipeworks?"

"Yes! Can you get me in?"

Doon thought for a moment. "I think I can. If you come just at quitting time and wait outside the door, I'll stay out of sight until everyone has gone, and then I'll let you in."

"Tomorrow?"

"Okay. Tomorrow."

Lina stopped at home the next day only long enough to change out of her messenger jacket, and then she dashed across town to the Pipeworks. Doon met her just outside the door, and she followed him inside, where he handed her a slicker and boots to put on. They descended the long stone stairway, and when they came out into the main tunnel, Lina stood still, staring at the river. "I didn't know the river was so big," she said, after she found her voice.

"Yes," said Doon. "Every few years, they say, someone falls in. If you fall in, there's no hope of fishing you out. The river swallows you and sweeps you away."

Lina shivered. It was cold down here, a cold that she felt all the way through, cold flesh, cold blood, cold bones.

Doon led her up the path beside the water. After a while they came to an opening in the wall, and they turned into it and left the river behind. Doon led the way through winding tunnels. Their rubber boots splashed in pools of water on the floor. Lina thought how awful it would be to work down here all day, every day. It was a creepy place, a place where it seemed people didn't belong. That black river . . . it was like something in a bad dream.

"You have to duck here," said Doon.

They had come to a roped-off tunnel. "But there's no light in there," Lina said.

"No," said Doon. "We have to feel our way. It isn't far." He ducked under the rope and went in, and Lina did the same. They stepped forward into the dark. Lina kept a hand against the damp wall and placed her feet carefully.

"It's right here," said Doon. He had stopped a few feet ahead of Lina. She came up behind him. "Put your hands out," he said. "You'll feel it."

Lina felt a smooth, hard surface. There was a round metal knob, and below the knob, a keyhole. It seemed an ordinary door—not at all like the entrance to a new world. But that was what made things so exciting—nothing was ever how you expected it to be.

"Let's try it," she whispered.

Doon took hold of the knob and twisted. "Locked," he said.

"Is there a pan anywhere?"

"A pan?"

"The instructions said 'small steel pan.' Maybe that would have the key in it."

They felt around, but there was nothing—just the rocky walls. They patted the walls, they put their ears to the door, they jiggled the knob and pulled it and pushed it. Finally Doon said, "Well, we can't get in. I guess we'd better go."

And that was when they heard the noise. It was a scuffling, scraping noise that seemed to be coming from somewhere nearby. Lina stopped breathing. She clutched Doon's arm.

"Quick," Doon whispered. He made his way back toward the lighted tunnel, with Lina following.

They ducked under the rope and rounded a turn, then stopped, stood still, and listened. A harsh scraping sound. A thud. A pause . . . and then the sound of an impact, a short, explosive breath, and a muttered word in a gruff, low voice.

Then slow footsteps, getting closer.

They flattened themselves against the wall and stood motionless. The footsteps stopped briefly, and there was another grunt. Then the steps continued, but seemed to be fading. In a moment, from a distance, there was another sound: the chink of a key turning in a lock, and the click of a latch opening.

Lina made an astonished face at Doon. Someone had gone down the roped tunnel and opened the door! She put her mouth close to Doon's ear. "Shall we try to see who it is?" she whispered.

Doon shook his head. "I don't think we should," he said. "We should go."

"We could just peek around the corner."

It was too tempting not to try. They crept forward to the place where the tunnel turned. From there they could see the entrance to the roped tunnel. Holding their breath, they watched.

And in a minute, they heard a thump and click— the door closing, the lock turning—and footsteps once again, this time quick. A long leg stepped over the rope, and the person it belonged to turned and walked away. All they saw was his back—a dark coat, dark untidy hair. He walked with a lurching motion that struck Lina as somehow familiar. In a few seconds, he had vanished into the shadows.

When they came up out of the Pipeworks, they stripped off their boots and slickers and hurried out into Plummer Square, where they flopped down on a bench and burst into furious talk.

"Someone got there before us!" said Lina.

Doon said, "He was walking slowly when he went in—as if he was looking for something. And he walked fast when he came out . . ."

"As if he'd *found* something! What *was* it? I can't stand not to know!"

Doon jumped up. He paced back and forth in front of the bench.

"But how did he get the key?" he asked. "Did he find Instructions like the ones you found? And how did he get into the Pipeworks? I don't think he works there."

"There's something familiar about the way he walks," said Lina. "But I don't know why."

"Well, anyhow, he opened that door and we can't," said Doon. "If it *does* go somewhere, if it *does* lead out of Ember, he'll be telling the whole city pretty soon. He'll be a hero." Doon sat down again. "If he's found the way out, we'll be glad, of course," he said glumly. "It doesn't matter who finds it, as long as it helps the city."

"That's right," Lina said.

"It's just that I thought *we* were going to find it," said Doon.

"Yes," Lina said, thinking how grand it would have been to stand before all of Ember, announcing their discovery.

They sat without talking for a while, lost in their own thoughts. A man pulling a cart full of wood scraps went by. A woman leaned from a lighted window on Gappery Street and called out to some boys playing in the square below. A couple of guards, in their red and brown uniforms, ambled across the square, laughing. The town clock rang out six deep booms that Lina could feel, like shudders, beneath her ribs.

Doon said, "I guess what we do now is wait to see if there's an announcement."

"I guess so," said Lina.

"Maybe that door is nothing special after all," said Doon. "Maybe it's just an old unused supply closet."

But Lina wasn't ready to believe that. Maybe it wasn't the door out of Ember, but it was a mystery nevertheless—a mystery connected, she was sure, to the bigger mystery they were trying to solve.

CHAPTER 10

Blue Sky and Goodbye

Lina slept restlessly that night. She had frightening dreams in which something dangerous was lurking in the darkness. When the lights went on in the morning and she opened her eyes, her first thought was of the door in the Pipeworks—and then right away she felt a thud of disappointment, because the door was locked and someone else, not her, knew what was behind it.

She went in to wake Granny. "Time to get up," she said, but Granny didn't answer. She was lying with her mouth half open and breathing in a strange hoarse way. "Don't feel too good," she finally said in a weak voice.

Lina felt Granny's forehead. It was hot. Her hands were very cold. She ran for Mrs. Murdo and after that to Cloving Square to tell Captain Fleery she would not be coming to work today. Then she ran to Oliver Street, to the office of Dr. Tower, where she banged on the door until the doctor opened it.

Dr. Tower was a thin woman with uncombed hair and shadows under her eyes. When she saw Lina, she seemed to grow even more tired.

"Dr. Tower," Lina said, "my grandmother is sick. Will you come?"

"I will," she said. "But I can't promise to help her. I'm low on medicine."

"But come and look. Maybe she doesn't need medicine."

Lina led the doctor the few blocks to her house. When she saw Granny, the doctor sighed. "How are you, Granny Mayfleet?" she asked.

Granny looked at the doctor blearily. "I think ill," she said.

Dr. Tower laid a hand across her forehead. She asked her to stick out her tongue, and she listened to her heart and her breathing.

"She has a fever," the doctor told Lina. "You'll need to stay home with her today. Make her some soup. Give her water to drink. Put rags in cool water and lay them across her forehead." She picked up Granny's bony hand in her rough, reddish one. "What's best for you is to sleep today," she said. "Your good granddaughter will take care of you."

And all day, that's what Lina did. She made a thin soup of spinach and onions and fed it to Granny a spoonful at a time. She stroked Granny's forehead, held her hand, and talked to her about cheerful things. She kept Poppy as quiet as she could. But as she did all this, in the back of her mind was the memory of the days of her father's illness, when he seemed to grow dim like a lamp losing power, and the sound of his breathing was like water gurgling through a clogged pipe. Though she didn't want to, she also remembered the evening when her father let out one last short breath and didn't take another, and the morning a few months later when Dr. Tower emerged from her mother's bedroom with a crying baby and a face that was heavy with bad news.

In the late afternoon, Granny got restless. She lifted herself up on one elbow. "Did we find it?" she asked Lina. "Did we ever find it?"

"Find what, Granny?"

"The thing that was lost," Granny said. "The old thing that my grandfather lost . . ."

"Yes," said Lina. "Don't worry, Granny, we found it, it's safe now."

"Oh, good." Granny sank back onto her pillows and smiled at the ceiling. "What a relief," she said. She coughed a couple of times, closed her eyes, and fell asleep.

Lina stayed home from work the next day as well. It was a long day. Granny dozed most of the time. Poppy, delighted to have Lina at home to play with, kept toddling over with things she found—dust rags, kitchen spoons, stray shoes—and whacking them against Lina's knees, saying, "Play wif dis! Play wif dis!" Lina was glad to play with her, but after a while she'd had enough of spoon-banging and rag-tugging and shoe-rolling. "Let's do something else," she said to Poppy. "Shall we draw?"

Granny had drunk a full cup of soup for dinner and was falling asleep again, so Lina got out her colored pencils and two of the can labels she'd been saving—they were white on the back and made good enough drawing paper, if you flattened them out. With their sharpest kitchen knife, she whittled the pencils into points. She gave the green pencil and one can label to Poppy, and she herself took the blue pencil and smoothed out the other can label on the table.

What would she draw? Taking hold of a pencil was like opening a tap inside her mind through which her imagination flowed. She could feel the pictures ready to come out. It was a sort of pressure, like water in a pipe. She always thought she would draw something wonderful, but what she actually drew never quite matched the feeling. It was like when she tried to tell a dream—the words never really captured how it felt.

Poppy was grasping the pencil in her fist and making a wild scribble. "Lookit!" she cried.

"Lovely," said Lina. Then, without even a clear idea of what it was to be, she began her own picture. She started on the left side of the can label. First she drew a tall, narrow box—a building. Then more boxes next to it—a cluster of buildings. Next she drew a few tiny people walking on the street below the buildings. It was what she nearly always drew—the other city—and every time she drew it, she had the same frustrating feeling: there was more to be drawn. There were other things in this city, there were marvels there—but she couldn't imagine what they were. All she knew was that this city was bright in a different way from Ember. Where the brightness came from she didn't know.

She drew more buildings and filled in the windows and doors; she put in streetlamps; she added a greenhouse. All the way across the paper, she drew buildings of different sizes. All the buildings were white, because that was the color of the paper.

She set her pencil down for a moment and studied what she'd done. It was time to fill in the sky. In the pictures she'd done with regular pencils, the sky was its true color, black. But this time she made it blue, since she was using her blue pencil. Methodically, as Poppy scratched and scribbled beside her, Lina colored in the space above the buildings, her pencil moving back and forth in short lines, until the entire sky was blue.

She sat back and looked at her picture. Wouldn't it be strange, she thought, to have a blue sky? But she liked the way it looked. It would be beautiful—a blue sky.

Poppy had started using her pencil to poke holes

in her paper. Lina folded up her own picture and took Poppy's away from her. "Time for dinner," she said.

Sometime deep in the night, Lina woke suddenly, thinking she'd heard something. Had she been dreaming? She lay still, her eyes open in the darkness. The sound came again, a weak, trembling call: "Lina . . ."

She got up and started for Granny's room. Though she had lived in the same house all her life, she still had trouble finding her way at night, when the darkness was complete. It was as if walls had shifted slightly, and furniture moved to new places. Lina stayed close to the walls, feeling her way along. Here was her bedroom door. Here was the kitchen and the table—she winced as she stubbed her toe on one of its legs. A little farther and she'd come to the far wall and the door to Granny's room. Granny's voice was like a thin line in the dark air. "Lina . . . Come and help . . . I need . . ."

"I'm coming, Granny," she called.

She stumbled over something—a shoe, maybe— and fell against the bed. "Here I am, Granny!" she said. She felt for Granny's hand—it was very cold.

"I feel so strange," said Granny. Her voice was a whisper. "I dreamed . . . I dreamed about my baby . . . or someone's baby . . ."

Lina sat down on the bed. Carefully she moved her hands over the narrow ridge of her grandmother's body until she came to her shoulders. There her fingers tangled in the long wisps of Granny's hair. She pressed a finger against the side of Granny's throat to feel for her pulse, as the doctor had shown her. It was fluttery, like a moth that has hurt itself and is flapping in crooked circles.

"Can I get you some water, Granny?" Lina asked. She couldn't think what else to do.

"No water," Granny said. "Just stay for a while."

Lina tucked one foot underneath her and pulled part of the blanket over her lap. She took hold of Granny's hand again and stroked it gently with one finger.

For a long time neither of them said anything. Lina sat listening to her grandmother's breathing. She would take a deep, shuddering breath and let it out in a sigh. Then there would be a long silence before the next breath began. Lina closed her eyes. No use keeping them open—there was nothing to see but the dark. She was aware only of her grandmother's cold, thin hand and the sound of her breathing. Every now and then Granny would mumble a few words Lina couldn't make out, and then Lina would stroke her forehead and say, "Don't worry, it's all right. It's almost morning," though she didn't know if it was or not.

After a long time, Granny stirred slightly and seemed to come awake. "You go to bed, dear," she said.

"I'm all right now." Her voice was clear but very faint. "You go back to sleep."

Lina bent forward until her head rested against Granny's shoulder. Granny's soft hair tickled her face. "All right, then," she whispered. "Good night, Granny." She squeezed her grandmother's shoulders gently, and as she stood up a wave of terrible loneliness swept over her. She wanted to see Granny's face. But the darkness hid everything. It might still be a long time until morning—she didn't know. She groped her way back to her own bed and fell into a deep sleep, and when, hours later, the clock tower struck six and the lights came on, Lina went fearfully into her grandmother's room. She found her very pale and very still, all the life gone out of her.

CHAPTER 11

Lizzie's Groceries

Lina spent all that day in Mrs. Murdo's house, which was just like theirs, only neater. There was one couch, and one fat chair covered in fuzzy striped material, and one big table, only Mrs. Murdo's table wasn't wobbly like theirs. On the table was a basket, and in the basket were three turnips, each of them lavender on one end and white on the other. Mrs. Murdo must have put them there, Lina thought, not just because she was going to have them for dinner, but also because they were beautiful.

Lina sat sideways on the couch with her legs stretched out, and Mrs. Murdo covered her with a soft gray-green blanket. "This will keep you warm," she said, tucking it around Lina's legs. Lina didn't really feel cold but she did feel sad, which was in a way the same. The blanket felt good, like someone holding her. Mrs. Murdo gave Poppy a long purple scarf to play with and made a creamy mushroom soup with potatoes, and all day Lina stayed there, snuggled under the blanket. She thought about her grandmother, who had had a long and mostly cheerful life. She cried some and fell asleep. She woke up and played with Poppy. The day had a strange but comforting feel to it, like a rest between the end of one time and the beginning of another.

On the morning of the next day, Lina got up and got ready to go to work. Mrs. Murdo gave her beet tea and spinach hash for breakfast. "The Singing's coming up soon," she remarked to Lina as they ate. "Do you know your part?"

"Yes," said Lina. "I remember it pretty well from last year."

"I rather like the Singing," said Mrs. Murdo.

"I love it," Lina said. "I think it's my favorite day of the year." Once a year, the people of the city came together to sing the three great songs of Ember. Just thinking of it made Lina feel better. She finished her breakfast and put on her red jacket.

"Don't worry about Poppy, I'll take care of her," said Mrs. Murdo as Lina headed for the door. "When you come back this evening, we'll talk about how to proceed."

"Proceed?" said Lina.

"Well, you can't live by yourselves, just the two of you, can you?"

"We can't?"

"Certainly not," said Mrs. Murdo sternly. "Who's to take care of Poppy while you go off delivering messages? You must move in here with me. I have an empty bedroom, after all, and quite a nice one. Come and look."

She opened a door at the far end of the living room, and Lina peeked in. She had never seen such a beautiful, cozy room. There was a big, lumpy bed covered with a faded blue blanket, and at its head four plump pillows. Next to the bed was a chest of drawers with drawer handles shaped like teardrops and a mirror attached to the top. The carpets on the floor were all different shades of blue and green, and in the corner was a sturdy square table and a chair with a back like a ladder. "This will be your room," said Mrs. Murdo. "Yours and Poppy's. You'll have to share the bed, but it's big enough."

"It's lovely," Lina said. "You're so kind, Mrs. Murdo."

"Well," said Mrs. Murdo briskly, "it's just common sense. You need a place. I have one. You go on now, and I'll see you this evening."

Three days had passed since Lina and Doon had seen the man in the Pipeworks, and there hadn't been any special announcements. So if that man had discovered a way out of Ember, he was keeping the news to himself. Lina couldn't understand why.

As Lina ran through the city with her messages on her first day back to work, it seemed to her that the mood of the people was even gloomier than before. There were long, silent lines at the markets, and knots of people gathered in the squares, talking in low voices. Many shops—more each day, it seemed—displayed signs in their windows saying "Closed" or "Open Mon. Tues. only." Every now and then, the lights flickered, and people stopped and looked up in fright. When the flickering ended and the lights stayed lit, people just took a breath and walked on.

Lina delivered her messages as usual, but inside she felt strange. Everywhere she ran, she heard the same words, like a drumbeat, in her mind: *alone in the world, alone in the world.* It wasn't exactly true. She had Poppy. She had friends. And she had Mrs. Murdo, who was somewhere between a friend and a relative. But she felt as if she had suddenly gotten older in the last three days. She was a sort of mother herself now. What happened to Poppy was more or less up to her.

As the day went on, she stopped thinking *alone in the world* and began thinking about her new life at Mrs. Murdo's. She thought about the blue-green room and planned how she would arrange her pictures on the walls. The one she'd drawn with her blue pencil would look especially nice, because it would match the color of the rugs. She could bring her pillows from home and add them to the ones on the bed, and then she'd have six altogether—and maybe she could find some old blue dresses or shirts and make pillow covers for them. The blue-green room, the orderly apartment, the meals cooked, and the blankets tucked in cozily at night—all this gave her a feeling of comfort, almost luxury. She was grateful for Mrs. Murdo's kindness. I am not ready yet to be alone in the world, she thought.

Late that afternoon, Lina was given a message to take to Lampling Street. She delivered the message and, as she was coming back out onto the street, caught sight of Lizzie coming out the door of the Supply Depot—her orange hair was unmistakable. "Lizzie!" Lina called out.

Lizzie must not have heard her. She kept on going. Lina called again. "Lizzie, wait!" This time it was clear that Lizzie had heard, but instead of stopping, she walked faster. What's the matter with her? Lina wondered. She ran after her and grabbed the back of her coat. "Lizzie, it's me!"

Lizzie stopped and turned around. "Oh!" she said. Her face was flushed. "It's you. Hi! I thought it was . . . I didn't realize it was you." She smiled brightly, but there was a distracted look in her eyes. "I was just going home," she said. Her arms were wrapped around a small bulging sack.

"I'll walk with you," said Lina.

"Oh," said Lizzie. "Oh, good." But she didn't look pleased.

"Lizzie, something sad has happened," Lina said. "My grandmother died."

Lizzie gave her a quick sideways glance, but she didn't stop walking. "That's too bad," she said absently. "Poor you."

What was wrong with her? Lizzie was ordinarily so interested in other people's misfortunes. She could be sincerely sympathetic, too, when she wasn't wrapped up in her own troubles.

Lina changed the subject. "What's in the sack?" she asked.

"Oh, just some groceries," said Lizzie. "I stopped at the market after work."

"You did?" Lina was confused. She had seen Lizzie not two minutes ago leaving the storeroom office.

Lizzie didn't answer. She began walking and talking quite fast. "It was so busy today at work. Work is so hard, isn't it, Lina? I think work is much harder than school, and not as interesting. You do the same thing every day. I get so *tired,* don't you, running around all day?"

Lina started to say that she liked running and hardly ever got tired, but Lizzie didn't wait for her to answer.

"Oh, well, at least there are some good things about it. Guess what, Lina? I have a boyfriend. I met him at work. He really likes me—he says my hair is the exact color of a red-hot burner on a stove."

Lina laughed. "It's true, Lizzie," she said. "You look like your head is on fire."

Lizzie laughed, too, and lifted one hand to fluff her hair. She puckered her lips and fluttered her eyelashes. "He says I'm as beautiful as a red tomato."

They were crossing Torrick Square now. It was crowded in the square. People had just left work and were lining up at the shops and hurrying along with packages. A cluster of children sat on the pavement, playing some sort of game.

"Who is this boyfriend?" asked Lina.

But just at that moment, Lizzie tripped. She'd been strutting along being beautiful, not paying attention to her feet, and the edge of her shoe caught on an uneven place in the pavement. She staggered and fell, and as she fell she lost her grip on the sack. It hit the ground and toppled sideways, and some cans spilled out. They rolled in all different directions.

Lina reached for Lizzie's arm. "Did you hurt yourself?" she asked, but Lizzie went scrambling after the cans so quickly it was clear she wasn't hurt. Wanting to help, Lina went after the cans, too. Two had rolled under a bench. Another was going toward the children, who were on their feet now, watching Lizzie's wild spider-like motions. Lina picked up the cans under the bench, and for a second her breath stopped. One of them was a can of peaches. "Peaches," it said right on it, and there was a picture of a yellow globe. No one she knew had seen a can of peaches in years. She looked at the other one. It was just as amazing—"Creamed Corn," it said. Lina remembered having creamed corn once, as a thrilling treat, when she was five years old.

There was a shout. She looked up. One of the children had picked up a can. "Look at this!" he cried, and the other children gathered around him. "Applesauce!" he said, and the children murmured, "Applesauce, applesauce," as if they had never heard the word before.

Lizzie was on her feet. She had all the cans except for the two in Lina's hands and the one the child had picked up. She stood there for a moment, her eyes flicking back and forth from Lina to the children. Then she smiled, a bright fake-looking smile. "Thanks for helping me," she said. "I found these on a back shelf at the market. What a surprise, huh? You can keep those." She waved the back of her hand at the children, waved again at Lina, and then took off, holding the sack by its neck so it hung beside her and banged against her legs.

Lina didn't follow her. She walked home, thinking about Lizzie's sack of cans. You simply did not find cans of peaches and applesauce and creamed corn on the back shelves of markets. Lizzie was lying. And if the cans hadn't come from a market, where had they come from? There was only one answer: they had come from the storerooms. Somehow, Lizzie had gotten them because she worked in the storeroom office. Had she paid for them? How much? Or had she taken them without paying?

Mrs. Murdo had cooked a dinner of beet-and-bean stew for them that night. When Lina showed her the two cans, she gasped in astonishment. "Where did you get these?" she asked.

"From a friend," said Lina.

"And where did your friend get them?"

Lina shrugged. "I don't know."

Mrs. Murdo frowned slightly but didn't ask any more questions. She opened the cans, and they had a feast: creamed corn with their stew, and peaches for dessert. It was the best meal Lina had had in a very long time—but her enjoyment of it was tainted just a little by the question of where it had come from.

The next morning, Lina headed for Broad Street. Before she started delivering messages today, she was going to have a talk with Lizzie.

She spied her half a block from the storeroom office. She was sauntering along looking in shop windows. A long green scarf was wound around her neck.

Lina ran up swiftly behind her. "Lizzie," she said.

Lizzie whirled around. When she saw Lina, she flinched. She didn't say anything, just turned around and kept walking.

Lina caught hold of one end of the green scarf and jerked Lizzie to a halt. "Lizzie!" she said. "Stop!"

"What for?" Lizzie said. "I'm going to work." She tried to pull away, but she didn't get far, because Lina had a firm grip on her scarf.

Lina spoke in a low voice. There were people all around them—a couple of old men leaning against the wall, a group of chattering children just ahead, workers going toward the storerooms—and she didn't want to be overheard. "You have to tell me where you got those cans," she said.

"I told you. I found them on a back shelf at the market. Let go of my scarf." Lizzie tried to wrench her scarf out of Lina's grip, but Lina held on.

"You didn't," Lina said. "No market would just forget about things like that. Tell me the truth." She gave a yank on the end of the scarf.

"Stop it!" Lizzie reached out and grabbed a handful of Lina's hair. Lina yelped and pulled harder on the scarf, and the two of them scuffled, snatching at each other's hair and coats. They knocked against a woman who snapped at them angrily, and finally they toppled over, sitting down hard on the pavement.

Lina was the first one to laugh. It was so much like what they used to do in fun, chasing each other and screaming with laughter. Now here they were again, nearly grown girls, sitting in a heap on the pavement.

After a moment, Lizzie laughed, too. "You dope," she said. "All right, I'll tell you. I sort of wanted to anyway." Lizzie leaned forward with her elbows on her knees and lowered her voice. "Well, it's this," she said. "There's a storeroom worker named Looper. He's a carrier. Do you know him? He was two classes ahead of us. Looper Windly."

"I know who he is," said Lina. "I took a message for him on my first day of work. Tall, with a long skinny neck. Big teeth. Funny-looking."

Lizzie looked hurt. "Well, I wouldn't describe him *that* way. I think he's handsome."

Lina shrugged. "Okay. Go on."

"Looper explores the storerooms. He goes into every room that isn't locked. He wants to know the *true situation,* Lina. He's not like most workers, who just plod along doing their jobs and then go home. He wants to find things out."

"And what has he found out?" Lina asked.

"He's found out that there's still a little bit left of some rare things, just a few things in rooms here and there that have been forgotten. You know, Lina," she said, "there are *so many* rooms down there. Some of them, way out at the edges, are marked 'Empty' in the ledger book, and so no one ever goes there anymore. But Looper found out that they're not all empty."

"So he's been taking things."

"Just a few things! And not often."

"And he's giving some to you."

"Yes. Because he likes me." Lizzie smiled a little smile and hugged her arms together. I see, Lina thought. She feels *that* way about Looper.

"But Looper's stealing," said Lina. "And Lizzie—he isn't just stealing things for you. He has a store! He steals things and sells them for huge prices!"

"He does not," said Lizzie, but she looked worried.

"He does. I know because I bought something from him just a few weeks ago. He has a whole box of colored pencils."

Lizzie scowled. "He never gave me any colored pencils."

"He shouldn't be giving you anything—or selling things. Don't you think everyone should know about this food he found?"

"No!" Lizzie cried. "Because listen. If there's only one can of peaches left, only one person gets to have it, right? So why should everyone know? They'd just end up fighting over it. What good would that be?" Lizzie reached out and put a hand on Lina's knee. "Listen," she said. "I'll ask Looper to find some good stuff for you, too. I know he will, if I ask him."

Before she had time to think, Lina heard herself saying, "What kind of good stuff?"

Lizzie's eyes gleamed. "There's two packages of

colored paper, he told me. And some cough medicine. And there's three pairs of girls' shoes."

It was treasure. Colored paper! And cough medicine to cure sickness, and shoes . . . she hadn't had new ones for almost two years. Lina's heart raced. What Lizzie said was true: if everyone knew there were still a few wonderful things in the storerooms, people would fight each other trying to get them. But what if no one knew? What difference would it make if she had the colored paper, or the shoes? She suddenly wanted those things so badly she felt weak. A picture arose in her mind's eye—the shelves at Mrs. Murdo's house stocked with good things, and the three of them happier and safer than other people.

Lizzie leaned closer and lowered her voice. "Looper found a can of pineapple. I was going to split it with him, but I'll give you a bite if you promise not to tell."

Pineapple! That delectable long-lost thing that her grandmother had told her about. Was there anything wrong with having a bite of it, just to see what it was like?

"I've already tasted peaches, applesauce, and a thing called fruit cocktail," said Lizzie. "And prunes and creamed corn and cranberry sauce and asparagus . . ."

"All *that*?" Lina was astonished. "Then there's a lot of special things like that still?"

"No," said Lizzie. "Not a lot at all. In fact, we've finished all those."

"You and Looper?"

Lizzie nodded, smiling smugly. "Looper says it's all going to be gone soon anyway, why not live as well as we can right now?"

"But Lizzie, why should *you* get all that? Why you and not other people?"

"Because we found it. Because we can get at it."

"I don't think it's fair," said Lina.

Lizzie spoke as if she were talking to a not-very-bright child. "You can have some, *too*. That's what I'm *telling* you. There are still a few good things left."

But that wasn't the unfairness Lina was thinking of. It was that just two people were getting things that everyone would have wanted. She couldn't think how it should have been done. You couldn't divide a can of applesauce evenly among all the people in the city. Still, something was wrong with grabbing the good things just because you *could*. It seemed not only unfair to everyone else but bad for the person who was doing it, somehow. She remembered the hunger she'd felt when Looper showed her the colored pencils. It wasn't a pleasant feeling. She didn't *want* to want things that way.

She stood up. "I don't want anything from Looper."

Lizzie shrugged. "Okay," she said, but there was a look of dismay on her small pale face. "Too bad for you."

"Thanks anyway," said Lina, and she set off across Torrick Square, walking fast at first and then breaking into a run.

CHAPTER 12

A Dreadful Discovery

About a week after he and Lina had seen the man come out the mysterious door, Doon was assigned to fix a clog in Tunnel 207. It turned out to be easy. He undid the pipe, rammed a long thin brush down it, and a jet of water spurted into his face. Once he'd put the pipe back together, he had nothing else to do. So he decided to go out to Tunnel 351 and take another look at the locked door. It was strange, he thought, that no announcement about a way out of Ember had come. Maybe that door had not been what they thought it was.

So he set out for the south end of the Pipeworks. When he came to the roped-off passage in Tunnel 351, he ducked in and walked along through the dark, feeling his way. He was pretty sure the door would be locked as usual. His mind was on other things. He was thinking of his green worm, which had been behaving oddly, refusing to eat and hanging from the side of its box with its chin tucked in. And he was thinking about Lina, whom he hadn't seen for several days. He wondered where she was. When he came to the door, he reached absently for the knob, and what he felt startled him so much that he snatched his hand back as if he'd been stung. He felt again, carefully. There was a *key* in the lock!

For a long moment, Doon stood as still as a statue. Then he took hold of the doorknob and turned it. Very slowly, he pushed on the door. It swung inward without a sound.

He opened it only a few inches, just enough to peer around the edge. What he saw made him gasp.

There was no road, or passage, or stairway behind the door. There was a brightly lit room, whose size he could not guess at because it was so crowded with things. On all sides were crates and boxes, sacks and bundles and packages. There were mounds of cans, heaps of clothes, rows of jars and bottles, stacks of light-bulb packages. Piles rose to the low ceiling and leaned against the walls, blocking all but a small space in the center. In that small space, a little living room had been set up. There was a greenish rug, and on the rug an armchair and a table. On the table were dishes smeared with the remains of food, and in the armchair facing Doon was a great blob of a person whose head was flopped backward, so that all Doon could see of it was an upthrust chin. The blob stirred and muttered, and Doon, in the second before he stepped back and pulled the door closed, caught a glimpse of a fleshy ear, a slab of gray cheek, and a loose, purplish mouth.

That day, Lina had more messages to carry than ever. There had been five blackouts in a row during the week. They were all fairly short—the longest was four and a half minutes, Lina had heard—but there had never been so many so close together. Everyone was nervous. People who might ordinarily walk to someone's house were sending messages instead. Often they didn't even come out into the street but beckoned to a messenger from their doorway.

By five o'clock, Lina had carried thirty-nine messages. Most of them were more or less the same: "I'm not coming to the meeting tonight, decided to stay home." "I won't be in to work tomorrow." "Instead of meeting me in Cloving Square, why don't you come to my house?" The citizens of Ember were hunkering down, burrowing in. Fewer people stood around talking in groups under the lights in the squares. Instead, they would pause briefly to murmur a few words to each other and then hasten onward.

Lina was on her way home to Mrs. Murdo's—she and Poppy had moved in with all their things—when she heard rapid footsteps. Startled, she turned and saw Doon racing toward her.

At first he was so out of breath he couldn't speak.

"What is it? What *is* it?" said Lina.

"The door," he panted. "The door in 351. I opened it."

Lina's heart leapt. "You did?"

Doon nodded.

"Is it the way out?" Lina whispered fiercely.

"No," Doon said. He glanced behind him. Clutching Lina's arm, he pulled her into a shadowy spot on the street. "It doesn't lead out of Ember," he whispered. "It leads to a big room."

Lina's face fell. "A room? What's in there?"

"Everything. Food, clothes, boxes, cans. Light bulbs, stacks of them. Everything. Piles and piles up to the ceiling." His eyes grew wide. "And someone was there, in the middle of it all, asleep."

"Who?"

A look of horror passed over Doon's face. "The mayor," he said. "Conked out in a big armchair, with an empty plate in front of him."

"The mayor!" Lina whispered.

"Yes. The mayor has a secret treasure room in the Pipeworks."

They stared at each other, speechless. Then Doon suddenly stamped hard on the pavement. His face flushed red. "*That's* the solution he keeps telling us about. It's a solution for *him*, not the rest of us. He gets everything he needs, and we get the leftovers! He doesn't care about the city. All he cares about is his fat stomach!"

Lina felt dizzy, as if she'd been hit on the head. "What will we do?" She couldn't think, she was so stunned.

"Tell everyone!" said Doon. He was shaking with anger. "Tell the whole city the mayor is robbing us!"

"Wait, wait." Lina put a hand on Doon's arm and concentrated for a minute. "Come on," she said at last. "Let's go sit in Harken Square. I have something to tell you, too."

At the north end of Harken Square stood a circle of Believers, clapping their hands and singing one of their songs. Lately they seemed to be singing more loudly and cheerfully than ever. Their voices were shrill. "Coming soon to save us!" they wailed. "Happy, happy day!"

Near the Gathering Hall steps, something unusual was happening. Twenty or so people were pacing around and around, carrying big signs painted on old planks and on big banners made of sheets. The signs said "WHAT solutions, Mayor Cole?" and "We want ANSWERS!" Every now and then the demonstrators would yell these slogans out loud. Lina wondered if the mayor was paying any attention.

Doon and Lina found an empty bench on the south side of Harken Square and sat down.

"Now, listen," said Lina.

"I *am* listening," said Doon, though his face was still red and the look on his face was stormy.

"I saw Lizzie coming out of the storerooms yesterday," Lina said. She told him about the cans, and Lizzie's new friend, Looper, and what Looper was doing.

Doon pounded his fist on his leg. "That's *two* of them doing it, then," he said.

"Wait, there's more. Remember how I thought there was something familiar about the man who came out the door? I've remembered what. It was that way he walked, sort of dipping over sideways, and also that hair, that black hair all unbrushed and sticking out. I've seen him twice. I don't know why I didn't remember who it was right away—maybe because I've only seen him from the front. I took a message for him on my first day."

Doon was jiggling with impatience. "Well, who was it, *who was it*?"

"It was Looper. Looper, who works in the storerooms. Lizzie's boyfriend. And Doon—" Lina leaned forward. "It was a message to the *mayor* that he gave me, and it was this: 'Delivery at eight.'"

Doon's mouth dropped open. "So that means . . ."

"He's taking things from the storeroom for the mayor. And he's giving some to Lizzie, and selling some in his store."

"Oh!" cried Doon. He slapped his hand against his head. "Why didn't I get it before? There's a hatch in the ceiling near Tunnel 351. It must go right up into the storerooms. Looper comes through there! *That's* what we heard that day, remember? A sort of scraping—that would have been the hatch opening. Then a thud—his sack of stuff dropping through—and then a sound like someone jumping down and landing hard on the ground."

"And then walking slowly—"

"Because he was carrying a load!"

"And walking quickly on the way out because he'd left it all for the mayor." Lina took a deep breath. Her heart was drumming and her hands were cold. "We have to think what to do," she said. "If this were an ordinary situation, the mayor would be the one to tell."

"But the mayor is the one committing the crime," said Doon.

"So then we should tell the guards, I guess," said Lina. "They're next in authority to the mayor. Though I don't like them much," she added, remembering how she'd been so roughly hustled down the stairs from the roof of the Gathering Hall. "Especially the chief guard."

"But you're right," Doon said. "We should tell the guards. They'll go down into the Pipeworks and see for themselves that we're telling the truth. Then they can arrest the mayor and have all the stuff put back in the storerooms, and *then* they can tell the city what's been going on."

"That's a much better idea," said Lina. "Then you and I can get back to what's more important."

"What?"

"Figuring out the Instructions. Now that we know that the door we found wasn't the right one, we have to *find* the right one."

"I don't know," said Doon. "We might be all wrong about those Instructions. They could just be about some old Pipeworks tool closet." He made a sour face. "'Instructions for Egreston.' Who's Egreston? Or Egresman? Or whoever it was? Why couldn't he have been just an especially stupid Pipeworks guy who needed instructions to find his way around?" He shook his head. "I don't know. I think maybe those Instructions are just hogwash."

"Hogwash? What's that?"

"It means nonsense. I read it in a book in the library."

"But they can't be nonsense! Why would they have been kept in a box like that? With the strange lock?"

But Doon didn't want to think about the Instructions right then. "We'll figure it out tomorrow," he said. "Right now, let's go find the guards."

"Wait," said Lina, catching hold of the sleeve of his jacket. "I have one more thing to tell you."

"What?"

"My grandmother died."

"Oh!" Doon's face fell. "That's so sad," he said. "I'm sorry." His sympathy made tears spring to Lina's eyes. Doon looked startled for a moment, and then he took a step toward her and wrapped his arms around her. He gave her a squeeze so quick and tight that it made her cough, and then it made her laugh. She realized all at once that Doon—thin, dark-eyed Doon with his troublesome temper and his terrible brown jacket and his good heart—was the person that she knew better than anyone now. He was her best friend.

"Thanks," she said. "Well." She smiled at him. "Let's go and talk to the guard."

They crossed the square and climbed the steps of the Gathering Hall. Sitting at the big reception desk outside the door of the mayor's office was the assistant guard, Barton Snode, the same one Lina had encountered her first time here. Snode looked bored. His elbows were on the desk, and his chin was moving very slowly from side to side.

"Sir," said Doon, "we need to speak with you."

The guard looked up. "Certainly," he said. "Go right ahead."

"In private," said Lina.

The guard looked puzzled. His small eyes darted back and forth. "This is private," he said. "No one here but me."

"But anyone could come along," said Doon. "What

we have to say is secret, and very important."

"Very important?" said Snode. "Secret?" His face brightened. Grunting, he raised himself up from his chair and motioned them into a narrow hallway off to the side of the main hall. "What is it?" he said.

They told him. As they spoke, interrupting each other to make sure they got in all the details, the guard's eyebrows gradually lifted higher and higher over his eyes. "You *saw* this room?" he said. "This is true? Are you sure?" He was chewing faster now. "You mean the mayor . . . you mean the mayor is . . ."

At that moment, a little way down the hall, a door opened. Through it came three more guards, including—Lina spotted him by his beard—the chief guard. They strode forward, talking to each other in low voices, and as they passed, the chief guard threw a quick glance at Lina. Does he recognize me? Lina wondered. She couldn't tell.

Barton Snode finished his sentence in a husky whisper. "You mean . . . the mayor is *stealing*?"

"That's right," said Doon. "We thought you should be informed, because who else can arrest the mayor? And once you've done that, the guards can put all the things he's stolen back where they came from."

"And then tell the city that a new mayor has to be found," added Lina.

Barton Snode leaned heavily against the wall and rubbed a hand over his chin. He seemed to be thinking. "Something must be done," he said. "This is shocking, shocking." He started back toward his desk, and Doon and Lina followed. "I will make a note," he said, taking a pencil from the desk drawer. Lina watched as he wrote slowly on a scrap of paper: "Mayor stealing. Secret room."

When he'd finished, he let out a satisfied breath. "Very good," he said. "Action will be taken, you may be sure. Some sort of action. Quite soon."

"Good," said Doon.

"Thank you," said Lina, and they turned to leave.

The three guards were standing by the main door of the Gathering Hall as Doon and Lina went out. The chief guard moved aside to make way for them, and they went through the door and out onto the wide front steps. Lina glanced over her shoulder. Before the door swung closed, she saw the chief guard striding toward the reception desk, where Barton Snode was standing up, leaning forward, his eyes shining with important news.

CHAPTER 13

Deciphering the Message

Doon headed for home, and Lina went in the opposite direction across Harken Square. The little group of Believers had gone, but the protesters with their signs continued to pace back and forth. A few of them were still shaking their fists in the air and yelling, but most of them tramped silently, looking tired and discouraged. Lina felt a bit that way, too. Once Doon said he'd seen a door, she was sure that the door he'd found and the door in the Instructions were the same. She had had such hopes for that door in the Pipeworks. But hoping so hard had made her jump to conclusions. She'd gone a little too fast. She always went fast. Sometimes it was a good thing and sometimes not.

Now Doon thought the Instructions were nothing important after all. She didn't want him to be right. She didn't believe he was, even now. But her thoughts felt like a mess of tangled yarn. She needed someone wise and sensible to help her sort things out. She headed for Glome Street.

Though it was nearly six o'clock, she found Clary still in her workroom, at the far end of Greenhouse 1. It was a small, crowded room. Pots and trowels cluttered a high table at one end. Above the table were shelves full of bottles of seeds, and boxes of string, wire, and various kinds of powders. Clary's desk was a rickety table, littered with scraps of paper, all of them covered with notes in her neat, round handwriting. Two rickety chairs went with the rickety table, one on each side. Lina sat down facing Clary. "I have to tell you some important things," she said. "And they're all secret."

"All right," said Clary. "I can keep secrets." She was wearing a patched shirt that had faded from blue to gray. Her short brown hair was tucked behind her ears, and a bit of leaf clung to it on the right-hand side. She folded her arms in front of her on the desk. She looked square and solid.

"The first thing is," Lina began, "that I found the Instructions. But Poppy had chewed them up."

"The Instructions," said Clary. "I'm not familiar with them."

Lina explained. She went on to explain everything—how she'd shown the Instructions to Doon, what they had figured out, how he'd searched the Pipeworks and found the door, and what he'd seen when he opened the door.

Clary made an unhappy sound and shook her head. "This is very bad," she said. "And sad, too. I remember when the mayor was first starting out. He has always been foolish, but not always wicked. I'm sorry to know that the worst side of him has won out." Clary's dark brown eyes seemed to grow deeper and sadder. "There is so much darkness in Ember, Lina. It's not just outside, it's inside us, too. Everyone has some darkness inside. It's like a hungry creature. It wants and wants and *wants* with a terrible power. And the more you give it, the bigger and hungrier it gets."

Lina knew. She had felt it in Looper's shop as she hovered over the colored pencils. For a moment, she felt sorry for the mayor. His hunger had grown so big it could never be satisfied. His huge body couldn't contain it. It made him forget everything else.

Clary let out a long breath, and a few of the scraps of paper on her desk fluttered. She ran her fingers through her hair, felt the bit of leaf, and plucked it out. Then she said, "About these Instructions."

"Oh, yes," said Lina. "They might be important, or they might not be. I don't know anymore."

"I'd like to see them, if you'd let me."

"Of course you can see them—but you'll have to come home with me."

"I'll come now, if that's all right," said Clary. "There's plenty of time before lights out."

Lina led Clary up the stairs and into her new bedroom at Mrs. Murdo's. "Nice room," Clary said, looking around with interest. "And I see you have a sprout."

"A what?" said Lina.

"Your bean," said Clary, pointing at the little pot of dirt on the windowsill.

Lina bent to see what Clary was talking about. Sure enough, the dirt was heaving up a little. She touched the pushed-up part, brushed away the dirt, and discovered a pale green loop. It looked like a neck, as if a creature in the bean were trying to escape but hadn't yet managed to pull its head out. Of course she already knew that plants grew from seeds. But to have put that flat white bean in the dirt, to have almost forgotten about it, and now to see it forcing its way up into the air . . .

"It's doing it!" she said. "It's coming to life!"

Clary nodded, smiling. "Still amazes me every time I see it," she said.

Lina brought out the Instructions, and Clary sat down at the table to study them. She puzzled over the patchwork of scraps for a long time, tracing the lines with her finger, murmuring the parts of words.

"What you've figured out so far seems right to me," she said. "I think 'ip ork' must be 'Pipeworks.'

And 'iverb nk' must be 'riverbank.' So this bit must be 'down riverbank'—then there's a big space here—'to edge.' Edge of what, I wonder? And does it mean 'down riverbank' as in 'walk alongside the river'?"

"Yes, I think so," Lina said.

"Or does it mean go down the riverbank itself, down the bank toward the water? Maybe 'edge' means 'edge of the water.'"

"It couldn't mean that. The bank goes straight down like a wall. You couldn't go down to the edge of the water, you'd fall in." Lina pictured the dark, swift water and shivered.

"This word," said Clary, putting a finger on the paper. "Maybe it isn't 'edge,' maybe it's something else. It could be 'hedge.' Or 'pledge.' Those don't make much sense. But it could be 'ledge' or 'wedge.'"

Lina saw that Clary was no better at deciphering the puzzle than she was. She sighed and sat down on the end of her bed. "It's hopeless," she said.

Clary straightened up quickly. "Don't say that. This torn-up piece of paper is the most hopeful thing I've ever seen. Do you know what this word is?" She pointed to the word at the top of the paper, *Egres.*

"Someone's name, isn't it? The title would be 'Instructions for Egreston,' or maybe 'Egresman,' or something like that. The person the instructions were for."

"I don't think so," said Clary. "If you add an s to

this word, right where this tear in the paper is, you get 'Egress.' Do you know what that means?"

"No," said Lina.

"It means 'the way out.' It means 'the exit.' The title of this document is 'Instructions for Egress.'"

When Clary left, there was still over an hour before lights out. Lina raced across the city to Greengate Square. She glanced in the window of the Small Items shop, where Doon's father was reaching for something on a shelf, and then she dashed up the stairs and knocked on the door of Doon's apartment. Right away, she heard quick steps and Doon opened the door.

"I have something exciting to tell you," Lina said breathlessly.

"Come in, then."

Lina went across the cluttered room to stand by a lamp. She pulled from her pocket a tiny piece of paper on which she had written "Egres." "Look at this word," she said.

"It's from the title of the Instructions. Someone's name," said Doon.

"No," said Lina. "It's meant to be 'Egress,' with two s's. I showed the Instructions to Clary, and she told me. It means 'the way out.'"

"The way out!" cried Doon.

"Yes! The way out. The exit. It's instructions for the way out of Ember!"

"So it *is* real," Doon said.

"It is. We have to figure out the rest. Or as much of the rest as possible. Can you come now?"

He darted into his room, emerged with his jacket, and they ran.

"All right," said Lina. They were on the floor of the blue-green room at Mrs. Murdo's. "Let's take the first line." She moved her finger along it slowly.

1. Exp
   riv   ip   ork .

"We know that 'ip ork' is Pipeworks," she said. "'Exp' could be 'expand,' or 'explore,' or 'expose' . . ."

"There's a big space between 'Exp' and the rest," said Doon. "There must be more words in there."

"But who knows what they are? Let's move on." Lina swept her straggly hair impatiently back from her face. "Look at number two."

2.   ston   marked with E by r
      dge

Lina put her finger on *ston*. "What could that be?"

"Maybe 'piston,'" said Doon. "That's part of a machine, like the generator. Or maybe it's 'astonish.' Or it could be . . ."

"I bet it's just plain 'stone,'" said Lina. "There's a lot of stone in the Pipeworks."

Doon had to admit this was probably right. "So then," he said, "it would be 'stone marked with E. . . .'" He frowned at the next bit. "This must be 'river's edge.' 'Stone marked with E by the river's edge.'"

They looked at each other in delight. "E for Egress!" cried Lina. "E for Exit!"

They bent over the document again. "There's not much left of this next line," said Doon.

3.   adde down iverb nk
            to edge appr   eight
    low.

"Just this part—which must say, 'down riverbank to edge' . . . something."

"'Edge of water' would make sense. But right after 'edge' there's 'app.' What would that be?" Doon sat back on his heels and gazed up at the ceiling, as if the answer might be there. Lina muttered, "down riverbank to edge, edge." She thought of Clary's guesses about that line. "Maybe it's 'ledge,'" she said. "'Down riverbank to ledge.' There could be a ledge down near the water."

"Yes, that must be right. There's a stone marked with E, and down the riverbank at that point there's a ledge. I think we're getting it."

Once again they crouched over the page, their heads close together. "Okay," Doon said. "Line 4."

```
4.                              acks to the
    wat  r,            find door of bo
       ker. Ke           hind small steel
    pan      the right        . Rem
      ey, open do  .
```

"This is where it says 'door,'" Lina said. "Somehow the door is by the ledge. Does that make sense?"

"And there's that 'small steel pan'—what can that mean? What would a pan have to do with anything?"

"But look, but look." Lina tapped the paper urgently. "Here it says 'ke' and here it says 'ey.' It's talking about a key!"

"But what is it a door *to*?" said Doon, sitting back. "Remember, we thought about this before. A door in the bank of the river would lead *under* the Pipeworks."

Lina pondered this. "Maybe it leads to a long tunnel that goes way out beyond Ember, and then gradually up and up until it comes out at the other city."

"What other city?" Doon glanced up at the drawings tacked to the walls of Lina's room. "Oh," he said. "You mean *that* city."

"Well, it could be."

Doon shrugged. "I suppose so. Or it could be another city exactly like this one."

That was a gloomy thought. Both of them felt their spirits sink a little at the idea. So they turned back to the task of deciphering.

"Next line," said Lina.

But Doon sat back on his heels again. He stared into the air, half smiling. "I have an idea," he said. "If we *do* find the way out, we'll need to announce it to everyone. Wouldn't it be splendid to do it during the Singing? Stand up there in front of the whole city and say we've found it?"

"It would be," Lina said. "But that's only two days away."

"Yes. We have to hurry."

They were bending again over the glued-down fragments when Doon remembered that he should check the time. It was a quarter to nine. He barely had time to get home.

"Come again tomorrow," said Lina. "And while you're at work, look for the rock marked with E."

That night, Doon had trouble sleeping. He couldn't find a comfortable position on his bed. It seemed to be made up of nothing but lumps and wrinkles, and it squeaked and groaned every time he moved. He flailed around so much that the noise woke his father, who came to his room and asked, "What *is* it, son? Nightmares?"

"No," said Doon. "Just can't sleep."

"Are you worrying? Frightened of anything?"

Doon wanted to say, Yes, Father. I'm worried because the mayor of our city is taking for himself the things that people need, and I'm afraid because any day our lights could go out forever. I'm worried and afraid a lot of the time, but I'm also excited because I think there *is* a way out, and we might find it—and all those feelings are whirling around in my head, which makes it hard to sleep.

He could have told his father everything. His father would have plunged in with great enthusiasm. He would have helped them decipher the Instructions and expose the mayor's thievery; he would even have come down into the Pipeworks and helped search for the rock marked with E. But Doon wanted to keep these things to himself for now. Tomorrow, the guards would announce that an alert young boy had uncovered the mayor's crime, and his father, hearing the announcements along with the rest of Ember, would turn to the person next to him and say, "That's my son they're talking about! My *son!*"

So in answer to his father's question, he simply said, "No, Father, I'm all right."

"Well, then, see if you can't lie still," said his father. "Good night, son," he added, and closed the door.

Doon smoothed out his covers and pulled them up to his chin. He closed his eyes. But still he couldn't sleep.

So he tried a method that had often worked for him before. He would choose a place he knew well—the school, for instance—and imagine himself walking through it, picturing it as he went in minute detail. Often his thoughts would wander, but he would always bring them back to the imaginary journey, and something about doing this would often make him sleepy. This night he decided to retrace his explorations of the Pipeworks. He held his mind to the task for a long time, picturing, with all the clarity he could muster, everything he had seen in that underground realm—the long stairway, the tunnels, the door, the path along the river, the rocks along the path. He felt sleep drawing closer, a heaviness in his limbs, but just as he was about to give in to it, he saw in his mind's eye the wrinkled rocks that bordered the river at the west end of the Pipeworks, the rocks whose strange ridges and creases had reminded him of writing. His eyes flew open in the dark, his heart began to hammer, and he gave up on sleeping and lay in a state of terrible impatience for the rest of the night.

CHAPTER 14

The Way Out

The next day was Song Rehearsal Day. Everyone was let off from work at twelve o'clock to practice for the Singing. It was a slow morning for messages. Lina had a lot of time to sit at her station in Garn Square and think. She put her elbows on her knees, rested her chin in her hands, and stared down at the pavement in front of the bench, which was worn smooth by the many feet that had passed there. She thought about the mayor, down in his room full of plunder, gorging on peaches and asparagus and wrapping his huge body in elegant new clothes. She thought of his great stack of light bulbs and shook her head in bewilderment. What was he thinking? If he still had light bulbs when everyone else in Ember had run out, would he enjoy sitting in his lit room while the rest of the city drowned in darkness? And when the power finally ran out for good, all his light bulbs would be useless. Possessions couldn't save him—how could he have forgotten that? He must be thinking the same way as Looper: everything was hopeless anyhow, so he'd live it up while he could.

She leaned back against the bench, stretched her legs out, and took a long breath. Very soon, the guards would storm into the secret room and seize the mayor as he sat stuffing himself on stolen goodies. Maybe they already had. Maybe today the stunning news would come: Mayor Arrested! Stealing from Citizens! Maybe they'd announce it at the Singing, so everyone could hear it.

No one came with any messages to be delivered, so after a while Lina left her station and found a step to sit on in an alley off Calloo Street. She pulled back her hair and braided it to keep it from sliding around. Then she took from her pocket the copy of the Instructions she'd made just after she sent her note to the mayor. She unfolded it and began to study it.

This is what she was doing when, a little before twelve o'clock, she looked up to see Doon running toward her. He must have come straight from the Pipeworks—he had a big damp patch of water on one leg of his pants. He spoke in an excited rush. "I've been looking all over for you!" he said. "I've found it!"

"Found what?"

"The E! At least it looks like an E. It *must* be an E, though you wouldn't know it if you weren't looking for it. . . ."

"You mean the rock marked with an E? In the Pipeworks?"

"Yes, yes, I found it!" He stood breathing hard, his eyes blazing. "I'd seen it before, but I didn't think of it as an E then, just a squiggle that looked like writing. There are all these rocks that look like they're covered with writing."

"Which rocks? Where is it?" Lina was on her feet now, bouncing with excitement.

"Down at the west end of the river. Near where it goes into that great hole in the Pipeworks wall." He paused, trying to catch his breath. "And listen," he said. "We could go there right now."

"Right now?"

"Yes, because of rehearsals. Everyone's going home, so the Pipeworks will be closed and empty."

"But if it's closed, how will we get in?"

Grinning, Doon produced a large key from his pocket. "I ducked into the office on my way out and borrowed the spare key," he said. "Lister—he's the Pipeworks director—was in the bathroom practicing his singing. He won't miss the key today. And tomorrow, everyone will be off work." He did an impatient shuffle. "So come on," he said.

The town clock struck the first of its twelve noontime booms. Lina stuffed her copy of the Instructions back in her pocket. "Let's go."

The Pipeworks was empty and silent. Lina and Doon went up the hallway past the rows of boots and the slickers hanging on their hooks. They didn't take any of these for themselves. This was not a Pipeworks tunnel they were about to enter, they were sure; it wouldn't be dripping with water or lined with spurting pipes.

They went down the long stairway and out into the main tunnel, where the river thundered alongside the path, its dark surface strewn with flecks of light.

Doon led the way along the river's edge. As they neared the west end, Lina saw the rocky outcroppings Doon had described to her. They were strange bulging shapes creased with lines like the faces of the very old. Not far beyond, Lina could see the place where the river disappeared into a great hole in the Pipeworks wall.

Doon knelt down beside a clump of stones. He ran a finger over their convoluted surface. "Look here," he said. Lina stooped down and peered at the deeply carved lines. It was hard to see the E at first, because it was surrounded by such a tangle of other lines, and because she was expecting it to be an E drawn with straight strokes. But once she saw it—an E drawn with curving lines, a script E—she was sure it had been carved on purpose: it was centered on its stone, and its lines were deep and even.

"So from here we should look down at the river," said Doon. "That's what the Instructions said, 'down riverbank to ledge.'"

He lay on his stomach next to the rock and inched forward until his head hung out over the edge of the path. Lina watched him anxiously. His elbows stuck up on either side of him, and his head, bent down, was nearly invisible. He stayed that way for long seconds. Then he shouted, "Yes! I see something!" and scrambled to his feet again. "You do it," he said. "Look at the riverbank right below us."

Lina did as he had. She lay down and pulled herself forward until her head was over the edge. Eight feet or so below her, she saw the black water churning by. She tucked her chin in and looked at the riverbank. It was a sheer rock wall, straight up and down and slick with spray, and at first that was all she saw. But she kept looking and before long could make out short iron bars bolted into the bank, one below the next, almost directly below her. They were like the rungs of a ladder. They *were* a ladder, she realized. The bars provided a way to climb down the riverbank. Not a very appealing way—the bars looked slippery, and the water below was so terribly fast. And because of the dimness and the flying spray, she couldn't actually see if there was a ledge at the bottom or not. But the E was clearly an E, and the bars were clearly a ladder. This must be the right place.

"Who'll go first?" said Doon.

"You can," Lina said, getting to her feet and stepping away.

"All right." Doon turned so that his back was to the river, and he eased himself carefully over the rocks, feeling for the first rung with his foot. Lina watched as he sank out of sight, little by little. After a few moments his voice called up from below: "I'm down! Now you come!"

Lina inched backward, just as Doon had, letting one foot dangle over the edge, lower and lower, until it touched the first rung of the ladder. She shifted her weight to that foot, clinging with cold fingers to a ridge in the rock, and lowered herself slowly until she was standing on the rung with both feet. Her heart was beating so hard she was afraid it would shake her fingers loose from their grip.

Now she had to move downward. She felt for the next rung with her foot, found it, let herself down. It would have been easy if it hadn't been for the river waiting below to swallow her.

"You're almost here!" called Doon. His voice came from right below her. "There's a ledge—one more rung and you'll feel it."

She did feel it, solid beneath her foot. For a second, she stood there, still clutching the ladder. The surging water was only inches below her now. Don't think about it, she told herself. She moved sideways two steps to stand next to Doon, and there in front of them was a rectangular space carved out of the river wall, rather like the entry hall of a building. It was perhaps eight feet wide and eight feet high, and would have been invisible from anywhere else in the Pipeworks. You had to have climbed down the riverbank to see it.

They stepped into this entry hall and walked a few steps. Enough light to see by came from the tunnel behind them.

Lina stopped. "There's the door!" she said.

"What?" said Doon. The water roared so loudly they had to shout to be heard.

"The door!" Lina yelled happily.

"Yes!" Doon yelled back. "I see it!"

At the end of the passage was a wide, solid-looking door. It was dull gray, mottled with greenish and brownish blotches that looked like mildew. Lina put her palms against it. It was metal, and it felt cold. The door had a metal handle, and just below the handle was a keyhole.

Lina reached into the pocket of her pants for her copy of the Instructions. She unfolded it, and Doon looked over her shoulder. Together they squinted at the paper in the dim light from the main tunnel.

"This is the part, right here," she said, pointing:

```
3.            adde  down  iverb nk
        to  edge appr          eight
     low.
4.                          acks to the
     wat  r,          find door of bo
       ker. Ke              hind small steel
     pan      the right          . Rem
      ey, open do  .
```

Lina ran her finger along line number 3. "This must say, 'Something something down riverbank to ledge approximately eight feet below.' That's what we've just done. Then four is something about . . . 'backs to the water, find door . . . something.' And then 'Ke hind'—that must be 'key behind,' and then there's the small steel pan. Do you see a small steel pan?"

Doon was still studying the paper. "It says 'right.' We should look to the right of the door."

And quite easily they found it. It wasn't a pan at all, but a small square of steel embedded in the wall. "A steel *panel*," said Lina. She ran her fingers across it and felt a dent at one side. When she pressed there, the panel sprang open easily and silently, as if it were glad to have been finally found. Inside, a silver key was hanging on a hook.

Lina reached for it and then drew her hand back. "Shall I do it?" she said. "Or shall you?"

"You do it," said Doon.

So she took the key from its hook and put it in the keyhole. She turned it and felt a click. She grasped the door handle and pushed, but nothing happened. She pushed harder. "It won't budge," she said.

"Maybe it opens outward," said Doon.

Lina pulled. The door still didn't move. "It *has* to open," she said. "We unlocked it!" She pulled and pushed and hauled on the handle—and the door moved, not inward or outward but sideways. "Oh, *this* is how it goes!" cried Lina. She pulled the handle to the left, and with a deep rasping sound, the door slid away, into a slot in the wall. Behind it was a space of utter darkness.

They stared. Lina had expected to see something when the door opened. She had thought there would be light behind it, and a path or road.

"Shall we go in?" said Lina.

Doon nodded.

Lina stepped across the threshold. The air had a dank, stuffy smell. She turned to the right and put her right hand against the wall. It was smooth and flat. The floor, too, was smooth.

"There might be a light switch," she said. She patted the wall just inside the door, from the floor to as high as she could reach, but found nothing.

Doon turned left and felt on the other side, with the same result. "Nothing," he said.

Very slowly, keeping a hand to the wall and tapping the floor cautiously with their feet before every step, Doon and Lina made their way in opposite directions. Each of them soon came to a corner and turned again. Now they were going deeper into the dark. They both had the same thought: Is the way out of Ember a long dark tunnel? Must we go mile after mile in absolute darkness?

But suddenly Lina gave a yelp of surprise. "Something's here on the floor," she said. Her foot had banged against a hard object. She knelt down and touched it cautiously with her hands. It was a metal cube, about a foot square. "It's a box, I think. Two boxes," she added as she explored farther.

Doon took a step toward her in the darkness, and his knees banged into a hard edge. "There's something else here, too," he said. "Not a box." He ran his hands along it. "It's big and has a curved edge."

"The boxes are small enough to lift," said Lina. "Let's take them out where it's lighter and see what they are. Come and help."

Doon made his way to Lina and picked up one of the boxes. They walked back through the door and set the boxes down a few feet from the river's edge. They were made of dark green metal and had gray metal handles on top and a kind of latch on the side. The latches opened easily. Lina and Doon raised the hinged lids and looked inside.

What they saw puzzled and disappointed them. Lina's box was full of smooth white rods, each about ten inches long. At the end of each one, a little bit of string poked out. In Doon's box were dozens of small packets wrapped in a slippery material. He opened one and found a lot of short wooden sticks, each with a blue blob on the end. Both boxes had a label on the inside of the lid. The label on Lina's box said "Candles." The label on Doon's said "Matches," and under it was a white, inch-wide strip of some kind of rough, pebbly material.

"What does 'Candles' mean?" Lina said, puzzled. She took out one of the white rods. It felt slick, almost greasy.

"And what does 'Matches' mean?" said Doon. "Matches what?" He took one of the small sticks from its packet. The blue stuff on the end was not wood. "Could it be something to write with? Like a pencil? Maybe it writes blue."

"But what's the point of a whole box of tiny pencils?" asked Lina. "I don't understand."

Doon frowned at the little blue-tipped stick. "I don't see what else it could be," he said finally. "I'll try writing something with it."

"On what?"

Doon looked around. The floor was too damp from the spray of the river to write on. "I could try it on the Instructions," he said. Lina handed them to him. Carefully, he rubbed the blue end of the stick along the edge of the paper. It didn't leave a mark. He rubbed it along his arm. No mark there, either.

"Try this white stuff," Lina said, pointing to the white strip inside the lid of the box.

He scraped the blue tip across the rough surface. Instantly, the end of the stick burst into flame. Doon cried out and flung the stick away. It landed on the floor a few feet off, where it burned brightly for a moment and then sputtered out.

They stared at each other, their mouths open in astonishment. There was a strange sharp smell in the air that smarted in their noses.

"It makes fire!" said Doon. "And light!"

"Let me try one," said Lina. She took a stick from the box and ran it across the rough strip. It blazed up fiercely, but she managed to hold on to it for a moment. Then she felt the heat on her fingers and let go, and the flaming stick dropped over the ledge and into the river.

"Fire sticks," said Doon. "Are they what saves Ember?"

"I don't see how they could be," said Lina. "They're so small. They go out too fast." She shivered. This was not turning out the way she'd thought it would. She held up one of the white things. "Anyway, what are these for?"

Doon shook his head in bewilderment. "Maybe a candle is a kind of handle," he said. "Maybe you tie the stick on with the string, and then you can hold it longer while it burns."

"It would still go out just as fast," Lina said.

"Yes," said Doon. "But it's all I can think of. Let's try it."

With a great deal of effort, they looped the string of a rod around one of the sticks. Lina held the rod while Doon scraped the blue tip into flame. They watched the stick flare brightly, making shadows jump up behind them. The wood turned black, and the charred firestick crumbled and dropped to the ground. But the light didn't go out. The string itself had caught fire. As they watched, it sputtered and smoked and then burned steadily, filling the little room with a warm glow.

"It's the movable light," said Doon in awe.

All Lina's excitement flooded back. "And now, and now—" she said, "we can go back into the room and see what's there."

They went back down the passage to the doorway and stepped inside. Lina held the movable light at arm's length before her. In its flickering glow they saw something made of silvery metal. They walked slowly around, examining it. It was long and low, filling up the center of the room. One end of it came to a point. The other end was flat. Across the open middle stretched two metal strips. Four stout ropes were attached to the outside, one at each end and one on each side. And on the floor of the thing were two poles, each flattened at one end.

"Look," said Lina. "There's a word on its side." They squatted at the pointed end and held the flame near the word. It said, in square black letters, "BOAT."

"Boat," repeated Doon. "What does that mean?"

"I don't know," said Lina. "And here's another word, on these poles: 'Paddles.' The only paddle I know is the one Mrs. Polster uses on kids who misbehave in school."

Once again, she took her copy of the Instructions from her pocket and consulted it, holding it in the light of the flame. "Look," she said, "right here: 'oat' must be 'boat.'"

5.		oat,		stocked with
	nec		uip	ent. Bac
	ont	s	eet.	

"And the next part must say, 'stocked with necessary equipment,'" said Doon. "That must be what's in the boxes."

"Then there's this." Lina ran her finger along the next line.

> 6. Usi   opes, lowe
>   ter. Head dow st   . Us pa
> av   cks and assist over rap .

"This word must be 'ropes,'" she said. "Then 'lower' . . . and then . . . would this word be 'downstairs'? Maybe it says, 'head downstairs'?"

"That doesn't make sense," said Doon. "There aren't any stairs, except the ones that go up." He frowned at the word, and then he took a short, sharp breath. "Downstream," he said. "The word must be 'downstream.' It must say something like, 'Use the ropes to lower the boat, and head downstream.'" He looked up at Lina and spoke in a voice full of wonder. "The boat goes on the water. It's something to ride in."

They stared at each other in the flickering light, realizing what this meant. There was no tunnel leading out of Ember. The way out was the river. To leave Ember, they must go on the river.

CHAPTER 15

A Desperate Run

"But this can't be right," said Doon. "If the river is the way out of Ember, why is there just one boat? It's only big enough for two people."

"I don't know," said Lina. "It *is* strange."

"Let's look around some more."

They stood up. Doon went back to where they'd left the boxes and got another candle. He brought it into the boat room and lit it, and the room grew twice as bright. Right away they saw what they hadn't noticed before: in the back wall was a door almost as wide as the whole room. When they went up to it they could see that it, too, was a sliding door. Doon took hold of the handle that was on the right and pulled sideways, and the door rolled smoothly open to reveal more darkness.

They stepped in. They could guess from the echoing sound of their voices when they spoke that they were in a tremendous room, though the ceiling was low—they could see it just over their heads. The candlelight glinted off something shiny, and as they went in farther they could see that the room was filled with boats, row upon row of them, all just like the one in the first room. "There must be hundreds," Lina whispered.

"Enough for everyone, I suppose," said Doon.

They wandered around a bit, but there wasn't really much to see. All the boats were the same. Each one contained two metal boxes and two paddles. The room was cold, and the air felt heavy in their lungs. The candle flames burned weakly. So they went back to the small room and slid the door closed behind them. "I guess," said Lina, "that this first boat is meant as a sort of sample. We learn what's what on the one that has signs. 'Boat.' 'Paddles.' 'Candles.' 'Matches.'"

They went back out to the river's edge. Lina blew out her candle and began closing up the boxes they'd opened.

Doon blew out his, too. "I'm going to take my candle with me," he said, "to look at later. I want some matches as well." He took a packet of matches from the box and tucked it inside his shirt.

Lina returned the boxes to the boat room and slid the door closed. Then she and Doon stood together on the ledge and gazed down. Less than a foot below, the river rushed by. A short distance down-stream it plunged into the dark mouth in the wall and disappeared.

"Well," he said, "we've found it."

"We've found it," Lina repeated, wonderingly.

"And tomorrow, at the start of the Singing," said Doon, "we'll stand up in Harken Square and tell the whole city."

When they came up out of the Pipeworks, it was nearly six o'clock. They hadn't realized they'd been down there so long; both Doon's father and Mrs. Murdo would be wondering where they were. They stood for a moment under a lamppost, just long enough to agree on a time to meet the next day and plan their announcement. Then they hurried home. When Doon's father asked why he was so late, he said his song rehearsal had gone long. He wanted to shout out to his father, *We've found the way out! We're saved!* But he held himself in for the sake of his moment of glory. Tomorrow, when his father saw him on the steps of the Gathering Hall, he would be so overcome with surprise and pride that he would go weak in the knees, and the people standing next to him would have to catch him and hold him up.

And the announcement about the thieving mayor! That would probably happen tomorrow, too. Doon had almost forgotten it in the excitement of finding the boats. The mayor's arrest and the city's rescue, both at once! It was going to be an amazing day. Racing thoughts kept Doon awake almost until morning.

The day of the Singing was a holiday for the entire city; all the stores and other businesses were closed. This meant that Doon didn't have to go to the Pipeworks. His father didn't have to go to his shop, either, but he was going to go anyhow. If he wasn't in his shop, fussing with his merchandise, he didn't know what to do with himself.

Doon dawdled over his breakfast of carrot sticks and mashed turnips, waiting for his father to go. He wanted to get ready for the journey down the river. They probably wouldn't leave for a few days—he and Lina would make their announcement tonight, and people would need time to get organized before they could leave the city—but he was too excited to sit around doing nothing.

As soon as his father left, Doon slipped the case off his pillow. This would be his traveling pack. He put in the candle and the matches. He put in the key he'd borrowed from the Pipeworks office. He put in a good-sized piece of rope that he'd found at the trash heaps and had been saving for years and a bottle for water. He put in an ancient folding knife that his father had given him, which had come down through generations of his family and which he used to chop off his bangs when they got so long they tickled his eyelids. He put in some extra clothes, in case he got wet, and some paper and a pencil, so that he could write a record of the journey. Along with these things, he crammed in a small blanket—it might be cold in the new city—and a packet of food: six carrots, a handful of vitamins, some peas and mushrooms wrapped in a lettuce leaf, two boiled beets, and two boiled turnips. That should be enough. Surely, when they got to where they were going, the people who lived there would give them something to eat. He tied the top of the pillowcase in a knot, and then he untied it again. He might want to add something else.

He stood in the middle of the apartment and looked around at the jumble of stuff. There was nothing else here that he wanted to take with him— no, there was one thing. He went back into his room. From beneath his bed he pulled out the pages of his bug book. He leafed through it. The white spider. The moth with the zigzag pattern on its wings. The bee, striped brown and yellow on its rear end. He looked at his drawings for a long time, memorizing their beauty and strangeness. Tiny fringes of hair, minute claws, jointed legs. Should he take this with him? There might not be creatures like this where they were going. He might never see such things again.

But no, he'd leave it behind—his pack should be small and light. He put the bug book back under his bed and pulled out the box where he kept the green worm. He drew back the scarf to check his captive one more time. Several days before, the worm had done a curious thing: it had wrapped itself up in a blanket of threads. Since then it had hung motionless from a bit of cabbage stem. Doon had been watching it carefully. Either it was dead, or it was undergoing the change that he'd read about in a library book but could hardly believe was true—the change from a crawling thing to a flying thing. So far, the bundled-up worm had shown no signs of life.

But now he saw that it was wriggling. The whole wrapped-up bundle, which was shaped like a large vitamin pill, bent slightly from side to side, then was still, then bent back and forth again. Something was pushing at the top end of it, and in a moment the threads there split apart and a dark furry knob emerged. Doon watched, holding his breath. Next came two hairlike legs, which clawed and plucked at the blanket. In a few minutes the whole creature was out. Egress, thought Doon with a smile. The creature's wings were crushed flat against its body at first, but soon they opened, and Doon saw what his green worm had become: a moth with light brown wings. He lifted the box and carried it to the window. He opened the window and held the box out into the air. The moth waved its feathery feelers and took a few steps along the wilted cabbage leaf. For several minutes, it stood still, its wings trembling slightly. Then it fluttered up into the air, rising higher and higher until it was just a pale spot against the dark sky.

Doon watched until the moth disappeared. He knew he had seen something marvelous. What was the power that turned the worm into a moth? It was greater than any power the Builders had had, he was sure of that. The power that ran the city of Ember was feeble by comparison—and about to run out.

For a few minutes he stood by the window, looking out over the square and thinking again about what to pack for his journey. Should he put in anything like nails or wire? Would he need money? Should he take some soap?

Then he laughed and struck a hand against his head. He kept forgetting that the entire population of the city would be with him on the trip. If he needed something he didn't have, someone would surely be able to supply it.

So he tied a knot in his pillowcase and was about to close the window when he caught sight of three burly men wearing the red and brown uniform of the city guards striding into the square. They stopped and looked around for a moment. Then one of them confronted old humpbacked Nammy Proggs, who was standing not far from the entrance to the Small Items shop. The guard towered over her, and she twisted her head sideways and squinted up at him. Doon could hear the guard's voice clearly: "We're looking for a boy named Harrow."

"Why?" said Nammy.

"Spreading vicious rumors" was the answer. "Do you know where he is?"

Nammy hesitated a moment, and then she said, "Went off to the trash heaps just a minute ago." The guard nodded curtly and beckoned to his companions. They marched away.

Spreading vicious rumors! Doon was so stunned that he stood still as stone for a long minute. What could they possibly mean? But there was only one answer. It had to be what they'd told the assistant guard about the mayor. Why were they calling it a vicious rumor? It was the truth! He didn't understand it.

He did understand, though, that Nammy Proggs had done him a favor. She must have seen that the guards meant him no good. She had protected him, at least for the moment, by sending the guards to the wrong place.

Doon forced his mind to slow down and think. Why did the guards think he and Lina were lying? Obviously, they hadn't investigated the room in Tunnel 351. If they had, they'd have known he and Lina were telling the truth.

He could think of only one other possibility. The guards—at least some of them—already knew what the mayor was doing. They knew about it and wanted it to stay a secret. And why? It was clear: the guards, too, were getting things from the storerooms.

It had to be the answer. For a moment, the fear he'd felt when he saw the guards was replaced by rage. The familiar hot wave rose in him, and he wanted to grab a handful of his father's nails or pot shards and throw them against the wall. But all at once he remembered: if the guards were after him, they'd be after Lina, too. He had to warn her. He dashed down the stairs, his anger turning into power for his running feet.

After discovering the room full of boats, Lina had come home to Mrs. Murdo's with the sound of the river still in her ears. It was like a huge, powerful voice, roaring at the top of its lungs. Deep inside herself Lina felt an answering call, as if she, too, contained a drop of the same power. She would ride on the river— she could hardly believe it—and it might take her to the shining city she had dreamed of, or it might drown her. What she had imagined before—the smooth, gently sloping path leading out—now seemed childish. How could the way into a new world be so easy? She dreaded going on the river, but she was ready for it, too. She longed to go.

She slept that night in the beautiful blue-green room, in the big, lumpy bed with Poppy next to her.

She felt safe here. Mrs. Murdo came in and tucked the covers around her. She sat on the edge of the bed and sang an odd little song to Poppy—something about rock-a-bye baby, in the treetops. "What are treetops?" Lina asked, but Mrs. Murdo didn't know. "It's a very old song," she said. "It's probably nonsense words."

She said good night and went out into the living room, where Lina could hear her humming quietly as she tidied up. She was so orderly. She never left her stockings draped over the back of a chair, or her sewing spread out all over the table. Lina closed her eyes and waited for sleep.

But her thoughts kept tumbling around. So much was going to happen tomorrow—the whole city would be in an uproar. People would stream down into the Pipeworks to see the boats. They'd be excited, shouting and laughing and crying, packing up their belongings, and surging through the streets. If they couldn't all fit into the boats, there would be fights. Some people might get hurt. It was going to be a mess. She'd have to keep her little family close around her—Poppy, Mrs. Murdo, and Doon, and perhaps Doon's father and Clary. Through it all, she would hold tight to Poppy so no harm could come to her.

It seemed she had barely closed her eyes when she felt Poppy's hard little heels banging against her shins. "Time-a get up! Get up!" Poppy chirped.

She got out of bed and dressed herself and Poppy. In the kitchen, Mrs. Murdo was mashing potatoes for breakfast. How lovely, Lina thought, to have breakfast cooked for her—to hear water bubbling in the pot, and to find a bowl and a spoon set out on the table, and vitamins lined up neatly beside a cup of beet tea. I could live here forever, Lina thought, before she remembered that in a day or two they would all be leaving.

There was a sudden banging on the front door. Mrs. Murdo dried her hands and went to answer it, but before she'd taken three steps the banging came again. "I'm coming, I'm coming," Mrs. Murdo cried, and when she opened the door, there was Doon.

His face was flushed, and he was breathing hard. He had a bulging pillowcase slung over his shoulder.

He looked past Mrs. Murdo to Lina. "I have to talk to you," he said. "Right now, but . . ." He threw a doubtful glance at Mrs. Murdo.

Lina scrambled up from the table. "In here," she said, towing him toward the blue-green room.

When she had closed the door, Doon told her what had happened. "They'll come for you, too," he said, "any minute. We have to get out of here. We have to hide from them."

Lina could hardly make sense of what he was saying. They were in *trouble*? Her legs went shaky at the knees. "Hide?" she said. "Hide where?"

"We could go to the school—no one would be there today—or the library. It's almost always open, even on holidays." He hopped impatiently from foot to foot. "But we have to go *fast,* we have to go *now.* They have *signs* up about us all over the city!"

"Signs?"

"Telling people to report us if they see us!"

Lina felt as if a swarm of insects was inside her head, buzzing so loudly she couldn't think. "How long do we have to hide? All day?"

"I don't know—we don't have time to think about it. Lina, they could be outside the door *this minute.*"

The urgency in his voice convinced her. On the way through the living room she gave Poppy a quick kiss and called, "Bye, Mrs. Murdo. We have some emergency work to do. If anyone comes asking for me, say I'll be back later." They were down the stairs before Mrs. Murdo could ask any questions.

Once in the street, they ran. "Where to?" Lina said.

"The school," Doon answered.

They took Greystone Street, staying within the shadows as much as they could. As they passed the shoe shop, Lina saw a white piece of paper stuck up on the window. She glanced at it and her heart gave a wild jump. Her name and Doon's were written on it in big black letters:

DOON HARROW AND **LINA MAYFLEET**

WANTED FOR SPREADING VICIOUS RUMORS

IF YOU SEE THEM,

REPORT TO MAYOR'S CHIEF GUARD.

BELIEVE NOTHING THEY SAY.

REWARD

She snatched the poster off the window, crumpled it up, and tossed it into the nearest trash can. In the next block, she tore down two more, and Doon ripped one off a lamppost. But there were too many to get them all, and they didn't have time to waste.

They ran faster. On this holiday, people slept late, and because the stores were closed, the streets were nearly empty. Still, they took the long route all the way out by the beehives to avoid Sparkswallow Square, where a few people might be standing around and talking. They ran past the greenhouses and up Dedlock Street. As they crossed Night Street, Lina glanced to her left. Two blocks away, a couple of guards were crossing to Greengate Square. She tapped Doon's shoulder and pointed. He saw, and they ran faster. Had they been noticed? Lina thought not; they would have heard a shout if the guards had seen them.

They got to the school and went in through the back door. In the Wide Hallway, their footsteps echoed on the wooden floor. It was strange to be here again, and to be here alone, without the clatter and chatter of other children. The hallway with its eight doors seemed smaller to Lina than it had when she was a student, and shabbier. The planks of the floor were scuffed gray, and there was a cloud of finger smudges around the doorknob of every door.

They went into Miss Thorn's room and, out of habit, sat at their old desks. "I don't think they'll look for us here," said Doon. "If they do, we can crawl into the paper cabinet." He set his pack down next to him on the floor.

For a while they just sat there, getting their breath back. They hadn't turned the light on, so the room was dim—the only light came from beneath the blind over the window.

"Those posters," Lina said after a while.

"Yes. Everyone will see them."

"What will they do to us if they catch us?"

"I don't know. Something to keep us from telling what we know. Put us in the Prison Room, maybe."

Lina ran her finger along the B carved in the desktop. It felt like a very long time since she'd last sat at this desk. "We can't hide in here forever," she said.

"No," said Doon. "Just until it's time for the Singing. Then when everyone is gathered in Harken Square, we'll go and tell about the boats and the mayor. Won't we? I haven't really thought about it—I haven't had a chance to think at all this morning."

"But the guards are always there at the Singing, standing next to the mayor," said Lina. "They'd grab us as soon as we opened our mouths."

Doon's eyebrows came together in a dark line. "You're right. So what will we do?"

It was like finding yourself on a dead-end street, Lina thought. There was no way out. She stared blankly at the things that had once been her daily companions—the teacher's desk, the stacks of paper, *The Book of the City of Ember* on its special shelf. The old words ran through her head: "There is no place but Ember. Ember is the only light in the dark world." She knew now that this wasn't true. There *was* someplace else—the place where the boats would take them.

As if Doon had read her thoughts, he looked up. "We could go."

"Go where?" she said, though she knew right away what he meant.

"Wherever the river leads," he said. He gestured to the pillowcase sack. "I packed up my bag this morning—I'm all ready. I'm sure I have enough for you, too."

Lina felt her heart shrink a little. "Go by ourselves?" she said. "Without telling anyone?"

"We *will* tell them." Doon was on his feet now. He went to the cabinet and got a sheet of paper. "We'll write a note explaining everything—a note to someone we trust, someone who'll believe us."

"But I can't just leave," said Lina. "How could I leave Poppy? And not even say goodbye to her? Not know where I'm going, or if I'm ever coming back? How could *you* go without saying goodbye to your father?"

"Because," said Doon, "once they find the boats, the rest of Ember will follow us. It's not as if we're leaving them forever." He strode across the room and rummaged in Miss Thorn's desk. "Who shall we write the message to?"

Lina wasn't sure about this idea, but she couldn't, at the moment, think of a better one. So she said, "We could write it to Clary. She's seen the Instructions. She'll believe what we say. And she lives close by—just up in Torrick Square."

"Okay," said Doon. He pulled a pencil from the desk drawer. "Really," he said, "this is a perfect idea. We can get away from the guards and leave our message behind us. *And* we can be the first ones to arrive in the new city! We *should* be the first, because we discovered the way."

"Well, that's true." Lina thought for a minute. "How long do you think it will take before the rest of them find the boats and come? It's a lot of people to get organized." She numbered on her fingers the things that would have to happen. "Clary will have to get the head of the Pipeworks to go down with her and find the boats. Then she'll have to make the announcement to the city. Then everyone in Ember will have to pack up their things, troop down to the river, get all those boats out of that big room, and load themselves in. It could be a big mess, Doon. Poppy will need me." She pictured frenzied crowds of people, and Poppy tiny and lost among them.

"Poppy has Mrs. Murdo," said Doon. "She'll be fine. Really. Mrs. Murdo is very organized."

It was true. The thought of taking Poppy with her on the river, which had darted into Lina's mind, darted out again. I'm only being selfish, she thought, to want to have her with me. It's too dangerous to take her. Mrs. Murdo will bring her in a day or two. This seemed the most sensible plan, though it made her so sad that it cast a shadow over the thrill of going to the new city. "What if something goes wrong?" she said.

"Nothing will go wrong! It's a good plan, Lina. We'll be there ahead of everyone else—we can welcome them when they come, we can show them around!" Doon was bursting with eagerness. His eyes shone, and he jiggled up and down.

"Well, all right," Lina said. "Let's write our message, then."

Doon wrote for a long time. When he was finished, he showed what he'd written to Lina. He'd explained how to find the rock with the E, how to go down to the boat room, even how to use the candles.

"It's good," she said. "Now we have to deliver it."

She paused a moment to see if she had any courage inside her. She found that she did, along with sadness and fear and excitement. "I'll deliver it," she said. "I'm the messenger, after all. I know back ways to go, where no one will see me." An idea struck her. "Doon, maybe Clary will be home! Maybe she would keep us safe and help us tell what we know, and we won't *have* to leave right now."

Doon quickly shook his head. "I doubt it," he said. "She's probably with her singing group, getting ready. You'll just have to leave the note under her door."

Lina could tell from his tone of voice that Doon didn't really want Clary to be home. She supposed he had his heart set on their going down the river by themselves. Doon glanced up at the clock on the schoolroom wall. "It's a little after two," he said. "The Singing begins at three. After that, everyone will be in Harken Square and the streets will be empty. I think we can get to the Pipeworks safely then—why don't we leave about a quarter after three."

"You still have the key?"

Doon nodded.

"So after I've delivered the note to Clary, I'll come back here," said Lina.

"Yes. And then we'll wait until three-fifteen, and then we'll go."

Lina got up from the cramped desk and went to the window. She moved the blind a little and peered out. There was no one in the street. The dusty school-room was very quiet. She thought about Doon's father, who would be frantic when he saw his son's name on those posters and then realized later that Doon had disappeared. She thought about Mrs. Murdo, who might already have seen the posters, and who would be frightened if guards came looking for Lina and terri-fied if Lina didn't come home by nightfall. She tried not to think about Poppy at all; she couldn't bear it.

"Give me the note," she said to Doon at last. She folded the piece of paper carefully and put it in the pocket of her pants. "Back soon," she said, and went out of the room and down the hall to the rear door of the school.

Doon went to the window to watch her go. He moved the blind aside just enough to see out into Pibb Street. There she was, running in that long-legged way, with her hair flying. She started across Stonegrit Lane. Just before she reached the other side, Doon's breath stopped in his throat. Two guards rounded the corner from Knack Street, directly ahead of her. One of them was the chief guard. He leapt forward and shouted so loudly Doon could hear him plainly through the glass: "That's her! Get her!"

Lina reversed her direction in an instant. She raced back down Pibb Street, turned down School Street toward Bilbollio Square, and vanished from Doon's sight. The guards ran after her, shouting. Doon watched, sick with horror. She's much faster than they are, he told himself. She'll lose them—she knows places to hide. He stood frozen next to the window, hardly breathing. They won't catch her, he thought. I'm sure they won't catch her.

CHAPTER 16

The Singing

When Lina heard the guards shout, terror shot through her. She ran faster than she ever had before, her heart pounding wildly. Behind her, the guards kept up their shouting, and she knew that if other guards were nearby they would come running. She had to find a hiding place. Ahead of her was Bilbollio Square—was there a spot she could duck into? And like an answer, Doon's words came back to her: "The library. It's almost always open, even on holidays." She didn't have time to think. She didn't ask herself whether Edward Pocket would be willing to hide her, or whether there would even *be* a good place to hide in the library. She just ran for the passageway that led to the library door and darted down it.

But the library door wouldn't open. She turned the knob frantically, she pulled and pushed, and then, at the same time that she heard the running footsteps of the guards coming into the square, she saw the small handwritten sign stuck to the door: "Closed for the Singing." The guards were very near now. If she ran, they would see her. She flattened herself against the wall, hoping they wouldn't think to look in the library passage.

But they did. "Here she is!" yelled one of the guards. She tried to shoot past him, but the passage was too narrow, and he caught her by the arm. She pulled and twisted and kicked, but the chief guard had her now, too. He gripped her other arm with fingers that felt like iron. "Stop your struggling!" he shouted.

Lina reached up and grabbed a handful of his wiry beard. She pulled with all her might, and the chief guard roared, but he didn't let go. He yanked her forward, almost off the ground, and the two guards dragged her across the square at an awkward, lopsided pace that made her stumble over her own feet.

"You're hurting me!" Lina said. "Don't hold so tight!"

"Don't you tell us what to do," said the chief guard. "We'll hold you tight till we get you where you're going."

"Where is that?" said Lina. She was so enraged at her bad luck that she almost forgot to be afraid.

"You're going to see the mayor, missy," said the chief guard. "He'll decide what to do with you."

"But I haven't done anything wrong!"

"Spreading vicious rumors," said the guard. "Telling dangerous lies calculated to cause civic unrest."

"It's not a lie!" she said. But the guard gripped her arm even more tightly and gave her a shove so she stumbled sideways.

"No talking," he said, and they walked the rest of the way in grim silence.

A few people had already gathered in Harken Square, though the workers were still getting it ready for the Singing. Street-sweepers crossed the square back and forth, pushing their brooms. Someone appeared at a second-floor window of a building on Gilly Street and unfurled one of the banners that was always displayed for the Singing—a long piece of red cloth, faded after years of use but still showing its design of wavy lines, representing the river, the source of all power. That was for "The Song of the River." There would be a banner on the Broad Street side of the square, too, this one deep yellow-gold with a design like a grid to represent "The Song of the City," and another banner on the Otterwill side for "The Song of Darkness," perfectly black except for a narrow yellow edge.

The guards marched Lina up the steps of the Gathering Hall and through the wide doorway. They took her down the main corridor, opened the door at the end, and gave her one last push, a push that caused her to stagger forward in an undignified way and bump up against the back of a chair.

It was the same room she'd been in that other, much happier day—her first day as a messenger. Nothing had changed—the frayed red curtains, the armchairs with the upholstery worn thin, the hideous mud-colored carpet. The portraits on the wall looked down at her sorrowfully.

"Sit there," said the chief guard. He pointed at a small, hard-looking chair that faced the large armchair. Lina sat. Next to the chair was the small table she remembered from before, with the china teapot and a tray of china teacups with chips around their edges.

The chief guard left the room—to find the mayor, Lina supposed. The other one stood silently with his arms folded across his chest. Nothing happened for a while. Lina tried to think about what she would say to the mayor, but her mind wouldn't work.

Then the door to the front hall opened, and the mayor came in. It was the first time Lina had seen him up close since she had delivered Looper's message to him. He seemed even more immense. His baggy face was the color of a mushroom. He wore a black suit that stretched only far enough across his vast belly for one button to connect with its buttonhole.

He moved ponderously across the room and settled into the armchair, filling it completely. Next to his chair was a table, and on the table was a brass bell the size of a fist. The mayor gazed for a moment at Lina with eyes that looked like the openings of tunnels, and then he turned to the guard.

"Dismissed," he said, waving the back of his hand at him. "Return when I ring the bell."

The guard left. The mayor swung his gaze back to Lina. "I am not surprised," he said. He lifted one arm and pointed a finger at Lina's face. "You have been in trouble before. Going where you shouldn't."

Lina started to speak, but the mayor held up his hand. It was an oddly small hand, with short fingers like ripe pea pods.

"Curiosity," said the mayor. "A dangerous quality. Unhealthy. Especially regrettable in one so young."

"I'm twelve," said Lina.

"Silence!" said the mayor. "I am speaking." He wriggled slightly from side to side, wedging himself more firmly into the chair. He'll need to be pried out of it, Lina thought.

"Ember, as you know," the mayor went on, "is in a time of difficulty. Extraordinary measures are necessary. This is a time when citizens should be most loyal. Most law-abiding. For the good of all."

Lina said nothing. She watched how the flesh under the mayor's chin bulged in and out as he spoke, and then she turned her eyes from this unpleasant sight and looked carefully around the room. She was thinking now, calculating, but not about what the mayor was saying.

"The duties of a mayor," said the mayor, "are . . . complex. Cannot be understood by regular citizens, particularly children. That is why . . . ," he went on, leaning slightly forward so that his stomach pushed farther out along his lap, "certain things must remain hidden from the public. The public would not understand. The public must have faith," said the mayor, once again holding up his hand, this time with a finger pointing to the ceiling, "that all is being done for their benefit. For their own good."

"Hogwash," said Lina.

The mayor jerked backward. His eyebrows came down over his eyes, making them into dark slits. "*What?*" he said. "Surely I heard you incorrectly."

"I said hogwash," said Lina. "It means—"

"Do not presume to tell me what it means!" the mayor cried. "Impudence will make things worse for you." He was breathing heavily, and his words came out with spaces between them. "A misguided child . . . such as yourself . . . requires . . . a forceful lesson." His short fingers gripped the arms of the chair. "Perhaps," he said, "your curiosity has led you to wonder . . . about the Prison Room. What could it be like, eh? Dark? Cold? Uncomfortable?" He made the smile that Lina remembered from Assignment Day. His lips pulled away from his small teeth; his gray cheeks folded. "You will have a chance to find out. You will become . . . closely acquainted . . . with the Prison Room. The guards will escort you there. Your accomplice—another known troublemaker—will join you, as soon as he is located."

The mayor turned to look for the bell. This was the moment when Lina had planned to make a dash for freedom—she thought she had a slim chance to succeed if she moved fast enough—but something happened in that instant that gave her a head start.

The lights went out.

There was no flicker this time, just sudden, complete darkness. It was fortunate that Lina had already planned her move and knew exactly which way to go. She leapt up, knocking over her chair. With her arm, she made a wide swipe and knocked over the table next to the chair as well. The furniture thumping to the floor, the teapot shattering, and the mayor's enraged shouts made a clamor that covered the sound of her footsteps as she dashed to the stairway door. Was it unlocked? She reached for the knob. Grunts and squeaks told her that the mayor was struggling to rise from his chair. She turned the knob and pulled, and the door sprang open. She closed the door behind her and leapt upward two steps at a time. Even in the pitch dark, she could climb stairs. In the room, the bell clanged and clanged, and the mayor bellowed.

When she got to the first landing, she heard the

guards shouting. There was a crash—someone must have fallen over the toppled chair or table. "Where is she?" someone yelled. "Must have run out the door!" Did they know which door? She didn't hear footsteps behind her.

If she could make it to the roof—and if from the roof she could jump to the roof of the Prison Room and from there to the street—then maybe she could escape. Her lungs were on fire now, her breath was burning her throat, but she climbed without stopping, and when she came to the top, she burst through the door to the roof and ran out.

And that was when the lights came back on. It was as if the blackout had been arranged especially for her. I am so lucky, she thought, so extremely lucky! Ahead of her was the clock tower. She went around to the other side of it. No dancing on the roof this time.

A low wall ran along the edge of the building. Lina approached it cautiously and peered out over the swarm of people assembling in Harken Square. Directly below her was the entrance of the Gathering Hall, and as she watched, two guards dashed out the door and down the steps. Good—they had gone the wrong way! They must think she'd escaped into the crowd. For the moment, she was safe. The clock in the tower began to chime. Three great booms rang out. It was time for the Singing to begin.

Lina gazed down at the people of Ember, gathered

to sing their songs. They stood so close together that she could see only their faces, which were lifted up toward the sky, with the hard bright lights shining down on them. They were silent, waiting for the Songmaster to appear on the Gathering Hall steps. There was a strange hush, as if the city were holding its breath. Of the whole Ember year, Lina thought, this hush before the Singing was one of the most exciting moments. She remembered other years, when she had stood with her parents, too short to see the Songmaster's signal, too short to see anything but people's backs and legs, and waited for the first note to thunder out. She felt her heart move at that moment, every year. The sound would rise in waves around her like water, almost as if it could lift her off the ground.

Now suddenly the moment came again. From hundreds of voices rose the first notes of "The Song of the City," deep and strong. She felt as she had all the years before: a quivering inside, as though a string under her ribs had been plucked, and a rush of joy and sadness mixed together. The deep, rumbling chords of the song filled Harken Square. Lina felt that she might step off the edge of the building and walk across the air, it seemed so solid with sound.

"The Song of the City" was long—there were verses about "streets of light and walls of stone," about "citizens with sturdy hearts," about "stored abundance never-ending." (Not true, Lina thought.) But at last,

"The Song of the City" wound down to its end. The singers held the final note, which grew softer and softer, and then there was silence again. Lina looked out at the lighted streets spreading away in every direction, the streets she knew so well. She loved her city, worn out and crumbling though it was. She looked up at the clock: ten minutes after three. Doon would be getting ready to leave for the Pipeworks. She didn't know whether he'd seen her being captured—if he had, he would be wondering if she'd been locked into the Prison Room. He'd be wondering if he should try to rescue her, or if he should go down the river by himself.

She should be hurrying to join him—but a sadness held her back, like a heavy stone in her chest. She bent her face into the palms of her hands and pressed hard against her closed eyes. How could she go away from Ember and leave Poppy behind? Because if she went, she must leave Poppy behind, mustn't she? How could she take her on a journey of such danger?

"The Song of the River" startled her when it began—the men's voices, low and rolling, swelling with power, and then the women's voices coming in above with a complicated melody that seemed to fight the current. Lina listened, unable to move. "The Song of the River" made her uneasy—it always had. With its rolling, relentless rhythm, it seemed to urge her onward, saying, Go down, go away, go now. The more she listened, the more she felt something like the motion of the river in her stomach, a churning, sickening feeling.

Then came "The Song of Darkness," the last of the three songs, and the one most filled with longing and majesty. The soul of Ember was in this song. Its tremendous chords held all the sorrow and all the strength of the people of the city. The song reached its climax: "Darkness like an endless night," sang the hundreds of voices, so powerfully the air seemed to shiver.

And at that moment, the lights once more went out. The voices faltered, but only for an instant. Then they rose again in the darkness, stronger even than before. Lina sang, too. She stood up and sang with all her might into the deep, solid blackness.

The last notes echoed and faded into a terrible silence. Lina stood utterly still. Will it end like this, she thought, at the finish of the last song? She felt the cold stone of the clock tower behind her back. She waited.

Then an idea came to her that made her skin prickle. What if she were to shout into the silence right now? What if she were to say, *Listen, people! We've found the way out of Ember! It's the river—we go on the river!* She could announce the astounding news, just as she and Doon had planned to do, and then—and then what would happen? Would the guards rush to the roof and seize her? Would the people in the square think her news was just a child's wishful thinking, or would they listen and be saved? She could feel the words pushing upward in her throat, she wanted so much to say them. She took a deep breath and leaned forward.

But before she could speak, a rumble of voices arose below. Someone shouted, "Don't move!" and someone else shrieked. The rumble rose to a roar, and then cries flew into the darkness from everywhere. The crowd was erupting into panic.

There was no hope of being heard now. Lina clutched the edge of the clock tower as if the tumult below might cause her to fall. She strained her eyes against the darkness. Without light, she could go nowhere. Lights, come back on, she prayed. Come back on.

Then she saw something. At first, she thought her eyes were tricking her. She closed them tightly and opened them again. It was still there: a tiny point of light, moving. As she watched, it moved along slowly in a straight line. Then it turned and moved in a straight line again. Was it on River Road? She couldn't tell. But suddenly she knew what it was. It was Doon, with a candle. Doon, going toward the Pipeworks in the dark.

And she wanted to go, too. She could feel it all through her, the urge to run and meet him and find the way out of Ember, to the new place. She listened to the shouts and wails of the terrified people in the square below. She thought of Mrs. Murdo down there in the dark, being bumped and pushed, with her arms wrapped tightly around Poppy, trying to protect her, and all at once everything seemed clear. Lina knew what she would do—if only the lights would come back on, if only this was not the very last blackout in the history of Ember. Watching the tiny light following its steady course, she made a wish with the whole force of her heart and mind.

Then the floodlights flickered—there was a great cry of hope from the crowd—and the lights came on and stayed on. Lina ran to the back edge of the roof, dropped easily down onto the roof of the Prison Room, and, seeing no guards in the crowd that was now streaming into the street, she jumped from there to the ground and joined the throng of people. She made her way down Greystone Street, going at the same pace as everyone else so she wouldn't stand out. When she came to the trash-can enclosure behind the Gathering Hall, she squatted down and hid. Her heart was beating fast, but she felt strong and purposeful now. She had her plan. As soon as she spotted Mrs. Murdo and Poppy on their way home, she'd put it into action.

CHAPTER 17

Away

At three-twenty, Doon took his pillowcase pack, left the school by the back door, and started up Pibb Street. He went fast—the lights had gone out for a few minutes just before three, and he was nervous about being outside. He planned to take the long way to the Pipeworks, out at the very edge of the city, to avoid any guards that might still be looking for him.

He was filled with dread about Lina. He wouldn't know what had happened to her until he got to the Pipeworks and she either showed up or didn't. All he could do now was run.

He raced down Knack Street. It was strange to be out in the city with the streets so utterly deserted. Without the people passing back and forth, the streets seemed wider and darker. Nothing moved but himself, his shadow, and his fleeting reflection in shop windows he passed. In Selverton Square, he saw a kiosk where the poster with his and Lina's names on it had been pinned up. Everyone in the city must have seen these posters by now. He was famous, he thought wryly, but not in the way he'd wanted. There would be no glorious moment on the Gathering Hall steps after all. Instead of making his father proud, he would cause him dreadful worry.

This thought made him so sad that his knees felt suddenly wobbly. How could he just vanish without a word? But it was too late now, he couldn't go back. If only there was some way to send him a message—and in a moment, he realized there was. He stopped, fished in his pack for the paper and pencil he had brought, and scribbled on it, "Father—We have found the way out—it was in the Pipeworks after all! You will know about it tomorrow. Love, Doon." He folded this in quarters, wrote "Deliver to Loris Harrow" in big letters on the outside, and pinned it to the kiosk. There! That was the best he could do. He would have to trust that someone would deliver it.

In the distance, he heard the faint sound of singing. He listened—it was "The Song of the River," just ending. *"Far below, like the blood of the earth, From the center of nowhere rushing forth,"* he sang under his breath. Like everyone in Ember, he knew the words of the three songs by heart. He sang along softly with the faraway singers:

> *"Making the light for the lamps of Ember,*
> *Older than anyone can remember,*
> *Faster than anything anyone knows,*
> *The river comes and the river goes."*

Up Rim Street now to River Road. He was halfway there. The singers were starting on "The Song of Darkness." It was his favorite, with its powerful, deep harmonies—he was a little sorry to be missing it. He went up the Pott Street side of empty Riverroad Square, where another poster hung crookedly on the kiosk, and he was headed toward North Street when suddenly the lights flickered and went out.

He jolted to a stop. Stand still and wait—that was his automatic response. In the distance he heard a dip in the sound of the singing, some startled voices breaking the flow, but then the song rose again, defying the darkness. For a moment all thoughts vanished from Doon's mind; there was nothing but the fearless words of the song:

> *"Black as sleep and deep as dreaming,*
> *Darkness like an endless night.*
> *Yet within the streets of Ember*
> *Bright and bravely shines our light."*

He sang, standing still in the blackness. When the song ended, he waited. The lights would surely come back soon. For a few minutes there was silence, and then, far away but piercingly clear, he heard a scream. More screams and shouts followed, the sounds of panic. He felt the panic himself, like a hand taking hold of him, making him want to leap up and fling himself against the dark.

But suddenly, with a flash of joy, he remembered: he didn't have to wait for the lights to come back on. He had what no citizen of Ember had ever had before—a way to see in the dark. He set his pack down, untied the knot at the top, and groped around inside until he felt the candle. Down in a corner, he found the little packet of matches. He scraped a match against the pavement, and it flared up instantly. He held the flame to the string on the candle, and the string began to burn. He had a light. He had the only light in the entire city.

The candle didn't cast its light very far, but it was enough to see at least the pavement in front of him. He went slowly along Pott Street, then turned left on North Street. At the end of the street was the wall of the Pipeworks office.

When he got to the Pipeworks entrance, no one was there. A little cloud of moths came to flutter around the flame of his candle, but otherwise nothing moved in Plummer Square. There was nothing to do but wait. Doon blew the candle out—he didn't want to use it all up in case the lights stayed off a long time— and squatted down on the pavement, setting down his bundle and leaning against one of the big trash cans. He waited, listening to the distant shouts—and at last the lights blinked, blinked again, and came on.

Lina was nowhere in sight. If the guards had found her and taken her . . . But Doon preferred not to think about that yet. He would wait for a while—she would have been delayed by the blackout if she was on her way. He couldn't see the clock tower from here, but it was probably not quite four o'clock.

What if she didn't come? The Singing was over, the people were dispersing throughout the city, and the guards, no doubt, would soon resume their search for him. Doon clasped his arms together and pressed them hard against his stomach, trying to stop the queasy fluttering.

If she didn't come, Doon had two choices: he could stay in the city and do what he could to save Lina, or he could go in the boat by himself and hope Lina could somehow free herself and tell the people of Ember about the way out. He didn't like either of these plans; he wanted to go down the river, and he wanted to go with Lina.

Doon stood up and hoisted his sack again. He was too restless to keep sitting. He walked down

to Gappery Street and looked in both directions. Not
a single person was in sight. He walked to Plummer
Street, thinking that perhaps Lina was coming by way
of the city's edge, as he had, to avoid being seen. But no
one was there; he didn't even see anyone when he went
past Subling Street to the very end of the city. He had
to decide what to do.

He went and stood in the doorway of the
Pipeworks. Think, he said to himself. Think! He was
not even sure he *could* make the river journey by himself. How would he get the boat into the water? Could
he lift it without help? On the other hand, how could
he help Lina if she was in the hands of the mayor's
guards? What could he possibly do that would not just
get himself caught, too?

He felt sick. His hands were cold. He stepped out
of the doorway and scanned the square once again.
Nothing moved but the moths around the lights.

And then down Gappery Street Lina came running. She came slantwise across the square, and he
dashed to meet her. She was hugging a bundle to her
chest.

"I've come, I'm here, I almost didn't make it," she
said, breathing so hard she could barely talk. "And
look." She folded back the blanket of her bundle. Doon
saw a curl of brown hair and two wide frightened eyes.
"I've brought Poppy."

Doon was so glad to see Lina that he didn't mind

at all that Poppy was coming with them, making a risky journey even riskier. Relief and excitement flooded through him. They were going! They were going!

"Okay," he said. "Come on!"

With his borrowed key, he opened the Pipeworks door, and they hurried past the yellow slickers on their hooks and the lines of rubber boots. Doon dashed into the Pipeworks office long enough to replace the key on its hook, and then they pulled open the stairway door and started down. Lina stepped slowly because of Poppy, and Poppy clung to her neck, unusually quiet, sensing the strangeness and importance of what was happening. At the bottom of the stairs, they came out into the main tunnel and walked down the path to the west until they came to the marked rock.

"How are we going to get Poppy down there?" Doon asked.

Lina said, "I'll fasten her to my chest." Setting Poppy down, Lina took off the coat and the sweater she was wearing. With Doon's help, she made her sweater into a sling for Poppy, tying its sleeves behind her neck. Then she put her coat back on and buttoned it up.

Doon looked doubtfully at this bulky arrangement. "Will you be able to climb down, carrying her like that? Will you be able to reach around her and hold on to the rungs?"

"Yes," said Lina. Now that she had Poppy with her, she felt brave again. She could do whatever she needed to.

Doon went down first. Lina followed. "Stay very still, Poppy," she said. "Don't squirm." Poppy did stay still, but even so it was not easy going down the ladder with her extra weight. Lina's arms were just long enough to reach past Poppy and hold on to the ladder. She descended very slowly. When she got to the ledge, she stepped sideways, gripped the hand Doon held out for her, and, with a deep breath of relief, came into the entryway.

They walked to the back of the entry hall, and Doon opened the steel panel and took out the key. He slid aside the door to the room where the single boat was, and they went in. Doon took his candle from his sack and lit it. Lina unwrapped Poppy and sat her down at the back of the room. "Don't move from there," she said. Poppy put her thumb in her mouth, and Doon and Lina set to work.

Doon's sack went in the pointed end of the boat, which they decided must be the front. They put the boxes of candles and matches into the rear of the boat. It was clear they'd been designed to go there; they fit snugly.

The poles labeled "Paddles" were a mystery. Lina thought maybe they were weapons, meant for fending off hostile creatures. Doon thought they might fit across the boat somehow to make railings to brace yourself against, but he couldn't get them to work in this way. Finally they decided just to leave the paddles in the bottom of the boat and figure out what they were for as they went along.

Doon dripped a bit of wax on the floor and stood his candle up in it, so he'd have both hands free. "Let's see if we can lift the boat," he said.

With Doon at the rear and Lina at the front, they found they could lift the boat with ease. It was amazingly light, even with the boxes and pack inside it. They set it down again. The next step was to get it in the water somehow, and then get in it themselves.

"We can't just drop it in," Lina said. "The river would grab it right away."

"That must be what the ropes are for," said Doon. "We lower it in by holding on to the ropes. And tie the ropes to something to keep it from moving."

"To what?"

"They must have put a peg or something in the wall to tie it to." Doon went back out to the edge of the river and got down on his knees. Leaning over, he felt with one hand along the bank below. At first there was only smooth, slippery rock. He moved his hand slowly back and forth, up and down. River water splashed against his fingers. At last he felt something—a metal rod attached to the river wall, like the rungs of the ladder they had climbed down. "I've found it," he called.

He got up again and went back to the boat room. "Let's carry the boat out," he said. He and Lina lifted it and, taking small steps, moved it forward. As they went out the door, Poppy began to wail.

"Don't cry!" Lina called to her. "Stay right there! We'll be back in a second."

They carried the boat right to the edge of the water and set it down carefully, its front end pointing downstream. Doon knelt again, feeling for the metal rod. "Hand me the end of the rope," he said.

Which rope? Lina thought for a second. She realized it had to be the one attached to the side of the boat nearest her—that would be the side closest to the riverbank when they put the boat in. She uncoiled the rope, ran it around the boat, and handed its end down to Doon, who lay on his stomach with his head hanging over the edge and knotted the rope to the metal rung in the wall. He got to his feet again, wiping water from his face.

"Now," Doon said, "we can put the boat in the water."

Another wail came from the boat room. "I'm coming," Lina called, and dashed back for Poppy. She hoisted her up and spoke into her ear, in the voice she used for announcing an exciting game: "We're going on an *adventure*, Poppy. We're going for a *ride,* a ride in the water! It will be fun, sweetie, you'll see." She blew out the candle Doon had left and carried Poppy to the river's edge.

"Are we ready?" said Doon.

"I guess we are." Goodbye to Ember, Lina thought. Goodbye to everyone, goodbye to everything. For a second, a picture of herself arriving in the bright city of her dreams flashed into her mind, and then it faded and was gone. She had no idea what lay ahead.

She set Poppy down against the wall of the entry passage. "Sit here," she told her. "Don't move until I tell you to." Poppy sat, her eyes wide, her plump legs sticking out in front of her.

Lina took hold of the rope at the rear of the boat. Doon took hold of the rope at the front. They heaved the boat up and stretched sideways to swing it out over the water. It tipped alarmingly from side to side. "Let it down!" yelled Lina. They both let the ropes slide through their hands, and the boat fell and hit the water with a slap. It bounced and rocked and pulled against its tether, but Doon's knot held. The boat stayed in place, waiting for them.

"Here I go!" Doon cried. He bent over, gripped the rim of the boat with one hand, turned backward, and stepped in. The boat tipped sideways under his weight. Doon staggered a step, and then found his balance. "All right!" he yelled. "Hand me Poppy!"

Lina lifted Poppy, who began to howl and kick at

the sight of the bucking boat and the churning water. But Doon's arms were right there, and Lina thrust her into them. A second later, she jumped in herself, and then all three of them were tossed to the floor of the boat by its violent rocking.

Doon managed to get to his feet. He hauled on the rope that held the boat to the bank until he was close enough to reach the knot. He struggled with it. Water splashed into his face. He yanked at the knot, loosened it, pulled the rope free—and the boat shot forward.

CHAPTER 18

Where the River Goes

For a second, Lina saw the banks of the river streak by. Ahead was the opening of the tunnel, like an enormous mouth. They plunged into it and left the light of the Pipeworks behind. In complete darkness, the boat pitched and rolled, and Lina, in the bottom of it, banged from side to side, gripping Poppy with one arm and grabbing with the other hand for anything to hold on to. Doon slid into her, and she slid into the boxes. Poppy was shrieking wildly.

"Doon!" Lina shouted, and he shouted back, "Hold on! Hold on!" But she kept losing her grip on the edge of the boat and being flung sideways. She was terrified that Poppy would slam into the metal bench, or be torn from her arms and tossed into the river.

The boat hit something and shuddered, then raced on. It felt like being swallowed, this rushing through the dark, with the river roaring like a thousand voices.

Lina's legs were tangled with Doon's, and Poppy's arms were so tight around her neck that she could hardly breathe. But it was the dark that was most terrible—going so fast into the dark.

She closed her eyes. If they were going to smash into a wall or plunge into a bottomless hole, there was nothing she could do about it. All she could do was hold tight to Poppy. She did that, for what seemed a long time.

And then at last the current slowed, and the boat stopped thrashing about so wildly. Lina managed to sit up, and she felt Doon moving, too. Poppy's shrieks turned to whimpers. The darkness was still complete, but Lina sensed space above and around her. Where were they? She had to *see*.

"Doon!" she said. "Are you all right? Can you find us a candle?"

"I'll try," Doon said. She felt him scramble past her to the back of the boat, and she heard a scrape as he pulled a box out from its place under the bench. "Can't find the latch!" Doon said. Then a second later, "There, I've got it. This is the matches, so this one must be candles." More scraping and banging. The boat lurched, Lina slid forward. Doon slid, too, and slammed into her back. He gave a yell of rage.

"Dropped the match! Hold on, I almost had it." Long seconds of scrambling and clattering. Then a light flared up, and Doon's shadowed face appeared above it. He touched the match to a candle, and the light grew steadier.

It was only a small flame, but it cast glints of light on the tunnel walls and the silky surface of the water. The tunnel had an arched ceiling, Lina saw, like the tunnels of the Pipeworks, but it was much wider than those tunnels. The river ran through it like a moving road.

"Can you light another?" Lina asked. Doon nodded and turned back to the boxes, but once again the boat struck something, causing a spray of water to slap into them and put the candle out.

It was several minutes before Doon managed to light it again, and more before he finally had two burning at once. He jammed one of them into a space between the bench and the side of the boat, and he held the other in his hand. His hair was flattened against his forehead, and dripping. His brown jacket was torn at the shoulder. "That's better," he said.

It was better—not only did they have light to see by, but the current was slower, and the boat sailed more smoothly. Lina was able to unwrap Poppy from her neck and look around. Ahead she could see that the tunnel curved. The boat swung into the curve, banged against the wall, straightened itself, and sped on. "Hand me a candle, too," she said.

Doon gave Lina the candle he was holding and lit another. They found places to wedge all three candles into the frame of the boat, so they could keep their hands free. For a while they rushed along almost silently, the river having become nearly as smooth as a sheet of glass.

Then suddenly the current slowed even more, and the tunnel opened out. "We've come into a room," said Lina. Far overhead arched a vaulted ceiling. Columns of rock hung down from it, and columns of rock rose from the water, too, making long shadows that turned and mingled as the boat floated among them. They glimmered in the candlelight, pink and pale green and silver. Their strange lumpy shapes looked like something soft that had frozen—like towers of mashed potatoes, Lina thought, that had hardened to stone.

Now and then the boat bumped into one of these columns, and they found that they could use a paddle to knock themselves free again. In this way they crossed the room to the other side, where again the passage narrowed and the current ran faster.

Much faster. It was as if the boat were being pulled forward by a powerful hand. The water grew rough again, and splashes of spray put out their candles. Lina and Doon huddled in the bottom of the boat with Poppy between them, their arms clasped around her.

They clenched their teeth and squeezed their eyes shut, and soon there was nothing in their minds but the roll and plunge of the boat and nothing in their bodies but the effort not to be thrown out. Once, the sound of the river rose to a crashing, and the front of the boat tipped downward, and they were pitched about so violently that it seemed they were tumbling down stairs—but that lasted only a few seconds, and then they were streaming onward as before.

Lina lost track of time. But a while later, maybe a few minutes, maybe an hour, the current slowed. The candles they'd stuck in the boat had been knocked overboard, so Doon lit new ones. They saw that they had come to another pool. There were no lumpy columns of rock here; nothing interrupted the wide flat surface of the water, which stretched out before them in the flickering light from their candles. The ceiling was smooth and only about ten feet above their heads. The boat drifted, as if it had lost its sense of direction. Using a paddle to poke against the walls, Doon guided the boat around the edge of the pool.

"I don't see where the river goes on," said Doon. "Do you?"

"No," said Lina. "Unless it's there, where it flows into that little gap." She pointed to a crack in the wall only a few inches wide.

"But the boat can't go there."

"No, it's much too small."

He poled the boat forward. Their shadows moved with them along the wall.

"Wanna go home," said Poppy.

"We're almost there," Lina told her.

"We certainly can't go back the way we came," said Doon.

"No." Lina dipped a hand in the water. It was so cold it sent an ache up her arm.

"Could this be the end?" said Doon. His voice sounded flat in this closed-in place.

"The end?" Lina felt a shiver of fear.

"I mean the end of the trip," Doon said. "Maybe we're supposed to get out over there." He pointed to a wide expanse of rock that sloped back into the darkness on one side of the pool. Everywhere else, the walls rose straight out of the water.

He poled the boat over to the rock slope. The boat scraped bottom here—the water was shallow. "I'll get out and see if this goes anywhere," said Lina. "I want to be on solid ground again, anyway." She handed Poppy to Doon and stood up. Holding a candle, she put one foot over the edge of the boat and into the cold water, and she waded ashore.

The way did not look promising. The ground sloped upward, and the ceiling sloped downward. As she went farther back she had to stoop. A few yards in, a tumbled heap of rocks blocked the way. She inched around them, turning sideways to squeeze through the narrow space, and crept forward, holding the candle out in front of her. This goes nowhere, she thought. We're trapped.

But a few steps farther along, she found she could stand up straight again, and a few steps beyond that she turned a corner, and suddenly the candlelight shone on a wide path, with a high ceiling and a smooth floor. Lina gave a wild shout. "Here it is!" she cried. "It's here! There's a path!"

Doon's voice came from far away. She couldn't tell what he was saying. She made her way back toward the boat, and when it came in sight she yelled again, "I found a path! A path!"

Doon scrambled out and waded ashore, carrying Poppy. He set her down, and then he and Lina took hold of the boat and hauled it as far as they could up the slope of rock. Poppy caught the excitement. She shouted gleefully, waving her fists like little clubs, and stomped around, glad to be on her feet again. She found a pebble and plunked it into the water, crowing happily at the splash it made.

"I want to see the path," said Doon.

"Go up that way," Lina told him, "and around the pile of rocks. I'll stay here and take things out of the boat."

Doon went, taking another candle from the box in the boat. Lina sat Poppy down in a kind of nook formed by a roundish boulder and a hollow in the wall. "Don't move from here," she said. Then she pulled Doon's bundle from under the seat of the boat. It was damp, but not soaked. Maybe the food inside would still be all right. She was hungry all of a sudden. She'd had no dinner, she remembered. It must be the middle of the night by now, or maybe even morning again.

She carried Doon's bundle ashore, along with the boxes of candles and matches, and as she set them down, Doon came back. His eyes were glowing, the reflection of a tiny flame dancing in each one. "That's it for sure," he said. "We've made it." Then his eyes shifted. "What's Poppy got?" he asked.

Lina whipped around. In Poppy's hands was something dark and rectangular. It wasn't a stone. It was more like a packet of some kind. She was plucking and pulling at it. She lifted it to her mouth as if to tear it with her teeth—and Lina jumped to her feet. "Stop!" she shouted. Poppy, startled, dropped the packet and began to cry.

"It's all right, never mind," Lina said, retrieving what Poppy had been about to chew on. "Come and have some dinner now. Hush, we're going to have dinner. I'm sure you're hungry."

In the light of Doon's candle, with Poppy squirming on Lina's lap, they examined Poppy's find. The packet was wrapped in slippery, greenish material and bound up with a strap. It wasn't wrapped very well; it looked as if someone had bundled it up quickly. The material was loose, and blotched with whitish mold.

Lina edged the strap off carefully. It was partly rotten; on the end of it was a small square buckle, covered with rust. She folded back the wrapping.

Doon took a sharp breath. "It's a book," he said. He moved his candle closer, and Lina opened the brown cover. The pages inside had faint blue lines across them, and someone had written along these lines in slanted black letters, which were not neat like the writing in the library books, but sprawling, as if the writer had been in a hurry.

Doon ran his finger under the first line. "It says, *They tell us we* . . . learn? . . . No, leave. *They tell us we leave tonight.*"

He looked up and met Lina's eyes.

"Leave?" said Lina. "From where?"

"From Ember?" Doon asked. "Could someone have come this way before us?"

"Or was it someone leaving the other city?"

Doon looked down at the book again. He riffled through the pages—there were many of them.

"Let's save it," said Lina. "We'll read it when we get to the new city."

Doon nodded. "It'll be easier to see there."

So Lina wrapped up the book again and tied it securely into Doon's bundle. They sat on the rock shelf for a while, eating the food Doon had brought. The candles wedged in the boat still shone steadily, and their light was cozy, like lamplight. It made golden shapes on the still surface of the pond.

Doon said, "I saw the guards run after you. Tell me what happened."

Lina told him.

"And what about Poppy? What did you tell Mrs. Murdo?"

"I told her the truth—at least I hope it's the truth. I caught up with her on her way home after the Singing. She'd seen the posters—she was terrified—but before she could ask questions, I just said she must give Poppy to me. I said I was taking her to safety. Because that's what I suddenly realized on the roof of the Gathering Hall, Doon. I'd been thinking before that I *had* to leave Poppy because she'd be safe with Mrs. Murdo. But when the lights went out, I suddenly knew: There *is* no safety in Ember. Not for long. Not for anyone. I couldn't leave her behind. Whatever happens to us now, it's better than what's going to happen there."

"And did you explain all that to Mrs. Murdo?"

"No. I was in a terrible hurry to get to the Pipeworks and meet you, and I knew I had to go while there were still crowds in the street, so it would be harder for the guards to see me. I just said I was taking Poppy to safety. Mrs. Murdo handed her over, but she sort of sputtered, 'Where?' and 'Why?' And I said, 'You'll know in a few days—it's all right.' And then I ran."

"So you gave her the note, then?" said Doon. "The one meant for Clary?"

"Oh!" Lina stared at him, stricken. "The message to Clary!" She put her hand in her pocket and pulled out the crumpled piece of paper. "I forgot all about it! All I was thinking of was getting Poppy and getting to you."

"So no one knows about the room full of boats."

Lina just shook her head, her eyes wide. "How will we get back to tell them?"

"We can't."

"Doon," said Lina, "if we'd told people right away, even just a few people . . . if we hadn't decided to be grand and announce it at the Singing . . ."

"I know," said Doon. "But we didn't, that's all. We didn't tell, and now no one knows. I did leave a message for my father, though." He told Lina about pinning his last-minute message to the kiosk in Selverton Square. "I said we'd found the way out, and that it was in the Pipeworks. But that's not much help."

"Clary has seen the Instructions," Lina said. "She knows there's an egress. She might find it."

"Or she might not."

There was nothing to be done about it, and so they

put the supplies back into Doon's pillowcase and got ready to go. Lina used Doon's rope to make a leash for Poppy. She tied one end around Poppy's waist and the other around her own. She filled her pockets with packs of matches, and Doon put all the remaining candles in his sack—in case they arrived in the new city at night. He filled his bottle with river water, lit a candle for himself and one for Lina, and thus equipped, they left the boat behind and crept up the rocky shelf to the path.

CHAPTER 19

A World of Light

As they squeezed past the rocks at the entrance to the path, Doon thought he saw the candlelight glance off a shiny place on the wall. He stopped to look, and when he saw what it was, he called out to Lina, who was a few steps ahead of him. "There's a notice!"

It was a framed sign, bolted to the stone, a printed sheet behind a piece of glass. Dampness had seeped under the glass and made splotches on the paper, but by holding their candles up close, they could read it.

Welcome, Refugees from Ember!
This is the final stage of your journey.
Be prepared for a climb
that will take several hours.
Fill your bottles with water from the river.
We wish you good fortune,
The Builders

"They're expecting us!" said Lina.

"Well, they wrote this a long time ago," Doon said. "The people who put it here must all be dead by now."

"That's true. But they wished us good fortune. It makes me feel as if they're watching over us."

"Yes. And maybe their great-great-great-grand-children will be there to welcome us."

Encouraged, they started up the path. Their candles made only a feeble glow, but they could tell that the path was quite wide. The ceiling was high over their heads. The path seemed to have been made for a great company of people. In some places, the ground beneath their feet was rutted in parallel grooves, as if a wheeled cart of some kind had been driven over it. After they had walked awhile, they realized that they were moving in long zigzags. The path would go in one direction for some time and then turn sharply and go the opposite way.

As they went along, they talked less and less; the path sloped relentlessly upward, and they needed their breath just for breathing. The only sound was the light *pat-pat* of their footsteps. Lina and Doon took turns carrying Poppy on their backs—she had gotten tired of walking very soon and cried to be picked up. Twice, they stopped and sat down to rest, leaning against the walls of the passage and taking drinks from Doon's bottle of water.

"How many hours do you think we've been walking?" Lina asked.

"I don't know," Doon said. "Maybe two. Maybe three. We must be nearly there."

They climbed on and on. Their first candles had long ago burned down to the last inch, as had their second candles. Finally, when their third ones were about halfway gone, Lina began to notice that the air smelled different. The cold, sharp-edged rock smell of the tunnel was changing to something softer, a strange, lovely smell. As they rounded a corner, a gust of this soft air swept past them, and their candles went out.

Doon said, "I'll find a match," but Lina said, "No, wait. Look."

They were not in complete darkness. A faint haze of light shone in the passage ahead of them. "It's the lights of the city," breathed Lina.

Lina set Poppy down. "Quick, Poppy," she said, and Poppy began to trot, keeping close at Lina's heels. The strange, lovely smell in the air grew stronger. The passage came to an end a few yards farther along, and before them was an opening like a great empty doorway. Without a word, Lina and Doon took hold of each other's hands, and Lina took hold of Poppy's. When they stood in the doorway and looked out, they saw no new city at all, but something infinitely stranger: a land vast and spacious beyond any of their dreams, filled with air that seemed to move, and lit by a shining silver circle hanging in an immense black sky.

In front of their feet, the ground swept away in a long, gentle slope. It was not bare stone, as in Ember; something soft covered it, like silvery hair, as high as their knees. Down the slope was a tumble of dark, rounded shapes, and then another slope rose beyond that. Way off into the distance, as far as they could see, the land lay in rolling swells, with clumps of shadow in the low places between them.

"Doon!" cried Lina. "More lights!" She pointed at the sky.

He looked up and saw them—hundreds and hundreds of tiny flecks of light, strewn like spilled salt across the blackness. "Oh!" he whispered. There was nothing else to say. The beauty of these lights made his breath stop in his throat.

They took a few steps forward. Doon bent to feel the strands that grew out of the ground, almost higher than Poppy's head; they were cool and smooth and soft, and there was dampness on them.

"Breathe," said Lina. She opened her mouth and took in a long breath of air. Doon did the same.

"It's sweet," he said. "So full of smells."

They held their hands out to feel the long stems as they waded slowly through them. The air moved against their faces and in their hair.

"Hear those sounds?" said Doon. A high, thin chirruping sound came from somewhere nearby. It was repeated over and over, like a question.

"Yes," said Lina. "What could it be?"

"Something alive, I think. Maybe some kind of bug."

"A bug that sings." Lina turned to Doon. Her face was shadowy in the silver light. "It's so strange here, Doon, and so huge. But I'm not afraid."

"No. I'm not either. It feels like a dream."

"A dream, yes. Maybe that's why it feels familiar. I might have dreamed about this place."

They walked until they came to where the dark shapes billowed up from the ground. These were plants, they discovered, taller than they were, with stems as hard and thick as the walls of houses, and leaves that spread out over their heads. On the slope beside these plants, they sat down.

"Do you think there is a city here somewhere?" Lina asked. "Or any people at all?"

"I don't see any lights," Doon said, "even far off."

"But with this silver lamp in the sky, maybe they don't need lights."

Doon shook his head doubtfully. "People would need more light than this," he said. "How could you see well enough to work? How could you grow your food? It's a beautiful light, but not bright enough to live by."

"Then what shall we do, if there's no city, and no people?"

"I don't know. I don't know." Doon didn't feel like

thinking. He was tired of figuring things out. He wanted to look at this new world, and take in the scent of it and the feel of it, and figure things out later.

Lina felt the same way. She stopped asking questions, drew Poppy onto her lap, and gazed in silence at the glimmering landscape. After a while, she became aware that something strange was happening. Surely, when she had first sat down, the silver circle was just above the highest branch of the tall plant. Now the branch cut across it. As she watched, the circle sank very slowly down, until it was hidden, except for a gleam of brightness, behind the leaves.

"It's moving," she said to Doon.

"Yes."

A little later, it seemed to her that her eyes were blurring. There was a fuzziness in the sky, especially around the edges. It took a while for her to realize what was making the fuzziness.

"Light," she said.

"I see it," said Doon. "It's getting brighter."

The edge of the sky turned gray, and then pale orange, and then deep fiery crimson. The land stood out against it, a long black rolling line. One spot along this line grew so bright they could hardly look at it, so bright it seemed to take a bite out of the land. It rose higher and higher until they could see that it was a fiery circle, first deep orange and then yellow, and too bright to look at any longer. The color seeped out of the sky and washed over the land. Light sparkled on the soft hair of the hills and shone through the lacy leaves as every shade of green sprang to life around them.

They lifted their faces to the astonishing warmth. The sky arched over them, higher than they could have imagined, a pale, clear blue. Lina felt as though a lid that had been on her all her life had been lifted off. Light and air rushed through her, making a song, like the songs of Ember, only it was a song of joy. She looked at Doon and saw that he was smiling and crying at the same time, and she realized that she was, too.

Everything around them was springing to life. A glorious racket came from the branches—tweedling notes, peeps, burbles, high sharp calls. Bugs? wondered Doon, imagining with awe the bugs that could make such sounds. But then he saw something fly from a cluster of leaves and swoop down low across the ground, making a clear, sweet call as it flew. "Did you see that?" he said to Lina, pointing. "And there's another one! And there!"

"There there there there!" repeated Poppy, leaping from Lina's lap and whirling around, pointing in every direction.

The air was full of them now. They were much too large to be insects. One of them lit nearby on a stem. It looked at them with two bright black eyes and, opening its mouth, which was pointed like a thorn, sent forth a little trill.

"It's speaking to us," said Doon. "What could it be?"

Lina just shook her head. The little creature shifted its clawlike feet on the stem, flapped its brown wings, and trilled again. Then it leapt into the air and was gone.

They leapt up, too, and threw themselves into exploration. The ground was alive with insects—so many that Doon just laughed in helpless wonder. Flowers bloomed among the green blades, and a stream ran at the foot of the hill. They roamed over the green-coated slopes, running, sliding, calling out to each other with each new discovery, until they were exhausted. Then they sat down by the entrance to the path to eat what was left of their food. They untied Doon's bundle, and Lina suddenly cried out. "The book! We forgot about the book!"

There it was, wrapped in its blotched green cloth.

"Let's read it out loud while we eat," said Doon.

Lina opened the fragile notebook and laid it on the ground in front of her. She picked up a carrot with one hand, and with the other she kept her place on the scribbled page. This is what she read.

CHAPTER 20

The Last Message

Friday

They tell us we leave tonight. I knew it would be soon—the training has been over for nearly a month now—but still it feels sudden, it feels like a shock. Why did I agree to do this? I am an old woman, too tired to take up a new life. I wish now that I'd said no when they asked me.

I have put everything I can into my one suitcase—clothes, shoes, a good wind-up clock, some soap, an extra pair of glasses. Bring no books, they said, and no photographs. We have been told to say nothing, ever again, about the world we come from. But I am going to take this notebook anyhow. I am determined to write down what happens. Someday, someone may need to know.

The Last Message

Saturday

I went to the train station yesterday evening, as they told me to, and got on the train they told me to take. It took us through Spring Valley, and I gazed out the window at the fields and houses of the place I was saying goodbye to—my home, and my family's home for generations. I rode for two hours, until the train reached a station in the hills. When I arrived, they met me—three men in suits—and drove me to a large building, where they led me down a corridor and into a big room full of other people—all with suitcases, most with gray or white hair. Here we have been waiting now for more than an hour.

They have spent years and years making this plan. It's supposed to ensure that, no matter what happens, people won't disappear from the earth. Some say that will never happen anyhow. I'm not so sure. Disaster seems very close. Everything will be all right, they tell us, but only a few people believe them. Why, if it's going to be all right, do we see it getting worse every day?

And of course this plan is proof that they think the world is doomed. All the best scientists and engineers have been pulled in to work on it. Extraordinary efforts have been made—efforts *that would have done more good elsewhere. I think it's the wrong answer. But they asked me if I would go—I suppose because I've spent my life on a farm and I know about growing food. In spite of my doubts, I said yes. I'm not sure why.*

There are a hundred of us, fifty men and fifty women. We are all at least sixty years old. There will be a hundred babies, too—two babies for each pair of "parents." I don't know yet which one of these gentlemen I'll be matched with. We are all strangers to one another. They planned it that way; they said there would be fewer memories between us. They want us to forget everything about the lives we've led and the places we've lived. The babies must grow up with no knowledge of a world outside, so that they feel no sorrow for what they have lost.

I hear some noises across the room. I think it's the babies arriving. . . . Yes, here they come, each being carried by one of those gray-suited men. So many of them! So small! Little scrunched-up faces, tiny fists waving. I must stop for now. They're going to pass them out.

Later
We're traveling again, on a bus this time. It is night, I think, though it's hard to be sure

because they have boarded up the windows of the bus from the outside. They don't want us to know where we're going.

I have a baby on my lap—a girl. She has a bright pink face and no hair at all. Stanley, who sits next to me, holds a boy baby, with brown skin and a few tufts of black hair. Stanley and I are the keepers of these children. Our task is to raise them in this new place we're going to. By the time they are twenty or so, we'll be gone. They'll be on their own, making a new world.

Stanley and I have named these children Star and Forest.

Sunday

The buses have stopped, but they have not allowed us to get out yet. I can hear crickets singing, and smell the grass, so we must be in the country, and it must be night. I am very tired.

What kind of place can this be, safe from earthly catastrophes? All I can guess is that it must be underground. The thought fills me with dread. I'll try to sleep a little now.

Later

There was no chance to sleep. They called us off the buses, and we stepped out into a *landscape of rolling hills, in full moonlight. "That's the way we'll be going in," they told us, pointing to a dark opening in the hill we stood on. "Form a line there, please." We did so. It was very quiet, except for the squalling of a few of the babies. If the others were like me, they were saying goodbye to the world. I reached down to touch the grass and breathed deeply to smell the earth. My eyes swept over the silver hills, and I thought of the animals prowling softly in the shadows or sleeping in their burrows, and the birds standing beneath the leaves of the trees, with their heads tucked under their wings. Last, I raised my eyes to the moon, which smiled down on us from a long, cold distance away. The moon will still be here when they come out, I thought. The moon and the hills, at least.*

The opening led us into a winding passage that ran steeply downhill for perhaps a mile. It was hard going for me; my legs are not strong anymore. We moved very slowly. The last part was the worst: a rocky slope where it was easy to miss your footing and slip. This led down to a pool. By the shore of the pool our group of aged pioneers gathered. Motorboats were waiting here for us, equipped with lanterns.

"When it's time for people to leave this

place, is this the way they will come?" I asked our pilot, who has a kind face. He said yes.

"But how will they know there's a way out, if no one tells them?" I said. "How will they know what to do?"

"They're going to have instructions," said the pilot. "They won't be able to get at the instructions until the time is right. But when they need them, the instructions will be there."

"But what if they don't find them? What if they never come out again?"

"I think they will. People find a way through just about anything."

That was all he would say. I am writing these notes while our pilot loads the boat. I hope he doesn't notice.

"It ends there," said Lina, looking up.

"He must have noticed," said Doon. "Or she was afraid he would, so she decided to hide it instead of taking it with her."

"She must have hoped someone would find it."

"Just as we did." He pondered. "But we might not have, if it hadn't been for Poppy."

"No. And we wouldn't have known that we came from here."

The fiery circle had moved up in the sky now, and

the air was so warm that they took off their coats. Absently, Doon dug his finger into the ground, which was soft and crumbly. "But what was the disaster that happened in this place?" he said. "It doesn't look ruined to me."

"It must have happened a long, long time ago," said Lina. "I wonder if people still live here."

They sat looking out over the hills, thinking of the woman who had written in the notebook. What had her city been like? Lina wondered. Like Ember in some way, she imagined. A city with trouble, where people argued over solutions. A dying city. But it was hard to picture a city like Ember here in this bright, beautiful place. How could anyone have allowed such a place to be harmed?

"What do we do now?" asked Lina. She wrapped the notebook in its covering again and set it aside. "We can't go back up the river and tell them all to come here."

"No. We could never make the boat go against that current."

"Are we here alone, then, forever?"

"Maybe there's another way in, some way that lets you walk down to Ember. Or maybe there's another river that runs the other way. We have candles now, we could cross the Unknown Regions if we found a way to get there."

This was the only plan they could come up with.

So, all day long, they searched for another way in. Under the brow of the hill, they found a hole where a stream wandered into the dark. The water was good to drink, but the hole was far too small for them to fit through. There were gullies full of shrubs, and Lina and Doon crawled among the leaves and prickly branches, but found no openings. Bugs buzzed around their ankles and past their eyes; brown earth stained their hands, and pebbles got into their shoes. Their thick, dark, shabby clothes got all full of prickly things, and since they were much too hot anyhow, they took most of them off. They had never felt such warmth against their skin and such soft air.

When the bright circle was at the top of the sky, they sat for a while in the shade of one of the tall plants on the side of the hill, in a place where the thick brush gave way to a clearing. Poppy went to sleep, but Lina and Doon sat looking out over the land. Green was everywhere, in different shades, like a huge, brilliant, gorgeous version of the overlapping carpets back in the rooms of Ember. Far away, Lina saw a narrow gray line curving like a pencil stroke across a sweep of green. She pointed this out to Doon, and both of them squinted hard at it, but it was too far away to see clearly.

"Could it be a road?" said Lina.

"It could," said Doon.

"Maybe there are people here after all."

"I hope so," said Doon. "There's so much I want to know."

They were still gazing at the far-off bit of gray when they heard something moving in the brush nearby. Leaves rustled. There was a scraping, shuffling sound. They stiffened and held their breath. The shuffling paused, then started up again. Was it a person? Should they call out? But before they could decide what to do, a creature stepped into the clearing.

It was about the same size as Poppy, only lower to the ground, because it walked on four legs instead of two. Its fur was a deep rust-red. Its face was a long triangle, its ears stood up in points, and its black eyes shone. It trotted forward a few steps, absorbed in its own business. Behind it floated a thick, soft-looking tail.

All at once it saw them and stopped.

Lina and Doon stayed absolutely still. So did the creature. Then it took a step toward them, paused, tilted its head a little as if to get a better look, and took another step. They could see the sheen of its fur and the glint of light in its eyes.

For a long moment, they stayed like this, frozen, staring at one another. Then, unhurriedly, the creature moved away. It pushed its nose among the leaves on the ground, wandering back toward the bushes, and when it raised its head again, they saw that it was holding something in its white teeth, something round and purplish. With a last glance at them, it leapt toward the bushes, its tail sailing, and disappeared.

Lina let out her breath and turned to look at Doon, whose mouth was open in astonishment. His voice shaky, he said, "That was the most wonderful thing I have ever seen, ever in my whole life."

"Yes."

"And it saw us," Doon said, and Lina nodded. They both felt it—they had been seen. The creature was utterly strange, not like anything they had ever known, and yet when it looked at them, some kind of recognition passed between them. "I know now," said Doon. "This is the world we belong in."

A few minutes later, Poppy woke up and made fretful noises, and Lina gave her the last of the peas in Doon's pack. "What was that, do you think, in the creature's mouth?" she asked. "Would it be something we could eat, a fruit of some kind? It looked like the pictures of peaches on cans, except for the color."

They got up and poked around, and soon they came across a plant whose branches were laden with the purple fruits, about the size of small beets, only softer. Doon picked one and cut it open with his knife. There was a stone inside. Red juice ran out over his hands. Cautiously, he touched his tongue to it. "Sweet," he said.

"If the creature can eat it, maybe we can, too," said Lina. "Shall we?"

They did. Nothing had ever tasted better. Lina cut the stones out and gave chunks of the fruit to Poppy. Juice ran down their chins. When they had eaten five or six apiece, they licked their sticky fingers clean and started to explore again.

They went higher up the slope they were on, wading through flowers as high as their waists, and near the top they came upon a kind of dent in the ground, as if a bit of the earth had caved in. They walked down into it, and at the end of the dent they found a crack about as tall as a person but not nearly as wide as a door. Lina edged through it sideways and discovered a narrow tunnel. "Send Poppy through," she called back to Doon, "and come yourself." But it was dark inside, and Doon had to go back to where he'd left his pack to get a candle. By candlelight, they crept along until they came to a place where the tunnel ended abruptly. But it ended not with a wall but with a sudden huge nothingness that made them gasp and step back. A few feet beyond their shoes was a sheer, dizzying drop. They looked out into a cave so enormous that it seemed almost as big as the world outside. Far down at the bottom shone a cluster of lights.

"It's Ember," Lina whispered.

They could see the tiny bright streets crossing each other, and the squares, little chips of light, and the dark tops of buildings. Just beyond the edges was the immense darkness.

"Oh, our city, Doon. Our city is at the bottom of a hole!" She gazed down through the gulf, and all of what she had believed about the world began to slowly break apart. "*We* were underground," she said. "Not just the Pipeworks. Everything!" She could hardly make sense of what she was saying.

Doon crouched on his hands and knees, looking over the edge. He squinted, trying to see minute specks that might be people. "What's happening there, I wonder?"

"Could they hear us if we shouted?"

"I don't think so. We're much too far up."

"Maybe if they looked into the sky they'd see our candle," said Lina. "But no, I guess they wouldn't. The streetlamps would be too bright."

"Somehow, we have to get word to them," said Doon, and that was when the idea came to Lina.

"Our message!" she cried. "We could send our message!"

And they did. From her pocket, Lina took the message that Doon had written, the one that was supposed to have gone to Clary, explaining everything. In small writing, they squeezed in this note at the top:

Dear People of Ember,
    We came down the river from the Pipeworks
and found the way to another place. It is green
here and very big. Light comes from the sky. You
must follow the instructions in this message and
come on the river. Bring food with you. Come as
quickly as you can.
                    Lina Mayfleet and Doon Harrow

They wrapped the message in Doon's shirt and put a rock inside it. Then they stood in a row at the edge of the chasm, Doon in the middle holding Poppy's hand and Lina's. Lina took aim at the *heart* of the city, far beneath her feet. With all her strength, she cast the message into the darkness, and they watched as it plunged down and down.

Mrs. Murdo, walking even more briskly than usual to keep her spirits up, was crossing Harken Square when something fell to the pavement just in front of her with a terrific thump. How extraordinary, she thought, bending to pick it up. It was a sort of bundle. She began to untie it.

ACKNOWLEDGMENTS

My thanks to the friends who read and commented helpfully on my manuscript: Susie Mader, Patrick Daly, Andrew Ramer, Charlotte Muse, Sara Jenkins, Mary Dederer, and Pat Carr. My gratitude to my agent, Nancy Gallt, who brought *The City of Ember* into the light, and my editor, Jim Thomas, who made it the best book it could be. And my love and thanks to my mother, my first and best writing teacher.

Turn the page
for a brand-new story
from Jeanne DuPrau
about the day
the Disaster began. . . .

On the Day of the Bombs

Eva Neale was not worried about war. She *had* been worried, earlier in the summer, when war was the only thing people talked about. But it was August now, and nothing had happened. Everyone still kept their TVs and radios tuned to the news, and the talk of high-level negotiations and red alerts and missile readiness went on in the background like a dull headache, but most people turned their attention elsewhere.

They'd done what they could: in the event of an attack, the plan was for the citizens of Arbor Valley to take shelter in the school gym. Eva imagined this might be rather fun. People would crowd in as they did for a basketball game, and maybe they *would* shoot some baskets, or maybe sing, and have a sort of picnic for a few days until the worst of the war was over. Because surely the war wouldn't come all the way to

Arbor Valley, which was a small and unimportant place.

On the last Saturday in August, Eva told her mother she was going to see her friend Kim, who lived in a town called Fallgrove several miles up the road. Fallgrove was a town like Arbor Valley, with houses scattered over many acres, and it happened that Kim's house was just over a ridge of hills that separated Fallgrove from Arbor Valley. If she didn't take the road but went up and over the hill instead, Eva could get to Kim's in only fifteen minutes or so.

This was what she set out to do. She and Kim were going to paint each other's fingernails for the first day of school. Eva's would be Sky Blue and Kim's would be Hawaiian Sunrise. Eva didn't dread the start of school as some kids did, even though it was said that eighth grade was much harder than seventh. School wasn't a contest to Eva—she didn't have to come out on top either in the learning part or the friends part. She did well when she could, and laughed easily when she couldn't.

"You're such a sunshine girl," her mother often said to her. "I'm a bundle of anxieties, and your father works so hard he's forgotten how to play. Where did *you* come from?"

"I don't know," Eva would say at these times, shrugging and smiling. "Heaven? Carol's Bargain Shop?"

Not that she was happy every moment. People being horrible to each other and to animals made her unhappy, which was why she turned off the war news when she could and never wanted to read the kind of book where a dog dies. She couldn't stand cauliflower; she loathed field hockey. But mostly it was easy for Eva to like things, faults and all.

She walked through the old part of her father's apple orchard, then along the irrigation ditch, over the three-strand barbed-wire fence, up the weedy hill, and on up toward the ridge. It was a hot day; the air was full of the scent of dry grass and of apples ready to be picked. Eva stopped for a moment and breathed it in. She looked out over the rows of trees with their red fruit, and beyond them to the square of lawn in the backyard of her house, and farther on to the school and the green football field, and she had one of those moments of love that came over her sometimes, especially in the late summer, when so much was ending and so much was ready to begin.

She took the path up a steep-sided gully, where in the winter a stream gushed down. Now the streambed was dry, just a tumble of rocks. She climbed, holding her hair back from her face so she wouldn't miss her footing. But in spite of that, a rock rolled when she stepped on it, and though she flung her arms out and bent sideways to keep her balance, her foot slipped and wedged itself between two stones. She fell, and she heard a crack as she went down. A pain shot through her ankle like an arrow, and then grew steady and fierce.

She sat up, braced her hands behind her on the prickly ground, and pulled herself an inch or so up the side of the gully. Moving even that much made the pain so bad she felt sick.

I have to move slow, she thought. Which is closer, home or Kim's?

Her heart was pounding, and her breath came in short gasps. Though the sun glared down on her, she felt cold.

She managed to haul herself up to the rim of the gully, but when she tried to stand, she collapsed again. She couldn't walk. She was afraid she'd faint if she tried. She'd have to slide or crawl if she was to get anywhere.

I can do it, she thought. I'll just rest a minute first.

She was facing west, looking out over the valley. Behind the distant hills she saw a flash of light in the sky—brilliant, blinding, like sun on metal. Then the edge of the sky darkened, and the darkness rose, a black fog. Another flash came, off to the north, and seconds later a long, deep thundering.

Then came the planes. They sped toward her in a fleet like a flock of crows, black, fast, slicing through the air. She flattened herself against the ground and covered her ears against their screaming, and they streaked over her head and were gone. In the west, the rising blackness hid the blue of the sky.

The war has come, she thought. I have to get home.

But she couldn't move.

The people of Arbor Valley saw the planes, too. Because they always kept the news on, they heard the announcement before the power went out: bombs had fallen on major cities all over the country, and warplanes, thousands of them, were approaching or already overhead, dropping explosives as they went.

Everyone followed the plan and rushed to the school gym. Eva's mother, remembering that Eva had gone to Kim's, was struck with terror for her daughter. But she remembered that the people of Fallgrove had made a plan similar to theirs: to take shelter in the church basement. Eva would go with Kim's family. She would be all right.

In the gym, they milled around, two hundred and twelve people of all ages, plus nineteen dogs and two cats. No cell phones worked. They burned candles for light, since the gym had no windows or skylights.

"We're about fifty miles from the city," said Hal

Martin, the high school history teacher. "Will there be dangerous radiation here, do you think?" He raised one eyebrow as he asked this, because he was embarrassed not to know.

"I think so," said Avis Archer, who worked in the post office. She had no idea if this was true. "We shouldn't go out."

"How long does radiation last?"

No one knew for sure. Andy Brown thought it lasted for years. Joe Stanley didn't think so.

"One thing I know," said Bud Davis, who owned the gas station. "After a bomb like that, there are firestorms driven by the wind."

"But would a firestorm come this far?" asked Eva's mother.

"If a firestorm is coming toward us, we have to get out," said Joe Stanley.

"Get out to where?" Bud Davis gave a hard laugh. "Outside where the fire is? We're better off staying here."

"But we need to *see*," said Eva's mother. "I can't bear not seeing what's happened."

The talk went around and around. People sat on the bleachers and on the glossy wood floor, leaning against the walls. Some of the older people lay down under the basketball hoops, using folded-up sweaters or jackets for pillows.

"We have to listen for the sound of more planes,"

said Sam Gomez. "And helicopters. There might be help coming."

"Or bombers," said Janet Tomanelli. "How will we know if they've come to rescue us or attack us?"

No one had an answer to this.

Eva's mother tried not to be anxious. In her mind, she pictured Eva in the church basement in Fallgrove, where maybe the lights were still on, Eva sitting with Kim's sensible mother, safe and not scared at all.

It wasn't true, though. Eva was on the hillside, curled up in the dry grass, having worn herself out shouting for help. No one came, and she understood why: they were shut inside the gym, according to plan. They couldn't hear her.

After a while, she sat up and tried to move. She scooted downhill a few inches on the seat of her pants, but she couldn't keep her leg from bumping against the ground, and when that happened, the pain shot through her and she felt sick and had to stop and rest.

A wind had started up. It rippled through the grass around her and brought with it the smell of smoke. Overhead, brown haze dimmed the sun.

Eva lowered her eyes and saw a sparrow land on a hillock of grass nearby. It seemed to look right at her, its eye catching whatever brightness was left in the air. Eva looked back, and when the bird sang its trilling song, she almost understood what it was saying, which came, she thought, from the heart of life.

I can stand the pain, she told herself. I have to get home.

On an aircraft carrier out in the ocean, miles from shore, Commander T of the Ninth Force sat at his computer monitor, looking at the pictures sent back by drones flying over the bomb sites. He was searching for places where life still stirred, places jet bombers might target.

"Anything yet?" asked Airman J, who would be flying one of the bombers. He was a young man with a face as round as a full moon and a dreamy nature. When war was expected and all young men in his country had to sign up with the military, he had joined the air force because he wanted to know what it was like to fly.

Commander T shook his head. "Visibility about zero," he said. "Smoke, dust, hard to see through." He moved the controls and sent the drones south.

Looking over the commander's shoulder, Airman J watched as the grainy gray view wheeled around to show more swirls of gray. Every now and then a break in the clouds revealed a landscape of moving rubble—wind sweeping the wrecks of buildings and trees, and sometimes orange lines of fire crawling ahead of the wind.

"Firestorms," Commander T commented. He turned the drones inland.

Airman J wondered what his own country might look like right now. He thought of the house he'd grown up in, where his parents still lived—if they were alive. It was a small house outside the city—far enough outside? Weathered wood, blue-painted window frames, a few yellow wildflowers in spring. His mother, buttoning her coat as she hurried out the gate; his father with his small round glasses, bending over his books . . .

"Here we go," said Commander T. "Looks like some minor population centers in this area here."

Airman J saw a line of green. A valley, he thought, east of the mountains, where it might have been protected from the worst of the blasts.

"We'll send someone there." He looked over his shoulder at Airman J. "You."

In the gym, the little kids ran wild at first, thrilled by the big, echoing space. Sam Gomez, a coach at the elementary school, found a couple of basketballs for them to play with, but soon they were fighting over them, shrieking and wailing, so he took the balls away.

The older kids didn't want to play basketball, or race each other, or entertain themselves much at all. A few of them walked up the bleachers and then down again, over and over, but most of them clumped together by the side door, talking in low voices or dozing, keeping themselves apart from the adults' nervous conversation.

As the hours went by, some people got hungry, and Karen Peabody, who had helped organize the gym shelter project, got out paper plates from the boxes of stored supplies. Those who wanted to eat spooned up cold baked beans, cold chili, and cold macaroni and cheese.

Eva's mother couldn't eat, though. Her stomach was too uneasy.

"Come on," said Eva's father. "Just a few of these peanut butter crackers." To him, love and food were close relatives. In the fall, he made apple pies with cinnamon sauce and vanilla ice cream and held an apple pie party for the family, including aunts, uncles, cousins, and neighbors. "Have some of this dried fruit at least," he said to Eva's mother.

She shook her head. "I can't, Mark," she said. "Not until I know."

"Kim's family is dependable," said Eva's father. "I'm sure she's all right."

But Eva's mother felt as if no one would ever be all right again.

Eva had forgotten about the fence. There it was, a little way down the hill—a row of posts with wire strung between them, marking the end of her father's property.

On the way up the hill, she'd gone through the fence just by bending over, putting one foot between the top wire and the middle one, and then stepping all the way through. She couldn't do that this time. She'd either have to slide under the lowest wire—which was impossible, there wasn't enough room, the barbs would scrape her—or haul herself along the fence all the way to the south gate, nearly a quarter of a mile away.

At the thought of this, she felt her will go limp. It was too far. She couldn't make it. Maybe it would be better to lie down right here and wait to be found.

Then another possibility occurred to her. Where the fence crossed the gully, there was space beneath it, enough so that she might be able to lie on her back in the dry streambed and wriggle under the bottom wire. It would still be an ordeal—to reach the gully, she'd have to scooch twenty or thirty yards across the field, slide down the bank, which was rough with roots and prickles, and lie flat against the stones, which would bruise her back.

For a moment, Eva felt the urge to crumple into a ball and wait for whatever might happen. Instead, she made her slow way across the field, slid down the bank, lay down in the gully, and slithered under the fence. And it was an ordeal, but afterward, she felt a moment of pure happiness at her accomplishment.

Another fifteen minutes or so, and she was down

off the hillside and in the apple orchard. The pain in her leg was slightly better, although her ankle looked terrible, swollen and turning violet. She could hop between the trees—three or four hops, and then she would cling to a trunk and rest for a few seconds. Almost there. Just through the orchard, down the lane, up Walnut Street, across the playing field, and then she would pound on the gym door and they would let her in.

In the distance she heard the roar of engines. She stopped moving, holding on to the gnarled trunk of a tree, and looked up. Not a flock of fliers this time—only one. It flew low toward the valley, straight at her as if it saw her, like a hornet aiming to sting.

Airman J flew through mile after mile of dust and smoke. As he went inland, the air became slightly clearer. He had an urge to fly home, but his home was on the other side of the world, and his plane would run out of fuel long before he could get there.

Up ahead to the right was a wide line of green— the valley the drones had photographed. He turned in that direction.

Bud Davis stopped in the middle of what he was saying. "Listen."

The people in the gym fell silent and in the silence

heard an engine. A steady rumble, coming closer. "A plane," said Ralph.

"Quick, outside! Signal for help!" cried someone, and right away someone else called, "No! It's an enemy plane!"

"We have to *see*!" Eva's mother ran for the gym's west door and had almost got to it before Bud stopped her and dragged her down.

The people in the gym huddled closer together as the plane flew over and the sound of its engine faded.

The plane passed over the valley and disappeared, and Eva made a desperate, lurching run, gasping at the pain, stumbling and picking herself up over and over. She was in the middle of the football field when the plane came again, this time from the east.

It sees me, she thought. She stopped where she was, looking up toward whatever might come at her. Something dropped from the plane. Eva squeezed her eyes shut. Her mind went blank.

The roar of the plane faded. There was no explosion. She opened her eyes, and she saw in the blue-gray sky a white flower opening. It grew tremendous, and at the base of it was a man, swinging from long threads. He floated toward the earth. Down by the far goalpost of the football field, he landed, rolled, tangled in his cords, and got to his feet, facing her.

Eva stood frozen, watching. The man reached into a pocket of his jacket and pulled out—a piece of white cloth. He waved it slowly back and forth as he took a step toward her, and then another, slowly closing the distance between them.

He wore some kind of military uniform. His face was round and young, and he looked frightened. He dropped the white cloth and put his two hands together as if he were praying, fingers pointing under his chin. He said, in English, "No . . . more . . . war." He paused, then added: "For . . . me."

If someone else—Bud Davis, say—had been the one out there on the football field that day, things would have turned out differently. But it was Eva, and not the everyday Eva but a wounded and exhausted and afraid Eva, an Eva with nothing left in her but her essential self, which was clear as a blue sky. She didn't question whether this man was telling the truth. She saw that he was.

"Follow me," she said, and she limped across the field to the door of the gym, where she pounded and called out, and when Bud opened the door with a gun in his hand, she stood in front of the soldier and cried out, "Don't shoot him!"

A few hundred miles away, Airman J's bomber plane, flying without a pilot, splashed down into the ocean, raising a wave that swept across the water for miles and slammed up against the side of the aircraft carrier, though not hard enough to attract any notice from Commander T.

For the people of Arbor Valley, the months that followed were terrible, as they were for survivors of the Disaster all over the world. Vast stretches of land were charred and poisoned. Fires burned everywhere, and a pall of smoke dimmed the sky for a long time. There was no water in the pipes, and no electricity traveled through the wires.

Ragged bands of people, many of them sick or injured, crept across the landscape, looking for water and food. The people of Arbor Valley, with others who had lived nearby, formed a convoy while they could still find cars with gas in them. Gradually they moved northward. They learned to find what they needed in the remains of old buildings, and some years later, when that was no longer possible, they looked for a place by a river, where they could build houses and grow food and begin to live like civilized beings again.

Eva was a grown woman by the time she and her people established their village. Though she always walked with a limp after the day of the bombs, she was otherwise healthy and strong. She was the one who came up with the name Sparks for the town they built, because it was a spark of light in a world that had become dark.

Airman J—people had come to call him simply Jay—lived out his life in the village and was never for one moment sorry that he'd decided, that day in his plane, not to drop the bombs he was carrying, but to drop himself instead.

Turn the page
for a special preview of
the second BOOK OF EMBER.

"A deftly constructed fable." —*San Francisco Chronicle*

The PEOPLE of SPARKS
the second BOOK OF EMBER

New York Times Bestselling Author
JEANNE DuPRAU

CHAPTER 1

What Torren Saw

Torren was out at the edge of the cabbage field that day, the day the people came. He was supposed to be fetching a couple of cabbages for Dr. Hester to use in the soup that night, but, as usual, he didn't see why he shouldn't have some fun while he was at it. So he climbed up the wind tower, which he wasn't supposed to do because, they said, he might fall or get his head sliced off by the big blades going round and round.

The wind tower was four-sided, made of boards nailed one above the next like the rungs of a ladder. Torren climbed the back side of it, the side that faced the hills and not the village, so that the little group of workers hoeing the cabbage rows wouldn't see him. At the top, he turned around and sat on the flat place behind the blades, which turned slowly in the idle summer breeze. He had brought a pocketful of small stones up with him, planning on some target practice: he liked to try to hit the chickens that rummaged around between the rows of cabbages. He thought it might be fun to bounce a few pebbles off the hats of the workers, too. But before he had even taken the stones from his pocket, he caught sight of something that made him stop and stare.

Out beyond the cabbage field was another field, where young tomato and corn and squash plants were growing, and beyond that the land sloped up into a grassy hillside dotted, at this time of year, with yellow mustard flowers. Torren saw something strange at the top of the hill. Something dark.

There were bits of darkness at first—for a second he thought maybe it was a deer, or several deer, black ones instead of the usual light brown, but the shape was wrong for deer, and the way these things moved was wrong, too. He realized very soon that he was seeing people, a few people at first and then more and more of them. They came up from the other side of the hill and gathered at the top and stood there, a long line of them against the sky, like a row of black teeth. There must have been a hundred, Torren thought, or more than a hundred.

In all his life, Torren had never seen more than three or four people at a time arrive at the village from elsewhere. Almost always, the people who came were roamers, passing through with a truckload of stuff from the old towns to sell. This massing of people on the hilltop terrified him. For a moment he couldn't move. Then his heart started up a furious pounding, and he scrambled down off the wind tower so fast that he scraped his hands on the rough boards.

"Someone's coming!" he shouted as he passed the workers. They looked up, startled. Torren ran at full speed toward the low cluster of brown buildings at the far end of the field. He turned up a dirt lane, his feet raising swirls of dust, and dashed through the gate in the wall and across the courtyard and in through the open door, all the time yelling, "Someone's coming! Up on the hill! Auntie Hester! Someone's coming!"

He found his aunt in the kitchen, and he grabbed her by the waist of her pants and cried, "Come and see! There's people on the hill!" His voice was so shrill and urgent and loud that his aunt dropped the spoon into the pot of soup she'd been stirring and hurried after him. By the time they got outside, others from the village were leaving their houses, too, and looking toward the hillside.

The people were coming down. Over the crest of the hill they came and kept coming, dozens of them, more and more, like a mudslide.

The people of the village crowded into the streets. "Get Mary Waters!" someone called. "Where's Ben and Wilmer? Find them, tell them to get out here!"

Torren was less frightened now that he was surrounded by the townspeople. "I saw them first," he said to Hattie Carranza, who happened to be hurrying along next to him. "I was the one who told the news."

"Is that right," said Hattie.

"We won't let them do anything bad to us," said Torren. "If they do, we'll do something worse to them. Won't we?"

But she just glanced down at him with a vague frown and didn't answer.

The three village leaders—Mary Waters, Ben Barlow, and Wilmer Dent—had joined the crowd by now and were leading the way across the cabbage field. Torren kept close behind them. The strangers were getting nearer, and he wanted to hear what they would say. He could see that they were terrible-looking people. Their clothes were all wrong—coats and sweaters, though the weather was warm, and not nice coats and sweaters but raggedy ones, patched, unraveling, faded, and grimy. They carried bundles, all of them: sacks made of what looked like tablecloths or blankets gathered up and tied with string around the neck. They moved clumsily and slowly. Some of them tripped on the uneven ground and had to be helped up by others.

In the center of the field, where the smell of new cabbages and fresh dirt and chicken manure was strong, those at the front of the crowd of strangers met the village leaders. Mary Waters stepped to the front, and the villagers crowded up behind her. Torren, being small, wriggled between people until he had a good view. He stared at the ragged people. Where were *their* leaders? Facing Mary were a girl and a boy who looked only a little older than he was himself. Next to them was a bald man, and next to him a sharp-eyed woman holding a small child. Maybe she was the leader.

But when Mary stepped forward and said, "Who are you?" it was the boy who answered. He spoke in a clear, loud voice that surprised Torren, who had expected a pitiful voice from someone so bedraggled. "We come from the city of Ember," the boy said. "We left there because our city was dying. We need help."

Mary, Ben, and Wilmer exchanged glances. Mary frowned. "The city of Ember? Where's that? We've never heard of it."

The boy gestured back the way they had come, to the east. "That way," he said. "It's under the ground."

The frowns deepened. "Tell us the truth," said Ben, "not childish nonsense."

This time the girl spoke up. She had long, snarled hair with bits of grass caught in it. "It isn't a lie," she said. "Really. Our city was underground. We didn't know it until we came out."

Ben snorted impatiently, folding his arms across his chest. "Who is in charge here?" He looked at the bald man. "Is it you?"

The bald man shook his head and gestured toward the boy and the girl. "They're as in charge as anyone," he said. "The mayor of our city is no longer with us. These young people are speaking the truth. We have come out of a city built underground."

The people around him all nodded and murmured, "Yes" and "It's true."

"My name is Doon Harrow," said the boy. "And this is Lina Mayfleet. We found the way out of Ember."

He thinks he's pretty great, thought Torren, hearing a note of pride in the boy's voice. He didn't look so great. His hair was shaggy, and he was wearing an old jacket that was coming apart at the seams and grimy at the cuffs. But his eyes shone out confidently from under his dark eyebrows.

"We're hungry," the boy said. "And thirsty. Will you help us?"

Mary, Ben, and Wilmer stood silent for a moment. Then Mary took Ben and Wilmer by the arms and led them aside a few steps. They whispered to each other, glanced up at the great swarm of strangers, frowned, whispered some more. While he waited to hear what they'd say, Torren studied the people who said they came from underground.

It might be true. They did in fact look as if they had crawled up out of a hole. Most of them were scrawny and pale, like the sprouts you see when you lift up a board that's been lying on the ground, feeble things that have tried to grow in the dark. They huddled together, looking frightened. They looked exhausted, too. Many of them had sat down on the ground now, and some had their heads in the laps of others.

The three village leaders turned again to the crowd of strangers. "How many of you are there?" Mary Waters asked.

"About four hundred," said the boy, Doon.

Mary's dark eyebrows jumped upward.

Four hundred! In Torren's whole village, there were only three hundred and twenty-two. He swept his gaze out over this vast horde. They filled half the cabbage field and were still coming over the hill, like a swarm of ants.

The girl with the ratty hair stepped forward and raised a hand, as if she were in school. "Excuse me, Madam Mayor," she said.

Torren snickered. Madam Mayor! Nobody called Mary Waters Madam Mayor. They just called her Mary.

"Madam Mayor," said the girl, "my little sister is very sick." She pointed to the baby being held by the sharp-eyed woman. It did look sick. Its eyes were half closed, and its mouth hung open. "Some others of us are sick, too," the girl went on, "or hurt—Lotty Hoover tripped and hurt her ankle, and Nammy Proggs is exhausted from walking so far. She's nearly eighty years old. Is there a doctor in your town? Is there a place where sick people can lie down and be taken care of?"

Mary turned to Ben and Wilmer again, and they spoke to each other in low voices. Torren could catch only a few words of what they said. "Too many . . ." ". . . but human kindness . . ." ". . . maybe take a few in . . ." Ben rubbed his beard and scowled. Wilmer kept glancing at the sick baby. After a few minutes, they nodded to each other. Mary said, "All right. Hoist me up."

Ben and Wilmer bent down and grasped Mary's legs. With a grunt, they lifted her so that she was high enough to see out over the crowd. She raised both her arms and cried, in a voice that came from the depths of her deep chest, "People from Ember! Welcome! We will do what we can to help you. Please follow us!" Ben and Wilmer set her down, and the three of them turned and walked out of the cabbage field and toward the road that entered the village. Led by the boy and the girl, the crowd of shabby people followed.

Torren dashed ahead, ran down the lane, and got up onto the low wall that bordered his house. From here, he watched the people from underground go by. They were strangely silent. Why weren't they jabbering to each other? But they seemed too tired to speak, or too stupid. They stared at everything, wide-eyed and drop-jawed—as if they had never seen a house before, or a tree, or a chicken. In fact, the chickens seemed to frighten them—they shrank back when they saw them, making startled sounds. It took a long time for the whole raggedy crowd to pass Torren's house, and when the last people had gone by, he jumped down off the wall and followed them. They were being led, he knew, to the town center, down by the river, where there would be water for them to drink. After that, what would happen? What would they eat? Where would they sleep? Not in my room, he thought.

JOURNEY THROUGH
THE BOOKS OF EMBER
from bestselling author
Jeanne DuPrau!

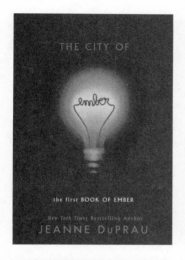

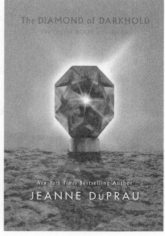

felt she knew what was best for someone, there was no shying away from letting them know it. Or from using her wily passive-aggressive skills to get her way, particularly with her kids and grandkids.

Like a truth teller affirming Anamaría's thoughts about her mom's meddling, her mom's voice stopped Anamaría seconds before her finger hit the *end call* icon on the dashboard screen.

"God has a plan for you, nena. I know He does." Her mami's tone softened with concern at the same time it sharpened with the conviction of her faith. "Dios te bendiga, mi vida."

Before she could reply to her mother's usual "God bless you, my life" farewell, the call was disconnected.

God has a plan for you. The sage advice replayed in Anamaría's head as she rubbed her thumb over the *AM Fitness* logo imprinted on the side of her water bottle. This—AM Fitness—had to be that plan. She sure hoped so, anyway, because it was her only focus now.

The black-and-red script in a font meticulously selected because of its strong, energetic vibe indicative of the brand she sought for her burgeoning business reminded her of how far she'd come. Sure, it had taken her awhile, but she was finally in a good place.

Her heart had mended. Her conviction that she'd made the right decision by staying behind had solidified. Her anger at Alejandro's mulish behavior had dissipated to mere indifference. Well, until his surprise return.

A surprise she refused to let derail her.

Ignoring her trembling fingers and the annoying jitters in her stomach, she tugged the keys from the ignition, grabbed her backpack, then left the safety of her vehicle.

Like many in this older Midtown neighborhood, the Mirandas' was a modest, single-story stucco house. Theirs was painted the same welcoming soft peach as the privacy wall, with dark gray hurricane shutters bookending the windows. Alejandro and his younger brother, Ernesto, had spent their entire lives here. Until their father, in a fit of anger Anamaría felt certain he'd never meant, threatened to ban Alejandro from their home if he chose to turn his back on running the restaurant that was their familia's legacy.

Despite the threat, Alejandro had boarded that plane to Spain. Off to seek fame and fortune on his own terms. Without his father's blessing. Without her.

As she stepped onto the sidewalk, the humid breeze snagged a few strands of hair that had fallen loose from her ponytail, blowing them across her cheek. She tucked them behind her ear and squared her shoulders, then paused in front of the wide wooden door nestled in the privacy wall's alcove. Overhead, sprawling bougainvillea with their deep green leaves and bright fuchsia flower petals climbed the slanted overhang in a colorful canopy. The sweet-smelling vines offered shade to those who entered, but the plant's sharp thorns were as prickly and harmful as the memories of Alejandro she had struggled to uproot from her heart.

Shit, if she was honest with herself, she'd admit that the sweat dotting her upper lip was a nervous reaction to seeing Alejandro again after all these years, not the hot island climate. That didn't mean anyone else needed to know.

All she had to do was put on her game face. Channel her I-don't-give-a-damn attitude that challenged any sexist, chauvinistic firefighters at work to question her abilities when it came to saving their asses. Treat this visit like another routine 911 call. Alejandro, another random patient she might need to load in the back of her . . . or, bueno, his mom's sedan . . . for the short drive to the emergency room at Lower Keys Medical Center if need be.

So what if instead of her firefighter gear she wore exercise clothes, having come directly from a private workout with a guest at the Casa Marina Resort. Her sundress from church was a balled-up, wrinkled mess inside her gym bag. No way was she wasting twenty minutes driving to her place in Stock Island, just outside of Key West, and back to freshen up. Not for him.

She refused to care whether or not she looked her best for the man who had walked away from her so easily.

Straightening her spine, Anamaría reached for the weathered metal door handle.

Her plan was simple. Get in and out quickly. Keep chitchat to a minimum. Remain professional and focused on her job—not the man—while she checked Alejandro's vitals and the pin sites of the external fixator keeping his surgically aligned tibia shaft in place while his compound fracture healed.

No doubt Alejandro had come back kicking and screaming. Metaphorically speaking anyway. That had been the general consensus during the conversation she'd tried to tune out around the table at her familia's mandatory weekly dinner the other night.

Nothing short of desperation and the need for assistance with his daily care—with a heavy dose of maternal insistence, no doubt—could have finally brought the prodigal Miranda son home.

Anamaría figured Alejandro wanted to be back in Key West about as much as she wanted him here.

That would be . . . not at all. As in zip. Zero. Zilch. Nada.

If luck was on her side, her visit now would be a quick "all's well" checkup. With Señora Miranda's fears for her eldest's well-being calmed, Anamaría could be on her way having fulfilled her duty, intent on maintaining her distance until he left again.

Because he would leave again. Everyone knew that.

Only this time, when Alejandro Miranda boarded his flight to wherever his photography skills took him, he would not be taking her heart with him.

After having decided almost two years ago to quit waffling and just do it—her younger brother's wise, albeit borrowed-from-Nike advice—she was finally taking steps to make her true career dreams a reality. Thanks to social media influencer mentoring from her brother Luis's fiancée, AM Fitness had started getting more buzz, Anamaría's platforms were accruing more followers and subscribers, and, most recently, a talent agent had offered her representation.

There was absolutely no time for distractions or strolls down a memory lane plastered with Dead End signs.

Alejandro Miranda was her past.

Anamaría's eyes were focused on the future.

All she had to do was get through this one awkward meeting. Then they could go their separate ways again.

A tiny pang of regret seared a hot trail through Anamaría's chest.

Stubbornly she stomped on the hurtful sparks like the dying embers of a careless fire. She didn't have time for regrets. Instead, shoulders back, head high, she pushed through the wooden door, ready to face the man who had shattered her once tender heart.

Sitting on the worn floral-print sofa in his familia's living room, Alejandro Miranda cursed the bad luck that had dragged his ass back to Key West. The island home he'd left behind over a decade ago, by choice and by force.

His mami sat on one side of him, his abuela on the other, their dark eyes pools of concern. Across from him, his sister-in-law, Cece, and two-year-old niece, Lulu, perched on the matching love seat pushed against the opposite wall, their gazes trained on him expectantly. His brother, Ernesto, leaned against the armrest, hovering at his wife's side, uncertainty pinching his brow.

Trapped by their intent stares and unspoken expectations, Alejandro jabbed his fingers through his hair in frustration. Being back in his childhood home made him think about that old copy of Thomas Wolfe's *You Can't Go Home Again* he'd found at a secondhand bookstore in London several years ago. The title had initially grabbed him, but it was the words on the pages inside that really resonated.

According to Wolfe, you could never return to your old life, your old ways, even your old hometown, and find things the same. Ha! The guy obviously hadn't tried going back to a Cuban familia rooted in tradition.

Sure, some things had changed. Cece and Ernesto had been about to start high school, barely making heart eyes at each other, when Alejandro had flown the restrictive coop his papi ruled. Curly-haired, pudgy-cheeked Lulu hadn't even been a thought in her parents' pre-pubescent minds. Now they were a family of three, with another about to arrive. And he had missed it all.

But the old portrait of his papi, mami, Ernesto, and him, snapped at the Sears studio twenty-plus years ago, still hung in its clunky frame on the pale blue wall above the love seat. A throwback frame you wouldn't find in any gallery that displayed Alejandro's prized photographs today.

Worse, the strange mix of disappointment and hope on his mami's, abuela's, and Ernesto's faces weighed as heavily on his shoulders now as it had back then.

Twelve years away and still he sensed their keen desire for him to quit shirking his responsibilities. To come back and work alongside his papi, preparing to take over the restaurant someday. A life sentence that would shackle Alejandro's dream of traveling and photographing the world.

It was the reason why he had stayed away for so long. Well, one of several.

"Your papi is sorry he couldn't be here to welcome you home," his mom said. She slid to the edge of the sofa, leaning forward to plump the leaf green throw pillows cushioning his injured left leg resting on top of the rattan coffee table.

"Por favor," he muttered. "Let's not pretend. If I hadn't been stupid enough to fall off that rock ledge in El Yunque and wind up in this damn—"

"¡Oye! Language!" Ernesto interrupted. He jerked a thumb at his daughter, busy murmuring something to the baby doll cradled in her tiny arms.

¡Carajo!

The second *damn* nearly slipped out before Alejandro swallowed it. He wasn't used to having a kid around. Unless they were the subject of his photograph, and then his camera kept him occupied and at a professional distance.

He dipped his head in apology at his brother and Cece.

"If I hadn't wound up in this position," Alejandro continued, "I'd be on my way to Belize for my next shoot. Not . . ."

Not here, surrounded by the people he had let down. Girding himself for when his father came home from Miranda's, their familia restaurant that was his pride and joy. The legacy Alejandro had spit on by walking away.

"Gracias a Dios que estás bien," his abuela said softly.

Yeah, thank God he was okay. If "okay" meant slipping down a fucking waterfall and busting the shit out of his leg, then being forced to return to the home he could no longer claim as his to face the people he was destined to disappoint.

He squelched the sarcastic retort. It would only hurt his familia. Instead, he bit his tongue and sagged back against the worn sofa cushions. His leg ached, signaling the time neared for him to swallow another over-the-counter pain pill. He'd given a hard pass to the opioid and acetaminophen with codeine the doc had tried prescribing post-surgery in Puerto Rico. No way would he risk developing any sort of dependency or addiction. There'd been a time after his divorce when he'd come way too close to relying on the bottle to dull his thoughts. Years later, that flirtation with dependency still haunted him.

"How are you feeling, hijo?" His mami finger-combed his hair, a gentle caress that reminded him of times past. When he'd lain on this same couch or the double bed in his room and she'd soothed him when he was sick.

"Your face is pale," she complained. "And you feel a little warm. Are you hurting?"

He shook his head, lying but unwilling to cause her more distress. His jaw clenched tightly against the ache radiating from two of the pin sites high on his shin, a couple inches below his knee.

"Kiss it better, 'Buela," his little niece suggested.

Despite the fatigue and disillusion crushing him, Lulu's cuteness drew his smile. Her pudgy cheeks plumped even more when she grinned back at him.

"I'm not sure that's going to work, chiquita, but thank you for suggesting it." He winked, pleased when a cute giggle burst from her mouth. She hugged her bald baby doll to her chest, twisting from side to side.

Her innocence reminded him of the toddler he'd photographed once in a remote Costa Rican village. Spending time with the villagers and volunteers as they toiled at constructing a rustic school building and the eco-brick steps leading up a slight incline to the site had been a humbling experience. One of many he was thankful for over the years.

Cece caressed Lulu's curly hair, her expression gentle with maternal love when she looked over at him. "It's good to see you, Ale. Even if it is like this."

She thrust her chin at the Ilizarov external fixator with its four rings and multiple wires piercing his shin, holding his tibia in place. Lulu had already been warned to keep her distance from the cyborg-looking contraption after racing over to greet him and nearly bumping against the rings.

Carajo, just thinking about the agony her knocking into his leg would have caused made him wince.

"Gracias," Alejandro replied to Cece.

He wanted to tell her it was good to be here. But they all knew it would be a lie.

Unlike them, he had always itched to be outside, not cooped up at the restaurant. He was more interested in seeing their small island from behind the lens of his camera. Capturing the beauty, wonder, and details so many missed in the busyness of life.

Making his own way in the world, not following someone else's.

His eyes drifted shut on the past. The differences between them that still held true today. The differences that disappointed them, especially his father.

This visit was only for a short time. Until he was healed enough to have the external fixator rings and pins removed, allowing him more mobility. Then he'd be able to handle the stairs at his town house in Atlanta and he'd be fine on his own. As he had been for years.

Getting out of the wheelchair meant getting back to the job that gave his life purpose. And helped silence the occasional cry of loneliness that howled in the dark of night when his defenses were low.

"I still think we should have driven straight to the emergency room when we arrived here," his mami said, concern lacing her words.

He swiveled his head on the back sofa cushion to meet her worried gaze. "Let me rest a few minutes; then I'll remove the dressings and clean the sites. I'm sure everything's okay. I'm just tired."

"Bueno, I would feel better if you saw a professional." His mami ran her fingers through his hair once again. The familiar gesture both soothed and left him longing for a simpler past.

"Don't be silly. I'm fine," Alejandro assured her.

"Humph, so I am silly for worrying about my son now, ha?" she demanded with a sniff. "That's what you think of me?"

Arms crossed as he leaned against the far wall, Ernesto returned Alejandro's exasperated grimace. They were familiar with this routine. When their mami was like this, you'd better pack your bags. Elena Miranda had a first-class ticket for you on a guilt trip you couldn't avoid.

The fact that he'd held firm in not returning all these years, despite her heavy-handed attempts to lure him home, spoke of the yawning distance separating Alejandro and his father. The bridge connecting them having long been burnt to the ground.

"A mother should not want what is best for her children?" his mami droned on.

"I didn't say—"

"Bueno, since you refused to go see the doctor, I asked someone to come see you."

If he didn't feel like death warmed over, he might have laughed at her over-protective nature. "Mami, few doctors make house calls anymore. Not the ones my insurance company will cover anyway."

"I didn't call a doctor. I called familia."

Fatigue weighing on him, Alejandro slowly shook his head, not following. They didn't have any physicians in their family. "What do you mean?"

Her brow furrowed, his mami exchanged a worried glance with his abuela, then shot a "don't say anything" parental warning at his brother, who in turn threw an apologetic grimace Alejandro's way.

Why did he suddenly feel like everyone else shared some kind of insider info he wasn't privy to?

Unease slithered down his spine.

"We only need someone with medical experience to properly clean your wounds and tell me if I should make you go to the hospital," his mami said. "When the physical therapist comes later this week, I can ask any new questions I have."

"Someone with . . . wait. . . ." Alejandro shot a "what the hell, how could you let her" glare at his traitorous brother.

Ernesto ducked his head, a sure sign he knew what their mami was up to but refused to, or more like was wise enough not to, get in her bulldozing way.

"Mami," Alejandro's voice sharpened. "Who did you call?"

Her eyes narrowed at his gruff tone. A warning for him to curb his disrespect.

The stubbornness tightening his mami's lips and the calming hand his abuela laid on his forearm answered Alejandro's question as if the two women had spoken.

Dread descended like a dark storm cloud rolling in from the ocean.

"Por favor, tell me you didn't—"

A sharp knock on the front door interrupted him. Before anyone could move, the hinges creaked in protest as the door slowly opened.

The rich, lilting voice that haunted his dreams, no matter how hard he tried to banish it, called, "Hola!" as Anamaría Navarro stepped inside.

"Anamawía!" Lulu squealed.

Dark curls bouncing, his niece hopped off the love seat. Her pink sandals slapped the gray and white tile as she ran with open arms toward the woman he hadn't spoken to since their last uncomfortable Skype video chat over a decade ago. The night she unequivocally confirmed his worst fear, discarding him like chum tossed overboard.

Lulu's skinny arms wrapped around Anamaría's thighs in a tight squeeze. Joy lit his ex's hazel eyes, sucker-punching him with vivid memories of her greeting him with a similar glee.

She bent to rub a hand on his niece's back, her long dark ponytail swooping over her shoulder. "Hola, Lulu, this is a nice surprise."

Lulu craned her neck to peer up at Anamaría, adoration dawning over her cute face. Damn if Alejandro couldn't help but understand exactly how the kid felt. No matter how often he called himself a fool for yearning for someone who obviously hadn't felt the same.

"Tío Ale, tiene an owie," Lulu announced. Like the Frankenstein contraption encircling his leg wasn't clue enough.

"Yes, he does have an owie," Anamaría answered. "A pretty big one. But your abuela and abuelita are going to take good care of him. Just like they do with you."

"Will you come pway wif me soon?"

"I hope so. I need me some Lulu time." Anamaría hunkered down and tugged one of Lulu's curls, eliciting a sweet giggle from the child.

The closeness between the two—the niece he'd only seen the one time Ernesto and his family had visited him in Atlanta and the woman who'd basically said he wasn't enough for her—felt like a poisonous lance in his side. He may not fit in here, but it was obvious Anamaría still did. Without him.

Holding her baby doll tightly against her chest, Lulu skipped back to her parents. "Anamawía gonna babysit me!"

"Not today. But we'll see when, mamita." Ernesto gave his daughter's butt a nudge to help her clamber onto the love seat.

"Text me, Cece, and I'll let you know when I'm free. I'm sure you two could use a date night before your bundle of joy arrives."

Cece circled a hand over her huge, beach ball–sized belly that stretched the material of her yellow blouse. A tired smile tugged up the corners of his sister-in-law's wide mouth as she murmured her thanks.

Anamaría sent Lulu a wink and rose from her haunches.

His shock at her arrival waning, Alejandro allowed himself to take in her figure, on gorgeous display thanks to a pair of form-fitting black leggings and a tight pink tank, the words *AM Fitness* in a black scrawling font across the front. With her matching black and pink Nike sneakers and slicked-back high ponytail, she looked primed for an athletic photo shoot. She could have easily replaced one of the models for the *Women's Health* spread he'd shot in the Bahamas last year.

The enthusiastic teenager he'd known and loved had matured into a vibrant woman. All lush curves and honed muscles, the latter no doubt hard earned from her work as a firefighter paramedic and fitness trainer.

Without acknowledging him, Anamaría made the round of hello kisses and hugs with Ernesto and his family, even tickling Lulu's baby doll under the chin, eliciting another precious giggle from Alejandro's niece.

His ex crossed to the sofa, the scent of the tropical lotion she had always preferred tickling his nose when she stooped to brush a kiss on his abuela's wrinkled cheek. The two exchanged warm smiles as his abuela patted Anamaría's hand with a murmured *Dios te bendiga, nena.*

The age-old wish for God's blessing may be a trite phrase easily tossed out by many. But in this house, with the mini altar in the far corner, its pillar candle lit during his abuela's daily prayer of the rosary, words of blessing held weight. His mami had already stopped at their altar earlier, giving thanks for her answered prayers for his return.

Anamaría hugged his mami, waved off the offer of a drink, set her black backpack on the tile floor next to the coffee table, and finally, *finally*, turned to him.

His body tensed, but he fought to maintain a neutral expression. To hide the anger, lingering bitterness, and disillusion of their past. All the while he greedily cataloged the features he had conjured in his dreams.

Her oval face with its high cheekbones, expressive hazel eyes, and slightly pointed chin remained as beautiful as ever. The faint crow's-feet lightly raying out from her eyes, telltale signs of laughter and days squinting under the bright Key West sun, added to her allure. The serious slant of her full lips made him ache for the enticing grin she'd so readily flashed at him in years past. And now easily shared with others in his familia instead. The round dark brown beauty mark an inch below the right corner of her mouth made him itch to press a kiss to it. Only, he was no longer free to do so.

That right had been taken away from him the moment she changed her mind and chose to stay here. Refusing to follow him to Spain after her papi's health had improved as promised.

The fact that Alejandro hadn't been enough for her had gutted him.

"So, I hear someone needs a little medical attention." Hands fisted on her hips, Anamaría got down to business, not even wasting time with a hello. Fine by him. The faster they got this unwanted reunion over, the better.

"I'm good. No need for you to be here," he told her.

"Alejandro!" His mami's dismayed gasp was accompanied by a slap of his thigh. "No seas rudo!"

Anamaría smirked, the quirk of her lips reminiscent of times she had teased him for getting in trouble in the past. "No worries, Señora Miranda. Making house calls and dealing with occasional rudeness is in my job description. Lucky for Alejandro, I'm in a generous mood."

Generous?

Please. It wasn't like she was the one who'd been wronged. Instead of the one who had reneged on their shared dream. Then pushed him away.

Seeing as how she was about to poke around the leg now throbbing like an alien had implanted itself under his skin and decided this was the perfect time to burst out, Alejandro kept his accusation to himself.

The sooner they got this over with and she left, the sooner he could go back to reminding himself that he was better off without any of the pressures and recriminations being back in Key West presented. Better off without her.

Anamaría bent to peer at his leg. Her cool hand touched his left knee above the top external fixator ring, a soft caress that sent heat searing through him. He tensed and sucked in a sharp breath.

Her intuitive gaze cut his way. Eyes narrowed, she stared back at him, ensnaring him like a helpless insect caught in a spider's silky web.

Something dark and primitive passed between them. Proof that while some things had changed in his absence, his instant reaction to the only woman he had ever loved remained brutally the same.

Lips pressed in an irritated line, Anamaría slid her glance away, breaking their connection as she leaned closer to peer at his injured leg. Her ponytail swung down to brush against his skin at the hem of his shorts. Lust made a beeline up his leg, straight to his crotch.

Fucking great. Annoyed, he folded his hands in his lap to cover himself.

"Okay, let's see what we're dealing with here," she said matter-of-factly, as if the spark between them hadn't singed her the same way it had him.

Shit, he already knew what he was dealing with. His own personal hell.

Her motions brisk, Anamaría unzipped her backpack, removed and opened a first-aid kit, then set it on the coffee table. She tugged on a pair of light blue medical gloves, the snap of the rubbery material against her skin loud in the quiet living room. Poor Lulu's eyes widened with apprehension.

Anamaría straightened, her impassive expression grating on his frayed nerves. "You ready?"

Was she kidding? Of course, he wasn't fucking ready. For a boatload of reasons he refused to admit out loud.

Unfortunately, there was no getting around this humiliation.

With a brisk nod, he braced himself for the discomfort her ministrations would bring—to his leg as well as to his traitorous heart.

Chapter 2

Heart pounding, Anamaría knelt between the floral sofa and wicker coffee table, her chest even with Alejandro's elevated leg. Even knowing what she was walking into, she hadn't been prepared for what greeted her.

Alejandro's handsome face was thinner, his skin slightly jaundiced rather than the usual sun-kissed bronze she'd seen in the pictures he occasionally posted on social media. His usually clean-shaven, angular jaw sported thick scruff, evidence that he hadn't shaved in at least a week. Pain pinched the edges of his mouth and shadowed his dark eyes in a broody expression she should not have found appealing.

Doggedly, Anamaría willed herself to concentrate on "the patient" and calm the nervous trembles humming through her. Steady hands were needed here. Both to ensure she didn't cause him more discomfort when she cleaned his pin sites and to dispel any question about whether or not being near him again might be a problem for her.

It wasn't. Not in the least.

She empathized with anyone who was injured, especially this

badly. It was part of why she'd chosen her profession. And she was damn good at what she did.

Forget that the last time they touched had been the night they'd said good-bye. Back when she'd thought he would change his mind about staying away for good. And he apparently thought she'd eventually be okay leaving everything behind. Their home. His familia. Hers.

Wrapped in a tight hug, she'd held on to him as they stood on the concrete seawall behind her parents' house in Big Coppitt Key. Above them, the midnight sky had sparkled with stars. A full moon shone its mercurial path over the dark open ocean at the end of the canal, disappearing in the distance. Just like he eventually would.

If she closed her eyes, Anamaría could sense the humidity and sorrow-laden air enveloping them. Smell the salty seawater mixed with the sweet scent of the bougainvillea trailing up the back stairs. Feel the harsh misery of her heart breaking.

Instead, she kept her eyes wide open, intent on doing her job, then getting the hell out of here.

Her fingers softly palpated the area a couple inches away from where one of the wires attached to the top ring on the external fixator pierced his skin. Two and a half weeks post-surgery, it was surprising to find bandages covering his pin sites. If there had been complications with healing, the surgeon in Puerto Rico wouldn't have, shouldn't have, let Alejandro travel.

"I'm assuming the bandages were placed here as a precaution to avoid germs during your trip home?" she asked.

When he didn't answer, she glanced at him from under her lashes.

Sweat beaded his upper lip and brow. Teeth gritted, his jaw muscles straining, he gave a jerky nod in response. Pain flashed like lightning in his nearly black eyes.

"Anamawía make Tío Ale better?" Lulu asked, her high-pitched voice breaking the tension filling the room as all the adults watched with varying degrees of concern.

"She's going to try, Mamita," Cece answered.

Try being the operative word here. Based on the tension radiating off Alejandro, he was either really pissed to see her or experiencing a higher degree of discomfort than he should. Maybe both.

As for him being pissed, he'd have to suck it up. She wasn't thrilled about their impromptu reunion, either. It had their scheming mothers written all over it.

But the pain from his injury . . . that she might be able to help. Not, however, with this particular audience breathing down her neck. All of them waiting for any sign that past hurts lingered. Or worse, a hint they'd been laid to rest and the potential for a new future for her and Alejandro still existed.

She'd bet her next Kelly day that her mom and Señora Miranda had already started praying a novena for the latter. And Anamaría, like most firefighters, wouldn't bet her monthly extra day off on anything less than a sure winner.

Pushing aside the irritating thought of their mothers' matchmaking, Anamaría turned back to her task. Not the person.

"Okay, everyone, while I'm sure Alejandro enjoyed the welcome home fiesta, we should move him to his room, where he'll be more comfortable," Anamaría announced. "After I finish checking his pin sites, Tío Ale needs to take a nap, like Lulu. Rest is important for his recovery."

Plus, getting him to his room would allow them a small measure of privacy. Not exactly what she personally wanted, but necessary for her to do her job correctly. Instinct told her Alejandro wouldn't answer her questions about his discomfort levels truthfully. Not in front of his worry-prone mother.

"Ernesto, can you help me?" Anamaría motioned toward the wheelchair parked in the combination dining-kitchen area.

It wasn't easy, but after a few grunts of complaint peppered with muffled curses, Alejandro settled into the chair, his left leg propped up on the elevated footrest. A light sheen of perspiration covered his haggard face, and she almost felt sorry for him.

Irritated at her reaction, she shoved her first-aid kit in her backpack, then slung the bag over her shoulder to wheel him toward the back of the house and the three bedrooms. Señora Miranda followed close behind them.

As they neared Alejandro's old room, Anamaría slowed her steps, hesitating.

Memories assailed her. Evil interlopers sabotaging her bid to remain aloof.

Study dates, movie nights, long afternoons spent perusing the latest pictures Alejandro had taken around the island and discussing their lofty dreams. Quick stolen kisses and innocent touches, because the bedroom door always remained open—Miranda and Navarro house rules.

Their last year of high school, when they'd both been ready, they had taken advantage of the rare opportunities when they'd had this house or her parents' place to themselves. Or stolen clandestine hours lying on a blanket, making out under the stars in the stern of her papi's boat when he left it docked in the backyard canal overnight, ready for an early-morning fishing trip.

Señora Miranda scooted around the chair to push open Alejandro's bedroom door, beckoning them in. Anamaría steeled herself and crossed the threshold, stepping inside the sanctuary where she'd once woven her life's dreams. In her naïveté not realizing the fragility of the threads that tied her and Alejandro together.

Comfort and dismay crashed against each other as Anamaría's gaze trailed around his room. The space remained unchanged. A shrine to the son who had walked away without a backward glance.

The same navy comforter draped the double bed pressed up against the far wall underneath the window overlooking the side yard. The same sturdy wood dresser sat to the right of the door, the matching dark-stained desk and bookcase on the left next to the closet. On the nightstand, the same framed picture of her mugging for him and his camera before they left for senior prom. Her framed copy sat in a box shoved high on a shelf in her hall closet.

Señora Miranda rolled a black carry-on suitcase into the closet, then tugged the bifold door closed again.

Anamaría shut off the flood of useless memories. She had no time for foolishness.

"Okay, let's get you into bed." As soon as the unintentionally suggestive words left her mouth, Anamaría bit the inside of her lips, attempting to squelch an embarrassed curse.

"I don't remember you being this forward," Alejandro teased. He glanced at his bed, then back to her. Despite his lecherous smirk, his jaw muscles clenched, his discomfort obvious. Either at their awkward situation or due to his injury.

"Stop being a wiseass. Here, I can—"

"I've got it." The veracity of his words was negated by his sharp hiss of breath when he grasped his injured leg to lower it off the footrest.

"Are you done being a tough guy?" she berated. "Let me help you before you hurt yourself."

Señora Miranda stepped toward them, but Anamaría shook her head. If he was in as much pain as she surmised, he wouldn't be much help getting into bed. The last thing they needed was the older woman injuring her back trying to heft his weight.

"Wait a second," she ordered, reaching down to lower the footrest to make the transition easier. "Now, put your hands on my shoulders for support."

Bending her knees, she lowered to a half squat in front of his chair, his right knee in between her legs. She gritted her teeth, ignoring her pulse blipping at the anticipation of him touching her again.

Several seconds ticked by without Alejandro making a move to follow her instructions. Anamaría glanced at him from under her lashes.

A deep groove etched the space between his brows at his stubborn frown.

She huffed, then matched him scowl for scowl. "Look, I carried a two-hundred-pound dummy over my shoulder down two flights of stairs during drills yesterday. I think I can handle another dummy—"

"Fine," he grumbled.

Palms up, Anamaría crooked her fingers in a "come on" gesture at him. The sooner they got this over with, the better.

With a disgruntled sigh, Alejandro set his hands on her bare shoulders. One of his thumbs slipped under her tank top strap to slide against her skin. Warmth seeped into her chest, and she barely kept her eyes from fluttering closed.

"Now, using only your right leg and my shoulders, push yourself to a stand. Do *not* put any pressure on your left. Got it?" she ordered.

"I couldn't even if I wanted to," he muttered.

He shifted, then froze on a hiss. His fingers dug into her shoulders, disgruntled pain filling his black-coffee eyes. His piercing gaze darted to his mom, then back to Anamaría in a silent plea for her to not say anything. Keep the degree of his discomfort a secret from his mom.

Anamaría answered with a faint, affirmative tuck of her chin. "Okay . . . one. Two. Three."

His muffled groan punctuated the end of her count as he shifted his weight onto his right foot and bent forward. The muscle in his thigh flexed with the exertion and she grasped his waist to both steady and support him. The hard jut of his hip bones pressed into her palms, proof of his recent post-accident weight loss.

Hunched over, he pressed the side of his face against her temple, his breathing labored. The urge to hug him closer, give thanks that the idiot was actually safe, consumed her. This close, his woodsy, patchouli scent assailed her senses, setting her body tingling in places it had absolutely no business tingling.

Jaw clenched, she ignored the unwelcome reactions, focusing on the task at hand.

Together they shuffle-twisted toward the mattress in a move

that had them imitating two middle schoolers at their first dance, awkwardly holding each other at arm's length. Leaving room for the Holy Spirit between them, like the nuns at St. Mary's used to warn the students.

With his fingers still clenching her shoulders, she guided his hips, turning him so he could sit on the edge of his bed. Without impressionable little Lulu around to hear, Alejandro didn't bother whispering his curses as he pushed himself farther onto the mattress while Anamaría carefully held his injured leg aloft.

Señora Miranda slid several cushiony pillows beneath his knee, careful of the top Ilizarov ring. She hovered over her son, mumbling prayers and Spanish platitudes about her precious niñito's misery. Typical Cuban mami hovering, no matter her children's ages.

Seizing her window of opportunity, Anamaría put part one of her impromptu plan into action. "Señora Miranda, would you mind bringing Alejandro some water? It's important for him to stay hydrated."

"Ay, sí, I will get it right away. Anything else, nena?" his mom answered.

"Maybe a small snack. I'm sure he'll need to take his pain medicine soon. Right?" She directed the question to Alejandro.

Lips pinched with obvious discomfort, he nodded.

"¿Un sandwich de jamón y queso?" his mom asked.

"A ham and cheese sandwich would be great. Grilled, maybe?" Anamaría suggested, intent on getting his mom out of the room for as long as possible.

Not that Anamaría had any keen interest in being alone with him. But something wasn't right, and he'd made it clear he didn't want his mom to know.

As soon as the older woman left and the slap of her Kino sandals on the tile floor faded, Anamaría leveled a stern stare Alejandro's way.

"Truth. On a scale of one to ten, what's your pain level?"

"One," he grunted as he pushed his hands into the mattress and tried shifting his position on the bed. His sharp intake of breath and full-body wince belied his answer.

"Try again, and don't bullshit me. After what you've been through, this is no time to play he-man."

"I was always more of a Batman fan, remember? You know, dark and dangerous. Lots of toys to play with." His full lips twisted in what resembled more of a sneer than his cocky grin. The angles and planes of his haggard yet still remarkably handsome face taut with anguish.

Heaving a beleaguered sigh, Anamaría set her backpack on the low dresser.

"Look, cut the crap, okay? It's obvious neither one of us really wants to be here." Her back to him, she unzipped her bag, purposefully keeping her gaze away from the square mirror hanging on the eggshell-painted wall over the dresser. "Me, in this room. And you, anywhere on the entire island. But we can't change that, so don't make it any harder or more uncomfortable than it needs to be. Let me do my damn job and appease your mother, then we don't have to see each other again. Deal?"

The words sliced her throat like shards of her broken heart forcing their way up. Doggedly, she reminded herself of her vow to no longer allow a ghost from her past to haunt her present.

"You look good," he said, his voice gruff.

Her stupid heart tripped, then lurched into a higher gear. She clenched her fists, cursing the injustice of her reaction to his words.

Unwilling to let him see the effect his too little–too late declaration had on her, Anamaría ducked her head, pretending to search for something inside her backpack.

"Hate to be the bearer of bad news, but you look like death warmed over," she countered.

If death sported a week's worth of sexy scruff covering a square jaw and highlighting his angular cheeks and full lips, plus a head of thick black wavy hair, windblown and mussed in a carefree style some paid hundreds of dollars in hair product to achieve.

Not that she had noticed or anything.

Behind her, Alejandro gave a hoarse chuckle. The raspy sound sent an unwanted shiver of awareness skittering down her spine.

"What are you talking about? I just got off a cruise," he complained.

"Practically a stowaway. Leave it to you to hitch a ride on a cruise ship because you're not medically cleared to fly."

"Where there's a will, there's a way."

And he'd obviously had no will to return home until he'd been forced.

She'd known this already. Still, hearing his confirmation hurt. Not that she'd let him know.

Shoving aside her wallet inside her backpack, she grabbed the first-aid kit. "Well, unlike the rest of the passengers, you neglected to disembark with a relaxed smile and new tan lines. And that souvenir of yours . . . it kinda blows."

"I didn't bring this contraption on my leg home by choice," he mumbled. "Believe me, I've been better."

That made two of them.

A peek at his reflection in the mirror found him hunched forward, tracing a finger along the top Ilizarov ring.

"I'm wondering, is this is a new look or were you already going for gaunt and haggard before you went and slipped off that rock ledge while you were . . ." She set the kit and the bottle of sterile water on the dresser top. "Exactly what *were* you doing in the El Yunque National Forest, climbing up the side of a waterfall alone, anyway?"

When he didn't answer, she glanced in the mirror again, surprised to find him staring back at her.

Dark eyes hooded, he lay sprawled on top of the comforter, a white-and-navy-checked pillowcase covering the pillow tucked behind his back, matching the two under his knee. His lanky frame was too thin. His skin too sallow. And damn it, his magnetism too strong.

A couple months ago, his image on her cell phone screen had

appeared larger than life. Mimicking the photographs that made him a sought-after talent. Broad shoulders and chest evident under a formfitting gray tee tucked into a pair of black jogging pants cinched at the ankles. Muscular arms looped around a young guy on his left and a strikingly beautiful woman on his right, Alejandro shot a cocky, confident grin at whoever snapped the photo captioned "Ready to celebrate a successful shoot on location at El Morro, Viejo San Juan, Puerto Rico" followed by the camera and Puerto Rican flag emojis.

He didn't post pictures of himself very often. When he did, she occasionally allowed herself a glimpse. Or two. Nothing more.

Even then, she couldn't help noting the laugh lines radiating from the corners of his nearly black eyes. The faint grooves on either side of his mouth. Testaments to the laughter in his life. The joy he found wherever he was and in the people he spent time with.

The fact that she wasn't one of them shouldn't . . . couldn't . . . *didn't* bother her. Not anymore.

The mystery woman's infatuated expression as she gazed up at him meant nothing to Anamaría. Her life and his had been separate for a decade. No longer the inseparable duo their classmates, familia, and friends had dubbed them.

He kept himself busy off photographing the world. Making a name for himself. Cavorting with people from all walks of life— celebrities and up-and-comers, hardworking villagers and unsung heroes in communities across the globe.

She was the one who had stayed in place. Marking time without realizing it. Unable to fully commit to either of the two serious relationships she'd been involved in. Silencing her secret dreams for too long.

But she was done with that. Over the past two years, she'd put her dating life on hold to dive 110 percent into her business. Now *she* was going places, too.

"When I set off to explore El Yunque, it was not with this outcome in mind." He gestured at his leg.

"Accidents like yours rarely are. But I see them all the time on the job," she answered, relieved to return her focus to his injury. Not their broken past.

"The rainforest has been hit hard by hurricanes in recent years. I wanted to document some of the change."

Anamaría stepped toward the bed. "We've had some harsh years with hurricanes here in the Keys, too. Big Pine really took a beating from Hurricane Irma."

"Yeah, I saw video and images online." Alejandro shook his head in commiseration. "Thankfully, El Yunque's slowly coming back to life. When I finished my job in Puerto Rico, I stuck around for a bit before I was supposed to move on to Belize. That day, I planned an easy hike. Thinking I'd unwind to the coquís singing their high-pitched frog song from the trees. A cool mist on my face from the rush of water tumbling over the rocks. Then I spotted an iguaca."

"Huh? You mean, an iguana?"

"No, it's my tibia that's banged up, not my head." The corners of his wide mouth curved in a teasing grin she nearly found herself returning.

"An iguaca," he enunciated the word. "It's Taino for 'parrot.' Because of the efforts of those working at the Iguaca Aviary, the endangered Puerto Rican parrot population has started increasing. Still, you don't see many. And when you do . . ."

"You can't help but capture its photograph," she finished, knowing him almost as well as she knew herself. Or so she'd once thought.

The reminder was a sobering one.

His camera had been like an extension of his hands. Always there, somehow finding the perfect moment, a beautiful or moving image the average eye may have missed, but his never did.

"So, you were snapping pics of this endangered bird and decided you could fly off the edge of the waterfall along with it."

"Well, it wasn't quite—"

"Only, gravity had other ideas," she said, barely quelling the stark fear tightening her chest at the image of him toppling over the mottled gray and black rocks, his blood mingling with the water spilling off the jagged, slippery surface.

Driving an ambulance, she had witnessed her fair share of death and carnage, far too often the result of foolish thinking. She didn't have to rely on her imagination to conjure any number of potential accidents when a daredevil like Alejandro went hiking on his own. The idea of him or any of her loved ones being the victim on a call she responded to at the station made her blood run colder than the springs she'd once tubed down in Central Florida.

"Not quite," Alejandro countered. "I followed the parrot up a rock ledge I'd seen another hiker traverse. Actually got some incredible pictures of him in flight. A few other beauties with him perched on a tree limb." He arched an impudent brow, far too sexy for someone in need of a bath, a shave, and a fatten-me-up Cuban mami meal. "I was feeling pretty satisfied with my Spidey climbing talents. Right up until my damn foot slipped and my non-superhero status became clear."

A laugh bubbled up her throat at his self-deprecating grumble and perturbed grimace. Anamaría slapped a hand over her mouth to smother it.

"The only good thing was that I managed to save my camera from any damage." He cradled his hands to his chest as if protecting a priceless object.

Anamaría snorted in disbelief as she sat on the edge of his bed facing him, careful not to bump his leg. "So, your camera's fine, but your tibia shaft didn't fare nearly as well. Why does that not surprise me?"

"Hey, anything for the best shot." He spread his hands wide, his shoulders rising and falling with a shrug. "You know how it is. No pain, no gain."

"Uh-uh. That's my line as a fitness instructor," she countered. "Sounds much better when I say it."

"Depends on your perspective."

"And we've always had different ones." Coño, the jab slipped out before she could stop it.

Tension snapped in the air. The old accusation hung between them like overripe mangos left to rot on the branch.

"Forget I said that," she offered, raising a hand to stem any argument from him. "It does no one, least of all us, any good to go there. The past is . . ."

"The past," he completed her thought when she let her voice trail off.

Regret and the staunch determination to ignore it warred inside her, wounding her with each strike.

Alejandro's sober gaze ensnared hers. "I had no idea she called you. If I'd known what she was thinking, I would have—"

"Been unable to stop her," Anamaria interrupted. "She's a force of nature, that woman. Much like my mami."

"Dios mío, deliver me from meddling mamis. One of many things I don't miss about Key West." His head dropped back to thump against the wall behind him.

If she were a glutton for punishment, she'd ask what the other "many things" might be. But there was no need to confirm her place of honor on his undoubtedly long "don't miss" list. That fact had become cruelly apparent the second she'd found out about his marriage to some swimsuit model. Less than six months after his and Anamaría's final video chat.

Dios, she would never forget the day her mom had sat her down at the familia dinner table. Her mami's face shadowed with remorse. Brown eyes shiny with unshed tears. Her hands twisting with unease, afraid of how her baby girl would react.

The news of Alejandro's new wife had hit Anamaría like an unexpected backdraft, a whoosh of heated air and flames blowing over her. Incinerating her silly adolescent dreams and young love until they were nothing but a pile of smoke-tinged ashes.

Not that Alejandro needed to know how decimated his actions had left her. Or the errant choices she'd made in the ensuing years.

Her days of self-sabotage, of unwittingly falling into the trap of holding herself back, were over. She had her eyes on the future now. Not the past.

"Yeah, well, get used to that meddling and hovering," she warned him, scooting a little closer to peer at his injury. "If you're stuck here while you convalesce and get back on your feet, odds are that'll be at least a couple months. Longer if you're hardheaded and don't take care of yourself or follow your doctor's orders. Like I'm guessing you haven't been?"

His bland expression didn't fool her.

"Thought so," she muttered.

"Believe me, I'm not pleased about having to drop or postpone my bookings for the next few months. I should be enjoying Belize. Not cooped up here. And after my mother's move today, I am all for doing whatever it takes to speed up my recovery and get the hell out of here."

Of course he was. Leaving "the Rock" had always been his goal. She'd simply thought he meant to eventually return, and not by force.

Her mistake.

"That's news I'm sure your doctor will approve of." Opening the first-aid kit, Anamaría set a handful of cotton balls on the lid, adding medical tape and gauze to the supplies. "Let's see what we're dealing with. That way we can make sure you're back out there snapping the next Alejandro Miranda award-winning photograph as soon as possible."

"So, you heard about those . . . the awards?" he clarified when she tilted her head in confusion.

"Por favor." She rolled her eyes at his failed attempt at modesty. "The way news travels around this island? In our comunidad? Who didn't hear, whether they wanted to or not?"

He waved off her backhanded praise, but his lips curved in a cocky tilt she would have tickled into a howl of laughter in the past. Not today, though.

"I'm surprised they didn't hold a freaking parade," she went on. "Although it probably would have been awkward when the guest of honor didn't bother showing."

His playful grin dissolved. Lips pressed together in a tight line, he rubbed a hand at the scruff on his cheeks, looking oddly uncomfortable with the truth.

A sliver of guilt for her rudeness pricked her conscience. A bigger person would congratulate him on his success. Compliment his magazine covers, gush over the breath-taking, cinematic images he'd taken across the world.

She wanted to be that kind of ex. Given a little more time to get used to having him home, grudgingly, she might get there. Maybe. At least, she could pretend better.

Bending her head, she concentrated on an easier task, carefully removing the medical tape that attached a piece of gauze around one of the pin sites.

"How 'bout we try this again," she suggested. "Truthfully, how's your pain?"

A puff of warm breath teased the tendrils of hair that had escaped her ponytail as Alejandro blew out a weighty sigh. "Is there some kind of doctor-patient confidentiality? I have a rep to protect."

"Quit being a smartass," she grumbled, shooting him a droll glance before pulling back another piece of medical tape. "Come on, fess up or I can't help you properly."

"Fine. But my mom worries enough as it is, so whatever we don't have to tell her, let's keep it that way." He waited for her nod before continuing. "It's holding steady at a seven."

"That's not good."

"Ha! You're telling me," he grumbled, wincing when she gently palpated his skin around the top pin sites.

"Oh, believe me, I haven't even begun my bad patient lecture." And she planned to relish every word.

Ten minutes later, Señora Miranda had yet to return with Alejandro's snack. His mood had lightened, based on his irreverent quips, and Anamaría had finished cleaning each of the pin sites, relieved to find most of them healing well. One at the top of his shin was a little more tender than the others, not that his tough-guy act had let him admit it. She'd had to pester him for info. About that and his refusal to take stronger pain relievers.

"You have got to stay on top of your meds," she warned him. Not for the first time. Unfortunately, his hardheaded nature had failed to mellow with maturity. Reminding herself to stay in para-medic mode was all that kept her from throttling him in frustra-tion. "If you don't, you're only chasing the pain and the medicine won't be able to do its job. It's basic first aid one-oh-one."

"Has anyone told you, you have a remarkable bedside manner?"

"Stop it," she grumbled, fully aware his teasing was a diversion-ary tactic.

Head tipped back to rest against the wall again, he eyed her under hooded lids. "I'm sure everyone you help sends your boss glowing reviews. Am I right?"

"My Captain," she corrected with a reproachful glare. "And flattery won't stop me from lecturing you."

He flashed her another tired grin, this one tinged with chagrin because he knew he'd been caught.

"Or stop me from siccing your mom on you if necessary." So much for remaining impersonal.

Where was his mami anyway?

Anamaría would lay money on odds that the older woman was purposefully taking her time grilling that sandwich, intent on leaving them alone in the bedroom as long as possible. My, how times had changed. In many ways.

"Hey now, play fair," he complained, nudging her knee with his fingers.

Irritated by his ability to so easily fall back into the banter they had once shared, pecking away at her steadfast resolve to keep him at a distance, Anamaría tugged off her medical gloves with a snap. She dropped them along with the other trash in the plastic waste bag she had brought, then jerked the ends closed in a tight knot.

"I'm not playing," she argued, her frustration hitting its limit.

"This isn't funny. You didn't have to witness the palpable fear on your mom's face when she told us about your accident."

He blinked, clearly taken aback by her brusque tone. "Hey, I didn't mean—"

"You didn't hear the tremble in your abuela's voice when a group of us gathered at the Grotto after mass last Sunday to pray a healing rosary in your name." Anger spiked and Anamaría gave it free rein, slamming her first-aid kit shut. "Or try to answer Lulu's questions about why her 'buela was so sad."

"Okay, I get it."

"I don't think you do. You never have."

He reared back at her accusation, banging his head against the wall and wincing in pain when his left leg slipped off the pillow propping it up.

Remorse flooded through her.

"What the hell's that supposed to mean?" he ground out, pushing her hands away when she tried to help him readjust his position.

She should stop pushing.

Back away from this argument.

Leave before she said too much.

But the words she'd kept bottled inside flowed from her like water from a fire hydrant cranked open on the street. "It means, how do you think they felt that time you were nearly trampled by a bull in Spain? Or when you had that hang-gliding fiasco somewhere in South America?" She gripped the plastic kit tightly to keep herself from grabbing his shoulders and shaking some sense into him. "Or the moped accident in Thailand? Or, let me see, what else was there? Oh, the—"

"I said, I get it," he repeated, impatience hammering his words.

"Are you sure?" She jerked her head, punctuating her question, and her ponytail swished over her shoulder.

"Yes, I'm sure." Jaw tight, lips pressed in an angry line, he glared back at her.

"Do you really understand how your actions affect those who

love you?" Those who also longed for him to come home. A group she no longer belonged to. For her own good.

Her question hung between them, challenging him with its truth.

Several tense seconds later, his shoulders slackened. His dark eyes shifted, becoming deep pools of disappointment and . . . was that regret?

No. No way would she let herself fall for that.

"Yes, I do," he murmured. "Believe me, I understand how the people we love are often the ones who hurt us the most."

Wait, was that some kind of dig at her? Indignation burned deep in her chest, scalding her heart. Questions screeched like bitter banshees in her head. Crying out for answers.

Why, in all these years, had there been no effort on his part to make peace with his father?

Why had he walked away and never looked back? Then stayed away for so damn long?

Why hadn't she, their comunidad, their island, been enough as his home base? A safe port to drop anchor after his travels.

Why? Why? Why?

The question reverberated in her head, yet she refused to ask. Refused to care about the answers anymore. They didn't matter. Couldn't matter.

Alejandro laid a hand over one of hers. She flinched, surprise catching her breath. A rough callous on his palm scraped her skin, and prickles of awareness skittered up her forearm, arcing across her breasts.

"I didn't mean to cause them—*anyone*—any distress," he said.

His face pinched with contrition, he squeezed her hand as if willing her to believe him.

She tried. Part of her wanted to. But her sense of self-preservation wrapped around her like a force field, protecting her battered soul.

"I'm not the one you owe that apology to," she said. "You and I were done a long time ago. We've both moved on. But your familia, that's—"

"Ay, look at you two." Señora Miranda swept into the room carrying a serving tray with two plates and bottles of water. "It makes my heart so happy to see you together again."

Anamaría hopped off the bed as if she and Alejandro were still two teens, caught in the middle of something illicit.

"Mami, no te metas," he cautioned.

"Don't get in the middle of what?" His mother's wide-eyed expression telegraphed the opposite of innocence.

As Anamaría shoved her supplies inside her backpack, she caught Alejandro's resigned gaze in the mirror. They might not agree about the past, but it was obvious they agreed on one important point in the present: They were not happy about their mothers entertaining the idea that the two of them might reconnect.

That ship had sailed. And, like the famed *Atocha* Spanish galleon of centuries past, it had crashed against the Keys' ocean reef, sinking to the sandy depths. Buried in a watery grave. Only there was no sunken treasure to recover here. Despite the gleam in Señora Miranda's eyes.

"Come, I made you un san'wich, también, nena." She waved Anamaría over to the bed. "Your mamá told me that you met a client right after mass this morning, then came straight here. Tienes que tener hambre."

No, she wasn't hungry. More like frustrated. By his presence. By her inability to remain aloof. She didn't need to eat. What she needed was to get out of here.

And yet she couldn't be rude and refuse his mom's invitation. Based on the triumphant gleam in the older woman's eyes, Señora Miranda had counted on Anamaría's ingrained manners.

His mom patted the edge of Alejandro's bed, indicating Anamaría should sit.

He hitched a shoulder, the twist of his lips miming that there was no use arguing.

As she stared at the insistent mother and insufferable son, a flashbulb flicked on inside Anamaría's head, blinding her with clarity.

Dios mío, she might be in deeper trouble than she had anticipated. One meddling Cuban mami was hard to outwit. Two teaming up?

This called for reinforcements. As in, her brothers and their
partners.

First though, she'd have to finagle her way out of this impromptu, unwelcome lunch date with her hardheaded, sinfully
sexy, wanderlust-driven ex.

Chapter 3

Alejandro jolted awake with a start. The jerky motion jostled his leg, and a stab of pain shot from his tibia up his thigh.

Digging the heels of his palms into his eye sockets, he pressed against the headache pounding a sledgehammer in his head. *Fuck,* he felt like shit.

He scrubbed the sleep from his eyes, then squinted out his window. Based on the varying shades of orange and red streaking the purplish-blue sky above their neighbor's Spanish tiled roof, he'd been zonked out for several hours. Sunset neared. One of his favorite times of day to grab his camera and explore whatever city, town, or village he found himself inhabiting.

Thanks to his sucky luck, his exploring was curtailed for the time being.

Grumbling under his breath, he snatched the water bottle his mom had left on the nightstand earlier. His gaze caught on the prom night photograph of Anamaría. Hazel eyes laughing, lush lips spread in her wide, engaging smile, she quirked her finger in a come-here motion. Had it been a video, he would have heard her *get over here and kiss me; you know you wanna* right before he snapped the picture.

An order he had eagerly obeyed moments later.

The photograph was one of his favorites of her. One of countless images he'd never been able to delete from his computer. Or his memory.

Her love of life, the positivity she saw in almost everything, her desire to share that positivity making a real difference for others . . . they shone like an aura around her, drawing you inexorably to her.

His ego bruised, his heart battered by her admission that she didn't know when she'd be ready to follow him to Europe once her papi was better, he'd purposefully left the photograph behind the morning he'd headed to the airport. Convinced he didn't need her with him. Assuring himself he'd be fine on his own.

A month later, he'd printed himself a new copy. Wallet sized this time, so he could carry her with him wherever he went.

Once, he'd thrown it away in a drunken rage.

Then found himself digging in the trash for her photograph hours later.

Through his closed bedroom door, a familiar deep, rumbling voice carried down the hall from the living room.

Papi was home.

In a Pavlovian reaction, his stomach automatically twisted with years' old dread and misgivings. His hands fisted at his sides, anticipating their inevitable confrontation.

The last memories with his papi involved pointed barbs exchanged in anger. Emotion-fueled words thrown out, unable to be reeled back in. Worse, others left unsaid.

Guilt over his disgraceful part in their rift had kept Alejandro away. At first anyway.

Later, as the impasse widened, the thought of more rejection and recrimination from his father had silenced him.

A light tap sounded on the door.

The breath stalled in his chest, his apprehension rising. He didn't know what to expect from the man he'd only seen in the background of video chats with his mom. Their exchanges limited to inane platitudes like, *Doing okay, and you?* Never sharing anything meaningful.

Alejandro had giving up trying before he'd even left.

Now the man who had never understood him, and made it clear he didn't care to, waited on the other side of his bedroom door.

"Come in!" Alejandro called, clearing the scratch from his throat when his voice caught on the last word.

"¿Estás despierto, hijo?" His mami poked her head inside.

Relief melted the steely resolve keeping him upright and he sagged back against his pillows at this small reprieve from the anticipated disagreement. "Sí, I'm awake."

A benevolent smile curved her lips, deepening the crow's-feet around her eyes, as she pushed the door open and entered.

She had changed out of the rust-colored slacks and tan cotton blouse she'd worn when she and Ernesto had picked him up at the Miami port for the three-hour drive home. Now the sight of her plumping figure draped in a familiar bata lulled the nervous energy jittering up and down his torso.

God, he'd missed seeing her like this. Shuffling around in fluffy slippers and a short-sleeved housedress that hung to mid-shin. Its maroon material decorated with white lilies and greenery in one of the floral patterns she tended to prefer. A thin black headband held the sides of her chin-length brown bob away from her face, leaving the pearl stud earrings he'd sent for her birthday a couple years ago to wink a welcoming hola at him.

"Your papi arrived a few minutes ago," she told him. Her overly perky voice signaled her worry over the father-son reunion. Much like him. "He brought dinner home from the restaurant. ¿Tienes hambre?"

As if on cue, Alejandro's stomach growled loudly, answering her question. He pressed a hand to his belly and checked the time on his sport watch. Seven P.M. Of course. For as long as he could remember, Miranda's closed at 4:00 PM on Sundays, allowing employees the evening with their families before the week started again.

Papi usually brought food from the restaurant, so they could avoid going from the restaurant's kitchen to the one at home.

"Anamaría said you should eat with every pain pill. Even a little. Your papi brought your favorite, ropa vieja y congrí."

Just the mention of the shredded flank steak sautéed to perfection with onions, peppers, garlic, spices, and tomato sauce, with sliced green olives and capers sprinkled in for extra flavor, had Alejandro's mouth watering. Ropa vieja paired with congrí, the savory black beans and rice concoction cooked together in the same pot, had been, hands down, his go-to meal growing up.

He'd sampled the dish in five-star restaurants across the globe, but no one, not even a Michelin chef, could serve him a plate that made his taste buds sing like his papi's dish. Which was the same with pretty much anything Victor Miranda whipped up.

The man was a freaking whiz in the kitchen.

Like Alejandro when he held a camera in his hands.

Too bad his papi hadn't considered the two professions the same caliber back when Alejandro was starting out. Apparently still couldn't, based on his absence at Alejandro's last exhibit a couple years ago in Atlanta. Mami, Abuela, and Ernesto had made the trip. Papi had remained noticeably absent.

"The restaurant needs him," Alejandro's mother had explained.

Alejandro had shrugged off the excuse. They both knew the real reason his papi refused to acknowledge Alejandro's success.

"I appreciate the food, Mami, pero I'm tired from the trip," he told her. Truth, but also the coward's way of avoiding his dad. "Would you mind if I ate here instead of joining you in the dining room?"

His mami's hopeful smile dipped, the corners trembling before she rallied. "Of course, hijo. Anamaría said you should rest."

One of the litany of orders his ex had rattled off before racing out the door as if the hounds of hell, or more like two harpies resembling their matchmaking mothers, nipped at her heels.

He would have fled, too, given the opportunity.

"Gracias, Mami. Maybe I'll feel better enough to join you soon."

Shuffling quickly toward his bed, she sat on the edge and tightly grasped both of his hands with her smaller ones. "I know coming here is not what you wanted, hijo. And I wish your return home would not have been because of this." She tilted her head, indicating the RoboCop contraption encircling his injured leg. "But I have prayed for you to be here with us again."

"Mami, por favor," he warned.

The weight of her expectations. Hers, his abuela's . . . everyone's desire for him to relegate his passion to mere hobby status and prepare to take the reins of Miranda's. It was all like a heavy shroud hovering over him. Threatening to smother his dreams.

It had been like this since the first time he begged off a shift at the restaurant to take pictures during the annual powerboat races. Papi had scoffed, relegating Alejandro's photography to nothing more than a waste of time. Child's play when there were responsibilities to uphold.

"Talk to him, mijo. This is where you belong," his mom insisted now.

The sorrow etched on her slightly lined face brought the bitter taste of guilt to his tongue. The knowledge that the animosity between father and son hurt her as much as him made the situation even worse.

"I'm sorry, but I don't belong here." Tugging his hands free of hers, he clasped them on his lap and leaned back against the pillow behind him. Distancing himself from her disappointment. "I love you, Mami, but I can't be who you want me to be."

"Ay, Ale, I simply want you to be happy. It's what I pray for every day." Cupping his face with her hands, his mami leaned forward to place a kiss on his forehead. The tender gesture sent a pang of nostalgia through his chest.

"I *am* happy. I have a good life. I'm proud of the work I do," he assured her.

"We are, too."

Yeah, if by *we* she meant her and his abuela. Maybe Ernesto and Cece. Because his papi sure wasn't.

As if she could read his thoughts, his mami's shoulders rose and fell on a sad sigh he felt in his soul. She gave Alejandro's cheeks a gentle pat, then rose to leave.

Her slow, defeated steps reminded him why he should not have come. Part of why he had stayed away for so long. There was no mending the rift between him and his father. Being here only made things uncomfortable for the rest of his familia.

"Bueno," she said, pausing in the doorway without turning to look at him. "I will bring a tray with your food after I serve your father."

The door closed behind her and Alejandro jammed a fist into his mattress. Damn it, he'd known coming here would be a mistake.

There had to be another option. His gaze trailed around the room while his mind raced through different ideas. All of which he'd considered before boarding the cruise ship. None of which were plausible.

His attention caught on the empty shelf above his desk. His baseball trophies had once been proudly displayed there. Until the summer his dad had laid down his first ultimatum: baseball camp or photography. There was no time for both when Alejandro was needed at the restaurant. Aware of how much his father enjoyed sharing their love of the game together, hurt by the blatant disregard for Alejandro's burgeoning creative interest, he'd tossed his first barrage of artillery in their battle by quitting the high school varsity team.

Anamaría's younger brother, Enrique, who together with Alejandro had created the varsity's best double-play duo . . . Enrique at second and him at first base . . . had been dumbstruck by Alejandro's rash decision. She'd reacted with the same level of shock.

Alejandro had figured his papi would give in. Allow his son to choose his own path, learn to juggle his responsibilities while exploring photography more. But Victor Miranda wasn't one to back down. Neither was his firstborn son.

Scrubbing his hands over his face, Alejandro groaned with frustration as he tried to wipe away the hurtful memory. It'd been years since he thought about that summer. Or the slew of head-to-head battles against his old man that had come after, with collateral damage to those around them.

Like his mami and his abuela, who worried and prayed for the rift to mend. Even Ernesto, who hadn't understood Alejandro's need to get out from under their dad's archaic rule, had been caught in the crossfire, torn between staying close with his only brother and respecting their father. Eventually, with Alejandro out of the picture, Ernesto had stepped into the role of Miranda's successor. A role that didn't have Ernesto feeling like he'd been strapped into a straitjacket. Unlike Alejandro.

A sigh weighty with recrimination blew through his lips and he turned away from the unwanted memories this house, this room, evoked.

Outside his bedroom window, Mother Nature continued her nightly artwork. Peach and orange and purple streaks slowly melted away, leaving an inky blue sky. The end of his first day back on the Rock.

He'd made it through the gut-clenching reunion with Anamaría relatively unscathed. Without revealing how she still made his pulse race, his body perk up with need. Foolish as that may be. Her obvious closeness with his familia bugged the hell out of him. Reminded him with sharp clarity of her ultimate choice . . . familia over him.

One difficult first meeting down, one more to go. Tipping his head back, Alejandro stared up at the swirls of eggshell white paint on the ceiling. At least, he'd put off dealing with his dad until tomorrow.

The thought set a mental clock in motion ticking down the

hours, minutes, seconds until the next unavoidable detonation between them.

Another soft knock rapped on his door.

"Come in." He schooled his features, trying to summon what he hoped resembled a welcoming smile, to greet his mother. Only, when the door pushed open, it wasn't his mami on the other side.

Victor Miranda, his rotund figure stiff and unyielding, stood in the doorway carrying the same metal and wicker serving tray from lunch. A somber expression blanketed his round face and full jowls, deepening the grooves bracketing his mouth on either side of his thick mustache.

"Oh, hi, I wasn't ex-expecting you," Alejandro stammered.

Shit, this was not how he'd wanted his first confrontation—damn it, conversation—with his dad to go down. Him sitting like a lame duck in his childhood bed. His papi serving him the food he'd cooked at the restaurant Alejandro had turned his back on.

No, the restaurant he had denigrated *and then* turned his back on.

"Your mamá says you should eat something and take your medicine," his dad announced.

No *Hola, hijo, it's good to see you.*

No *It's been too long.*

No *I fucked up all those years ago.*

Of course, those same statements could be uttered by Alejandro himself. He could attempt to make amends. Only why bother when a negative response was a guarantee.

"Gracias." Alejandro reached to take the serving tray from his father, keeping his tone neutral and eye contact minimal. "I appreciate dinner."

His favorite meal no less. Was it a peace offering? Or merely the easiest leftovers to pack up after the kitchen closed?

"I was bringing something for your mom and abuela." His dad hitched a beefy shoulder in an it's-no-big-deal shrug. His black mustache drooped over the sober slant of his mouth, his craggy face telegraphing the indifference Alejandro had come to expect during the smattering of times they'd seen each other on video chat.

Alejandro dug into the ropa vieja, his eyes closing on an inner sigh of blissful satisfaction when the tangy taste of the shredded flank steak, its sauce teeming with the perfect combination of tomato, spices, and garlic, exploded on his tongue. A bite of congrí had the black beans and rice mixture adding to the taste buds party in his mouth.

His papi cleared his throat, and Alejandro's eyes opened to find his old man watching him, a suspicious scowl angling his brows. His mustache twitched, as if his mouth itched to say something but refrained.

"It's delicious," Alejandro offered.

"You need to eat more. You're too skinny."

The gruff command was more insult than caring observation. But it was spot-on. In the weeks since his accident, Alejandro's appetite had nose-dived. Thanks in large part to a combination of pain-induced nausea and a semi-depressive, feeling-sorry-for-himself state of mind. The result was the loss of ten pounds on an already-lanky frame.

He tapped his fork against the edge of the ceramic plate. "With food like this and a bum leg, I'll wind up gaining too much weight. Being out of shape is a liability in my line of work."

Arms crossed in front of his burly chest, Alejandro's papi's scowl deepened, his dark brows threatening to become a unibrow. "It seems to me that there are worse *liabilities* in this thing you insist on doing. Especially when you are not careful."

Subtext, *you are never careful.*

Why was it that every word his papi said about Alejandro's career held an undercurrent of disdain? Making it clear that nothing his older son did met with the man's approval.

Truth was, his papi would never be satisfied with him until Alejandro set aside his "silly" aspirations and worked a respectable, steady job. One his abuelo, who had risked much to send Alejandro's dad and his older brother to the United States in search of a better life during the Peter Pan Operation in the early 1960s, would be proud of.

Setting down his fork, Alejandro reached for his bottle of water to wash down the sour taste of reality coating his mouth. "Look, I don't want to fi—"

"Your mamá told me that Anamaría was here today." His dad dipped his head toward the external fixator rings encircling Alejandro's left shin. "To check your injury."

Alejandro nodded slowly, unsure where his father might be going with this unexpected turn in their awkward conversation. Leery of bringing Anamaría into their discord, Alejandro stayed quiet.

"Ella es una nena buena," his dad said, repeating himself when Alejandro stared back at him blankly. "She is a nice girl. Do not—"

"Actually, she's a woman now. A firefighter paramedic and small-business owner."

His father's eyes narrowed at the interruption.

Alejandro gave himself a mental smack on the back of his head. Why did he feel the need to bait the man by correcting him?

The question whispered through his brain as if his mom or Ernesto sat on the bed beside him, muttering the words in his ear.

"She is familia. She always will be. It does not matter that you—" His papi's words cut off abruptly, as if he couldn't even be bothered to spit them out.

"That I what?" Alejandro pressed, picking at the scab over a wound that had never, probably would never, healed. "Accepted a paid internship, then worked my ass off to earn a dream job? That I chose to be true to myself and what fulfills me?"

His papi lurched forward a step, hands fisted at his sides. "No, that you refused to fulfill your responsibility to your familia. Our name. To the legacy your abuelo gave his life for!"

The familiar accusations pelted Alejandro like stones thrown at a sinner. His father's dark eyes flashed with hostility and resentment. His nostrils flared with his chest-heaving breaths.

Tension sizzled in the air of the small bedroom.

"I don't want to have this argument with you again," Alejandro said, both his urge to fight and his appetite evaporating. "It does neither one of us any good. And it will only hurt them." He jabbed his fork toward the front of the house, indicating the rest of their familia.

His father huffed his disdain.

Several seconds ticked by, the gulf between them widening.

Finally, Alejandro's old man gave a curt, tight-jawed nod. The most he would acquiesce.

With a bone-weary sigh, Alejandro laid his fork across his half-eaten meal. He wiped his mouth with the neatly folded paper towel, then reached for the bottle of pain pills on the nightstand.

"Gracias por la comida." He nudged the tray, emphasizing his thanks for the meal. "I'm going to try and wash up, then get more sleep."

It was as close to a dismissal as he could make without disrespecting his father in his own home. Again.

"I agreed to you coming here because your mamá and abuela were sick with worry," his papi admitted, head high, shoulders stiff with pride. "But you will not cause them, or Anamaría, any more trouble while you are here. And you will not toy with her feelings again. ¿Entiendes?"

Oh, he understood, all right. As far as Victor Miranda was concerned, his elder son couldn't get the hell off this island fast enough.

The unfairness of the blame laid solely at his feet made Alejandro's blood boil with anger.

Why was he the bad guy when she was the one who had reneged on their plan to see the world, find their place in it, together? When he simply hadn't settled for a life he'd always made clear he didn't want to live? When he had followed his father's edict and stayed away from where he was no longer welcome.

But the questions remained unspoken. This was an old argument he would never win. Not with her. And never with his father.

"Look, I'm here only as long as I have to be." Alejandro popped two pills in his mouth, then washed them down with a gulp of water. "I don't plan on seeing Anamaría again. She's safe from me."

His father humphed and took the meal tray off Alejandro's lap, then strode from the room without another word. Not that there was anything left to say. His papi had made his feelings clear. He hadn't wanted Alejandro to return. There would be no fatted-calf celebration for this prodigal son.

Feeling like he'd aged fifteen years in the last fifteen minutes, Alejandro leaned back against the pillow behind him and closed his eyes.

First Anamaría, now his papi. What a fucking messed-up first day back.

At least he'd told his dad the truth. He had absolutely no intention of seeing Anamaría while he was here. Being around her stirred up too many emotions, too many what-ifs he preferred to ignore.

The only wrinkle in this plan would be whether or not their mothers stayed out of it. Then again, when had a determined Cuban mami ever stayed out of her children's business?

Shit. Alejandro thumped his head against the wall behind him. The answer to that question would be *never*, which did not bode well for his bid to recuperate in solitude.

Not. At. All.

Chapter 4

"So, nena, how was Alejandro when you saw him earlier today?" Anamaría's mom asked.

Seated across their familia's dinner table, Anamaría's younger brother laughed, turning it into a fake cough at her glare.

Her obvious annoyance didn't stop Enrique from rubbing his thumb against his fingertips, indicating she and her two older brothers would have to pay up as losers in their wager. Not a single plate was filled yet and already their mami had started henpecking about Alejandro's return. Anamaría had bet they'd make it half-way through the meal, at least until someone went in for seconds. Luis and Carlos had placed their money on dessert and during cleanup—like there'd been any chance at all their mom would wait that long. Ha!

Pay up, losers, Enrique mouthed, his eyes laughing at her.

She wrinkled her nose and was about to mouth, *Bite me,* when Sara leaned toward her on Anamaría's right.

"Ignore him. He's being infantile," Luis's fiancée advised.

"But you still love me," Enrique shot back with a cheeky wink.

"Not nearly as much as she loves me." Luis, Anamaría's closest sibling, older by barely a year, set his glass of water on the table so he could wrap his arm around Sara's pale shoulders. "Right, cariño?"

The endearment brought a pleased blush to Sara's cheeks. Luis hugged his fiancée closer. Sara laid her head on his shoulder and gazed adoringly up at him. Anamaría's brother's bronze skin and black, close-cropped hair were a striking difference to Sara's peachy coloring and wavy blond tresses, but the couple was a perfect match when it came to their temperaments.

The secretive half smile that had garnered Sara over half a million social media followers broadened into a pleased grin when Luis brushed a lock of hair off her forehead and dropped a kiss on her nose. She tipped her chin and he obliged, pressing his lips to hers.

Anamaría marveled at the change in her formerly sedate, guarded brother thanks to his relationship with the gregarious social media influencer who managed to pull him out of his shell. Bringing him back to the land of the living after he suffered a devastating loss years ago. One that had torn Luis and their younger brother apart. Until Sara.

Luis's life wasn't the only one changed thanks to Sara. With her soon-to-be sister-in-law as her business mentor, Anamaría's AM Fitness brand and online presence had grown exponentially over the past year. She'd taken Sara's advice and transferred it into hard work, garnering a sizeable increase in athletic-training clients, social media buzz, and, most recently, a potential agent.

"Bleh! Kissy-face mushy stuff!" little Ramón complained from the other end of the table. "My papi and mami do that all the time."

"And one day, you'll understand why, hijo." Seated next to the younger of his two sons, Anamaría's burly oldest brother, Carlos, ruffled Ramón's dark hair, then linked fingers with his wife, Gina, in between their dinner plates. The high school sweethearts exchanged an innocent peck on the lips, with Carlos adding a loud *muah* for special effect.

Their eight- and six-year-old sons' scrunched faces matched their loud groans of "Gross!"

Nudging her nephew José with her left elbow, Anamaría hunched closer with a conspiratorial grin. "At almost nine you think it's gross, but let's see how you feel when you're nineteen."

"That's so ooooold!" he whined, drawing laughter from the adults around their familia's table.

Anamaría chuckled as she grabbed the dish of oven-fried chicken Sara passed her. Dios mío, at nineteen she'd been—

Don't go there.

It did no good to think about that time.

Too bad the pesky memories of her nineteenth birthday wouldn't be deterred.

By the time that particular December fifteenth had rolled around, Alejandro had been gone nearly six months. Impressed by his work, the photographer had offered to make the temporary apprenticeship that had lured Alejandro away a permanent, paying job.

Alejandro was thriving in Europe . . . traveling and taking amazing pictures and learning more about his craft . . . living his dream.

The morning of her birthday, he called. As he had every birthday morning since she'd turned fourteen. Only this time they'd wound up fighting about her enrolling in spring classes instead of flying out to join him.

"I don't get it. What about coming out here?" he had asked.

"I just . . . I'm not ready yet," she hedged. "I can't go."

She broke off, that supersize tsunami wave of fear and doubt gaining momentum, crashing over her like it did every time she thought about leaving the island, her familia.

What if something happened to Papi or Mami, one of her brothers, or someone else she loved while she was away? God forbid they were gone before she made it home! She had lived that loss before when her abuelo suffered his fatal stroke during her eighth-grade trip to DC.

Papi's heart attack the week before her and Alejandro's high school graduation had unearthed the devastation she'd hidden after her grandfather's death. Faced with her mami's and abuela's gut-wrenching sorrow over the loss of their father and husband, she had buried her own. Nearly losing her papi had made it all come flooding back.

"I just . . . I need more time," she told Alejandro. "Caring for Papi over the summer, taking my health and nutrition class during the fall semester. They gave me a sense of purpose. I think I want to earn my EMT certification."

"Are you kidding—" His huff of frustration blew through the phone line. "And then what?"

"I'm not sure," she had admitted softly, torn and confused. She had stared at their prom picture on her nightstand. Missing him desperately. Afraid to leave when she felt so unsettled inside.

He was so sure about himself and what he wanted. While she . . . she'd felt lost. Like a boat unmoored in stormy waters.

"So, what are you saying? Are you considering fire college, like your brothers and dad?"

His words had been more accusation than question. An unfair reaction that had her throat tightening with unshed tears.

"I don't know. Maybe? I'd make a good paramedic. But I'm also enjoying experimenting with healthy recipes for Papi, so I might be interested in studying nutrition."

"Okay, can't you do that online, from here?"

But where would "here" be? He hopped around from photo shoot to photo shoot.

She was trying to find the right path for herself. Aimlessly following her globe-trotting boyfriend around like a groupie, without having some purpose in her own right, didn't feel like the right solution.

"Can't you come home for the holidays?" she had asked, hoping it would help them reconnect. "Then we can—"

"No. How can you even ask me that? You know what my father said. I'm not coming back. Not until he apologizes. You promised to come with me. Are you giving up on me, too?"

Dios mío, how his words had stung. The unfairness had fractured her tender heart.

Going away for the summer was one thing. That, bueno, that was an adventure.

Going away for good like he wanted? That was incomprehensible.

He'd been unfair. Changing the game plan by applying for the apprenticeship without telling anyone. Accepting without even discussing it with her.

Yes, the apprenticeship had proven fortuitous for Alejandro. She couldn't, wouldn't, begrudge him what had been the opportunity of a lifetime.

For her, though, things had been different. And he wouldn't or couldn't understand.

What should have been a happy birthday morning call had ended with their first big fight. Unknowingly, the beginning of a long, drawn out, agonizing end that had left her heart battered and bruised.

"Are you done?" José nudged the platter of chicken she held aloft, pulling her back to the present. The memory of Alejandro's terse disappointment as they hung up dissipated.

"Uh, yeah," she mumbled. "Here you go."

Her nephew took the platter, his skinny arms wobbling with the weight. On either side of him, her mom and Anamaría steadied it, waiting while the young boy grabbed a chicken leg. After serving herself, Anamaría's mom passed the dish off to Carlos.

"Elena tells me that Alejandro will be home for a few months recovering." Like a dog with a pernil bone, savoring the pork shoulder flavor and unwilling to let it go, Anamaría's mom swung the conversation back to her current favorite topic. "Is that right?"

"Probably," Anamaría answered.

"It was nice of you to go spend time with him today," her mom continued gnawing.

"I didn't spend time with him. I went because Señora Miranda was worried about infection setting in after his trip."

"¿Se ve bien?"

Reaching for the amarillos—happily noting that the sweet plantains had been sautéed with a mist of olive oil instead of the usual pan-fried technique, per her heart-healthy suggestion—Anamaría forked a few slices on her plate and played dumb. "Does who look good? Señora Miranda? You saw her just the other day."

"Ay, nena, don't be silly. I'm asking about Alejandro. How does he look? Handsome, I'm sure."

Anamaría swung her irritated gaze around the table at her knuckleheaded brothers. What happened to helping deflect their mami's anticipated Cuban Inquisition like they had all agreed in their sibling text thread?

Clueless Carlos was occupied scooping off some of the giant-sized pile of congrí little Ramón had served himself, with Gina rushing him before the mix of black beans and rice toppled off their youngest's plate. Enrique and her papi had their heads together, from the sounds of it swapping opinions about something that had gone down at one of the city's fire stations. Luis and Sara were still busy canoodling like teenagers.

So much for bailing her out if needed. Fine.

Experience cautioned her to say as little as possible during her mom's inquisition. Less chance of inadvertently mentioning something that could be misconstrued or used for ammunition later.

"Alejandro looks like a man foolish enough to climb up the side of a rocky waterfall, alone mind you, while chasing a silly bird. Only to slip and wind up breaking his tibia. Idiota."

"¡No seas mala!" her mom chided.

"I'm not being mean. You asked. I told the truth. The fool's lucky he didn't break his neck instead."

"¡Ay, nena, por favor!" Her mom made the sign of the cross, kissing her fingertips at the end. "I hope you did not put that idea in Elena's mind. She worries enough about ese nene."

"Only he's not a boy anymore. He's a grown-ass man—"

"Oye, what's with that kind of language at our familia mesa?" Her mami scowled over the plate of amarillos as she berated Anamaría for breaking one of their family table rules.

"Bottom line, Alejandro's an *adult* who should know better." She hoped her lecture earlier today made him think twice in the future. Then again, he'd always been hardheaded.

"Bueno, I think you should—"

"Abuela, will you give me some amarillos, please?" Ramón asked his grandmother.

Anamaría could have kissed her nephew for the interruption, especially since her siblings were useless. She'd have to treat the cutie to a sundae at Dairy Queen off White Street after baseball practice this week.

Too bad, her mami was a woman on a mission. Forking a few slices of sweet plantain, she plunked them on her younger grandson's dinner plate and went back to her henpecking. "I know Elena was comforted by your visit. You should stop by the Mirandas' tomorrow. Check on Alejandro again. It will put Elena at ease to know her son is healing properly."

Anamaría tucked her chin to hide the eye roll that would elicit another warning for bad manners. "Tomorrow's Monday; I'm sure the orthopedist he plans to follow up with here has office hours. Alejandro should see a doctor, not a paramedic, if he's concerned."

"Sí, that may be so," her mami pressed. "Pero sería más fácil si tú—"

"No, it would *not* be easier for me to do *anything* for him." Anamaría's harsh tone stopped the other conversations around them.

Coño, so much for keeping her cool and not giving any indication that Alejandro's return affected her one way or another. Her mami would pounce on the slightest whiff of perceived interest or emotional attachment on Anamaría's part. Like the meddling wasn't bad enough already.

From his place at the head of the table, Papi arched a thick black brow in question. He didn't voice a reprimand. He didn't have to. Anamaría could hear his usual "your mami means well" advice in her head. Words he calmly repeated whenever she complained during their weekly papi-hija dates over lunch, ice cream, or café con leche. A tradition that had started when she was in elementary school and still continued.

She hoped her current expression had him hearing her typical "but she's driving me crazy" grievance. When he answered with an almost imperceptible disappointed shake of his salt-and-pepper head, some of the fight drained out of her.

Across the table, Enrique straightened in his seat with an apologetic grimace. She evil-eyed him for not having her back like he had promised. But she was equally pissed at herself. They had all anticipated her mom's inquisition. Anamaría shouldn't have let her mami's nagging about Alejandro get her insides scrambled and her patience spread thin.

"Perdóname," she apologized. "I am not available tomorrow. My day's filled with classes and private training sessions. Plus, Sara and I are supposed to go over plans for our trip this weekend."

Beneath the table, Anamaría knocked knees with Sara, counting on Luis's fiancée to take the hint and jump in.

"Oh, yes!" Sara piped up. "My agent wants to meet with AM and there are some reps from an up-and-coming athletic wear company I'd like her to meet while we're in Manhattan. She'd be a perfect fit to promo their merchandise. There might even be the potential for her to do some travel as a spokesperson."

Ay, Dios, por favor. Anamaría closed her eyes as she whispered the prayer under her breath. "Please, God, let things pan out." Landing an agent and securing a sponsorship would propel AM Fitness to a higher level of exposure and networking.

"See, even if I wanted to, I don't have the time," Anamaría told her mother. "If Alejandro wants someone to check his pin sites, maybe Enrique can stop by."

"I'm on duty at the— Ow!" Her brother yelped when her sneaker connected with his shin. She glared at him, hoping mental telepathy was a real thing because right now she was cataloging the number of times she had covered for Enrique's ass when they were kids and he pulled some dumb stunt. Often involving Alejandro. Her brother owed her.

"But I'll give him a call. Let him know I'll swing by Tuesday morning when I get off shift," Enrique volunteered. "I need to tease his as—butt anyway. It'll be good to catch up."

"Gracias, Enrique." Their mom gave her youngest son a benevolent smile, then swept her penetrating gaze back to Anamaría. "Forgiveness . . . es una bendición, nena . . . sí, a true blessing. I give thanks every day that your brothers have reconciled."

In her peripheral vision, Anamaría caught Luis's water glass salute to Enrique, who answered with a ghost of his usually cheesy smirk. She agreed, it really was a blessing her brothers had finally healed the years' old rift between them. Luis had found the peace he deserved. And yet, with Enrique . . . the hollow expression on his *GQ* handsome face whenever the topic came up, like now, made it clear her younger brother still harbored some guilt over the tragic accident that had driven him and Luis apart. Only, he never talked about whatever weighed him down.

"Learn from your brothers. Forgive the past," her mami counseled. "I fear you will not be truly happy until you do."

Anamaría gazed into her mami's eyes, the admonition tempered by a mother's soulful desire for her child's happiness. Around them the others ate quietly, respectful of their matriarch's heartfelt admission. For several moments, the tinny clink of silverware against well-worn ceramic plates was the only sound in a room typically filled with boisterous conversation.

Little Ramón sent Anamaría a commiserating raised-brow, big-eyed, uh-oh look as he shoveled congrí into his mouth. Even at the age of six he could sense something serious going down and was probably relieved to not be the focus of his abuela's attention. Smart kid.

Anamaría shot him a playful wink, though the truth in her mami's words stung. Forgive and let the past go. Anamaría's desire to simultaneously hug Alejandro and punch him in the gut proved she hadn't succeeded in achieving either of her mom's suggestions. But she would.

Until then, admitting even the tiniest bit of attraction would be like waving a red flag in front of a bull, encouraging her mami's insistence on pushing Anamaría and Alejandro together.

No gracias. It had taken her long enough to recognize her own self-sabotage when it came to her love life. The last thing she needed was her mother's interference.

"I have moved on, Mami. You have to accept that. My only focus now is my business."

Sara placed a comforting hand on Anamaría's forearm, and she glanced up in time to catch Gina's thumbs-up. Their supportive gestures calmed Anamaría's bubbling anxiety. She had to give it up for her brothers. They might drive her crazy sometimes with their bonehead antics, but they sure knew how to pick fantastic sisters for her!

Being surrounded by her loving familia and reminding herself that her mami only wanted what was best for all her children tempered Anamaría's aggravation with the whole conversation. She didn't want to squabble over this . . . over him . . . anymore.

"Look, I wish Alejandro well, but that's all. Por favor, Mami, you need to let it be. Now, thanks to Sara's help"—Anamaría smiled her gratitude—"my dream of expanding AM Fitness, helping others develop healthier eating habits and get in better shape on a wider scale, is becoming a reality. That's enough for me right now. Estoy bien. Really, I'm good," she repeated when her mother's brows arched high with doubt.

Damn that Cuban mami radar that seemed to pick up on even the smallest of blips.

Anamaría reached for her glass of water, swallowing the truth. Good was not the same as great. Which she would be, soon. Especially when things really kicked off with AM Fitness and she was too busy to think about anything else. Like how messed up her personal life was.

But that personal life could not involve or be influenced by Alejandro anymore.

For his own sake, and the rest of his familia's, she hoped his return signaled a chance for him and his father to reach an understanding.

Alejandro being back in Key West for this short time had absolutely nothing to do with her. She planned to keep it that way. Her sights set on business, not her heart.

She hoped her mami understood and the matchmaking had come to an end. The problem was, experience told her that convincing her mother wouldn't be that easy.

"We'll see you at eleven on Thursday, Señora Gómez." Anamaría waved good-bye to the older woman who was on her way out of St. Mary's Fellowship Hall after Monday's seniors Zumba class.

"¡Sí! I will keep you in my prayers while you're on duty!" Señora Gómez made a sign of the cross, pressing a kiss to her fingertips at the end. Then, in a blur of aqua leggings and a bright yellow short-sleeved tee, the older lady headed out into the humid, late-April midday sun.

Several other regular attendees called out adios or good-bye or blessings after gathering their belongings from the tables pushed off to the side to create a makeshift workout floor in the center. One first-timer, a widow who had mentioned her recent move to Key West to live with her son's family after her husband's death, approached Anamaría.

"Are you sure there's no fee involved?" the older woman asked, pulling a light blue hand towel from the brightly patterned Lilly Pulitzer bag slung over her shoulder.

"Positive," Anamaría answered. "Father Miguel and I have agreed upon a flat rate for my teaching the class twice a week. I've been a parishioner here my whole life. Many of the ladies who attend have known me since I was in diapers. We're like family, and this gives me a chance to use my training to help others."

Over the woman's shoulder, Anamaría watched Señora Miranda stroll toward the kitchen and office area, the opposite direction of the door to the parking lot. Usually she hurried out after class, on her way to the restaurant where she helped her husband with Miranda's busy lunch shift.

"Perhaps a donation to the church then?" the newcomer suggested. She dabbed the sheen of perspiration on her pale forehead and cheeks, then pressed the hand towel to the area above her navy scoop-necked tee. "I must share, this past hour, meeting the other ladies and witnessing your positive energy, it's the most uplifting I've felt since . . ." Her voice faltered. A shadow fell over her face, deepening the lines tracing across her forehead. "Since my dear Harry passed."

Moved by the admission, Anamaría gave the woman's hand a reassuring squeeze. "I'm happy you've joined us then. Getting those endorphins flowing can improve your psyche; I promise. And most of the ladies who come are always looking for volunteers for one church committee or charity or another. There's no shortage of friends to be made and good deeds to keep you busy here at St. Mary's."

The woman's light gray eyes crinkled with her appreciative smile, lifting the cloud of sorrow from her features. "Thank you, dear. I do look forward to coming back on Thursday. Now, did I hear you say the class days change from week to week?"

Anamaría explained how the time always remained 11:00 A.M., but the days of the week varied depending on her shift at the fire station. She removed a blue folder from her backpack and handed a flyer with the AM Fitness April–June class calendar to the newcomer.

"Feel free to contact me with any questions. And please share the info with anyone who might be interested," she said. "I'm always looking for new clients who'd like some one-on-one diet and exercise assistance. Or who enjoy outdoor group workouts."

"I certainly will. My daughter-in-law's an elementary school teacher at Poinciana. I'll be sure to sing your praises to her and her friends."

"Much appreciated."

With a loose-fingered wave, the woman turned to leave, her white tennis shoes squeaking on the hall's cream-and-brown vinyl flooring.

As soon as the door closed, Anamaría began gathering her supplies from the six-foot folding picnic table pushed against the back wall. She slid the Bluetooth speaker that connected to the Zumba playlist on her phone into its protective Bubble Wrap sleeve, then placed the speaker inside her workout duffel along with a box of tissues and the stack of unused AM Fitness sweat towels she kept on hand for clients.

A quick glance at her Apple watch confirmed she had a little over an hour before she and Sara were scheduled to meet at Starbucks. Plenty of time—

"If our class keeps growing like this, we might have to ask about using the school gym."

Anamaría twisted around at Señora Miranda's comment.

Smiling her pleasure, Alejandro's mom strolled closer. A black headband tucked the sides of her brown bob away from her face, and she had changed from exercise leggings and a T-shirt into a pair of black pants and a red polo with the Miranda's logo stitched in black above her left breast.

"A crowded class is a good problem to have, verdad?" Anamaría replied.

"Yes, very true." Señora Miranda set her purse on the folding table next to Anamaría's duffel. "Gracias, again, for soothing an old woman's worries yesterday."

"It was nothing." Anamaría waved off the thanks, crossing to grab another tissue box from a table along the adjacent wall. "Anything to make you feel better."

"Por favor, I meant my mamá. I am not quite so old yet."

Relief ribboned its way through Anamaría at Alejandro's mom's exaggerated scandalized expression. On the drive from her home in Stock Island to Smathers Beach for her sunrise yoga class, she'd been running through her schedule for the day. Feeling guilty about refusing to check on Alejandro like her mother had suggested. Yet still certain the less time she spent with him, the better off she would be.

If luck was with her, after her familia dinner last night, the Cuban mami grapevine had been activated. With her mom passing along the info to Alejandro's that Anamaría had absolutely no interest in their matchmaking.

Still, she'd been prepared to sidestep any prodding or pushing Señora Miranda had in mind before class. To Anamaría's surprise, Alejandro's mami had kept mum about her son. Until now.

A girl had only so much luck, apparently.

"Bueno, I only wanted to say thank you, and remind you not to be a stranger." Alejandro's mom took the box of tissues and dropped it into Anamaría's duffel before zipping the bag closed and handing her the strap. "Stop by the restaurant soon. Victor has a surprise for you."

"A surprise?"

"Sí. He finally added your healthy suggestions to the permanent menu."

"What?" Anamaría froze in pleased shock, her excuse for avoiding Miranda's now that Alejandro had returned faltering at his mother's unexpected news. "Are you . . . they're no longer just an occasional addition to the daily special chalkboard?"

Señora Miranda shook her head, sending the curled ends of her brown bob brushing her red shirt collar.

Excitement flickered through Anamaría like Fourth of July sparklers. She'd been trying to convince Señor Miranda to consider permanently adding some of her healthy Cuban food recipes to the menu for a while now. A long while. To no avail.

"When did this happen?" she asked.

"Apparently yesterday, before dinner. Or else I would have

told you when you stopped by to check on Alejandro. We believe in you, nena. We always have." Señora Miranda's round cheeks plumped even more as her grin broadened. "You know how set my Victor is in his ways. But I was sure he would come around to your ideas eventually. It is good for business. And it is a way for us to support you. He even added your website address to the new menus."

"¿De veras?" she asked, nearly asking for a pinch to make sure this wasn't a dream.

Miranda's was on many must-try lists for Key West visitors. Having her website on the menu was fantastic free advertising.

"Sí, really."

Overwhelmed by Señor Miranda's gesture, Anamaría pressed a hand over her chest, where joy had her heart dancing a Zumba grapevine. She'd done it! She'd actually convinced one of the staunchest "tradition is tradition; there's no need for change" men she knew to add her healthy options to his long-standing menu. Victor Miranda's hardheadedness was legendary. Same as his elder son's.

But she also hadn't stopped trying to change the older man's mind. Unlike Alejandro.

"Like I said, we believe in you, nena." Señora Miranda spread her arms, inviting Anamaría in for a tight hug.

As they embraced, the familiar scent of the older woman's cinnamon and vanilla lotion wafted over Anamaría while her words echoed a hurtful memory.

How could you be like him. I thought you believed in me. In us.

Dios, how Alejandro's unfair accusation had hurt. She *had* believed in his talent. The same with his mother, abuela, and brother.

He was the one who had given up on all of them.

The close ties she had maintained with his entire familia, despite her hurtful breakup with their son and brother, spoke of their strong connection. She had never understood how Alejandro could walk away from his loved ones so easily. Only seeing his mother, abuela, and brother if they visited him. Or how he could risk severing those ties for good. As he'd done with his father. And her.

"I should be on my way now," Señora Miranda said. "But I know Victor would love for you to come by and sample something on your special menu. ¿Sí?"

"I will," Anamaría promised as she slipped on her backpack and hefted her duffel over a shoulder. "I'll try to go see him before I leave this weekend. If not, definitely early next week."

"¿Adónde vas?"

"Sara and I are going to New York. She's speaking at a social media influencer event on Saturday, and I'm planning to meet with her agent and do some networking."

"Good for you." Señora Miranda looped an arm through one of Anamaria's, giving it an encouraging squeeze. "But you are not thinking of moving up there, are you?"

Anamaría shook her head with a vehement no that sent her long braid swaying across her shoulder blades. "Not at all. Not even Miami holds any appeal to me. My home is here. Siempre."

"Always. I like the sound of that. And I'm sure your parents do, too. Bueno, I know you like to visit with Padre Miguel on your way out, but I must go help with the lunch rush. Dios te bendiga, nena." Alejandro's mom leaned closer to exchange cheek kisses, and Anamaría returned the familiar "God bless you" farewell.

She stayed in the doorway, waving good-bye as the woman who'd always been like a second mother to her pulled her gray sedan out of the parking lot onto Windsor Lane before turning onto Truman Avenue.

After locking the Fellowship Hall door, Anamaría did a quick merengue step and fist pump in celebration. Señor Miranda had finally . . . fiiiiiinally . . . changed his mind!

The Miranda patriarch was not a man easily swayed. Victor's unyielding temperament had benefitted him during his rise from a humble home catering business entrepreneur to a well-known and respected local business owner. Master chef of the restaurant created in the image of the one his father had built in Havana. Miranda's was Victor's homage to the memory of the father who, like many parents in Cuba when Castro took over, had given up much to provide his children with a better future. That same strong will that made him a success was in large part why the older man remained at odds with Alejandro. Both equally as proud and obstinate.

And yet he had changed his mind. The fact that Miranda's now listed *her* recipes on their rarely altered, traditional menu was a huge coup for her.

Walking on a cloud nine of epic proportions, Anamaría made her way to the basilica.

Fifteen minutes later, after stopping to chat with Father Miguel, Anamaría set her duffel inside the back of her Honda Pilot and closed the hatch. Squinting under the bright midday sun, she opened the driver's side door and was greeted by the trill of a cell phone ringing.

She slid behind the steering wheel and dug her hand in the side pocket of her backpack before it fully registered that the music wasn't actually her ringtone. Strange. The high-pitched notes continued, and she twisted to give the empty back seat a quick glance. The music trilled on, coming from the open trunk area.

Climbing out of her SUV, she made her way to the rear.

By the time she lifted the hatch, the music had stopped. A light breeze cooled the sheen of perspiration on her brow as she perused the regular contents in her trunk. A basket of rolled yoga mats, another with aqua-colored foam yoga blocks, a battery-powered jump starter and air compressor for roadside emergencies. She grabbed her duffel to check underneath it, and the music started up again. As she slid the bag closer, the music volume increased.

What the hell?

Unzipping her duffel, she found a cell phone in a black protective case, its screen illuminated, wedged between a stack of towels. The words *Victor Miranda—ICE* flashed across the tiny screen.

Her stomach nose-dived.

The only person she knew who would have Victor Miranda as her "in case of emergency" contact would be . . .

No freaking way.

Anamaría slid her finger across the phone's screen to answer, already suspecting the person on the other end. "Hello, Señora Miranda?"

"Ay, nena, I am *so* happy to hear your voice." Señora Miranda breathed a huge sigh through the speaker. "Gracias a Dios my phone is safe with you."

"Yes, I have it." Ironically enough. Or maybe not.

Anamaría pulled the cell away from her ear, glancing from it to her unzipped duffel, wondering how the device could have gotten inside. Then she remembered Señora Miranda taking the tissue box from her and putting it inside Anamaría's bag. Probably along with the cell phone.

Bemused, she shook her head as she brought the phone back to her ear. "I'm about to leave the church. Do you want me to drop it off at Miranda's for you?"

"Actually, Victor needs me to run a few errands. Would you do me a favor and drop my phone by the house? I will swing by later."

"You don't need it now? I can meet you—"

"No, no, that's okay. It would be better if you leave it there."

Where she would run into Alejandro.

Surprised, and yet somehow not so surprised, by Señora Miranda's blatant maneuvering, Anamaría plopped down on her SUV's black bumper. She twisted the hair at the end of her long braid around a finger, contemplating whether or not the mamis would actually stoop this low. The meddling would never go to this bizarre extreme, would it?

"¿Hola, Anamaría, estás ahí?"

"Yeah, I'm still here." Unsure whether she wanted to tip her imaginary cap at the inventive idea or shake her fist at the brazenness.

In the background she heard the usual cacophony of raised voices in the restaurant's kitchen, Victor's deep bass carrying over everyone else's.

"I have to go, nena," Señora Miranda said. "Thank you for dropping off my phone. Te lo agradezco."

Oh, she might appreciate it all right, but what Anamaría would appreciate was the trickery coming to a stop.

The call disconnected and Anamaría sat there, scratching her head in disbelief. Clearly telling her own mother that her and her best friend's plan to rekindle a romance between their two children was a fruitless idea had not worked.

Some way or another Anamaría had to make that message clear.

As much as she didn't want to think of them as being on the same side, she and Alejandro might have to come up with their own plan for putting a stop to their moms' matchmaking.

If not, for the next few months they'd both be dodging annoying parental meddling like this.

Stomping back to the driver's side door, Anamaría plopped down on her seat and cranked the car's engine. She'd return Señora Miranda's phone, but instead of the anticipated happy reunion, she'd see about brokering a truce with Alejandro long enough to get their mamis off their backs.

Chapter 5

"Whatcha doing, Tío Ale?" Lulu pedaled her pink tricycle up to Alejandro's wheelchair under the covered back patio at his parents' house. She craned her neck to look at the iPad resting on his lap.

"Sorting through pictures from a photo shoot I did for a magazine."

"Wif lelephants?"

He grinned, charmed by her toddler speak. "Yep, with elephants."

Eyes as dark as his and wide with wonder, she pointed a pudgy finger at the screen where a picture of a baby elephant played on the muddy banks of a slowly trickling river. Lulu placed her small hand on his thigh and pressed closer, her mouth open in a cute "oh" of surprise. Thankfully, she'd ridden up on his right side, away from his injured leg.

Alejandro slid one arm around her back, welcoming her. He angled the iPad, giving her a better view of the screen. "I was in South Africa, taking pictures at an elephant sanctuary."

Lulu scrunched her face in confusion. "¿Qué es eso?"

"It's a place where they take care of elephants when they're hurt out in the wild. Or, if their mamá is ki—" He broke off.

Shit, he didn't want to make her cry or scare her by talking about dead mothers and poachers.

"If their mamis can't be with them," he hedged. "Then, the caregivers release them into the wild again when the elephants grow up or get better."

"Like Anamawía wif you?"

Alejandro blinked in surprise at the guileless question. "Um, well . . ."

Damn, out of the mouths of babes. Lulu was probably talking about his injury. However, Anamaría *had* kind of released him into the wild when they graduated from high school and she'd opted not to join him.

Similar to the released elephants who never forgot their caregivers, he'd never been able to forget her.

And he had tried. Damn, how he had tried.

Packing his schedule with every gig imaginable on the guise of gaining experience. Working crazy long hours. Carousing until late into the night and early morning. Staring at the bottom of far too many bottles. Hell, he'd even tried an ill-fated, short-lived marriage to a woman who eventually recognized the truth when he didn't.

She would never have his heart. It wasn't his to give.

Problem was, the one who actually possessed it had laid anchor somewhere he would never, *could* never, call home again.

The tense exchange last night with his father had solidified Alejandro's conviction that the two of them could not live in Key West. Their perspectives were diametrically opposed. Always had been. Always would be. Alejandro leaving again was better for everyone, especially the rest of his familia, who would forever be caught between his father and him.

Lulu set her little chin on the wheelchair's padded armrest, gazing up at him with innocent eyes. All chubby cheeked, eyelashes naturally thick and long in a look many models paid money to emulate, her pink lips curved in a sweet smile . . . his niece was a heartbreaker, all right. Ernesto would have his hands full when Lulu hit adolescence.

Kinda strange to think . . . she'd be the first of the next generation of Mirandas walking the halls of Key West High. Following in Ernesto's and his footsteps.

Nostalgia for the moments missed tightened his chest, and Alejandro found himself imagining being here to witness the antics his precocious niece might try to pull. Along with wistful thoughts came the daunting reality of actually being responsible for an impressionable teen. Talk about stressful responsibility.

Remembering some of the stunts he had gotten away with, and those he hadn't, alongside Anamaría and her brothers made him shudder. Carlos, the jokester, had already graduated and been connected at the hip with Gina by the time Alejandro and other Navarros reached high school, but occasionally he joined the melee. Back then saintly Luis had tried to be the voice of reason, with Enrique usually egging them on to cross the line and Anamaría balancing out the two. Alejandro joined the fray, practically considered another sibling.

Until that memorable July Fourth weekend, the summer before their sophomore year, when he and Anamaría had shared their first kiss. Unable to ignore his growing feelings, he'd been a lovesick fool hoping he'd been correctly reading her signs of interest. After that, the two of them had started spending more one-on-one time together. Much to her brothers' dismay and both of their mothers' elation.

"Anamawía tooked cares of your big owie, huh?" Lulu's question drew his attention back to the present. She pointed at his left leg, resting on the elevated footrest, and shook her head. "No Band-Aids anymores."

"You're right." He combed his fingers through her brown curls, marveling at their baby softness. "It's getting better."

Now that he was done traveling, the bandages had been removed and the pin sites were left to air out. The whole contraption reminded him of an X-Men experiment gone awry with its four metal rings spanning his shin and the K-wires poking into his skin, in one side and out the other, keeping the pieces of his tibia in place until the bone healed. Only his X-men rendition lacked the cool factor of Wolverine's claws. Instead he was more like Professor X, stuck in a chair but without the mental telepathy power.

What he wouldn't give to know what had been going on inside Anamaría's head yesterday. If seeing him again had caused the same deluge of pleasurable and troublesome memories to rain down on her.

"Can I sees more lelephants?" Lulu touched the iPad screen. Like many kids these days, she already knew that sliding her finger across the glass would scroll to the next picture.

Now an adult elephant joined the baby in the river. A stream of water shot from her extended trunk in a glistening shower that sparkled in the sunlight and left ripples undulating across the river's surface.

"A mamá lelephant!" Lulu exclaimed. She lunged closer, and her tricycle tipped over.

"Whoa!"

He lunged to his right to grab her. The armrest jabbed his ribs as he wrapped his arm around her waist, catching her before she fell. A jolt of pain shot up his left leg at the jerky motion. The bike clattered to the cement floor. Its handlebars with their pink rubber grip twisted, leaving one jutting up in the air like the front wheel.

"Uh-oh." One hand clinging to his armrest, the other splayed on his bare right knee, Lulu gazed up at him with wide dark eyes. "I awmost felled."

Her serious expression made him chuckle. Thankfully, since he had dutifully followed Anamaría's advice and taken his medicine as prescribed, the discomfort in his shin dulled to an ache.

"Here, let's see if you can get up here to look at the pictures. Careful, though, okay?"

Lulu nodded solemnly.

He handed his iPad to his niece, then grasped her under the armpits and lifted her up onto his lap with her legs and white sneaker–clad feet dangling to the right. She fluffed the skirt of her floral sundress with one hand while holding the tablet with the other. The bright pink material was a splash of color against his black basketball shorts and gray T-shirt. A shot of welcome color in the dreariness of his current situation.

She wiggled a few times, snuggling her warm body into his chest as she made herself comfortable, and he found himself amazed by how easy it was for a child to worm her way into a person's heart.

"You good?" he asked, ducking his head to peer at her face.

"Sí," she answered, already scrolling through the pictures in his most recent *National Geographic* folder. "Ooh, pretty!"

A stunning South African sunset filled the tablet screen. Blurring brushstrokes of varying shades of orange and red filled the darkening purplish sky above rolling plateaus on the famous Garden Route. Having grown up taking pictures of the breathtaking Key West sunsets, he'd always found himself snapping a sunset pic at least once during his travels, no matter where he went.

Seldom did the resulting photograph compare to those he'd taken at home. But he kept searching for the place that would eventually usurp Key West as his favorite. There had to be somewhere for him.

Lulu continued scrolling until she reached the last picture in the file. "More, por favor."

Alejandro obliged, closing that file and opening the one from his stay on a wildlife reserve following his shoot at the elephant sanctuary. He'd spent a month assisting the team with their conservation efforts, including monitoring the Big Five.

His niece oohed over the series of lion cubs wrestling and aahed when she spotted the leopard cub napping with its mother. She asked him the name of the big gray animal with a spiky horn, bumbling the pronunciation of *rhinoceros* with her toddler jargon.

Alejandro answered her questions while his gaze traveled the familiar setting of his childhood backyard. The bougainvillea vines climbing the privacy fence were thicker. The flamboyán tree with its orange-red flowers spread its branches taller and wider, still a great spot for candid shots of a particular dark-haired beauty who'd been his first model. Not that he'd be taking any more of her.

The grassy area where he and Ernesto had played football and tossed a baseball back and forth felt smaller, though he knew it was he who had changed, not the yard's size. The wicker patio furniture where he and the Navarros hung out was different, the old set damaged by either a hurricane or the usual wear and tear of a humidity-laden climate with frequent rainy weather.

The rumble of cars driving down Laird Street in front of the house and nearby Bertha Street around the corner melded with the occasional puttering of mopeds creating a familiar white noise from his childhood. A bird squawked from the flamboyán, and another answered from the flowering geiger tree in the Morales yard next door, and a musical conversation ensued.

Absently, he wondered if the Morales familia were still their neighbors. Or if, like many other Conchs born and raised on the island, they had left behind the rising cost of living and ventured to the Central Florida area. Their girls had been younger than Ernesto but had to be at least college age by now. Grown up while he'd been gone.

A light breeze lifted the afternoon's humidity and carried a hint of the salty ocean and seaweed draped shore less than a mile away. Overhead, the rhythmic whirr of the ceiling fan created a lulling effect that soothed his tension. His eyelids grew heavy, but he blinked away the tiredness. Hell, he'd already slept more in the past two-plus weeks than he had in ages.

Lulu stopped scrolling. Her hand plopped on to the iPad screen at the same time her body went slack in his lap. Her head lolled against the front of his shoulder, and he realized his niece had fallen asleep. Alejandro had no idea if she was on some kind of schedule and this was her regular nap time or not. That would be his luck to throw the kid off her routine, mess things up for Cece, who was at a doctor's appointment and might welcome a nap when she returned. His poor sister-in-law had looked like she was ready to pop. Though her due date was supposedly still three or four weeks away.

Glancing at his watch, he realized it was almost twelve. His abuela should have called Lulu in for lunch already. Unless Abuela had dozed off while watching her telenovela in the living room.

Having adopted a "when in Rome" mentality over the course of his travels, a habit that taught him a respectful appreciation for different cultures and traditions, Alejandro figured it wouldn't hurt to join his abuela and niece in a siesta. One of the many customs he welcomed when spending time in Spain.

Resting his cheek on top of Lulu's head, he let his eyes drift shut. His body needed to heal. His mind needed a break from the onslaught of unwanted memories and thoughts of mistakes made. A short nap in the backyard where he'd once hung out with his closest friends, with the blessing of his cute niece in his arms and his medicine working its magic, sounded like a solid plan.

As was often the case when his defenses were down, his last thought before sleep claimed him was of that same dark-haired beauty with a long braid, a beguiling grin, and a beauty mark on her chin begging for his kiss.

The screech of the sliding glass door rubbing against the metal grate roused Alejandro from his nap. Straightening in the wheelchair, he rubbed at the crick in his neck and blinked, squinting against the bright sun.

Lulu shifted in his lap, murmuring in her sleep. Instinctively he cradled his niece's limp body tighter in his arms and hunched over to press a kiss to the top of her head. He glanced at the back door, a smile for his grandmother on his lips. His friendly greeting wobbled when Anamaría stepped over the threshold instead.

"Hey, sleepyhead," she said softly.

Her lips curved in an inviting grin, she moved toward him, her long braid swinging behind her. His ultimate fantasy come to life.

Dressed in another pair of figure-hugging black leggings, this time paired with a white and black AM Fitness tank over a bright pink exercise bra, the color complementing her white and pink Nikes, she was on her way either to or from a workout. Lucky clients.

He pushed the inane sentiment away. Jealous thoughts about her never led him to healthy mental places.

"She's out like a light," he murmured, gently rubbing his hand up and down the baby-soft skin on Lulu's arm.

"She wasn't the only one," Anamaría teased.

The humorous glint in her hazel eyes, especially after her abrupt departure yesterday, was a welcome surprise, and he couldn't resist joining her banter. "Oh, my abuela's asleep inside, too?"

"Ha!" Anamaría's lips curved with her husky laugh.

Lust raced through him. It gained momentum as he thought about the number of times over the years he had imagined kissing those lips. Nuzzling his nose along her smooth jawline to blow a heated breath in her ear. A move she had readily admitted turned her on. The urge to find out if it still did pulsed through him.

As if she somehow divined the illicit path his thoughts had veered down, the open expression on Anamaría's tanned face slipped. Her gaze skittered away to the wide back lawn. But not before he caught the confusion puckering her brow, stealing away the carefree smile she'd offered him moments ago.

"How is your leg today?" she asked, her tone suddenly all business. No pleasure. "Any discomfort with that top pin site?"

He shook his head. "It's fine. Better now that I'm staying on top of the meds."

"Good. If you want to dial those back, I recommend talking to your orthopedic doc first. Maybe the physical therapist."

She strolled a few feet away to lean a shoulder against one

of the wooden support beams for the patio's slanted roof. Arms crossed, she eyed him dispassionately before swiveling to face the backyard.

So different from the last time they'd sat out here together. Him on the love seat; her on his lap, arms lazily looped around his neck. Ernesto and Enrique cracking jokes from their deck chairs. Luis, already working for the city fire department by then, shaking his head at their younger brothers' foolishness. All of them laughing and swatting away mosquitos as dusk descended, loath to go inside where their parents chatted after a shared familia dinner a couple weeks before graduation.

"Is your first PT appointment still Wednesday?" Anamaría asked, firmly entrenched in paramedic mode. Proof she wasn't currently wrestling with the same useless nostalgic meanderings.

"Yeah. Midmorning. They confirmed via text earlier."

"Who's your at-home physical therapist?"

"I don't remember." He waved a hand at the sliding glass door, careful not to jostle Lulu but frustrated by this inane conversation. "It's written down on a notepad inside. Doesn't matter."

"Make sure you follow their instructions. And like I said, definitely take your pills before—"

"Got it."

"Good. Because if you don't—"

"I'll be hating life even more than I do right now." As if that were possible.

She tucked her chin, one haughty brow arched as if she were scolding a recalcitrant patient. "You'll be swearing up a storm, paying for that tough-guy mentality your entire PT session. And after. Count on it."

"Yes, Captain." Fingers pressed together, he tapped his hand near his temple in a mock salute.

"Don't be a smartass," she warned, an edge creeping into her voice.

Good. Anything was better than her bland indifference.

Oh, he knew he shouldn't needle her. Hell, she'd gone out of her way to allay his mom's overboard concern yesterday. And that was more than likely the only reason Anamaría was back for another visit today.

Still, her apathy was almost fucking worse than the silence that had divided them all these years. In his current state, there was no way for him to avoid the recalcitrant doubts and regrets about her . . . about them, his familia.

Usually he'd get lost in the challenge of a job, of capturing the perfect photograph. The one that spoke of whatever inspiring story he sought to share through his work. Behind his camera he could forget about everything else, *everyone* else, except whatever or whoever he eyed through his lens.

Being back here brought far too many memories crashing over him like a storm-driven wave on the protected coral reef. Making it impossible for him to continue ignoring what he and Anamaría once had together. How her decision to not join him in pursuing the dream they'd woven together had blasted them apart.

Lulu mumbled in her sleep, shifting to burrow her face in Alejandro's chest. His iPad slid off her lap, and he grabbed ahold of it, tucking the tablet between his hip and the side of the wheelchair. Gently, he rubbed a hand up and down her back and shushed her back to sleep.

"So, what do you think of her?" Anamaría asked, surprising him with the personal question. "I know you haven't spent much time with Lulu since she was born."

Only those few days early last year when Ernesto, Cece, and Lulu had flown to Atlanta for a long weekend.

"She's changed so much," he admitted, scooping up one of her white sneakers in his palm. "She was just over a year when I met her. Stumbling around like a giraffe calf on wobbly legs. Freaking me out about her getting hurt 'cuz my town house is far from babyproof."

Anamaría chuckled, the sound like the light brush of her fingertips along his nape. Goosebumps shimmied down his neck, sweeping across his shoulders and spine.

Ignoring the unwanted sensation, he focused on his niece, gently finger-combing her soft curls. "Now she's riding a tricycle and talking in full sentences. It's . . . it's pretty amazing."

"They do grow up fast." A warm smile curved Anamaría's lips as she gazed at Lulu.

The fact that she had witnessed many of the momentous stages of his niece's young life while he'd been basically banished, relying on social media and video chats, smarted. Another reminder that he was an outsider in his childhood home.

"It's the same with Carlos and Gina's two boys, José and Ramón. Those little rascals are getting so big," she mused.

"Named for your father, huh?"

"Yeah, you should have seen his face when Carlos and Gina told him." Anamaría pressed a hand to her chest, her gaze lost in some memory that didn't include him. "Two of the rare times I've seen my papi tear up."

Alejandro understood why. Carlos and Gina's decision showed their deep respect for the Navarro patriarch. A man beloved by his familia, fellow firefighters, and many of the island's residents.

Unlike, say, the unforgivable lack of respect his dad felt Alejandro had shown by refusing to work at Miranda's. A living legacy of his grandfather. The man who, during the summer of 1962, sent his two sons from Cuba to the United States as part of the Peter Pan Operation. Two of the fourteen thousand–plus children whose parents had willingly said good-bye to them when Castro's regime took power, thinking they would all be reunited shortly. For many families who participated in *Operación Pedro Pan*, that reunion wound up taking years. For some, like Victor's father, it never came at all.

To Alejandro's dad, the success of Miranda's stood as a tribute to the man who had sacrificed so his familia could live their dreams of freedom and prosperity. Alejandro identified with that desire. The dream for more. For something different. Only in his own way. Something he wanted to believe his abuelo would have blessed had he survived to immigrate with his familia to the United States.

However, Alejandro's father did not agree. In Victor Miranda's mind, his elder son's actions proved him to be ungrateful. Selfish. As if Alejandro considered himself too good to work in a kitchen. Which couldn't be further from the truth.

It was ironic, actually. Alejandro and his father had both been sent away. One with a blessing, the other with a curse.

Anamaría had never truly grasped the finality of Alejandro's last argument with his dad. In part because she hadn't heard the steel conviction in his dad's threat. But also because she had never felt the slap of disdain from the man she idolized.

Her papi had always been her champion. As had her brothers. Growing up, she'd been their princesa. Granted, one who also threw a mean left hook and cursed the machismo common in their culture. But protected all the same. She and her papi shared a unique bond. One Alejandro had often secretly envied, but also one he knew had fed her fears after her dad's heart attack.

"How has your dad been?" Alejandro asked, remembering those difficult days following Señor Navarro's emergency surgery.

Anamaría hesitated, as if she sensed the two of them tiptoeing near the touchy subject of her decision to stay behind. She fingered the strands at the end of her long braid. A familiar, sometimes nervous, sometimes thoughtful gesture he remembered. The fact that he could no longer gauge which pricked his already-battered heart.

"He still hates being relegated to a desk, and Mami keeps trying to get him to retire. I think they'd both go crazy if he was home all the time."

"No one likes it when they're benched." Alejandro tapped an armrest with a fist, knowing all too well how her dad must feel.

She nodded. "Especially not someone who's spent his life running toward danger when most are running away."

The thought of her as one of those brave firefighters, putting *herself* in harm's way, filled Alejandro with admiration. And fear. Back in high school, she was always volunteering for service projects, so he had expected her to find some way to serve others no matter where the two of them settled. But she had never expressed interest in following in her father's and older brothers' footsteps. Until she had taken an active role in her papi's recovery.

"It's good to hear he's well," Alejandro said. *Really* good. The loss of the Navarro patriarch would have hit many in their community hard. Especially both of their familias.

"Thanks," Anamaría murmured. "I'm just glad he hasn't given us another scare."

Her gaze met his, and for a moment, Alejandro found himself transported back to the afternoon he'd gotten the call about Señor Navarro's heart attack. The fear hammering his heart as he and his parents raced to the hospital. The devastation on Anamaría's tear-streaked face when he arrived. The weight of her body as she collapsed in his arms, sobbing uncontrollably.

Thankfully, Señor Navarro had survived. Looking back, though, that day, without Alejandro realizing it, had been the beginning of the end for his dreams with Anamaría.

A bird squawked in the flamboyán tree and Anamaría swiveled on the support post toward the sound, breaking their connection to each other and the past.

"Everyone's doing well, gracias a Dios. Mami's—" She huffed out a laugh and tipped her head toward the sliding glass door. "A lot like yours. Still trying to keep us all on her leash. I know she does it out of love, but it drives my brothers and me crazy."

"Man, I get the third degree over the phone every time I call," he grumbled. "I've learned not to video chat when I'm shooting in rough locations."

Anamaría glanced over her shoulder with interest, but she didn't prod him to elaborate. Good. He didn't want to talk about his work. The less he brought her into his present-day world, the less he'd wish he could pick up the phone and share with her when he was off on his own again.

"How about the others?" he asked, bringing the conversation back to her familia. "It's been a while since Enrique and I touched base. I know Carlos and Gina have two kids; what about Luis?"

She grinned. That open, charismatic smile he now only saw in pictures. Damn if the real deal didn't pack a powerful wallop.

"Luis is still a saint. Annoying but true." She hitched a shoulder playfully. "He recently got engaged. Sara's amazing; love her already. And Enrique's . . . the best I can say is he's still Enrique. Pushing the extremes. At work and at play. Letting his artistic talents go to waste, if you ask me. I think he plans to stop by tomorrow after his shift."

Two old friends catching up. That's how anyone listening in might describe their conversation.

And yet unspoken questions they avoided asking each other lay in the murky abyss separating them. Mostly because they remained at an impasse.

She wanted what he couldn't give her. Stability, a home here on their island.

He wanted what she refused to consider. A life of their own outside of familia obligations, on their own terms.

The futility of picking at the scabs covering these old wounds, knowing no good would come of it and they'd wind up having to restart the healing process, alone, all over again, grated on raw nerves.

"Why are you here?" he blurted.

Anamaría's head drew back at his rudeness.

"Like you said, Enrique's dropping by tomorrow," Alejandro went on. "There's no need for you to play doctor with me."

She glared at his word choice. "I don't play when it comes to patients."

"I'm not your patient. You shouldn't feel obligated to check up on me," he argued, irritated that she did. It was the only reason she would be here.

Hip cocked, arms crossed defiantly, Anamaría scowled. "Believe me, any obligation I feel is not to you."

The harsh words pelted him. Despite his knowing he deserved them for baiting her, they still wounded. Worse, her animosity did little to cool his pent-up desire to taste her lips again rather than argue.

A move that would most certainly earn him a swift knee to the balls if he tried.

Not that he could while stuck in this damn wheelchair. Nor was he pathetic enough to make a fool out of himself by doing so anyway.

"Which brings me to a problem that we need to address. Apparently, your mom has upped her game." Anamaría's braid swung over her shoulder as she tossed an annoyed glance at the sliding glass door. "Moving beyond the typical verbal guilt trip and engaging in flat-out subterfuge."

Grasping the wheels on his chair, Alejandro maneuvered himself around sharply.

The move jostled Lulu, and she grumbled in her sleep, rubbing her nose on his T-shirt.

He shushed her with a few gentle pats, before lowering his voice to a harsh whisper as he glared at Anamaría. "What the hell has my mother done now?"

Chapter 6

Fifteen minutes ago when she had knocked on the Mirandas' front door, Anamaría had told herself to hand Señora Miranda's phone over to Alejandro's abuela and leave, then send out an SOS to her brothers for advice on how to disabuse both mothers of their over-the-top matchmaking shenanigans.

But after they exchanged hello cheek kisses, Alejandro's abuela had practically dragged her inside. Seconds later, Anamaría found herself being pushed toward the enclosed lanai leading to the back patio.

"Lulu will be very disappointed if you don't go see her," Abuela Julia insisted.

Guilt trips . . . had to be a skill Cuban mamis learned during pregnancy. And mastered throughout their kids' lives.

One look at the determined glint in the older woman's eyes and Anamaría caved. A little Lulu hug to brighten her day, a polite *take care of yourself* to Alejandro, and she'd be on her way.

Only she had peeked through the sliding glass door and discovered the two of them napping. Alejandro's lanky frame hunched over his niece. His arms wrapped around Lulu's tiny body in a protective embrace. Their dark heads and bronze skin tones so similar, they could easily be mistaken for father and daughter.

It wasn't a leap for her to wonder, if she and Alejandro had stayed together, would they have a precious little girl or boy of their own by now? Maybe two?

Dangerous territory for a woman who'd recently admitted to herself that she had subconsciously allowed their breakup and the ease with which he had moved on from her to negatively impact every other romantic relationship she'd had since.

"¡Vete, nena! Go say hello." From her seat on the living room sofa in front of her telenovela, Alejandro's abuela shooed Ana-maría out back.

Without a good excuse to avoid doing so, she had tugged open the sliding glass door and ventured into the turbulent waters of what might have been.

She may have let her guard down a little while talking about her family, but his rudeness reminded her there was no need to bother being polite, especially when they were alone and didn't have to pretend.

"What happened?" Alejandro asked, his voice pitched low to avoid waking Lulu, who had settled back to sleep on his lap after his initial outburst. Drool dribbled from a corner of her slightly open mouth, leaving a misshapen dark spot on his gray tee.

"Somehow her cell phone wound up conveniently in my gym bag after Zumba."

"What?" His dumbfounded expression matched her initial re-action to finding the cell earlier.

"I know, crazy, right?" She shook her head, bemused, though also miffed. "Then she called it from the restaurant, acting all surprised when I answered, only to ask if I didn't mind dropping the phone off here. Where, of course, your abuela insisted I come out back to say hello."

Alejandro jabbed a hand through his hair, mussing the black waves. She couldn't help noticing that he had shaved this morning. The devil-may-care scruff was gone from his cheeks and angular jaw, giving him a clean cut vibe that belied the reckless glint in his eyes. The dark circles shadowing under his eyes yesterday had lightened. Maybe, thanks to the pain meds she had insisted he take as prescribed, he'd finally been able to get a decent night's rest.

Men and their tough-guy bullshit. She saw it every day on the job.

"Are you kidding me?" he asked.

"Nope. Convenient, right?" she added, bobbing her head yes at his wide-eyed shock.

"No shit," he grumbled. "I mean, it's kinda genius. If it didn't involve us," he quickly added when she balked. "Un-fucking-believable."

He grimaced and cupped a hand over Lulu's ear, like the little girl could hear him curse while she slept. Anamaría smirked as she spun away to pace out her frustration.

"Believe it. I've tried being frank with my mom," she told him. "Last night during familia dinner, I—"

"You still do that?"

His question took her by surprise and she spun around before reaching the end of the patio's cement slab. Familia dinner had always been a Navarro tradition. One night a week, all of them sat down to break bread together. No excuses.

"Mm-hmm. The night fluctuates week to week now that we're all with the fire department. But none of us work green shift, so that helps," she answered.

There'd been a time when he had a reserved seat at their table. Now her older nephew filled the spot beside her.

A wistful glimmer shone in Alejandro's eyes. She told herself to ignore the answering pang in her chest and resumed her pacing back in his direction.

Alejandro's throat worked with a swallow. "That's . . . that's good to hear. Those dinners were always sacred to your mom. I think about them every now and then."

Struck by his admission, she sucked in a shaky breath and drew to another stop. "They still are. Anyway, um, at dinner yesterday I told Mami they need to quit with the matchmaking and meddling. It's a waste of their time. And ours. I figured she'd pass that message onto your mom and they'd back off. Based on this latest maneuver, that doesn't seem to be happening."

"This is crazy," he grumbled, grabbing the right armrest and planting his sneaker on the floor to lift his hips and shift his position.

The wheelchair creaked in protest and Lulu stirred, drawing Alejandro's attention. Somehow in his attempt to shield her while he found a comfortable position in the chair, his left foot slipped off the plate holding it aloft. His heel dropped onto the cement slab and he yelped in pain.

Anamaría rushed over, pushing Lulu's overturned tricycle out of the way to hunker down at his side. "You okay?"

"Yeah," he grunted, waving her off, but his pinched features had her scrambling around the front of the chair to inspect the metal rings and pins.

The muscles in his jaw tightened, Alejandro tucked Lulu closer to his chest with his right arm while he rubbed his left thigh and knee with the other hand.

"Don't play superhero. If there's something hurting, keeping it to yourself can lead to problems later," Anamaría warned.

He scowled, either still fighting his discomfort or annoyed with her for lecturing. Probably both. "I'll keep that in mind, when I talk to my *doctor.*"

"Wiseas—"

"Anamawía, guess what?" Lulu's sleepy question interrupted their verbal sparring.

Alejandro hunched forward to look at his niece at the same time Anamaría leaned in with a smile for the little cutie. With Anamaría crouched in front of the wheelchair, her face wound up mere inches from his. This close, she caught a whiff of Alejandro's woodsy cologne, its undertones of patchouli and citrus blending in an enticing aroma that was different, richer, than what he'd used as a teen. A tiny red scratch from his razor blade marred his tanned skin where his jawbone curved. In the past she would have teased him for rushing, then kissed it better.

The warmth of his exhale caressed her lips, and she couldn't stop her gaze from trailing to his mouth. Desire curled through her.

It had been so long since she'd felt his lips against hers. Tasted what she thought was the sweet promise of a future together. The night before he'd left for Spain, when the two of them had stood on the canal seawall in her parents' backyard and held each other. They had shared their last kiss then, though neither had known it at the time.

Ultimately, she had stayed behind. Confused. Unsure. Pining for him. Yet convinced she needed to find herself.

He'd gone off to a new life, easily rebounding after their breakup with that quickie wedding to a swimsuit model he met on a shoot. She had consoled herself by privately dubbing the marriage a total cliché.

As if his betrayal was fresh, hot anger bubbled in her chest, rising to burn its way up her throat. She drew back in her crouch, intent on distancing herself from him and the insanity of craving his kiss once more. The abrupt motion made her lose her balance, and she grabbed the wheelchair's armrest to avoid falling on her ass.

"Wait!" Lulu's tiny fingers circled Anamaría's wrist. "I wanna showed you sumping. Tío Ale's got lelephants on here."

The tyke dug out a slim, supersize iPad from between Alejandro's hip and the side of the wheelchair. Her tiny pointer finger tapped the screen. It came to life with a gorgeous photograph of a giraffe casually munching on tree leaves in a field of tall, wispy, dry grass. The animal with its distinctive spotted coat stood in partial shadow, the setting sun's rays spreading in radiant reddish-orange rays across the darkening sky and horizon.

Before Anamaría could fully appreciate the image, Lulu slid her finger across the screen. A treasure trove of pictures scrolled by until Lulu stopped on one.

"See. Lelephants. A mami and her bebé."

Anamaría gasped softly, awed by the stunning image of a mother elephant bent protectively over her offspring, their trunks tangling together. Another elephant bathed in the distance, a blurred figure that blended with the muted colors of the muddy riverbank and a looming rock formation. The play of light and shadow created by the sun's rays peeking over a far-off plateau and the camera angle chosen gave the image an ethereal quality. One that spoke of Alejandro's magical artistry. His ability to find beauty in the world, capturing it with breath-taking photographs that came to life.

"Pretty, huh?" Lulu asked.

Anamaría bobbed her head. A mixture of pride and sadness clogged her throat, making it impossible for her to speak. He was good. Like, really *really* good. It made it impossible for her to begrudge him for following his dream. For loving it more than he had loved her. Especially when his talent allowed him to share the stunning way he viewed the world with others.

"If you like this one, I can frame a copy for your bedroom," Alejandro offered his niece.

"Sí, p'ease." Lulu's toddler speak had him chuckling, their shared smile sweet, but hard to watch when it evoked unwanted what-ifs in Anamaría's heart.

There'd been a time when her room could have served as an Alejandro Miranda photograph exhibit. One on the wall over her bed. Another on her nightstand. A third keeping watch on her desk. Each taken at their favorite spots around Key West. Astro City across from Higgs Beach, the site of their first kiss with July Fourth fireworks illuminating the night sky above them. Sunset off Snipes Point on her papi's boat, the *Salvación*. One of her taken here, in his familia's backyard, laughing at some joke they had shared, the flamboyán tree a blur of fiery red behind her. He'd captured her staring directly at the camera. Her expression brimming with love and joy for the young man who evoked those emotions in her.

Until that had no longer been the truth.

Now all those photos were in a box in the back of her closet. And she . . . she did not need to be here, derailing her hard-earned professional momentum because a ghost from her past had suddenly decided to come back and haunt her.

"That picture will look great in your room, Lulu." Pushing off her knees, Anamaría rose from her haunches. "I should be going."

"Hey!" Alejandro reached for her hand, their fingers lacing together.

An electric current zigzagged up her wrist, into her arm. Anamaría stared down at their joined hands, despising the conflicting emotions rioting inside her.

"Don't let the moms stress you out," he said. "I'll talk to mine. Remind her that my stay here is temporary. My dad's already made it clear I'm not wanted here. She knows that. Besides, I've got jobs booked later in the year and I'm waiting to hear back on one I'm really excited about."

Of course, he was already planning his escape. Because his life was out there. Not here.

"And you"—he jiggled their joined hands—"I've seen your social media reach expanding. Which should translate to an uptick in clients and your business expanding. Neither one of us needs our family getting in our way, trying to stop us. They need to back the hell off."

He was right. Even though well-intentioned, the meddling was obnoxious. Their moms' warped way of showing how much they cared.

But he was also wrong: their moms weren't trying to stop her, or him, from succeeding. They only wanted—

"Wait, you follow me?" Her surprised question slipped out unbidden.

Alejandro blinked, a guilty expression chasing across his handsome face. "I . . . peek at your social media feed. Once in a while." He cleared his throat, his frown deepening. "And may have sampled a recipe, or two, from your website."

"Oh really?" The idea that maybe he hadn't been able to completely forget, the satisfaction his admission gave her, felt good.

Petty maybe, but definitely gratifying.

It made the years she had wasted settling for *mostly* happy feel not quite as one-sided.

Because until her cousin Vanessa's beachside tequila-fueled enough-is-enough speech during a girls' weekend in Miami two years ago, that's exactly how Anamaría had been living. Clocking in and out of the fire station alongside her brothers and Papi. Relegating AM Fitness to a side hustle she dreamed about growing but never did. Dating a few guys, kind of.

Empty margarita glass high in the air like a tipsy bikini-clad Lady Liberty on the shores of South Beach, Vanessa had laid out her ultimatums for Anamaría's new start in life.

Time to stop spinning her wheels and set up her website, post her videos, grow her damn business instead of simply paying it lip service.

Stop dating the wrong men. Like Henry, the sailor, destined to ship out after his tour of duty at the naval base. And Edgardo, the firefighter from Miami, biding his time in Key West until he landed a job with a station closer to his home, which he eventually did. Both were men who would inevitably leave her, as she cursed them for doing.

Alejandro released her fingers and rubbed at his now-smooth jaw. "To be honest, my mom mentioned that you were showing her how to use Instagram a while back, and I started checking out your feed. Then I hopped onto your YouTube channel. You've got something good going, AM. Smart play off your nickname for your business. I'm happy for you."

Not happy enough to send her a simple DM to say congrats. Although, who's to say she would have responded to a direct message from him. But she might have . . . what?

She didn't need praise from him. Now she buoyed herself. Or relied on her familia, who would never walk away from her.

Even when Luis and Enrique had been at odds with each other

for years after everything with Luis's ex, her brothers had never cut ties completely. Not that their mother would have allowed it.

Yeah, familia she could count on.

Love and men? Not so much.

"Tengo hambre," Lulu announced, setting the iPad on her lap and rubbing a hand over her tummy.

"You know what, chiquita? Me too. Why don't we raid the kitchen and see how we can fill your belly, huh?" Alejandro tickled her round stomach and Lulu squealed with glee. He barked with laughter, the deep timbre a foil for the little girl's high-pitched giggle.

Anamaría tore her gaze from the heartwarming play. Joining their fun, letting her guard down with Alejandro, would be like snipping off a piece of the fuchsia bougainvillea vines trailing along the backyard privacy wall. Beautiful, but if she tried to hold on to it, she'd wind up pricking her fingers on the sharp thorns.

"Do you, uh, you wanna eat with us?"

Anamaría's eyes fluttered closed at Alejandro's hesitant invitation. She knew she'd enjoy their company, but . . . "I need to be go—"

The sliding glass door rumbled open and she broke off.

"Lunch is on the table for everyone," Señora Miranda announced, all smiles and sunshine. No sign of guilt for her sneaky maneuver. "Come, let's eat together."

"Yay! I hung'y, 'Buela!" Lulu tucked the iPad back along Alejandro's hip, then wiggled to slide off his lap. She hop-skipped over to her abuela, who held out a hand for her precious granddaughter. Together the pair disappeared inside, leaving Anamaría and Alejandro alone.

"You don't have to stay," Alejandro said. "We can't let our mothers ride roughshod over us. At least, I don't intend to let that happen. And I definitely don't intend on letting mine disrupt either of our lives with her meddlesome plotting."

Anamaría stepped closer and dropped her voice, not putting it past Señora Miranda to eavesdrop. "Complaining about it hasn't seemed to work. You got any other ideas?"

"Like?" His baffled frown told her he remained clueless.

Great. She heaved a frustrated sigh and strode to the patio edge farthest from the sliding glass door and potentially prying eyes. "I haven't quite figured it out yet. But I do know, I am not up for surprises and forced meet-ups like this."

She didn't have the time or energy . . . or the heart, not that she'd admit that last one . . . to worry about thinking one step ahead of their moms. If she even could.

"I don't know how you put up with this all the time," he muttered, rolling his chair closer and stopping at her side.

"They mean well." Something her father reminded her of often.

"Doesn't feel like it. The nosiness and butting into your business. Always thinking they know what's best, the—"

"Caring about you?" Her annoyance swung like a heavy pendulum from their meddling moms to him and his rudeness. "Que ingrato."

"Pfff, ingrate?" he scoffed. "What? Because I don't like being manipulated?"

"No, because you're being a jerk about it."

"Look, you deal with your mom your way. I'll take care of mine." Palming the large tires, he spun his chair around, then pushed himself away.

Nuh-uh. He was not going to run away like he'd done before. Lunging forward, she latched on to one of the handgrips, dragging him to a halt.

"What the hell?" He twisted in his seat and swatted at her hand.

Anamaría held on tighter. "Don't be an ass and go hurting your mom's feelings. As bothersome as their hovering might be, it's their way of saying they want us to be happy."

"No, they want what they *think* will make us happy! But even if they can't or won't face the truth, you and I have." He eyed her with resentment, then muttered a curse and twisted around to plop back in his chair. "You made your choice clear years ago."

Outrage at his unfair accusation exploded inside her like an emergency flare shot in the air and she saw red.

"Are you seriously putting this all on me?" she ground out.

Pulse pounding in a bongo beat that freed the anger and disillusion she had long harbored, Anamaría circled his chair to stand in front of him, hands fisted on her hips.

Their breakup had been excruciating and drawn out. Months in the making. Precipitated by decisions he had made on his own.

She had spent those months praying he'd change his mind about never coming back. That he'd make amends with his father.

Alejandro had expected that she would drop her classes, leave her familia, and simply follow him. Without a real plan for herself.

Eventually, they had started allowing the silences between them to grow longer. The number of days between calls stretched. And then, like the quiet closing of a book that had come to an end, they finished with a vapid *We can't keep doing this* from her and a trite *It's not working anymore* from him.

She'd been forced to throw in the towel first because he hadn't been man enough to admit he was distancing himself from her. From everyone. Hell, he'd even stopped calling Enrique, and they'd been as close as brothers.

"You may not comprehend this," she ground out. "The hovering, the annoying over-protective behavior. I'd take all of that from my parents and brothers any day of the week over not having them in my life at all. You didn't get that back then. And it's apparent you're still clueless now."

Alejandro's lips pressed into a hard line. He stared at her, his chest rising, then falling with a deep breath before he finally spoke in a gravel-rough voice. "I didn't expect you to give them up. But I didn't expect you to give up on *me*, either."

She heaved a resigned sigh, dropping her head back to glare at the wispy clouds in the pale blue sky. Irritated at the universe in general and her ex in particular over this rehash of their last few arguments.

"Ale, you applied for and accepted a full-time, six-month internship without talking to me about it." She held her hands out as if laying their cards on the table, wanting him to finally give her a good reason for playing his so close to his chest and keeping everything a secret. His original flimsy excuse of thinking his news would be a welcome surprise didn't suffice. "Our summer trip turned into something indefinite and you expected me to be okay with that."

"You said you wanted adventure."

"Yes, along with a home. Here. Those two didn't . . . don't have to be mutually exclusive."

"They do for me. My father made that clear. Then, and now." The finality in his voice stifled her rebuttal.

His gaze slid past her to the sliding glass door, then down at his injured leg. She recognized the anguish of a son rejected by his father. Something Ale's ego would never allow him to admit.

Frustrated by the futility of their circular argument and the reality that more than ten years had passed without a damn thing changing, Anamaría turned away from him with a muttered curse.

A moped horn beeped somewhere nearby, startling a little yellow bird that squawked and flew out from between the flaming red petals of the flamboyán tree. A male voice called out, "Adiós!" and the moped's engine sputtered, then gained intensity as the driver accelerated away. Unknowingly fleeing the tense silence in their neighbor's backyard.

"AM, I don't want to fight with you anymore."

Alejandro's softly spoken confession whispered over her like a light breeze blowing in off the ocean. Refreshing, though momentary before the heavy humidity, much like their problems, descended again.

She peeked at him from the corner of her eye. Skeptical.

"I only plan on being here for a couple months. I don't want to spend that time upset with my mom, or my abuela. Or you, for that matter." He dipped his head and gestured toward her, palm up, sincerity in his dark eyes and broody expression.

Her breath caught with surprise at what sounded almost like a peace offering.

Could she do more than pretend she had moved on? Forgive and forget like her mami had advised?

Maybe. If he didn't start acting like a selfish ass again. And if she kept her heart completely out of the equation.

"Fine," she muttered. "I accept your apology."

"I didn—"

"Look, Sara and I are heading to New York this weekend. She's speaking at a conference. I'm meeting with her agent about representation and a potential sponsorship opportunity," Anamaría elaborated when Alejandro arched a brow in question. "If you and I are lucky, Enrique will pull some idiotic stunt while I'm gone and my mami will have her hands full with that. Leaving us . . . me . . . alone."

She hitched a shoulder and tilted her head with a half shrug. "That's our best option right now."

Ale nodded. "When E comes by tomorrow, I'll see if I can convince him to be the fall guy this time."

"My baby brother owes me. Remind him of that."

The faint smile on Alejandro's lips at her fisted salute to her brother was at odds with the thoughtful frown furrowing his brows as he absently rubbed his left quad and knee.

"You okay?" she asked, chalking her concern up to a hazard of her job.

"I'm fine. Supposed to take another pill with lunch. Actually, I was, uh, thinking about our strange role reversal."

Anamaría shook her head, unsure what he meant.

"Here you are, flying off to the big city. And here I am"—he tapped the padded armrest with a palm—"the one stuck here on the Rock."

"Only I've never felt 'stuck' here. I'll be happy to return on Sunday, with my familia excited to hear all about my trip."

Alejandro's mouth opened, then closed without him saying anything. His expression shuttered, and belatedly, she realized the unintended gut punch in her words. Evidence proving his point as to why he couldn't stay. Because unlike her, not all of his familia welcomed his return.

"I shouldn't have—"

"Forget about it." He waved her off. "It is what it is. You should go. Don't keep your client waiting."

He was right. There was nothing left for them to say to each other anyway.

"You talk to Enrique tomorrow. I'll give him a nudge, too." Her heart heavy, she moved toward the sliding glass door.

The cool AC air from inside kissed her heated skin as his husky voice stopped her.

"For what it's worth, good luck in New York. Whoever you're meeting with, they're crazy if they don't wanna work with you."

Crazy. Exactly how he made *her* feel.

Crazy with longing. Crazy with frustration. Crazy with what-ifs that could never be.

His words of encouragement brought a painful tightness in her chest.

He used to be her best friend. Her confidant. The one she shared all her exciting news with first.

She missed those innocent years. Missed him.

But they remained at the same fork in the road. And their decisions about which path to take hadn't changed.

"Gracias," she whispered, unable to look at him. Afraid he'd see the regret she was determined to hide. "Cuídate."

Not that he'd listen and actually take care of himself. Hard-headed man that he was.

Without waiting for him to respond, she hurried inside to say her good-byes. Time to focus on her trip and the opportunities that awaited.

Her future was out there. Not here.

Chapter 7

"For a guy who had the bright idea of cliff-diving onto a pile of waterfall rocks instead of the glistening pool of water a few feet to his left, you don't look half-bad."

Alejandro gave Enrique the finger as Anamaría's younger brother grinned and stepped back to the dresser.

"Douchebag," Alejandro grumbled. Planting his palms on either side of his hips, he pushed up, raising his butt to reposition himself more comfortably on his bedroom mattress.

"Seriously, you got lucky, bro." Enrique deftly removed his light blue latex gloves with a snap of the rubbery material.

Alejandro leaned against the pillow sandwiched between his back and the headboard, answering his friend with a lazy shrug. Luck was a fickle shit. Coming and going at its whimsy.

Case in point. His current position. Holed up in his childhood bedroom. Avoiding his father. Surrounded by memories of the one woman he'd spent his entire adult life trying—and failing—to forget.

Yeah, he was a lucky bastard all right.

"Three weeks post-surgery, I'd say you're healing well. When are you following up with Dr. Peterson?" Enrique tossed the gloves in the circular office-sized trash bin near the computer desk.

"Friday morning after . . ."

Alejandro trailed off, his attention caught on the five-by-seven framed photograph Enrique had lifted from one of the desk shelves.

"Damn, we look like freakin' babies here." Enrique held out the picture of their Little League baseball team back when they were in middle school. Enrique going into seventh, Alejandro and Anamaría rising eighth graders.

"That's 'cuz we were," Alejandro answered. "I picked up a camera for the first time that summer. And you. Shit, you'd already picked up your first girl and hadn't even hit puberty yet."

Enrique laughed and waggled his eyebrows. But didn't bother negating the truth.

A knock sounded on the bedroom door; then Alejandro's mom poked her head inside. "I am going over to the restaurant for lunch. Quieren venir conmigo?"

Her expectant gaze slid from Alejandro to Enrique, then back again.

Alejandro knew she wanted him to say yes, they would join her. But that was an answer he couldn't give.

The night he and his father had argued was the last time Alejandro had set foot in Miranda's. He wasn't sure when or if he'd be able to go back again. Not with the electrically charged fence standing between his papi and him.

Alejandro gave a single shake of his head. As if the small movement might hurt her feelings less.

The expectant hope in his mami's eyes faded. Guilt stampeded over his chest like a herd of wildebeests he'd photographed once.

Highly experienced with Cuban mami guilt and dashed expectations, Enrique replaced the old photograph and flashed the cheesy grin that had gotten him into and out of more trouble for as far back as Alejandro could remember.

"Actually, Señora Miranda," Enrique said, crossing the few

steps to drape an arm around her shoulders. He tucked her plump
body against his side, looping his other arm across her chest to
wrap her in a bear hug. Schmoozer. "I was hoping to kidnap
Ale. Introduce him to a friend of mine who owns an art gallery
downtown. Then run a quick errand. We'll grab a sandwich from
Sandy's on the way."

Just like when they'd been kids and he had to cover for whatever
tall tale Enrique spun, Alejandro worked to keep the surprise off
his face. This was the first he'd heard about an errand. Or meeting
some friend of Enrique's. But if playing along got him out of an uncomfortable meal at Miranda's, where his papi would not welcome
him, he'd gladly run every errand on Enrique's To Do list.

"You don't mind, do you, Señora M? I promise to have him
back in one piece," Enrique teased, apparently still a pro at but-
tering someone up to get his way. "No jumping off the bridge at
Bahia Honda like he convinced me to do that one time."

Alejandro's mami gasped, her eyes going as wide as Lulu's when
his niece had first seen the baby elephant photograph yesterday.

"Hey! That was all you, man! Mami, I never jumped. ¡Te lo
juro!" Alejandro pointed a finger at Enrique while holding up a
placating palm to his mother, repeating his promise. "I swear! I
didn't."

Enrique, the fool, grinned wider. "I'm kidding. It was a joke."

Alejandro's mom shot his buddy the pursed-mouth, eyebrow-
slanted frown of aggrieved mamis the world over.

Believing that E had actually made that jump wasn't too far-
fetched. There'd been a time in high school when Enrique had
teetered on the line between prankster and troublemaker. One
incident in particular nearly earned him a stint of community
service. Until their art teacher, of all people, stepped in with a
compromise that wound up changing Anamaría's baby brother's
trajectory. For a while anyway. Alejandro had never gotten the full
story behind why his friend had given up pursuing art and joined
the familia business, becoming a firefighter instead.

"Ay, nene, me vas a matar," Alejandro's mom admonished. He

was pretty sure E's mom had uttered a similar you're-killing complaint too many times to count.

"Mami blames me for most of her gray hair. I tell her she looks like the goddess she is." Enrique gave an impudent wink that had Alejandro's mami tsking and shaking her head, all while smiling indulgently.

Alejandro bit back a disbelieving grin. Some things never changed.

"In all seriousness, though," E said, crossing to the duffel he'd set on top of the dresser. "It'll do Ale good to get out of the house, move around a little, and get his blood flowing."

A tiny worry V added to the fine wrinkles in the space between his mami's brows.

Alejandro knew her lunch invitation stemmed from her desire for her husband and son to make amends. Unfortunately, not even Mother Teresa herself could have brokered a peace treaty between the two of them.

"It's too soon," Alejandro told his mom softly. "Por favor, don't push this."

Her lids fluttered closed on a soft sigh. "Está bien. Pero pórtense bien!"

"Aw, Señora M, we always behave!" Enrique complained.

"Ha!" Alejandro and his mom barked disbelieving laughs in unison. She wagged a finger at Enrique's bogus claim, her narrow-eyed glower reminding both men that no matter their age, they would always answer to their mamis.

She gave each of them a good-bye kiss on the cheek, adding a love pat on Alejandro's, then left for the restaurant.

Fifteen minutes later, Alejandro sat in the back of Enrique's black SUV, his left leg stretched out across the seat.

"Drive, Enrique, and be mindful of potholes." With a flick of his wrist, Alejandro motioned for his chauffeur to proceed.

"Yeah, that's not how this is gonna work, smartass." Enrique pushed the ignition button to start his Pilot, then glanced over his shoulder at Alejandro. "Now that we're out of the house, away from your mom's supersonic hearing, I've got two questions for you. Any chance of you and your dad burying the hatchet so you can quit visiting every other damn place on the planet except here? And what the hell are you doing to help my sister put an end to whatever schemes our moms keep inventing?"

Ignoring the first question, Alejandro leaned back against the passenger door and grinned at his buddy, feeling relaxed for the first time in weeks. "Funny you should ask. Anamaría wanted me to remind you about the number of times she's saved your sorry butt over the years."

By the time Enrique managed to find a parking spot on Eaton Street, a couple blocks from the Duval Street art gallery his friends owned, Alejandro had updated his buddy on the slim to none odds Alejandro and his dad would resolve their issues anytime soon. They'd spent the past two days giving each other a wide berth when they were both in the house. Speaking in brusque monosyllables and making minimal eye contact.

As for the meddling mothers, Enrique and Alejandro were still tossing around ideas. Testament to the Navarro siblings' bond, E hadn't even balked at the idea of him throwing his mom off Anamaría's and Alejandro's scent.

"I don't mind taking one for the team," Enrique reiterated, pushing Alejandro's wheelchair across the intersection at Simonton as they headed down Eaton toward Duval.

"If your mom's in a matchmaking mood, why not introduce her to your new girlfriend?" Alejandro suggested.

Enrique jerked the wheelchair to a stop. "Girlfriend? What the hell are you talking about?"

"C'mon. I'm sure you've got a line of women willing to volunteer to play make-believe with you. Just long enough to distract your mom. Cece's about ready to pop out the next grandkid. That's a definite distraction for my mom. Problem solved."

"Wrong. When did you get so dumb?" Enrique smacked the back of Alejandro's head.

"¿Qué carajo?" Alejandro cursed, rubbing the sting from his nape.

"Yeah, what the hell?" Enrique threw him a dirty look, then nearly gave Alejandro whiplash when he pushed the chair into motion again. "First of all, I am not gonna use a girl like that. And secondly, Luis and Sara tried pulling some fake relationship nonsense last year. That tangled mess did not fool our mom, and look how Luis wound up?"

"I thought they were engaged?"

"Exactly!" Enrique leaned over Alejandro's shoulder, eyeing him over the top of his sunglasses. "A state I do not plan on entering anytime soon. If at all."

"What? Don't be an idiot." Alejandro pushed Enrique's forehead to get him to back off. "We're not saying get engaged. Just let it slip to your mom that you're exclusive with someone. She'll glom on that like—"

"Like one of Carlos's boys with a bag of cotton candy at Children's Day in the park. Also equally as messy. No thanks."

They reached Duval, and Enrique wheeled Alejandro around the corner in front of St. Paul's Episcopal Church.

Alejandro gazed up at the towering concrete and steel building that stood like a beacon on the popular corner. Its wood-beam ceiling and stained-glass windows were a popular draw for worshiping locals and tourists alike. People also sought out the haunted graveyard tours through the cemetery tucked behind the building itself. Some believed the ghost of John Fleming, whose widow donated the land for the church in the 1830s, walked the grounds along with other spirits.

For a young aspiring adventure photographer, the church with its angles and tall spires and the grounds with their haunting history and looming shadows had been a familiar subject during Alejandro's adolescence. He'd even convinced Anamaría to join him for a few late-night photo ops here, despite her aversion to spooky places. Of course, that meant she stuck close to his side. Not that either one of them had minded.

"You got a better idea?" he complained to Enrique.

"Maybe. Whatever we do, it's gotta be legit. My mom'll smell a con before I even put it in motion. Somehow her all-knowing radar is even stronger since becoming an abuela. Carlos and Gina's boys don't stand a chance of getting away with half the shit we did as kids. Sneaking out, skipping class to go out on the boat? She even makes us all share our location on our cell phones."

Alejandro chuckled at his buddy's beleaguered grimace. If there was one Navarro kid who had truly tested his Cuban mami and knew what might work, it was Anamaría's younger brother. Too bad Alejandro's own doubt about the flawed fake girlfriend idea echoed Enrique's.

Damn it! He had to come up with something. No way could he spend the next three or four or— Shit, the idea of an interminable stay on the Rock, being confined to a mere three-by-five-mile area when there were so many interesting spots far away to explore, made his skin crawl as if a line of bullet ants marched up his arm. He'd rather deal with the mind-numbing pain of the Costa Rican insect bites than be stuck in Key West, living with his parents again, dealing with the sense of betrayal that festered in his gut.

"Here we are." Enrique stopped in front of a one-story building on the same block as the historic church. "My 'better idea' to occupy your mom. And remind mine that your life isn't here anymore. The last thing either of my parents want is one of us moving away. Especially their only daughter, la Princesa."

Confused by E's vague description of what he had in mind, Alejandro took in the storefronts searching for some type of clue.

In a row of stores and businesses, the building's butter yellow siding and white-trimmed windows invited passersby to peek inside and check out the various wares. The façade of the business they stood in front of was taken up by an expansive window and a glass door. The name *Bellísima* was etched in the window's right corner and emblazoned in a flourishing black script on a rectangular ceramic tile hanging near the door. The eye-catching window display featured two vibrant watercolor paintings of well-known Key West landmarks. The first a teeming Mallory Square during the nightly sunset festival with its orange sherbet sky and wispy deepening purple sky. The second canvas captured Ernest Hemingway's house with a smattering of tourists perusing the lush grounds. Propped on a doll-sized easel in between the framed paintings, a sign written in blood orange brushstrokes read: Local Artist.

"Before we go in, we gotta set something straight between us." Enrique stepped out from behind the chair, then backpedaled to make room for a middle-aged woman power walking with a baby stroller. As soon as she passed by, he moved to Alejandro's left. His back to the art gallery, Enrique lifted his black Ray-Bans to rest on top of his head. The bright noonday sun glinted off the dark lenses.

E's pretty-boy face—the likes of which Alejandro knew could sell bottles of men's cologne as easily as cold drinks on a hot day at Smathers Beach if Enrique wanted to go that route—turned sober. All signs of joking erased from his expression as Enrique crossed his arms and stared down at Alejandro.

"Here's the deal," Alejandro's once partner in crime said. "We've been friends for as long as I can remember. You've gotten me out of plenty of jams, and into a few."

"Ah-ah-ah!" Alejandro held up a finger, compelled to point out the truth. "You have to admit, anything I instigated is now a comical remember-when story. And most of those were at least partly your idea first."

Enrique clamped his mouth closed, neither agreeing with nor denying his ringleader status in their past antics. "Whatever. You know how this goes. My sister comes first. You're familia, but she's—"

"La Princesa."

A corner of Enrique's mouth quirked. "Word to the wise, she still hates it when we call her that. It's grounds for a gut punch that, believe me, does not tickle. Our dad's the only one who gets away with it."

Of course he did. That fact spoke of the bond Anamaría and Señor Navarro shared. Still. Always. Alejandro's mistake had been not realizing how that bond would keep her tethered here for good. Or rather, that she didn't consider herself tethered by the tiny island like he did.

"I get it," he told Enrique.

At least, the rational side of him now did. The emotional side that he channeled into his craft still hadn't come to grips with her rejection.

"I'm glad busting your leg made you drag your sorry ass back here. It's been too long," Enrique went on. "But Anamaría's in a good groove. Finally doing something about growing AM Fitness since she broke up with that loser who moved back to Miami. So, I'm saying this as fair warning—" Enrique hooked his thumbs in his front jeans pockets, his body language casual to anyone walking by, while his gaze hardened with a serious intensity. "Don't do anything to hurt her or mess with her head. 'Cuz this time, it won't matter where you fly off to. I will hunt you down. We clear?"

The assumption that Alejandro was the only one who'd done the hurting had frustration bubbling hot and frothy in his stomach, like milk for café con leche left in a pot on the stove to overflow.

No way would he admit that the sister his friend defended had done her own number on him. Doing so wouldn't change anything.

And yet that dedication to your familia, the Navarros, all kept sacred, having each other's back no matter what, accepting them for who and what they were . . . it was all Alejandro had ever wanted from his own dad. The one thing the old man couldn't give the son whose dreams differed.

Despite his disappointment, Alejandro couldn't begrudge Enrique looking out for his sister.

"Yeah, we're clear." Alejandro signaled his agreement with a chin jut. "Look, man, I'm here to heal and appease my mami and abuela's desire to fatten me up. I plan on getting to know my niece and meet this new little one Cece's about to have. Then, I am out of here. Chasing the next great photograph. Climbing the next waterfall."

"Without doing another piss-poor cliff-diving imitation. Please," Enrique wisecracked.

Their shared smirks broke the tension. Enrique leaned forward to clap him on the shoulder, and for the first time since he'd arrived back home Alejandro felt like his old self. When taking pictures had been about the joy of capturing the beauty around him, not the need to lose himself in his work to forget.

"You should join me on a shoot sometime. Maybe it would inspire you to paint something they'd let you show here." Alejandro peered through the gallery's front window, catching sight of a short man with shaggy black hair and a trendy vibrant blue suit peering at them from inside. The guy smiled and lifted a hand in greeting.

Enrique shook his head. "Naw. I don't show my work anymore."

"Sometime you're going to have to explain to me why the hell not."

"Doubtful. All that's behind me. But you . . . big-shot *National Geographic* cover photographer . . . you are another story. Which is why we're here." Stepping behind the wheelchair again, Enrique pushed Alejandro toward the door. "I connected with Logan Summers while I was in art school. He and his husband, Marcelo López, co-own Bellísima. And, you'll be pleased to know, Marcelo's a huge fan of your work. Naturally, I told him you're not a big deal. You put your pants on the same damn way we do. One leg at a time. And right now, even that's not happening 'cuz your decision-making skills when it comes to cliff-diving landing spots need improvement. Marcelo's opinion of you didn't budge though."

"I like him already," Alejandro joked.

"Remember, I know your childhood secrets and most embarrassing highlights." Enrique ducked down, whispering his idle threat in Alejandro's left ear.

"Back atcha, hermano."

"True. But I'm not the big shot with a rep to protect. You are." Enrique grinned like the sly dog he was. "Anyway, when I mentioned that you were in town for a while, Marcelo and Logan thought you might be interested in having a show. Here."

Alejandro craned his neck to gape up at Enrique, surprised by the unexpected offer.

"It'll keep you busy," Enrique said. "Out of the house. Away from meddling moms and abuelas."

Alejandro settled back in his chair, considering. Enrique's rationale made sense.

But a showing? On the island? It was something he'd dreamed of as a budding photographer. Wouldn't that be like thumbing his nose at his papi's expectations? Drawing attention to the work Alejandro had chosen over his abuelo's legacy?

The questions ran circles inside his brain, so it took him a few seconds to note that the guy in the suit now stood at the gallery's entrance, holding the door ajar. His pale blue eyes sparkled with excitement, their contrast with his deeply bronze skin creating a striking combination. Fingers splayed, he pressed a hand to his chest over his thin black tie and tipped forward in a slight bow.

"Marcelo López. Such a pleasure to meet you," he said, his words lilting with his heavier Spanish accent. "I am a huge fan of your work. Todos son una maravilla. Truly, all marvelous images."

"Ay, por favor, Marcelo, don't go stroking his ego so much or the rest of us won't hear the end of it," Enrique complained.

"Cállate," Marcelo chided, pressing a finger to his lips to shush Enrique. "It would be an absolute honor to feature Mr. Miranda's work here at Bellísima."

Alejandro laughed when Enrique answered with a loud groan.

"Please, call me Alejandro. Any friend of Enrique's is a friend of mine."

After exchanging handshakes, the three of them moved farther into the gallery. Alejandro's gaze roamed over the soft cream walls, admiring the watercolor paintings and still-life photographs in white frames expertly mounted and displayed. The dark-stained wood floor gave the space a warm feel, and the strategically placed cream-upholstered love seats and ottomans with wood accents invited visitors to relax and appreciate the artwork, as they would when they took home a piece.

Exactly the type of space he envisioned for his photographs. Allowing viewers to linger, taking their time connecting with the people and places, cultures and way of life. To connect with the emotions the images evoked and the moments often unnoticed. Or worse, taken for granted.

There'd been a time when he'd dreamed of showing his work at one of the numerous galleries on the island. He and Anamaría had talked about it while spinning their plans for the future. But he had crossed that idea off his bucket list years ago. Respecting his papi's directive that he never return.

Instead, his mami and abuela had flown to New York for his first show. He'd been so fucking excited that night. Yet also disappointed, missing two of the people he most wanted to impress.

He had expected his father to be a no-show. As he'd been for Alejandro's second exhibition a few years later in Atlanta. Ernesto and Cece had made that one.

Like his dad, Anamaría had been noticeably absent. There'd been no reason for her to attend since they'd broken up. No reason other than Alejandro secretly wanting her to be there.

But to finally have a show here . . . where their entire comunidad could attend. Where maybe, if Alejandro handled it respectfully, his father might finally see the value of Alejandro's talent and work. It was worth a shot.

Excitement coursed through him.

Not to mention, Enrique was right. Planning and preparing for an event like this would fill the time while Alejandro was stuck here. He'd be combing through his personal photographs. Considering themes and collections. Carefully selecting the perfect images. Deciding how best to display them. Publicity, promotion, invitations . . .

The list of tasks helping to keep his mind off the problems and people he couldn't change lengthened.

He'd be so busy, he might finally be able to shut off that reel of highlights, memories of him and Anamaría, playing on repeat in his mind. Being near her but not *with* her, not having his work to distract him, had him climbing the freaking walls. And it'd only been two days.

Shit, he needed this. More than Marcelo or Enrique realized.

And his mom. Damn, his mami would relish a chance to finally fulfill her wish to celebrate her elder son's success. Asking for her help might be enough to get her off matchmaking and on to party planning.

It was worth a try.

"So, Marcelo." Alejandro met the gallery owner's inquisitive gaze. "What did you have in mind? And how soon can we get started?"

Chapter 8

"I think everything went amazingly well. Don't you?"

Anamaría avoided Sara's inquisitive gaze by ducking her head to secure her airplane safety belt.

"Mm-hmm," she hummed, taking her time pulling the strap tight around her hips. Ignoring the matching tight band of worry squeezing her chest.

"The people from AllFit loved you! I knew they would." Sara bumped her shoulder against Anamaría's playfully. "Still, Arnold admitted he was surprised they sent your contract over so fast. I mean, we probably hadn't even washed the makeup off our faces and climbed into bed after dinner on Friday and he was already reading over their terms!"

It *was* pretty unreal.

Anamaría checked her arm for bruises again. Having pinched herself so many times the past couple of days thinking this all might be a dream.

Friday afternoon, she had signed with Sara's agent, Arnold Baker. A formality since they'd exchanged multiple emails and shared several phone calls. Sara trusted him; that meant Anamaría could, too.

That evening they'd met the reps from AllFit athletic wear for dinner and drinks at a trendy rooftop bar off New York's High Line. The bar was a backyard oasis in the middle of the bustling city. Greenery and potted flowers were strategically placed around the two bars that bookended the rooftop. A smattering of high-top tables, and pods of seating areas with low tables and comfy sofas and love seats. Muted mood lighting from burnished-metal open-bulb fixtures. The iconic skyline a mix of shadows and lights as the fading sun peeked out from behind tall buildings, casting its watercolor display of smoky orange and reds across the darkening sky as it whispered farewell to the evening.

Dios mío, the whole affair had been like a dream . . . the picturesque views, the energized yet relaxed atmosphere, the diverse mix of people networking or blowing off the week's steam. Or out on a date. Like the young couple who had snuggled in a loveseat nearby, oblivious to everyone else. Hands loosely clasped. Fingers lingering over a caress along a jaw or forearm, lips curved in secret, shared smiles. Their eyes only interested in each other's.

Like she and Alejandro had been once.

Now, same as on Friday evening, Anamaría shoved him out of her head. He had no business invading her thoughts like that anymore. She had more important matters to contend with and it did no good adding Alejandro to the tumultuous mix. The entire weekend had been a total whirlwind.

Early Saturday morning, Arnold had met Sara and her at their hotel, the historic Wyndham New Yorker, where the Social Media Summit was being held. The rest of the day, Anamaría barely had time to catch her breath. They'd immediately gone into Sara's panel and autograph session, followed by her two-hour presentation on working with an influencer. Both were great learning opportunities for Anamaría, who'd also taken on the role of bodyguard when mobs swarmed Sara with questions or requests for selfies around the hotel meeting room areas. Arnold stuck around, finding pockets of time to go over AllFit's contract, explaining lingo Anamaría found confusing, redlining specific terms and areas he and Sara recommended they negotiate with AllFit to change.

And the networking. Arnold and Sara seemed to know practically everyone at the conference. Anamaría hadn't shaken that many hands or delivered her AM Fitness elevator pitch to so many people in . . . bueno, ever.

After their hectic day, she and Sara had a hot second to change and give their cheeks a break from all the smiling, then they headed out for more networking over drinks and appetizers at a different rooftop spot. This one with a breathtaking view of the Empire State Building, the moon bathing it in silvery light from an inky, starless sky.

"Teaming with Brandon will be a huge boost for you," Sara went on, thankfully oblivious to the nervous jitters ricocheting in Anamaría's belly. "I was surprised he showed up at the mixer last night. I mean, when we spoke before our morning panel, he mentioned having other plans. I bet meeting you at lunch with AllFit changed his mind about skipping the mixer."

"Oh, I doubt that."

"Girl, he is smitten," Sara said, waggling her artfully threaded brows.

"Ha! Doubtful, though ego boosting," Anamaría said with a laugh.

A sandy blond–haired, blue-eyed swimmer, runner, and all-around fitness buff with a body most men would kill for and a boy-next-door personality women swooned over, Brandon Lawson was a social media influencer phenom. He floated around the same stratosphere as Sara. One Anamaría hadn't attained. Yet.

"I can't believe he offered to do an AllFit photo shoot together," Anamaría mused. His idea, shared over drinks the night before, had caught her off guard. In a holy-shit-I'm-game kind of way.

"I can. You, little sister, are what Arnold calls the complete package." Sara looped her right arm through Anamaría's left, giving her a squeeze. "Smart and willing to work hard, passionate about helping others, natural in front of the camera. With a body made for AllFit's workout gear. What I wouldn't give for your toned arms."

"Oye, it's more important to love the skin you're in and the body the good Lord gave you." The familiar refrain Anamaría shared with her clients tumbled easily off her tongue. Because she believed it. Something she and Sara had discussed during one of their early heart-to-heart chats about Sara's daily efforts to stay in recovery with her disease.

Now Sara's glossy lips spread in a pleased smile. "See? That's the perfect response for the perfect spokesperson of a line of athletic wear that prides itself on accommodating all sizes, all ages, and all levels of fitness."

A giddy, slightly hysterical giggle tickled Anamaría's throat, bursting out before she could stop it.

"I just might be."

The shock in her voice must have telegraphed itself on her face because Sara shook her head.

"Not might be, girl. You *are!*"

They shared matching grins as passengers filed past their first-class seats—Sara having insisted on upgrading them in celebration. Anamaría, unwilling to rain on her almost-sister's party mood by arguing over the wasted expense, wiggled her butt and settled into her wide, comfy seat. A little splurge now and again never hurt.

"So, what did your parents say when you told them that you're AllFit's newest spokesperson? And that Brandon Lawson might fly to Key West for a photo shoot?" Sara smoothed the skirt of her fuchsia sundress over her thighs.

"Um, I haven't. Actually." Anamaría flicked the seat-belt clasp up with her thumb, letting it fall closed with a tinny clank. "It's . . . it happened so fast. And we were . . . you know, in go mode so much. Plus, I'm not . . ."

Sara straightened in her aisle seat, head cocked in confusion so the tips of her blond hair brushed her collarbone. "Not what?"

"Nothing." Anamaría flicked the seat-belt clasp again, grappling with the inexplicable doubts she'd been trying to silence. "I just, um, I was thinking maybe I should wait and share the news in a few days. Not jinx it, or anything."

Could she sound more absurd?

Sara's confused expression slid into yeah-right territory. Anamaría couldn't blame her; she was in the same disbelieving boat as her friend. Stymied by her own reaction to a development she'd been working her butt off to achieve.

"Talk to me, girl," Sara coaxed, the candor in her blue-green eyes showing how easily she had stepped into the role of protective big sis, even though she and Luis weren't married yet.

Anamaría let her eyes drift shut, giving her a small reprieve from Sara's probing gaze. Sucking in a deep breath, she filled her chest, upper abdomen, then belly; then slowly released the air in reverse order, relieved to find the breathing exercise soothing the anxiety gnawing at her insides.

When she opened her eyes, she found Sara watching her intently.

"I'm fine," Anamaría assured her. "It's still sinking in. That's all. It doesn't seem real. Y'know?"

Sara nodded. "I get it. When I made the decision to move to New York, after signing with my first few sponsors, I had doubts. My mom had just been diagnosed with cancer, and I was dealing with my own health issue. But I was determined and focused. Like you." Sara pointed at her emphatically. "Girl, you are ready for this!"

Outside the window across the aisle, a team of Newark Airport employees transferred a hodgepodge of suitcases, duffel bags, and a set of golf clubs from a cart onto a belt moving toward the belly of their nonstop flight home to Key West.

Many of their fellow passengers were heading down for vacation. Excited for snorkeling, bike riding, sunset viewing, and relaxing on the beach. In need of an island getaway.

Anamaría was one of the lucky ones who lived in the Keys full-time. A local. A true Conch. Born and raised on her beloved island. Where she belonged.

AllFit had mentioned her traveling to trade shows. Mostly in the United States, occasionally in Europe if she could swing the time off from the fire department. The job was a dream. Especially since, after her aborted plans with Alejandro, she had never made it overseas. For lots of reasons.

Time. Money. Work. *Fear.*

Acknowledging that last reason drop-kicked her in the gut.

Common sense and her professional training told her a therapist could help her delve into the root cause of her fear. Regular therapy or counseling was an important part of self-care for many. She should stop dragging her feet and follow up with the therapist her familia's long-time general practitioner had recommended.

But she also knew that she gained strength and a sense of purpose from her familia. The security and comfort they provided. The unconditional love they offered. The certainty that they would never leave her by choice. And she in turn would never leave them. Not for good.

Sharing this news with them would make it more . . . real. As if signing a legal document with AllFit and Arnold hadn't.

For several years now Enrique had been harping on her to spread her wings. Stop keeping her feet rooted to the island like the gnarled mangroves growing in the marshes and the smattering of tiny islands dotting the area waters.

That was finally happening, which should have her jittery with excitement. Not nerves.

"What has you second-guessing yourself?" Sara prodded softly.

Anamaría leaned her head against the airplane wall, considering Sara's question. This new development wouldn't change anything she didn't already want to change. She remained in control. Only now she was taking the advice she gave her clients about moving out of their comfort zone to experience growth.

She was ashamed to think about how long she'd fallen into the trap so many women got caught up in. Holding themselves back because of someone else. Settling when they didn't have to. Sabotaging themselves and their opportunities. Often, as with her, without even realizing.

"It's okay to want this, isn't it?" she murmured. When Sara didn't respond, Anamaría swiveled her head away from the thin wall to face her friend. "Because I *do* want it. So badly it scares me."

The words were a scratchy whisper, weighty with dreams too long deferred. Goals she didn't want to hold back anymore. No longer willing to wait. Not for anyone.

Sara placed her hand over Anamaría's on the armrest between them and gave a gentle squeeze. "It's *more* than okay. You deserve this. Anyone who loves you, who knows and respects you. Anyone who's worthy of those from you in return will tell you the same."

Unbidden, Alejandro's last words to her tiptoed through Anamaría's mind, meandering lower to leave warm, mini footprints on her heart.

They're crazy if they don't wanna work with you.

Would he be as excited for her as Sara was? As the rest of her familia undoubtedly would be?

She didn't know. And it shouldn't matter either way.

Still, a tiny voice she'd been unable to completely silence whispered from a dark corner of her heart . . . it *did* matter. *He* mattered.

After their tentative truce the other day, she could no longer deny it.

"Why all the secrecy about your exhibition? I thought the idea was to give your mom a distraction?" Enrique tossed the question at Alejandro like a grenade over his shoulder as he maneuvered his SUV out of a tight downtown parking spot Monday afternoon.

At least, E hadn't asked in the middle of their meeting at Bellísima with Marcelo and Logan. Alejandro didn't want to discuss his dysfunctional familia drama in front of the other two men.

Who the hell was he kidding? He preferred to avoid the topic altogether.

Scooping up the verbal explosive, Alejandro lobbed it back toward the front seat. "Better question, why won't you consider an exhibition of your own? It's clear Marcelo's interested."

The stony silence that greeted his observation told Alejandro he'd hit a nerve.

No flip remark from E. No casual shrug of the shoulders in his devil-may-care way. His response was a telling white-knuckled grip on the steering wheel. His profile flinty angles of tight jaw, steely cheekbone, and a thin line of lips.

There had to be a juicy story behind Enrique's surprising decision to suddenly stop pursuing his passion after graduating from art school in Miami. Relegating his skills to painting geometric-shaped wood pieces with the beachy Key West themes tourists plunked down their money for, mementos they carted home, then often forgot about. Pieces Enrique could create blindfolded. One-handed.

But, as someone with his own secrets he preferred not to examine, Alejandro respected his friend's privacy. A concept neither one of their mothers seemed to understand.

Especially when it came to Alejandro and Anamaría.

Heaving a disgruntled sigh, he adjusted the seat-belt strap crossing his chest.

He hadn't seen or heard from his ex since she'd been coerced into delivering his mami's cell phone last week. That didn't mean she'd been far from his thoughts. Or that he hadn't been treated to a regular update about her comings and goings. His mami had been glued to Instagram, waiting for each new post about Anamaría's trip to New York so she could like or comment. Whether he wanted to see the pictures or not, his mami had shared them.

If he wasn't hearing about her trip, then his mom was regaling him with stories of AM Fitness expanding and the people whose lives Anamaría was changing for the better. From free Zumba classes at Saint Mary's to health and fitness presentations at the high school and fun runs around the city raising money for one charity or another. While he'd been off capturing images around the globe, Anamaría was busy making a difference here at home. Expanding her reach as she took on clients vacationing in Key West who hired her for virtual training sessions after they left.

Hell, even his staunchly traditional father had succumbed to the pressures of meeting his customers' changing preferences by adding some of Anamaría's healthier Cuban food options to the Miranda's menu. The man made a huge concession like adapting his beloved father's recipes but couldn't understand that his son wanted to honor their familia legacy in his own way.

Another sign of how Anamaría belonged here. While he did not.

As he sat sideways in the back of Enrique's SUV, Alejandro's gloomy thoughts blurred along with the sights of Key West's Old Town neighborhood through the passenger window opposite him. Refurbished old Conch houses with their wide verandahs, white picket railings, and gingerbread details invited visitors to pull up a rocking chair and find respite. Flamboyán trees with their fiery red miniature petals and vibrant fern-like leaves offered shade and eye-catching adornment for the small lawns. Their colorful petals dotted the cracked gray sidewalks as if pointillism artists had used the concrete as their canvas.

He itched to be out there again. Lazily strolling the streets of his childhood. His Canon cradled in his hands. His eyes absorbing the contrast of light and shadow, the intricate play of colors. The movement and emotion of the world around him a palpable force. Discovering an interesting mark and stopping to observe. Patience more a necessity than a virtue. His heart slowing to a dull thud as he waited, anticipated. Trusting the innate sensation that guided him. Certain it led him toward what every photographer sought—the decisive moment.

The millisecond when your breathing stilled, the camera shutter whirred, and you were gifted with the perfect image.

One in a stream of images many unpracticed eyes might say

were all perfect. He knew better. There could be only one. And that only if he was lucky.

Trusting his instincts had resulted in some of his most prized photographs. Like the one taken along the Malecón in Havana. A wave crashing against a seawall pockmarked from years of serving sentinel confronting the ocean's caustic brine. Wispy arcs and drops of salt water shimmering in the air, hovering over a lone fisherman who braved the elements, a slender fishing rod clutched in his weathered grip. His threadbare clothes and worn sandals as much a part of him as the unrestrained, life-affirming grin slashing across his dark complexion.

And yet even that spectacular photograph was rivaled by another. Several others. All taken in the stolen moments he'd carved out for himself during the week he'd spent on his familia's native island of Cuba for a magazine shoot.

He'd spent an afternoon slowly strolling the dusty streets in Centro Habana, a residential area dilapidated and crumbling though still teeming with life, juxtaposed in stark contrast with the tourist-filled posh hotels and museums of Parque Central and El Paseo del Prado. There, in Centro Habana, he'd eventually found the old establishment he'd heard tales of but had only seen in a faded, creased photograph framed in a place of honor beside a cash register that dinged each time a satisfied customer settled their bill in the restaurant built for its namesake.

This discovery had come after a morning excursion to Santiago de Las Vegas where his paternal grandparents had met, courted, and married before moving to Havana, where they opened the original Miranda's. Alejandro's father and uncle had been born in Havana, spending their early years watching their father hard at work building his dream. Until, desperate to give their sons a better life, one they could choose for themselves, Alejandro's abuelos had packed a small suitcase for each child and put them on a plane to the United States. Prayers and hope for the future whispered as the young boys headed toward uncertainty.

No one in his immediate familia knew Alejandro had spent

that too-brief time in Cuba several years ago. Nor of his search for their roots. The beginning of their legacy. The one his papi was convinced he had rejected.

But there, on the streets of Centro Habana, Alejandro had stood before the old restaurant. Long closed and left to withstand the harsh elements—but never forgotten. The single-story building lay in forlorn shambles. Windows hazy, most jagged and broken, like the dreams of many who once ate, drank, and celebrated within. The proud name scrawled over the arched door in a painted flourish mostly scraped away by Mother Nature's brittle nails. A photograph with stories to tell.

Another prized image featured an aging park in Santiago de Las Vegas with its circular fountain—derelict and long dried up. The shadows of his grandparents and countless others, meeting up with their friends at the park to promenade alongside each other, lingered. Another photograph with its own stories to tell.

And yet another, this one of his abuela's childhood home, still inhabited by a cousin Alejandro had never met but who had welcomed him like a long-lost son. Something his own father couldn't, wouldn't, do. The home's structure may have been a little dilapidated, but the heart and soul of those inside beat strong and proud.

Those photographs . . . moments of perfection gifted him through his camera lens . . . pieces of his familia that couldn't be snatched away from him . . . had remained on his laptop and saved in the cloud, for his eyes only. His personal treasures. Never shown to anyone. Until now.

Perhaps.

Was he brave enough to share them? Offer them up to the prying eyes of others who had no knowledge of their significance to him? More important, to a man who would more than likely think Alejandro unworthy of the connection they represented.

That uncertainty kept him from letting his mami in on his secret project. From one moment to the next he found himself either exhilarated by the reality of his first showing in his hometown and anxious about how his papi might take the news. Worried he would view it as another affront to everything Alejandro's abuelo had sacrificed for them.

Enrique slowed his vehicle to make a turn off Simonton into a parking area alongside a light tan–colored stucco two-story building Alejandro didn't recognize.

"I gotta grab something from my locker," Enrique said.

"Is this the new station?"

"Not so new anymore. We opened in 2015. Pretty sweet, huh?" The pride of two generations of firefighters rang in Enrique's voice.

Alejandro had seen pictures of the remodeled station. The Old Town Fire House's grand opening had been prominently covered by the *Key West Citizen*, and he occasionally checked the local newspaper's website for updates. Catching sight of familiar names and places gave him a taste of home when cravings hit.

Enrique pulled into a spot at the end of the building where the sidewalks along the perimeter and parking lot met in an L shape, leaving a large open area in the back corner behind the station. An outside stairway with a metal railing zigged, then zagged up to a red door on the second level. A firefighter in full gear and lugging a sandbag over one shoulder climbed the last step to the top landing, then immediately pivoted and headed back down. Several others milled about on the sidewalk near Enrique's SUV. Their helmets, jackets, and air tanks lay in discarded piles at their feet. Sweat streamed down the men's faces and plastered their gray KWFD T-shirts to their chests. Two greedily chugged bottles of water. The other sloshed his drink on top of his bald head, his shoulders slumped with exhaustion.

Off to the right, on the edge of the sidewalk, lay a monster-sized tire. At the far end, about fifty feet away, sat two five-gallon buckets.

"Looks like we caught the shift wrapping up their exercise drills," Enrique said as he put the vehicle in park. "I'll be right back."

Outside, he high-fived his hellos to the three firefighters who had finished the drill. They gathered around him, and the bald dude whose ripped arms and barrel chest stretched the material of his wet tee clasped Enrique's shoulder with a beefy hand. The older guy's deep mahogany skin glistened with sweat and the water he'd just dumped over his head as he motioned toward the building.

The welcoming smile on Enrique's lips melted into a grimace at whatever the big guy was saying. Alejandro followed their gaze to the firefighter descending the steps. Based on the guy's smaller size, he was probably a young rookie.

At the bottom of the stairs, the firefighter slung the bag of sand over the railing, then tugged at his chin strap. A second later he dropped to the sidewalk, his elbows bending and straightening in a quick series of push-ups. Enrique and the others approached the smaller firefighter, who paused, arms extended, his body in a straight plank position. The sun glinted off his helmet as he shook his head, then continued his workout.

The others waited a beat, the bald guy shaking Enrique's hand before they returned to gather their gear, then mosey up the stairs, clearly worn out by their drill.

Enrique stayed behind. He crouched beside the lone firefighter still racking up push-ups. Perhaps working off some kind of punishment or well-intentioned hazing. All with an idea of making him better, stronger. Safer. For his own good and the good of his fellow firefighters.

From his haunches, Enrique shot a glance back at his SUV. A frustrated scowl tugged at his brows. Alejandro leaned forward, straining to get a better look at the young firefighter, but it was impossible to tell who he was or why Enrique might be annoyed.

Several beats passed; then Enrique shook his head and rose to take the concrete stairs up by twos. By the time he reached the top, the other firefighter had hopped to his feet, his booted steps taking him toward the monster truck tire to the right of the SUV.

As the kid drew near, the name written on a wide piece of tape across the front of the bright yellow helmet became clear. *Navarro.*

Alejandro muttered a curse. This wasn't a kid or a rookie, and whatever kept Anamaría out here in this intense heat, she wasn't thrilled about it. Whereas the other firefighters had looked beaten up and ready for the showers, she strode toward the huge tire with determination. Underneath the shadow of the helmet's black-lined brim, Anamaría's tight jaw and stoic expression screamed back-the-hell-off.

As she drew even with the SUV, her boot toe caught on a crack in the sidewalk and she stumbled a step. Her mutinous expression faltered. In the last second before she turned her back to the SUV to continue the circuit of exercises, Alejandro could have sworn he caught grief on her face.

Anamaría squatted behind the supersize tire, her growl carrying on the humid breeze as she rose and hefted the black rubber, pushing and tossing it end over end until she reached the far edge of the sidewalk at least fifty feet away, where the five-gallon buckets awaited. There, she squatted to clasp the aluminum handles, then she lifted the buckets. Water sloshed over the sides as she took a jerky step, then another back toward Enrique's SUV. Dark splotches of water marked her path along the wide sidewalk like Hansel and Gretel's bread crumbs.

Alejandro stared at her, riveted.

Not by her display of strength as she lugged the heavy buckets weighing down her arms or tossed the monster truck tire, nor the sun glinting off the reflective stripes on her uniform reminding him of the danger she willingly placed herself in each shift.

It was the anguish in her hazel eyes as she stumbled to a finish that stole his breath. The sight of her beautiful face, creased with devastation and flushed with exertion. Her pinched lips and trembling chin. All sure signs that she neared her tipping point.

But he knew she wouldn't cry. Especially not when it would make her appear weak in front of the others. He remembered her grumbled curses at the machismo and sexism common in the two cultures that were so much a part of her familia's life—Cuban and firefighting. Though much less evident in their actual home.

This couldn't be hazing either. He'd bet his favorite lens she was too good at her job to warrant any kind of punishment. Something else had to be driving her to push herself to this extreme.

Stumbling to the end of the sidewalk, Anamaría dropped the buckets with a resounding *thunk*.

"Whyyyy?!" The word burst from her on a guttural groan as she staggered toward Enrique's SUV. She tore off her yellow helmet, dropping it carelessly to the ground before collapsing onto the hood.

Arms crossed to cushion her forehead, she lay there, the air tank strapped to her back rising and falling with each fatigued breath she heaved. Her head shook in denial of whatever hounded her.

All the while, he remained stuck in the back seat. Unable to go to her and offer comfort. As if he had the right to anyway.

Hating the impotence of his situation, Alejandro hunched down to look through the front windshield at the red door on the second-floor landing. Where the hell was Enrique? Why hadn't her brother stuck around long enough to dig out what was bothering her?

Any fool could see that *something* was obviously wrong.

Screw it! He jabbed the button to lower his back passenger window. "Hey!" he called out.

Anamaría didn't move.

"¿Oye, Princesa, estás bien?"

Her head shot up at the dreaded nickname. Bingo! She scanned the area, her rosy-cheeked face scrunched with fatigue and irritation.

"In here!" he called, waving his arm in between the front bucket seats to get her attention.

Her frown deepened, and she peered intently through the windshield. Surprised recognition widened her eyes when she spotted him.

Alejandro tipped his head toward his side of the SUV, beckoning her over.

Skepticism narrowed her eyes as she glared at him.

He motioned a more insistent *come here* with a hand and shot her an encouraging smile, hoping she'd give in. Also calling himself all kinds of stupid for wanting to be someone she counted on like he used to be.

With an audible huff, she pushed herself off the hood. Biting the fingertip of one protective glove, she tugged it off with her teeth, then spat it to the ground. The other glove got the same feral treatment. And damn if that wasn't hot.

Alejandro's blood pulsed, his gaze never wavering from hers. Unwilling to break their tenuous connection as she unbuckled her belt with deft fingers. She made short work of sliding the air tank and her heavy jacket off her shoulders, dropping the jacket at her feet to cushion the metal tank when she lowered it to the ground. Then she straightened, shoulders thrown back, chin high.

Hands on her hips, her baggy uniform pants pooling over her dusty boots, she faced him. All confident and proud . . . and shadowy pain.

Deep, gulping breaths made her chest rise and fall under her faded gray KWFD tee, the sweat-stained cotton material clinging to her sexy curves. Her lips trembled and she rolled them in, as if struggling to keep whatever she fought inside herself.

More than fatigue or over-exhaustion consumed her. He knew it as well as he knew the proper settings for a low-light photo session. Something *was* wrong.

He didn't beckon her again, though. He waited. Prayed she wouldn't shut him out. Hated the knowledge that, in her mind, he might deserve it. In spite of their tentative truce.

She took a step toward him . . . then another . . . her long braid no longer tucked under her jacket, swinging gently behind her. The breath he'd been holding released on a gush of air as she strode toward his open window. And him.

Chapter 9

"What are you doing here?" The question burst from Anamaría before she'd even reached Alejandro's side of her brother's vehicle.

Angling his torso toward the lowered SUV window, Alejandro dragged his gaze down her body, to the tips of her well-worn boots, and back up again. The lazy perusal might as well have been a physical brush of his fingertips the way her body reacted, awareness tingling in secret spots that had missed his touch.

"I'm watching you kick your own ass in this unbearable heat," he answered. "The smart ones escaped inside to the AC. What gives?"

What gives?

A two-word question with a million-word answer. Most of them too personal to share, even with him. Or, more like, especially with him.

"They'll be the ones sucking wind, bitchin' after running up a few flights of stairs when the time comes. Wimps."

Forget the fact she'd been the one to put them through four rounds of the stations, fifty push-ups between each, sticking around for two more on her own. The muscle-straining, stamina-testing exercises hadn't been enough to dilute the bitter mix of sadness and disappointment gurgling up her throat and knotting her gut.

Losing a victim on a call tended to bring the general mood down for everyone in the station.

Losing an otherwise healthy, middle-aged man to a massive cardiac infarction brought old ghosts swooping over her. The stark reminder of her papi's heart attack and the resulting aftermath raised goose bumps down her arms. Set her thoughts spinning with what-ifs and second guesses that had her rethinking decisions and dreams. The fear of losing a loved one always made her want to cling tighter to them, almost convincing herself that there was no need for change when she already lived a charmed life.

Why rock the boat by wanting more? By changing things unnecessarily?

Because settling was for suckers, damn it! And she'd been one of those long enough.

"Wimps, huh?" Alejandro asked. "You sure that's all?"

She hitched a noncommittal shoulder.

One of his dark brows quirked, pressing her for more. She ignored it. He'd lost the role of confidant ages ago.

"How's your PT going?" she asked, a not-so-subtle deflection.

"Hurts like hell."

A light breeze kicked up, cooling her skin and ruffling the dark waves of his hair. He combed his fingers through it, leaving a wavier piece sticking out at an odd angle. Her fingers twitched with the urge to smooth the piece into place. She ignored it.

One demon from her past was enough to wrestle with at the moment.

"The physical therapist's bubbly cheerleader routine annoys the crap out of me," he complained.

Anamaría nearly smiled at his grouchy petulance. "Suck it up, buttercup. You'll be thankful later."

"Spoken like someone who's not laid up with a cyborg-looking contraption holding together pieces of her leg."

"Also, someone who isn't dumb enough to scale the side of a waterfall and nose-dive onto the rocks," she countered.

"But who willingly runs into burning buildings like a super-hero answering the call for help."

She shook her head, still grappling with her and Jones's inability to revive the poor man earlier. The sounds of the defibrillator's charge as it pulsed his body, his teenaged daughter's sobbing pleas for them to do something, reverberated in Anamaría's head.

"I wouldn't necessarily call me a—"

"—and who signs contracts making her a new spokesmodel for an up-and-coming athletic wear company. Felicidades."

Her argument against being called anything close to a super-hero stalled in surprise at his congratulations.

Alejandro's dark eyes flashed with glee. "Ahhh, you didn't think I'd heard. Did you?"

"Are you kidding me?" She shook her head dubiously and hooked a hand over the lowered passenger window's edge. "On this island, with our mothers, and the way chisme passes between them and their friends? I'm not surprised you already know."

"This isn't cheap gossip," he answered. "It's good news. Of course they want to share. They're proud of you. Rightfully so."

She'd feel more proud if she could have revived that man today. Saved his daughter from facing her agonizing loss.

Anamaría shook off the guilt-driven thoughts, remembering what Luis had advised when he'd called to check on her from Station 3, where he was on duty. She and Jones had done everything by the book. They'd followed standing protocols set by the Medical Director to the letter. Sometimes, despite their best efforts, it was too late. There was nothing they could do.

Dwelling on the call. Doubting her decisions. Those could only lead to mistakes with the next person. Eyes fluttering closed, she rubbed her forehead, massaging the stress headache pounding inside.

"¿Qué te pasa?" Alejandro's hand covered hers on the door ledge. The soft caress of his thumb along the side of hers sent heat spreading up her arm, short-circuiting her resolve to remain unaffected by him.

"Nothing's wrong with me," she fibbed.

"You sure?"

Lips clamped shut, she dipped her chin in a brisk nod, unwilling to confide in him when he was a distressing thread weaving through the memories and emotions she struggled with.

"You want to play it that way? That's fine. But if you need to talk something out." His hand tightened briefly over hers. "I'm here."

"Uh-huh, sure." The skepticism automatically slipped out.

Sure he was here; for now. Until things got uncomfortable with his dad and Alejandro took off again, rather than work through their difference of opinion.

Or until adventure crooked its finger and lured him away, which she couldn't exactly blame him for given his talent. Although leaving didn't mean he couldn't eventually return home. That had been his decision.

Just as hers had been to wait for him. Lying to herself that she had moved on.

Not anymore.

Exhausted by the day's emotional toll, she dragged her hand out from under Alejandro's and took a step back, out of his reach. "I'm good. Thanks."

His doubtful expression told her he wasn't convinced, but he didn't press. "I thought you'd wanna know that I'm working on something. I'm not ready to say anything yet, but this should keep my mom busy enough to get her mind off matchmaking."

Something?

With the call earlier having dredged up the past, Alejandro's secrecy now had her reliving the shock when he confessed about having applied for and accepted the six-month apprenticeship in Spain, without telling her. The betrayal of him making a choice that affected both their lives, their plans, then not understanding why she'd been upset, still rankled.

"If you really want to know—"

"That's okay!" She threw up a stop sign with her hands as she edged backward toward the sidewalk. Him being here right now only compounded her difficulty with silencing past fears so they wouldn't sabotage her present. "I'm not involved with whatever you're cooking up to thwart your mom. And I don't plan to be."

Alejandro frowned, probably confused by her brush-off after the way they'd left things last week. But today, swarmed with harrowing memories, she was having trouble holding on to his olive branch offering.

"You do your thing." Like he always did. Like she was determined to do now. "And I'll do mine."

She took another step and backed into her brother with an *oof*.

"Everything okay?" Enrique asked.

"Yep. All done here." She spun and sidestepped around her brother, anxious to get away. "I should get back inside."

"Hey, you wanna—"

"Catch you later, E." She lifted a hand to wave but didn't turn around. He'd see the lie in on her face and she couldn't deal with an interrogation.

On the sidewalk, Anamaría bent down to grab her gear, then hightailed it to the station. Away from the temptation to fall into old habits like confiding in Alejandro and accepting the comfort he offered simply because she felt vulnerable at the moment. If she gave in, she'd only wind up getting hurt later. Unlike before, she knew better this time.

Anamaría waved good-bye to the last of her Morning Yoga on the Beach students, watching as they drove away in their cars and on their mopeds or hopped on their beach cruisers and pedaled down the wide sidewalk at Smathers Beach.

Once they had all departed, she turned to face the open ocean.

Instead of starting to pack up the yoga blocks she provided for students, she closed her eyes and tipped her chin into the light breeze. The bright ball of the morning sun hovering above the horizon left a dark circle behind her lids.

Inhaling deeply, she filled her lungs with the familiar waft of sulfur from the piles of seaweed washed up and drying on the shore. Many wrinkled their noses at the stench. To her, it mixed with the fresh, briny scent blowing in from the ocean, creating a smell she would always equate with home and the contentment that came with being where she belonged.

Toes wiggling in the wet sand. Ears tuned to the lap of barely there waves on the shore thanks to the reef, and the putter of a boat's motor out on the water. Skin dewy with humidity and perspiration. In her element.

Only this morning, the sense of serenity her yoga sessions typically brought eluded her.

When two belly-filling breaths and slow releases still hadn't quieted her unease, Anamaría dropped down onto the packed sand. She crossed her legs to sit in lotus position, elbows bent, the backs of her hands resting on top of her knees. The midmorning sun wrapped her in its welcome embrace, heating her bare legs and arms, kissing her cheeks.

She should be excited. Preparing for her first AllFit photo shoot tomorrow. The company had even upped the wow factor by working out the logistics for Brandon Lawson to come to Key West.

Forget butterflies. Baby seagulls like the little ones scampering across the sand flapped in her belly when she thought about the text message Brandon sent her last night:

Looking forward to some fun and sun with you tomorrow.

Even though he had a weekend event on his schedule, Brandon was flying down for a brief overnight trip before heading out west. According to her agent, Brandon had suggested the idea of them pairing up. A splashy way to announce her partnership with AllFit, seeing as how he'd been the company's face since its inception several years ago.

Sara had whooped with glee when Anamaría called her with the news. Of course her lovesick soon-to-be sister-in-law had jumped to unfounded conclusions.

"Brandon is hard to book. I told you I got an 'interested' vibe when you two connected over cocktails," Sara had said.

"Dios mío, por favor, not you, too," Anamaría had complained. The last thing she needed was another matchmaker in her familia.

Those baby seagulls in her stomach flapped harder at the complication even a hint of romance with Brandon would add to her current troubles.

Heaving a groan—the opposite of a yoga cleansing breath—Anamaría pushed up to her bare feet. After slapping the sand from her hands and butt, she gathered her supplies, then trudged up the beach, stopping to pick up an empty paper cup and toss it in the trash.

Supply basket stored in the back of her Honda Pilot, she tapped her Apple watch to disable the Do Not Disturb mode. Few things were worse than her mami interrupting yoga class in the middle of a chaturanga or a soothing child's pose with a nagging text about Anamaría not stopping by the house enough.

As if to prove her point, as soon as her watch was live it buzzed with notifications. *La Reina* and Señora Miranda's name flashed on the small screen.

"What are the two mamis instigating now?" Anamaría grumbled. She was not up for another meddling-mami intervention. Not today. She still had two more group classes, a private session, and her own workout. Plus, reviewing tomorrow morning's shoot with Sara.

Sliding onto the driver's seat, Anamaría fished for her cell phone in her backpack's side pocket. Seconds later, she was listening to Señora Miranda's worried voice mail.

"Ay, nena, I am sorry to bother you—"

"Then don't. Hang up, Mami." Alejandro's beleaguered voice cut through his mother's greeting.

"Shhh, es un mensaje!" Señora Miranda chided. "Where was I?

Ay, yes, my hardheaded son has told his physical therapist he no longer needs her services."

"Because I don't!" he cried in the background.

"¡Basta, Alejandro; enough! You are interrupting my message."

Normally, the familiar bickering between an exasperated adult child and the Cuban mami in whose eyes her kids were never fully grown would have had Anamaría crowing with laughter. But she sensed the reason behind the phone call and wasn't looking forward to confirming her intuition.

"Please come and talk some sense into him, so I can stop worrying," Señora Miranda pleaded.

Alejandro's "Unbelievable" groan in the background was a classic child-embarrassed-by-their-parent reaction. Thanks to her own mami, Anamaría could relate.

Undeterred, Señora Miranda pressed on, delivering the final nails in Anamaría's coffin. "We are home now, and I believe you should be finishing with your morning yoga class at Smathers Beach soon. I will wait for you to arrive. Gracias, nena, te lo agradezco."

Of course, the older woman was already saying she appreciated Anamaría stopping by their house. They all knew Anamaría wouldn't ignore a cry for help. Nor would she disrespect her elder by pretending she hadn't seen the voice mail until later today.

They were familia. Maybe not by blood, but by choice. Even if that choice was by virtue of their shared comunidad and years of friendship, instead of the anticipated marriage. The twinge of buried dreams jabbed at her heart.

Huffing out a resigned sigh, Anamaría started the car and buckled her seat belt.

The Miranda house was only a few minutes from here. With a little zigzagging off Atlantic Boulevard, she'd pass by on the way to her next group class on the Casa Marina Resort's grounds.

She could stop in, reassure Señora Miranda that her elder son's leg would not grow gangrene and fall off or whatever extreme scenario the older woman's worry gene envisioned happening.

She could also tell Alejandro to stop being a pain in everyone's ass and simply follow his doctor's advice. At least, until he was no longer under his parents' roof and his mami's watchful eye. Stop traumatizing the poor woman, so she'd stop SOSing Anamaría.

The secret plan to distract his mother he had mentioned yesterday needed to start today. Enough was enough.

Pulling away from the curb and making a U-turn, she drove west on South Roosevelt, following the curve in the road onto Bertha Street. Several turns later, she hit Laird Street, and shortly after the gravel edging the road and sidewalk crunched under her tires as she pulled to a stop in front of the Mirandas' house.

She ducked under a low-hanging bougainvillea vine in the privacy wall alcove and was two steps up the brick walkway trailing through the lush lawn when she drew to a surprised halt.

Alejandro stood on the front stoop, hunched over a pair of crutches that were jammed in his armpits for support. His wheelchair was nowhere in sight.

The stubborn mule probably shouldn't be upright, at least not without his wheelchair nearby if he suddenly tired and certainly not on his own.

Instinct and experience had her eyeing his Nike sneaker–clad feet, relieved to note that at least he was smart enough to keep his weight on his good leg. Although *smart* wasn't the word she would use to describe him at the moment.

As if sensing her disapproval, he straightened out of his hunch, his fingers clenched around the handgrips. His biceps flexed with tension, tightening the short sleeves of his navy T-shirt, already a little snug across his broad shoulders. His previously hollowed cheeks had filled out. A sign his papi, mami, and abuela's cooking was doing its job of fattening him up over the past week and a half.

Of course, based on the pecs outlined by his formfitting tee and the curve of his vastus medialis obliques visible under the hem of his athletic shorts, muscles honed by the miles he typically put on the racing bike she'd seen on his social media feed, there wasn't an ounce of fat on the irritating man's body.

Her pulse kicked up a traitorous notch at the thought of tracing the new hills and planes of his physique. Exploring the changes the years had wrought, taking him from young man to . . . she gulped . . . *all* man.

"You shouldn't have come." The annoyed twist of his full lips mimicked his tone.

She arched a brow and shot him an equally annoyed glower.

"It only encourages her," he complained.

"Nu-uh." Anamaría shook her head, refusing to let him put the blame on her. "That's what you're doing. By pushing her buttons."

Alejandro shifted on his right foot, shimmying his hips and shoulders as he tried to balance himself. His right crutch lifted as he careened dangerously to his left, flailing to keep his balance.

Anamaría hurried toward him, afraid the hardheaded idiot might fall and wind up doing more damage to his tibia.

"I got it," he growled, his jerky motions finally settling. "I don't need your help."

She pulled up short a few feet away. "Apparently, you don't need anyone's help. Is that it?"

The crutches squeaked under his weight, the rubber soles thumping on the mottled cream and chocolate tiles as he hobbled to the far edge of the covered porch.

"I told you yesterday, the PT was too damn perky. Between her Positive Patty routine and my mami's hovering and my dad's . . . I just . . . carajo, I can't take it right now!" He shoved a hand through his tousled hair, his frustration telegraphed in the tight grip he held on the back of his neck. "The PT left a sheet with some exercises. I'll be fine."

"As long as you do them properly. If not, you could wind up causing more damage." Anamaría glanced through the set of double-hung windows into the living room, expecting to see Señora Miranda or Alejandro's abuela watching their favorite morning show on Telemundo. While peeking at whatever was going on out front.

Instead, the familia sala sat oddly empty.

"Where's your mom?" Anamaría asked, squinting past the empty sala at the kitchen and lanai farther back in the house.

"She's helping Abuela put away some laundry in her room. Mostly, I think they knew I needed some space. It's like the walls here are closing in on me."

For someone used to living outside of the familia bubble, especially the one exacerbated by island life, being confined like he was could make the antsiness worse. "My mom giving me space is pretty rare; you should be thankful. At least, this gives me a few minutes to talk some sense into you."

Anamaría looked back at him in time to catch his eye roll. Despite her irritation at being summoned, she understood some of his frustration.

Her phone buzzed in her leggings hip pocket at the same time Sara's name lit up on her Apple watch. Anamaría ignored the call. "Please tell me that whatever plan you cryptically mentioned yesterday to distract your mother from her matchmaking is not this. Because if so, it's a dumb one."

He blew out an annoyed *pffft.* "Of course not. Do you think I'm an idiot?"

Hip cocked, Anamaría crossed her arms and silently stared back at him. "Do you really want me to answer that?"

"Whatever," he grumbled, waving off her jab by flapping an elbow as he held on to his crutches. "No, it's not my plan. If you really want to know . . ." His gaze slid to the window as if ensuring the coast was still clear. "I'm working with a gallery downtown to host an exhibit of my work."

"What?!" Joy flooded through her, pushing aside her exasperation with him. "Alejandro, that's incredible!"

Dios, the hours they'd spent strolling hand in hand downtown, admiring and critiquing gallery displays. Him confident that someday an Alejandro Miranda photograph would fetch the high prices marking many of the pieces.

"It's what you used to dream about." What *they* dreamed about together.

Nostalgia, bittersweet and aching, swelled in her chest.

"I did," he acknowledged with a dip of his head, swiping at the lock of hair that tumbled over his forehead, into his eyes. "Still do."

"Then what's wrong?"

Gaze glued to the tile at her feet, he rubbed a hand up and down his angular jaw, pensive. Uncomfortable . . . or, strange, maybe even uncertain?

That wasn't the Alejandro Miranda she'd known. Or the one that he ran off and became without her. *Uncertain* did not describe the man who scaled waterfalls and ran with the bulls and wielded a machete to help remote villagers forge a trail to a new water source in South America.

Seeing this side of the man who had become almost larger than life in the pictures she saw on social media and the stories his mami and abuela had shared with her over the years reminded Anamaría of the boy struggling with the desire to please his familia while being true to himself. The teen she had given her heart to, before he'd become the angry young man fighting for what he wanted in a way she couldn't go along with.

Caught up in her own struggle between what she had yearned for and what was reality, she watched Alejandro absently scratch at the several days' scruff darkening his jaw. His mussed hair and slightly wrinkled tee gave him a just-rolled-outta-bed vibe that he wore well. Like, dangerously well. Reminding her of other, more private activities they had shared when not gallery hopping together.

The thrill of young love, of sharing firsts with someone your heart assured you was *the* one. Lust curled through her, puckering her nipples at the delicious memory of his touch and the thought of the times since then when she secretly conjured him in her bed when she was alone with a certain battery-powered toy.

Conscious of her thin exercise bra material, she crossed her arms and angled away from the living room window, away from peeping eyes inside.

"Why haven't you said anything about the exhibit?" she asked, pulling her thoughts back to a much safer topic. "The Cuban mami grapevine would already be working overtime to spread the word. Forget matchmaking!"

"I don't know. I mean . . . shit, this is stupid." He blew out a harsh laugh, one hand tap-tap-tapping the metal crutch bar nervously. "You'd think I'd be past this by now."

"Past what?"

He stared at her intently for several beats, tension emanating from him. That strange uncertainty she would never attribute to him clouded his dark eyes.

"My work isn't something my father necessarily takes pride in. You know that," he admitted. His throat bobbed with a swallow and a shadow darkened his dejected expression even more. "I don't want him to take me having a local exhibit as another sign of me thumbing my nose at him, at Miranda's."

Anamaría's heart ached for him. For the son who, whether he admitted it or not, admired and looked up to his father, who couldn't bring himself to accept their differences. Ironically, they shared one important similarity, both having worked their way up from entry level positions in their respective professions. One going from dishwasher to successful restaurant owner; the other moving from apprentice to sought after, award-winning photographer.

"It doesn't matter." Alejandro lifted a shoulder, dropping it in a blasé move he might think would mask his disappointment.

Maybe it worked with others. But not with her. She knew him too well. Despite her years of trying to forget. "It's okay to admit that it does. Matter, I mean."

Angry lines creased his brow, but he didn't respond.

"I understand that he's always been tough on you. But I also know that he's capable of changing his mind. I've seen it. He's been open-minded with me."

Alejandro's frown deepened, his eyes filling with scornful anger the more she defended his father.

"Maybe if you—"

"You know what? Screw it!" Lifting his crutches, Alejandro

stomped them against the tile with an angry thump. "The owners of Bellísima were planning to be out of town all of July, so they didn't schedule a special display. They're willing to change their travel and host the opening night of my exhibition July Fourth weekend. That's pretty fucking incredible of them. I shouldn't be dragging my feet because of someone who won't even try to understand my perspective. I'm gonna give Marcelo and Logan a definitive yes."

"That's . . . that's good. I think you should." She honestly did. Maybe witnessing his son's success would stir Señor Miranda's benevolence.

"Mami and Abuela will be thrilled," Alejandro went on, as if still working to convince himself that this was the right decision. "Ernesto and Cece can bring Lulu. Maybe even the new baby. Plus, your parents and brothers. Even, well, everyone's welcome . . . if they're interested."

He stared at her. A silent, hopeful invitation. As if he doubted whether or not she would accept.

She could never tell him no. Not about something so important to him. His exhibition was a shared dream from their past. This was a chance for them to experience it together. Albeit, in a different way than anticipated.

A lump lodged in her throat, and she swiveled to face the open front yard again. The bougainvillea vines with their bright fuchsia flowers trailing up the inside of the privacy wall blurred. She blinked rapidly, willing away the sting of tears. It'd be hard, witnessing his achievement as an old friend, rather than his partner.

But coño, she did not want to be the bitter ex-girlfriend anymore. The one left behind, whose familia tiptoed around whenever his name came up.

She hadn't done herself any favors by settling into that role, even if it had happened unintentionally.

This was a chance for her to prove she had moved on. Prove to him, her familia, and, more important, herself.

"If I'm not on duty, I'll be there," she promised. "I wouldn't miss it for anything."

His shoulders relaxed, as if her acceptance removed some of the weight pressing on them.

"Bellísima's a beautiful space," she said, moving the focus off them and their past to a positive in their future.

"It is. Marcelo and Logan have a great eye."

"I'm sure your photographs are going to look amazing there."

He smiled, the excitement she had expected with his announcement finally dawning on his handsome face, softening his chiseled jaw. "Yeah, I'm already combing through my files, imagining different collections. Thinking about where they'd best fit in the space. Marcelo may bring in an art consultant he knows since we'll have to pull this together so quickly. That's why I'm roping in my mom. If I ask her to be in charge of the food and help with promo, she'll stay busy."

"Not, however, if she's also worrying about your recovery. Tossing your PT wasn't the brightest move."

"Again, with the nagging!" He gave an exaggerated groan and spun away on his good foot.

The rubber grip on the bottom of his crutches stuck to the tile, and his left crutch clattered to the floor. His injured leg swung out erratically, both arms and the lone crutch he still held flailing through the air as his torso wobbled from side to side in his fight to maintain his balance.

Anamaría lunged forward hoping to catch him before he fell.

"I got it— Ow!" Alejandro groaned as her knee accidentally banged into the top external fixator ring.

Her arms encircled his waist, inadvertently knocking the second crutch aside, sending it crashing to the floor with the other. His eyes widened with an almost comical combination of astonishment as she tightened her hold, hugging his body against hers in an intimate embrace.

They wound up chest to chest, her face buried in the warmth of his neck, his woodsy patchouli and citrus scent filling her lungs.

One of his arms wrapped tightly around her shoulders, the other around her hip, his hand cradling her butt cheek.

Her brain sounded an alarm, warning her to step back, put some distance between them. Instead, she fisted his T-shirt in her hands, unable to let go of him yet.

A car pulled into the neighbor's driveway, its squeaking brakes interrupting the charged silence on the Mirandas' front porch.

Alejandro cleared his throat, a low rumble that vibrated against her nose and cheek, still nestled in the crook of his neck.

"Damn, woman, if you wanted to sneak a feel, all you had to do was ask. Not tackle me," he teased.

Angling her head to peek up at him, she quirked a brow in challenge. "I'm not the one with a hand on someone's ass."

He winked, then had the audacity to flex his fingers on her butt cheek. Lust shot from her glute straight to her core, leaving her throbbing with desire.

"It's pretty hard to resist when a good-looking woman throws herself at me. Not that I mind."

"Uh-huh, I bet." She started to pull away, enjoying the titillating feel of being in his arms again way too much for her own good.

Alejandro's arm around her shoulder stiffened, holding her in place.

She started to object, but he ran a hand through the strands of her loose ponytail, his fingertips grazing the bare skin on her back between her sports bra and leggings, and her argument evaporated. Her pulse hitched as he twisted his wrist to wrap the length of her hair around his open palm like he used to do. Tethering himself to her. He lifted the tangled strands to his face and her eyes drifted closed, reveling in the rise of his chest pressing against hers as he sucked in a deep breath.

"Still using the same tropical shampoo you like, huh?" he murmured.

She nodded, not trusting her voice. Telling herself to step back. Put "friendly truce" distance between them.

But he sucked in another deep whiff of her shampoo, and she swore he stole the very breath from her.

"God, I've smelled this scent in my dreams so many times." His deep voice rumbled over her, a rich, husky caress. "Thought I caught a whiff of it once at an open-air market in India."

Tears burned her eyes, and she squeezed them shut even tighter.

His other hand slid from her butt to her lower back, leaving a trail of heat that burned with its intensity. She pressed closer. Not wanting to let go of him. Of this moment.

"Damn, I've missed you."

His gruff admission was her undoing. A hot tear leaked out of the corner of her eye to trail down the side of her face.

He'd missed her. Just not enough to come back. Not until he was forced to.

And, inevitably, he would leave again.

Her watch and phone buzzed with an incoming text message alert, a welcome intrusion stopping her from revealing an admission of her own that she would later regret.

Loosening her hold, she eased back, careful to hold him steady. "We should get you inside. I'm sure the PT didn't intend for you to ditch the wheelchair for good."

Alejandro nodded but slid his hand down the length of her ponytail one last time, his fingers threading through the strands. The familiar gesture tightened twin knots of desire and regret deep within her.

He held on to her shoulder to steady himself while she toed one of his crutches closer, then bent to pick it up. When she stooped to grab the second one, her phone buzzed with another incoming call. She handed him the crutch and caught Sara's name scrolling on her watch screen again.

"You mind if I take this?" she asked. "Sara's tried to reach me several times since I got here."

"Go for it."

Answering on her cell rather than via speakerphone on her

watch, Anamaría stepped to the far side of the porch. "Hey, Sara, what's up?"

"Hi. Listen . . . I don't want you to freak out about anything," Sara said, her harried voice sounding like she might be freaking out herself. "I'm working on a Plan B. So don't worry, okay?"

"What are you talking about? And, FYI, when you lead with 'don't freak out,' it usually makes someone do exactly that," Anamaría joked.

The crutches squeaked and she glanced over her shoulder to find Alejandro had moved closer. Just like one of their moms, he made no attempt to pretend he wasn't eavesdropping.

"I take it you haven't seen Craig's email to us?" Sara asked.

"The photographer for tomorrow's photo shoot? No. I've been, um, a little busy since my morning yoga class. Haven't paid attention to notifications."

Sara's heavy sigh blew through the phone speaker. "He got food poisoning, so he can't make the drive from Miami today. He's a no-go for the AllFit shoot in the morning."

"Oh crap! And Brandon's on his way here already, isn't he?" Anamaría slapped a hand over her forehead, the news making her do exactly what Sara had advised against, freak out. "Um, let me think who I could try locally. I know a few photographers; it's just a matter of whether or not one of them's available?"

"If worse comes to worst, I can take the pictures myself," Sara suggested. "Brandon and I have a good eye. So do you. We should be fine."

"In a pinch, I'd say okay. But with Brandon coming all this way, I'd hate to not use a professional if we can avoid that," Anamaría said. The guy was planning to give her first AllFit post a boost by sharing their pictures on his social media accounts, tagging her to help drive his followers to her feed.

"¿Qué pasa?" Alejandro whispered over her shoulder.

She waved him off, then stopped, an idea taking hold. A crazy one. But definitely their best option.

"Hey, Sara, give me a few minutes. I might have a solution."

"You do? What is it?" Sara asked, surprise raising her voice an octave.

"Let me see if it'll work first. I'll call you in about ten, when I'm on my way to the Casa Marina for another group class." After reassuring Sara that she did indeed have something up her sleeve, Anamaría disconnected the call. Tapping her cell on her chin, she stared blindly at the front yard as she considered the pros and cons of what she was about to propose.

"What's going on?" Alejandro asked.

Craning her neck, she peeked at him over her shoulder. "You're tired of being confined to the house. Watching telenovelas with your abuela. Right?"

Alejandro eyed her suspiciously but nodded and step-swung on the crutches to stand beside her on the patio's edge. He squinted down at her under the late-morning sun.

"Got any plans tomorrow?" she asked.

His "pffft" and accompanying scowl boded well for her scheme.

"I'm waiting to hear back from Marcelo about whether the art consultant he knows in Chicago is available. So, you're pretty much looking at my plans." He waved a hand down his front, then at the empty yard. "Although 'Buela's telenovela is really starting to heat up. El patrón is about to find out—"

"Okay, okay, stop!" she said on a laugh, holding up her hands. "Then I have a proposition for you."

"Oye, what kind of guy do you take me for?" He pressed a hand to his chest in mock horror. "First you feel me up, now you're propositioning me?"

"¡Ay Dios mío, por favor!" She bumped her shoulder against his, relieved that their up close and personal moment earlier hadn't made things awkward. "I'm in a bind, but I have an idea that'll get you out of the house, get me some fantastic photographs courtesy of the best photographer currently on the island—"

"Flattery will get you everywhere with me." He winked, that cocky grin of his flashing again.

"Thought so." She wrinkled her nose at him playfully. "And, my idea will stop our moms from trying to finagle a way to get us together. Mainly because we'll already be together."

"Hmm, I'm intrigued." Alejandro twisted to glance back inside the house where his mami and abuela now sat on the floral couch in front of the television, smiles wide as they waved at him.

Of course the two women were watching. They were probably taking notes to report back to her mami.

Anamaría checked the time on her watch, not wanting to arrive late for her next session. She quickly filled Alejandro in on Brandon's short time frame visit, their planned photo shoot at Higgs Beach and the White Street Pier, and the sick photographer.

"The wheelchair situation isn't ideal, but I'll manage," Alejandro said. "I'd want to get a rundown on any particular shots All-Fit has in mind. As well as what you and Brandon are thinking. Maybe Sara, too, since she's got experience with similar shoots."

"Are you sure? This is a big ask. And we're . . ." Anamaría trailed off, unsure how to describe what the heck they were now.

"We're two professionals helping each other. I haven't taken a picture since my epic swan dive and could stand to get out of here for a bit. You need my stellar skills. Win-win." He pivoted on his good leg to face her, lifting his crutches off the tile this time to avoid a replay of his earlier debacle.

He lifted a hand to cup her shoulder, but his gaze slid to the front window where his mami and abuela sat in plain view. Furtively watching as if Anamaría and Alejandro were their telenovela come to life.

His hand dropped back to the crutch handgrip.

Probably a good thing. Based on the way she had nearly combusted at his simple ass grab a few minutes ago.

"Okay, let me get your number and I'll text you Sara's. I'm booked with classes and private sessions, so I won't be available until midafternoon." Anamaría pulled her cell from her leggings pocket and handed it to him. As soon as he was done saving his information in her contacts, she stepped off the porch. Spinning around to point at him, she backpedaled across the grass. "Now *you* need to get inside and elevate that leg, so you're not in pain tomorrow because you overdid it today."

"I'm fine."

She shook her head. "Suck it up and call your PT. Stick with her for at least a couple weeks to make sure you know what the hell you're doing and don't reinjure yourself. Even if it's just to pacify your mom."

"Nag, nag, nag."

The playful smirk on his lips teased another curl of desire whisking through her.

"I think you should let her know about your you know what," she said, purposefully speaking in veiled words out of respect for his secret but not wanting to leave without letting him know she was in his corner. Even if it was in a different capacity than before. "It's a great opportunity, Ale. I'm excited for you. *Everyone* will be excited about your exhibit. He'll understand. Trust me. It takes time, but he *will* come around."

Alejandro's expression sobered at her reference to his father.

"I'm really happy for you, Ale," she offered. "Bellísima's lucky they're getting to show your work."

He dipped his head in thanks, though his joy had dimmed. "I appreciate it."

"And you're lucky that you'll get to work with me mañana." She winked, pleased at his bark of laughter as she sent him a loose-fingered wave and slipped out of the Mirandas' yard.

Inside her car, she lowered the windows and put the AC on high to cool off the interior; then, using the Bluetooth connection, she dialed Sara. As the phone rang, she hoped she'd made the right move by asking for Alejandro's help. Prayed that they could bank their lingering attraction for the short time he was here. Because clearly it wasn't extinguished.

On this tiny island, with parents as close as theirs, running into him was unavoidable. So, attempting some kind of friendly-ish relationship their moms accepted as the best outcome they could get was better than the stilted, uncomfortable conversations they'd had when he first arrived.

But getting close to him again, relishing the rush of desire when his strong arms wrapped around her and his heady scent made her woozy with desire. Giving into the thrum of a need long unquenched . . .

That would be unwise and foolish. If also temptingly delicious.

Chapter 10

"You don't know how relieved I was to get your call yesterday," Sara Vance told Alejandro as they made the short drive from his parents' house to Higgs Beach and the White Street Pier early the next morning.

Seated next to Luis Navarro's fiancée, with the front passenger seat in her Toyota RAV4 pushed as far back as possible to accommodate his injured leg, Alejandro cradled his trusty Canon in his lap. For the first time since his accident, he felt a little like his old self again. Pre–nose dive off the waterfall. Back when he didn't have to work so hard to avoid his dad. When regrets of what might have been were relegated to late at night or weak moments . . . not 24-7 with reminders all around him.

He smoothed his thumb over the camera's backside, saying hello to an old friend. The familiar itch to explore his location, determine the perfect spot with the right angles and lighting, and start capturing images started at his fingertips, then spread up his arms, into his chest. Invigorating him.

"I'm happy to help," he told Sara, eyeing the lush vegetation along the south side of Atlantic Boulevard. Mother Nature's early-morning sun peeked across the sky, soft and hazy. The ideal lighting for outdoor photography. "Actually, like Anamaría mentioned, I'm relieved to get out of the house and work on something productive."

Sara flashed a friendly smile, one that had earned "likes" from millions the world over. Her classic features, blue-green eyes, wavy blond tresses, and runner's physique gave her a girl-next-door appeal that had many companies paying for her to use and promote their products or services.

But Alejandro knew she was more than a pretty face. Sara Vance also possessed the keen mind of a successful entrepreneur. One who'd gone from small-time fashion and beauty blogger in college to sought-after social media influencer to the designer of her own clothing line. More important, to him at least, over the past year she had taken Anamaría under her wing, providing guidance and introducing her to contacts that were helping build the AM Fitness brand.

The irony of this outgoing people person who lived much of her life in front of the camera and connecting with individuals across the globe being engaged to the strong but silent, most introverted of the Navarro brothers wasn't lost on Alejandro. According to Enrique, Sara and Luis balanced each other, somehow fitting perfectly together.

If he still believed in soul mates and happily-ever-after, Alejandro guessed Luis and Sara would be the poster couple. For their sake, he hoped so.

Sara slowed her SUV as they approached the three-way stop where Atlantic Boulevard intersected with White Street. Off to their left the long concrete pier jutted out over the ocean.

"I have to admit, you did cross my mind when I first hung up with Craig yesterday. But with your injury and . . . given your history with Anamaría . . ."

Sara's blue-green gaze cut to him. He was sure she knew all about his and Anamaría's breakup. And since she had only heard the Navarro side of the story, more than likely she viewed him as the one to blame. Family loyalty was strong with the Navarros. He respected that. Even with him being on the wrong side of it when it came to protecting their Princesa.

To his surprise, though, Sara's watchful gaze didn't contain condemnation like his father's. More like caution, as if she was reserving judgment until she drew her own conclusion about him. Encouraged by her attitude, he opted to trust Luis Navarro's judgment and trust Sara with the truth.

"I'm sure you've heard about my history with Anamaría. For what it's worth, I'm excited for her and the opportunities she's worked to attain. She asked for my help, as a friend. No way would I or could I refuse. Because of our history. But also because I want what's best for her."

A car behind them beeped, and Sara eased away from the stop sign, heading toward the public parking spots along Higgs Beach.

She arched a light brown brow, her pensive glances between him and the road a little unnerving. "That's very commendable of you."

Having just met her, Alejandro couldn't tell if she was being serious or condescending.

"This isn't the type of shoot you'd usually book," Sara continued. "More small potatoes when compared to the magazine covers and inspiring cultural and geographical photography you're known for."

"Nah." He waved off her flattery. "Every job has potential. Honestly, when I'm on location, some of my favorite photographs are a result of me wandering the streets on my own time. Interacting with locals."

Sara pulled into an open parking spot by the West Martello Tower, the unfinished Civil War–era fort that housed the Key West Garden Club's botanical gardens. The redbrick structure, known for its archways and paths, lush gardens, and gorgeous views overlooking the Atlantic Ocean, was often a sought-after location for weddings and private events. Back in high school, one of Anamaría's girlfriends had held her quinceañera here.

Staring at the brick building's façade, Alejandro could easily picture the moment Anamaría had stepped into her familia's living room wearing that figure-skimming mermaid-cut sleeveless red gown. Her dark hair a mass of curls gathered in a fancy updo. He'd nearly swallowed his tongue, his hormones going haywire. Nearly embarrassing himself in front of her parents.

Thinking about their up close and personal encounter on his front porch yesterday, it was clear that his body still reacted the same way to hers.

Alejandro's gaze scanned the public beach off to the right, one of his adolescent playgrounds. Like countless other spots around the island, this place held so many memories of him and Anamaría.

How many times had they sat at one of the concrete picnic tables sharing a sandwich from Sandy's Café? Most Friday nights they'd hung out here with Enrique and a group of friends until ten o'clock rolled around and the cops shooed them off. Across the street a little farther down, at Astro City Park, he and Anamaría had shared their first kiss. July Fourth weekend, the summer before their sophomore year.

"Well then, if local pictures are your personal specialty, I guess White Street Pier and the beach are great locations." Sara's observation chased away his memories, bringing him back to the here and now.

"Definitely," he agreed. "And I can't get more local than a born-and-raised Conch as my subject."

The same girl who had starred in much of his early work.

They'd almost come full circle. Unfortunately, true to form, this circle would continue the same way, with him leaving to find the next great photograph that would fill the void inside him.

"Well, *one* Conch and one Malibu surfer," Sara reminded him, her eyes alight with excitement. "East and West Coast combining in social media greatness. Or at least, that's our goal."

Yes, it was, Alejandro reminded himself, despite his unease. He was all for Anamaría expanding her business, pleased he'd be helping her do that today. But he wasn't exactly interested in watching her "combine" with the golden boy surfer turned Iron Man triathlete who had been splashed across the cover of *Men's Health* with his surfboard last year.

From what Sara had shared over the phone yesterday, and Alejandro's own poking around the internet had confirmed, Brandon was considered by many to be a stand-up guy who took his personal training and work seriously. However, he also knew how to have a good time, usually with an equally fit, strikingly beautiful woman on his arm.

The thought of Anamaría becoming the next Brandon Lawson "it" girl had Alejandro squeezing his Canon in a death grip. Just as quickly as his jealousy reared its green-eyed head, though, he realized the folly of his reaction.

Anamaría was smart enough not to fall for a player, if that's what Brandon turned out to be. And if his good-guy reputation proved legit, then he was a better man than Ale was.

Either way, his pride and joy did not deserve to be manhandled in petty anger. This camera had gifted him with moments and memories that aided him in forgetting others that haunted him.

Accomplishments like nabbing the *National Geographic* cover last fall with the elephant sanctuary series that Lulu had marveled over while cuddling on his lap. Meaningful experiences like befriending the Costa Rican villagers who welcomed him into their homes and shared the humility and spiritual meaning behind their simple way of life via the article in *AFAR* magazine.

His momentous trip to Cuba, where he had connected with familia he'd never known, walked the streets where his abuelos had lived and loved, and visited his father's childhood home.

"Let me grab your wheelchair, and we can head down the pier." Sara pushed open the driver's side door and grabbed her woven shoulder bag off the console.

"We can leave it. I'll be fine using the crutches."

The look she shot him over her shoulder clearly screamed, *Yeah, right!*

"Really, I'm good," he assured her.

Sara bent down to peer back into the car at him. "Your mom and my future mother-in-law will not let me hear the end of it if you overdo things today. I'm not chancing that. Not to mention Anamaría already warned me to stay on guard if you're tiring or show any sign of discomfort. So, I'll wheel you down the pier and you can switch to crutches if you need to once we get started."

"Scary how quickly a Cuban mami can have you bending to her will, even when she's not around. Isn't it?"

"My Mexican nanny could give them a run for their money. I miss her every day she's been gone. Word to the wise, be thankful for your mom, even when she's pestering you." With a raised brow, I- know-what-I'm-talking-about look at him, Sara closed her door and moved around to the back hatch where she had stored his wheelchair.

Moments later, the bag with his backup Canon and several lenses rested on his lap as Sara pushed him past the African Cemetery commemorating the enslaved men, women, and children who lost their lives in 1860, then through the AIDS Memorial that ushered visitors onto the long pier.

Out on the water, the sun floated like a big beach ball bobbing on the horizon, bleeding varying shades of orange and red across a sky dressed in hues from the purple and blue spokes of the color wheel.

"Anamaría and Brandon should be here any minute," Sara told him. "I asked her to pick him up this morning, so that you and I could have a little more time to chat. Without her."

The wary note in Sara's voice had Alejandro angling sideways to peer up at her over the frames of his Carreras.

"Here's the thing," she said. "This is AM's first major sponsorship. None of us . . . Luis, Enrique, Carlos, Gina, and I—"

¡Carajo! His gut clenched as she rattled off the names of all the Navarro siblings and Carlos's wife, apparently all in group force mode with Sara as their spokesperson.

The pan tostado con huevo his mami had insisted he choke down before leaving the house, despite his assurances that he usually ate something lighter than the toasted Cuban bread and fried eggs before a shoot, settled like a rock in his stomach.

"—none of us want your involvement to derail her," Sara continued, "or the positive step that today should represent for her and AM Fitness. Enrique assures us that you wouldn't. Frankly, his threat to kick your ass if you hurt her holds little weight given your current condition."

"I'd still take him," Alejandro complained, settling into the wheelchair's backrest with a huff.

Sara actually laughed, as if he were joking. "I'm not getting in the middle of your male posturing. It happens often enough with Luis and his brothers. Anyway, Anamaría seems to think the two of you have buried the proverbial hatchet. And Luis . . ." Sara stopped pushing the wheelchair and looked down at him, a big sister's concerned warning in her serious expression. "Well, I'm sure you remember how protective Luis is of his loved ones. The same goes with me."

Alejandro nodded, coming to see why Anamaría was a fan of her soon-to-be sister-in-law. Sara had her back, like all the Navarros did for each other.

"I assure you," he told Sara, "there's nothing to worry about on my end. Enrique might talk a lot of crap about a lot of things, but he's right about one, I want what's best for Anamaría. Happy to have my Canon in my hands again. So, in the butchered words of Lebron James when he shocked the world and thrilled everyone in the 305 area by joining the Miami Heat, 'I'm taking my talents to Higgs Beach' with the intent on using my skills to help team AM Fitness. You have my word."

The friendly smile he recognized from the pics on Sara's Instagram feed greeted his promise. "Good answer. It makes my job as protector much easier."

"She doesn't need protecting from me." Hell, after yesterday, he was beginning to think it was him who needed protecting from her.

I've missed you. Shit, he still couldn't believe he'd dropped that stink bomb after she linebacker tackled him and nearly knocked him on his ass on the front porch.

Worse, his loose-lips admission hadn't even fazed her.

He, on the other hand, had fallen asleep and woken up thinking about the curve of her butt cheek cradled perfectly in his palm. Her full breasts cushioned against his chest. Her breath warm on his neck and the familiar, citrusy scent of her shampoo teasing his memories. His body so hard and ready and aching, no amount of alone time in the shower could satisfy him.

Tack on the idiocy of him waxing poetic as if he'd been pining for her all this time. *Thought I caught a whiff of it once at an open-air market . . .* qué carajo era eso?

Lust short-circuiting his brain. That's what the hell that was.

"If you ask me, you two have some unfinished business," Sara said.

Alejandro blinked with surprise at her conclusion. Relieved his sunglasses hid the truth—he agreed with her.

"But we're all professionals here," she continued, not waiting for his response to her prediction about him and Anamaría. "Luis also reminded us that we've all made stupid decisions in the past, himself included."

Alejandro gestured to the three-ring-circus contraption on his leg with a grimace. "My latest among many. Some with regret."

Sara's head tilted to the side, as if she was considering him. "I have to admit, I might come to like you." She grinned, then wagged a finger at him in a move reminiscent of his Cuban mami when she lectured, "Just remember, if it comes down to a choice between you or Anamaría—"

"I know," he interrupted. "You're Team AM, all the way."

She shrugged her pale shoulders, bared by her yellow sundress straps and, he made a note to ask if she had slathered on sunblock. "That's how we Navarros roll."

Yes, they did. All their generations looked out for each other.

Too bad the same couldn't be said with his familia. Not when it came to him and his dad. Alejandro had been home for almost two weeks. In that time, he and his papi hadn't exchanged more than a handful of words since that first night.

Sara pushed him the rest of the way down the length of the pier, stopping once they reached the top of the nearly twenty-foot wide compass painted in the center of the wide rectangular area. "Where do you want to set up?"

Alejandro scanned their surroundings. Off to the right two older gentlemen leaned against the waist-high concrete balustrade, a brown tackle box resting between them on the top rail, fishing poles in hand, a blue cooler at their feet. An older man and woman in shorts and matching "Life Is Better in the Keys" tees waved hello as they pedaled their rental bikes around the perimeter, then made their way back down the pier.

"Let's claim this spot." He pointed straight ahead, dead center between the two sides. "That way I can angle to get the open ocean and watercolor skies as a backdrop, without the sun shading out Anamaría or Brandon. You mind posing for a few test shots?"

"Sure!" Sara padded over, then hoisted herself up to sit on the two-foot-wide concrete railing. Knees bent, arms wrapped underneath them to keep her dress from blowing up in the wind, she tipped her face to the sky. "It's a gorgeous morning, isn't it?"

"Great conditions for photography," he answered, already peering through his camera lens, the rhythmic whirr with each press of the button a sound as naturally a part of him as the beat of his heart.

A sense of déjà vu tickled the back of his neck. Taking early-morning photographs off the White Street Pier with Anamaría as his model was nothing new. Back then he'd been practicing, learning, deleting . . . trying to hone his craft.

This time, he was here for *her*. To support her career aspirations, not his. Something Alejandro was ashamed to realize was a first.

He had always been certain about pursuing photography as a career.

Anamaría had been uncertain where her passion lay. He had

pushed her to join him, thinking she could find her place out there with him. But she had come into her own here. Her island roots, interwoven with those of her familia and their comunidad, had grown stronger, helping her to flourish.

"¡Buenos días!"

Anamaría's good morning cry coming from down the pier had Alejandro's finger slipping off his Canon's shutter button.

Today was important to her. That meant he'd do whatever the hell was needed to ensure its success.

She had encouraged him when he'd been starting out. Now, he had a chance to show his appreciation for the gift she'd given him back then by doing the same.

Chapter 11

"There they are." Anamaría pointed at Sara and Alejandro up ahead as she and Brandon Lawson strolled down the White Street Pier together.

Despite her trepidation about the forecast for potential morning showers, the weather had cooperated marvelously for her first AllFit photo shoot. Clear, picturesque skies with cotton candy clouds tinted by the sun's peachy, pinky rays greeted them and a salt water–tinged breeze chased away the humidity.

She called out a greeting to Sara, perched on the concrete balustrade ledge lining the perimeter of the large open area at the end of the pier. The few remaining jitters in Anamaría's belly settled as her gaze moved to Alejandro, sitting in his wheelchair, a padded black backpack unzipped on the ground near his feet. With his back to her, she couldn't tell for sure, but she'd bet he was already snapping pics and making adjustments.

Sara had worried that having him here might be a distraction. That Anamaría would feel awkward or strained, which would definitely affect the photos. Oddly, she found comfort in having him behind the camera for her first big shoot. She could almost pretend this was like all the other times they'd spent with him snapping pics of her for practice. No pressure. Only fun.

Beside her, Brandon gave his signature head toss to send his floppy bangs out of his eyes as he waved to Sara. Picking him up at his downtown hotel had been a good icebreaker for Anamaría and the well-known trainer, as Sara had wisely suggested. Turned out, Brandon was good friends with one of AllFit's founders and had been their "face" from the beginning, even after his status as a professional tri-athlete and go-to celebrity trainer had taken off. And yet, despite his notoriety as a leading social media influencer in his field, like Sara he was surprisingly down-to-earth.

"Good morning!" Sara hopped off the railing and spread her arms wide in welcome, the skirt of her yellow sundress billowing in the breeze. "Who's ready to take some pics that'll have followers racing to share and clamoring for more?"

Brandon laughed at the overly boisterous greeting. "That's the plan. Not a bad way to spend my first visit to Key West."

Alejandro palmed the wheelchair tires, swiveling himself around to face Brandon and her. He had swapped his wrinkled-tee look for a respectable short-sleeved button-down and chinos but hadn't bothered to shave again. His wind-tousled hair, trendy sunglasses, and scruffy beard gave him a roguish vibe that fit with his adventurous streak. Unfortunately for someone trying to squelch her unwanted attraction, his vibe stroked a lusty chord within her.

Sara strolled over to give Brandon a hug, making small talk about his flight down and his accommodations.

"AM, you ready?" Alejandro asked, his voice pitched low, drawing her closer so she could hear.

"Excited. Maybe a little nervous." She angled away from the others before admitting, "I don't want to screw this up."

"Just be yourself. The camera loves you. It always has."

She was certain his pep talk was simply meant to bolster her confidence, not touch her heart. Still, it did. "Ale, I really—"

"Here, let me introduce the two of you." Sara ushered Brandon over, interrupting Anamaría. Probably saving her from being the one who made the photo shoot awkward by letting old emotions color this new phase of their relationship.

Brandon approached, his hand extended. "It's great to meet you. I gotta say, after Sara mentioned your name last night, I Googled and am a new fan. Impressive work!"

The two men, both striking in their own way, shook hands, their conversation becoming a display of mutual admiration for each other's professional accomplishments.

Sara stepped behind Brandon to greet Anamaría with a hug and cheek kiss, then looped an arm through one of Anamaría's, leaning close to whisper. "Aren't we the lucky ones working with these two today? Although they could say the same about us, right?"

Anamaría grinned at her friend's cheeky assertion while she watched the two men.

One tall, golden sun-kissed blond, with a charisma and charm that drew countless followers and clients. His light aqua AllFit tank and navy running shorts putting the muscles honed from hours spent training his body on display for the appreciative eye to ogle.

The other all lanky muscles with a broody, life-on-the-edge aura. Ale must have spent time in the Mirandas' backyard because his skin had regained its bronze tan. The healthy glow and his thick, wavy hair were a foil for the flash of his rascally grin, a combination that made parts of her quiver with desire.

Brandon gestured at the external fixator rings, wincing when Alejandro explained his fall in El Yunque. This launched a "recovering from an injury" exchange of war stories between the two adventure seekers.

Sara led her away to step up onto the raised sidewalk lining the balustrade and railing, stopping to lean a hip against the concrete ledge near a Shallow No Diving sign. "You doing okay?"

"Mm-hmm, Brandon and I had a nice conversation this morning. Thanks for suggesting I give him a ride."

"I thought it might be good to break the ice. And Alejandro?"

Anamaría glanced at her ex, his head thrown back as he laughed at whatever Brandon was wildly gesturing about. This was the real Ale. On set, Canon in hand, enjoying the people and places he captured through his lens. Living his dream.

And now he was lending his talent to help her get closer to living hers before he left.

"It's all good. Alejandro's going to give us the best pictures of AllFit gear they've ever seen." She leaned against the railing and shot Sara a sly glance, punctuated with a waggle of her brows. "Because I'll be in them."

"That's the attitude I'm talking about. Go get 'em, girl." Sara slapped her on the butt, then motioned for her to follow as she called out to the guys, "Are you two done comparing war stories over there?"

Alejandro jiggled his camera. "I was just telling Brandon, I'm happy to get out of the house for a bit. Helping familia makes this opportunity a win-win."

Familia, huh?

Keeping their ex status out of the equation today worked for Anamaría. She was fine avoiding Brandon's potential questions about her and Alejandro's breakup. Talk about awkward conversation.

Sara cupped a hand around the edge of her mouth, as if letting him in on a secret. "In case Anamaría didn't already tell you, these two grew up together. Their families go way back."

"He's my younger brother's best friend," Anamaría chimed in. "They were joined at the hip in junior high and high school. Best four-to-three double-play combination on the varsity baseball team."

Until Alejandro had given up his favorite sport for photography.

His opening salvo in the battle of wills with his father. Unfortunately, Señor Miranda hadn't budged, and Ale had never played another varsity game.

"Some of us stayed here on the island; some went off seeking fame and fortune." She ruffled Alejandro's hair, trying to maintain a playful, brotherly love act. Only the softness of his thick locks sparked the urge to let her fingers linger, maybe take a stroll down to caress the scruff on his cheeks.

Anamaría yanked her hand back before she gave in to temptation. "Key West is often a port in the storm for those who wander off. Alejandro may have dropped his anchor here for the time being, but once he's healed, he'll be off chasing the next awe-inspiring photograph, making us all proud, right, Ale?"

"Who knows, I might find it right here." Alejandro's lips quirked and he lifted his camera to snap a picture of her. "Like that one." He snapped another. "Or how about that one?"

"Sto-o-o-o-op." The word was more a whiney laugh than a command.

She stiff-armed him and ducked her head, her ponytail swishing across her face. He grabbed her hand, his fingers tangling with hers.

"None of those dorky pics will make it on my social media feed," she warned.

"I don't know, dorky is one of your best sides. You two should see some of the ones I took when we were kids."

He chuckled at her wide-eyed, you-wouldn't-dare glower. Then he flat-out belly laughed when Sara chimed in with, "I have got to see them. Do you have any of Luis?"

Swiping at the strands of hair that had snagged on her Chap-Stick, Anamaría shook her head at him, recalling the irritating way he used to tease her when he didn't want to talk about something. Like his father. The camera was the shield Ale hid behind, randomly clicking away until she laughed and waved him off or body tackled him, so he'd stop.

Of course, body tackling often led to—

Sara sidled up to her and bumped their hips together, inadvertently bumping aside memories Anamaría needed to keep buried.

"Well, we are thrilled you agreed to fill in for Craig, aren't we?" Sara said. "Here, let's get a dorky sister pic."

An experienced selfie taker, having grown her own social media reach to over half a million followers, Sara dipped her chin and tilted her head the precise way she knew would give Alejandro her best angle, then she stuck out her tongue. Anamaría joined in with her own funny face.

The soft click of Alejandro's Canon answered.

"Hey now, I want in on the action." Brandon joined the fray, looping his arm around Anamaría's shoulders on her other side.

The three of them hammed it up for several minutes. Alejandro encouraging, pulling back to remove his sunglasses and check a setting, then snapping away again.

Eventually Sara begged off and moved to stand behind Alejandro. Brandon ducked down to scoop behind Anamaría's knees.

"O-kay!" she squealed, grabbing onto his shoulders when he swept her up in his arms and strode toward the cement balustrade.

"I say we need an 'I am woman' with the ocean behind her. What do you think?" he called out.

"Yes!" Sara answered.

"Go for it," Alejandro chimed in. "Pretend I'm not even here."

Ha! Fat chance of that happening.

Brandon set her down on the two-foot-wide surface, then gave it a slap with his open palm. "Hop up."

She hesitated, for some inexplicable reason suddenly awash with a wave of insecurity. She glanced at Sara, who smiled with encouragement, then at Ale. His earnest gaze held hers, telegraphing his belief in her.

Shit, this was going to be an excruciating experience for them all if she didn't get out of her head. Trust herself. More important, trust Alejandro. He was good at what he did.

So was she.

Energized by the self-truth, she scrambled to her sneakered feet, mindful of the small ledge. She smoothed down the hem of her racerback AllFit tank, the peach color matching the tiny stripe running along the outside seam of her black cropped leggings.

"Careful. We don't want you tumbling onto the rocks on the other side," Alejandro warned.

Hands on her hips, she sent him an are-you-kidding-me stare. "That's more your signature move, not mine."

Her teasing earned her a sexy grin that peeked from under the bottom edge of his camera.

Encouraged, she flexed her right biceps à la Rosie the Riveter and tilted her face toward the sun hovering over the hazy horizon.

"I love it!" Sara cheered. "Work it, girl! That peach tank really pops against the blue sky."

Anamaría hammed it up, blowing a kiss for the camera.

Without missing a beat, Alejandro pretended to snatch her kiss out of the air, lowering his hand to press his palm against his heart.

Her own heart stuttered, then hiccupped into a faster rhythm, at how naturally he executed their old move. Something he'd started one day when she'd blown him a kiss in the middle of the hallway in between classes at Key West High. Enrique had called him a sap. She'd fallen a little more in love with him for it.

She stared at him, confused by how easily he seemed to fall back into old habits. Joking with her, offering to be her sounding board after that tough call on Monday, teasing away her qualms. Making her feel like, in his world, she mattered.

The sounds of a Jet Ski motoring by . . . a seagull squawking overhead . . . Sara asking Brandon a question . . . it all faded into the background as a maelstrom of emotions, all tied to Alejandro, swirled through Anamaría.

His arms relaxed, lowering a fraction. His dark eyes peered back at her over the top of his camera. Intent. Questioning.

She had no answers, though. The clear path she'd planned for herself over the past couple of years had started to become a bit hazy.

It was absolute foolishness really. His being forced to come home changed nothing. At best, they might be friends when he left. That's all they could ever be to each other.

As if he read her thoughts and could see the line in the sand she made herself draw between them, Alejandro gently wiggled his camera as if to say, *Back to work*; then he disappeared behind it once again.

By now Brandon had walked over to talk to Sara, who tapped Alejandro on the shoulder to include him in whatever they'd been discussing. While Anamaría waited, her gaze slid to Higgs Beach where two bikini-clad girls dragged an orange kayak into the shallow water. Nearby on the sandy shore, two guys wearing long board shorts swatted a rubber birdie back and forth with short paddles.

More memories from her and Alejandro's past assailed her. Interlopers intent on sabotaging her morning.

The two of them hanging out with friends on the beach during the day. Him pushing her on a swing at Astro City when teens took over the park at night.

Later, when the group broke up, the two of them would drive around in his beat-up Corolla, often winding up parked in the back corner of the tennis courts where they made out. Both hot and bothered and not nearly satisfied by the time her curfew rolled around.

Doggedly, Anamaría closed her eyes, drawing a curtain on the images.

Damn him for waking up these old ghosts. She'd fought hard to put them to rest. To drive around her island home and not feel like a piece of her was missing.

She smoothed an unsteady hand over her slicked-back hair to her ponytail and sucked in a deep breath. The familiar briny scent of the ocean filled her lungs. The sun warmed her skin. The typical sounds of life along the ocean—birds and boat motors and people splashing in the water—soothed her.

"Look out, gorgeous, I'm joining you."

Brandon's playful warning was exactly what she needed to help her switch gears and refocus. Arm muscles bulging, he pushed himself up, then hiked a knee to step onto the balustrade beside her.

"Careful," she warned when he twisted at the waist to take in the shallow water lapping against the base of the pier.

Two pelicans bobbed on the tiny waves nearby, one clutching a squirming gray fish in its beak. The other bird dipped its head closer as if asking for a bite.

"I was thinking we might try that *Dirty Dancing* lift from up here. But we should probably save that move for the sandy beach," he suggested.

His boyish grin drew a laugh from her. "Uh, yeah, that's a better idea."

"No injuries on my watch, please," Sara threw in. "Señora Navarro would not approve if something happened to Anamaría. I'm all about gaining future-mother-in-law points, not losing them."

"And while I'm usually all for daredevil escapades, I'm already dealing with my pissed-off Cuban mami. I don't need a second one on my case," Alejandro added, his beleaguered tone drawing laughter from their group.

The light-hearted conversation allowed Anamaría to regain her internal footing.

Alejandro didn't seem encumbered by their past. She shouldn't be, either.

"Show me your moves, Princesa," he ordered, his camera poised and ready. "I know you got some."

She narrowed her eyes at his use of her familia's nickname. The second time this week. His cheeky grin told her he'd known it would get a rise out of her. Put her in kiss-my-ass mode. Just like when her brothers teased her and she set out to prove she was as capable as them.

Raising her fists, she shot Alejandro a squinty glare, ruining it with a playful smirk she couldn't hide. Grudgingly thankful for his prodding.

"Let's get ready to rumble," she told him, before swiveling to face Brandon.

Although her new AllFit partner stood a good eight inches taller and several inches wider, he mirrored her fighting stance. They faced off like two boxers at a weigh-in, expressions serious. For all of five seconds. As soon he crossed his eyes, she couldn't hold back a giggle, and their mugging for Alejandro's camera began in earnest.

Arms crossed, they stood back to back, her head barely reaching his shoulder blades. Brandon made a *pssst* sound, drawing her attention. She glanced up at him through her lashes and found him staring down at her, one brow arched in a pretty decent imitation of the Rock's signature look. Recognizing a challenge when she saw one, Anamaría swiveled to a wide-legged stand, shoulders back, chest proud. She lifted her arms at her sides and bent her elbows to display her "guns." Brandon flashed a *Wow!* face for the camera and gave her biceps a pretend squeeze.

"That's my girl!" Alejandro shouted, humor lacing his cry.

Anamaría started with surprise. *My girl?*

"Brandon, you going to let her show you up like that, or what?" Alejandro's baiting chatter shook her from her brief stupor. This was part of his job, cajoling his subjects, putting them at ease.

Brandon took the proverbial ball lobbed his way and ran with it. He dropped into a push-up position. She followed suit. Heads craned so they stared at each other, they did a set of ten. He switched to one-handed for the last two, and she raised a leg in the air for hers.

"Show-offs!" Alejandro teased.

Sara whooped her praise.

Feeding off their encouragement, Anamaría flipped over to do a V-up, her straight arms and legs shooting toward the sky until her fingers touched her toes. Brandon copied her. They held the pose, turning it into a who-can-stick-it-the-longest competition.

She won, though she'd bet a smoothie from the stand usually parked at Smathers Beach that Brandon let her.

It showed how well he didn't know her. There was no need for any guy to "let" her win; just ask her brothers. Or Alejandro.

"Looking good," he told them. "Rest for a second while I make some adjustments."

He fiddled with his camera, his brow furrowed in concentration. The humid breeze picked up, pushing his wavy hair onto his forehead, and he finger-combed it back absently, his gaze never leaving his camera's display screen.

Sara ducked down by his chair to peer at the images with him. Alejandro said something that broadened her smile. She looped an arm around his neck, bringing them cheek to cheek for a hug. It was an easy hop, skip, and a jump to picture him on another location, with another beautiful model, equally as tall and confident and experienced *and blond* as Sara.

Like the one he had married.

Jealousy—ridiculous and unwanted—burned in Anamaría's chest.

Brandon tugged softly on the end of her ponytail. "Hey, you, where'd you go off to?"

"Wha—? Oh, nowhere special."

Nowhere productive, either.

"You sure?"

She nodded, tamping down on her mind's negative meanderings. "So, LA's next for you?"

"Yep. Shame you're not heading to the expo with me. But I'm glad I made it down here." His blue eyes sparked with friendly interest.

"I really appreciate you doing this," she said. "You and Sara have gone out of your way for me."

"She's good people. Any friend of Sara's is a friend of mine." He tossed his hair out of his eyes with a little head jerk, then gazed down at Anamaría, his expression sincere. "She called it right by recommending AllFit take a look at you. I like what you've done with your business model for AM Fitness. The content you're sharing and posting on all your platforms aligns with the company's inclusive values. I'd say, you're a great addition to the team."

Anamaría returned his smile, pleased to know her hard work was paying off. "Thanks, I'm excited about taking this step with them."

"You know—"

"Okay, ready to get back to work?" Alejandro interrupted.

"If we have to," Brandon dead-panned, his easy laugh belying his troll tone.

He hopped off the balustrade, landing gracefully on the sidewalk in front of her. Tapping his shoulders, he motioned for her to climb on.

Anamaría frowned.

The last time she'd sat on a guy's shoulders, they'd been Alejandro's. During a beach party up the Keys at Bahia Honda with a group of friends, spring of their senior year. Enrique had proposed a game of chicken in the water. She and Alejandro had been eliminated early. Mostly because she'd given up, preferring to hang out with him off to the side, the gentle motion of the waves as she floated in his arms lulling her with a false sense of security.

Less than two months later, he'd been gone.

"Come on, I got you," Brandon encouraged. His back to her, he held his hands high for her to use for support.

Sara gave her two thumbs-up.

Alejandro didn't seem pestered by memories of them clowning around in a similar manner. Instead, his gaze bounced from their surroundings, over to her and Brandon, then back to his camera where he fiddled with the settings. Focused on his job, like she should be.

All righty then.

Gamely, she grabbed ahold of Brandon's hands. She hooked one leg, then the other over his broad shoulders, wrapping her shins around his hips and gripping his lower back with her sneakers.

As soon as she settled on top of him, he dropped down in a deep squat.

"Yikes!" she squealed, tightening her entire body and squeezing his hands in a death grip.

"Watch it, big guy. You're carrying precious cargo there."

Brandon and Sara laughed at Alejandro's warning.

Anamaría scrunched up her face like she'd done as a kid when her brothers told her she couldn't do something because she was a girl.

He clicked away without missing a beat. She caught the white slash of his devilish grin behind his camera, and she realized that no matter what, she was happy he was here.

Chapter 12

Several hours later, Anamaría emerged from the public bathroom on Higgs Beach to find Alejandro on his crutches, standing by himself in the shade of one of the elevated circular pavilions that rose the height of four steps from the ground. His camera bag nestled in the sand beside him, his trusty Canon in his hands. He'd been on his feet since they had moved from the White Street Pier to the beach at least an hour and a half ago when he vetoed the hassle of pushing the wheelchair through the sand.

While Ale and Sara had scoped out various locations around the public beach area, she and Brandon had changed into differ-ent AllFit workout clothes for the next set of pictures. Once ready, they'd spent the past hour plus hitting a volleyball back and forth on the sand court, clowning around in a kayak still on dry land, and strolling, then cartwheeling, down the smaller walking pier near the Casa Marina end of Higgs.

They had wrapped up a little while ago with Brandon and Sara talking Anamaría into attempting the *Dirty Dancing* lift, though she had balked at the idea of him trying to hold her aloft, arms raised above his head. It had taken three tries and a boat-load of trust on her part. Plus, Alejandro's threat of ratting out to her brothers that she'd been too chicken to attempt the lift properly.

Sara, like a good big sister, had swatted him on the back of the head and told him to be nice or she'd take one of his crutches. Anamaría had snickered at the threat, knowing it was all talk but appreciating the gesture.

"Sara and Brandon are buying waters inside," Alejandro told her as she approached him now. He motioned with his chin toward Salute! On the Beach, the popular Italian restaurant with killer ocean views; then he went back to studying his camera.

His right thumb repeatedly pressed a button and she realized he was toggling through the pictures.

"How do they look?" She stepped toward him, moving to his right, to avoid bumping the fixator rings on his left leg.

"Not half bad. If only the two of you were more photogenic." He side-eyed her with a bemused twist of his lips.

"Ha ha," she muttered, fake punching his arm in lighthearted protest.

"Hey now, don't hurt the injured hired help." He rubbed his biceps with a wounded expression.

"No seas un bebé. I barely tapped you."

He snorted. "You're calling *me* a baby? Who yelped like a young pup and nearly pulled out a chunk of Brandon's hair when she first tried that cheesy dance lift?"

This time, she really did punch him.

Annoyingly, he laughed at her, unfazed. "Ven pa'cá, take a look."

Following his request, she leaned closer. He did the same, angling the camera so she could better see the display screen. The back of his hand accidentally brushed across her left breast. Her nipples tightened in response, aching for more of his caress.

She eased back a fraction, self-preservation outweighing lust. Alejandro didn't even seem to notice.

He toggled a button on the back of the Canon and the screen lit up. The image of her leaning over the pavilion's round metal railing as she spread her arms and yelled, "I'm queen of the world!" filled the tiny rectangle. Alejandro had snapped it from the sandy beach below.

"I think you need to work on not being so shy," he teased.

She chuckled, instinctively leaning close again when he pressed the arrow backward.

Picture after picture flashed by. Unedited, obviously, but quality images. Silly ones and blooper reel–worthy ones. Some that should immediately be deleted. But others, even untouched . . . wow . . .

"Not too shabby," he mused. "I mean, I've got some great photography skills if I do say so myself."

"¡Ay, nene, por favor!" She dropped her head back to groan up at the sky. "The ego on this one. Unbelievable!"

"Here. Let me show you something."

He pressed a button and the screen filled with a collage of tiny images. They blurred as he toggled quickly through them, finally stopping and tapping on one. "Sí, esta. This one's my favorite. You have to post it. Or let me."

Alejandro's request should have prepared her. She, more than many, knew how seriously he took his work. He would not give his praise lightly. Especially when he was such a tough critic of his own work.

Still, when she peered at the screen, her breath hitched when she saw the photograph.

In the background, the baby blue sky was a watercolor painting of muted early-morning peachy orange and bloodred with cotton ball white clouds. She must have just tossed her head and the ocean breeze spread her long ponytail in a dark fan behind her. Fists on her hips, an I-got-this tilt of her chin, a determined gleam in her eyes, a mischievous quirk at one corner of her mouth completed her don't-mess-with-me expression.

She looked . . .

Coño, she looked pretty badass. Empowered. Confident. Brimming with a ready-to-take-on-the-world energy she encouraged others to adopt with her.

It was the AM Fitness brand come to life. Exactly what AllFit had mentioned appealed to them. And Alejandro had captured it in one frame.

Overwhelmed, she covered his hand with hers on the camera. "Thank you," she murmured.

"For what? The pictures?" His shirt sleeve brushed her bare arm with his no-big-deal shrug. "It felt good to work again. You did me a favor."

She blew out a breath and shook her head at his humility, unwilling to let him downplay what he had done for her today. "For seeing me this way."

Her thumb grazed the image on the tiny display screen. Alejandro looped his over hers as if they were playing thumb war. Only the emotion tightening her chest wasn't playful. More like blown away.

"This *is* you, AM. It's why so many people here in Key West love you. Why AM Fitness is growing. Why AllFit offered a contract. Why Brandon freaking Lawson flew down here to be part of your first shoot. There's no Photoshop or editing here. It's raw, real footage. Of you."

He glanced at her, pride swimming in his dark eyes. She blinked up at him, moved by his candor. Her knees suddenly weak, she sank down to perch on the raised pavilion's floor ledge, the metal railing cool against her back.

They sat in companionable silence for several moments. Absently, she drew an arc back and forth in the sand with her sneaker toe. At a loss for words after his heartfelt ones.

"We had some good times over there, didn't we?" His softly spoken question, nostalgia weaving through it in a rough stitch, drew her attention.

Lips rolled between his teeth, Alejandro stared across the street at Astro City Park, where a young woman chased a toddler around the base of the slide. His profile was all sharp cheek angles and planes above the several days' beard growth, his squinty eyes accented by laugh lines.

The boy she had loved, now the man she was trying to befriend, while also working to convince herself she no longer desired him.

"Yeah, we did," she answered, her throat tight with regret for what they hadn't been able to hold on to.

A seagull swooped over the volleyball net, snagging her gaze. It glided in front of them to land on its spindly feet about ten feet away where a couple in bikinis lounged on a yellow-and-blue-striped beach blanket. One of the women held a sandwich out to her partner, who leaned in and took a bite. They shared a chaste kiss; then one gently combed the other's brown hair behind her ear with an intimate smile.

A fond kinship warmed Anamaría's chest. There'd been a time when a picnic on this same beach had been one of her and Alejandro's favorite ways to spend a lazy afternoon together.

"Can I ask you a question?" Alejandro looped his camera strap around his neck, then grasped his crutches in one hand before lowering himself to sit beside her on the small ledge.

She slanted a cautious look at him. "Sure. Doesn't mean I'll answer, though."

"Fair enough." He rubbed a hand over the scruff darkening his jaw. "You got certified as a trainer while working on your EMT and paramedic training, then finished your degree in nutrition on-line while on the job with the fire department, what . . . five, six years ago?"

She nodded, wondering where he was going with this.

"How come you haven't ramped things up with AM Fitness sooner? I mean, listening to you talk with Brandon about what you do outside the fire station, not to mention all the volunteering and fundraising my mom talks about you doing in the community . . . it's clear you love everything AM Fitness stands for." He held up a hand like he anticipated her objection. "Not that you don't like being a paramedic. I saw the other day how much your job and the people you try to help affect you. But this . . ." He drew an open-palmed circle in the air in front of her. "Your cooking videos, live classes, and virtual clients, the excitement when you talk about going to race expos and giving exercise demos as part of AllFit's team. It feels different. You talk about it with a different energy. Why not pursue AM Fitness full-time?"

His insightful observation, one few made, caught her off guard. Her familia had encouraged her when it came to her interest in nutrition and athletic training, but as a side hustle. Her position alongside her brothers and Papi in the familia business, as they liked to call it, had never been questioned.

At least, she had never questioned it out loud. Definitely not with others.

"You know the job can be demanding. Some shifts take their mental, physical, or emotional toll on you. But it's what we Navarros do." Elbows bent, she gave an it-is-what-it-is shrug. "Exercising has always been a way to blow off steam. When people started asking me for workout advice, I educated myself. Learning about nutrition became important to me after Papi's heart attack. Then I found I could combine athletic training with my nutrition degree to help others, like I had with my dad. But taking it to another level? I wasn't sure I wanted to turn what helped me refill my well into a *job* job."

At least, that's what she had always told herself. Before she'd been able to admit that she'd been subconsciously waiting for something. Someone. Holding herself back, settling rather than pushing herself.

But even with this strange sort of truce she and Alejandro were trying to navigate together, she couldn't bring herself to reveal the full truth to him.

"What made you change your mind?" he pressed.

She took her time answering, weighing how much she wanted to say. "A little over two years ago I had a kind of eye-opening experience. A few months later, my cousin Vanessa and I had a frank conversation. And quite a few margaritas." She paused at his laugh, her mouth twisted with chagrin. "Believe me, the hangover the next morning was not fun. But, that night, I promised myself I would stop hesitating and go for it."

"Good for you."

"Yeah, it was. And kudos to Vanessa for giving me the kick in the pants I needed."

The strains of a country music song interrupted the calming beach atmosphere, intensifying to club level when a yellow Jeep screeched to a stop in a parking spot close by. Two guys, one as short and stocky as the other was tall and gangly, both wearing tropical board shorts and faded tees, hopped out. Two girls in bikini tops and booty shorts followed. Arms laden with towels, beach chairs, and a cooler, they made their way toward the shore, kicking up sand with their flip-flops, voices raised with their fun.

Alejandro's gaze tracked the group's path until they disappeared around the other side of the pavilion, all the while absently rubbing his left knee above the highest fixator ring. He had to be feeling some level of discomfort after their long morning but was probably too proud to say so. When he noticed her eyeing his motion, he stopped and tugged down the hems of his faded black cargo shorts.

"Here they come." He separated his crutches, grasping one in each hand; then he pushed up on his right foot.

Across the way, Sara and Brandon strolled out of the restaurant's main entrance into the covered outdoor seating area.

"He's a decent guy." Alejandro motioned toward Brandon, who waited for Sara to precede him through the gate in the low, brightly painted wooden fence surrounding the popular eatery. The two of them stopped, Sara leaning closer as Brandon lifted his cell phone for them to look at something on the screen.

"Seems like it," Anamaría said.

"Probably a good idea that the two of you paired up."

"Oh, we're not *pairing* pairing up. Not like that, anyway." Flustered by the wrong direction Alejandro was heading, she straightened, waving off whatever he might be implying. "We're professional acquaintances. Maybe moving into friend territory. That's all."

"You never know," Alejandro pressed.

"Nuh-huh, it's not happening." Anamaría shook her head emphatically. "I'm not messing things up with AllFit by trying to hook up with someone. This is business, and Brandon seems like he could be a good friend, nothing more."

"Look, all I'm saying is"—Alejandro gave a lazy one-shoulder shrug, as if his version of Cuban mami matchmaking wasn't weirding her out—"two people with common careers, working long hours closely together. It's been known to happen."

"Is that how you and your wife connected?" The question burned her tongue as she voiced it.

"Morgan?" Alejandro's wide eyes told of his surprise at Anamaría's blunt inquiry. That made two of them.

Worse, hearing him say the other woman's name hurt far more than it still should. Over the years, similar questions about him and Morgan Ritter, the statuesque model he had married shortly after breaking up with Anamaría, had clamored in her head. Begging for answers. Anamaría had remained in the dark, refusing to ask them. Refusing to even Google the woman.

"Uh, yes. Morgan and I met on a shoot. In Italy. Right after . . . well, a few months after you and I . . . after we ended." He spoke haltingly, as if fumbling for the right words. But his intense gaze never wavered from hers. "The relationship snowballed. Then, it, uh . . . as I'm guessing you already know . . . it melted fairly quickly."

A troubled expression stamped his face over the demise of his marriage. Remorse for allowing her jealousy to infect the positive experience they had shared together flared in Anamaría's chest. At the same time, both her heart and mind still struggled to make sense of how he could have forgotten about her and moved on so quickly.

"I guess I never understood how—were you—" She broke off, her eyes searching his, desperate for answers that would assuage her own anguish. The questions she had always wanted to ask remained stuck in her throat. Except for the one she hoped was true but whose confirmation would hurt the most.

"Were you happy with her? At least for a time?"

Alejandro heaved a sigh, his gaze moving to squint out at the open water behind her. A strange mix of regret and acceptance settled in his dark eyes. "Morgan wasn't the problem in our marriage. We both acted rashly, jumping into something way too soon. But, ultimately, the problem was me."

His answer gave rise to more questions. With Brandon and Sara making their way over, now wasn't the time to ask them.

"You've got something great going here," Alejandro said. "I'm happy for you, Princesa. You deserve it."

"Ay!" She scuffed at the sand near his left crutch, purposefully missing to avoid knocking it out from under him. "No one calls me that anymore unless they want some trouble!"

A shadow of his cocky grin answered her playful threat. "I'm not afraid of you."

"You should be. I can take you. Especially now."

He laughed at her, the rich sound drawing the attention of the two women nearby.

Anamaría didn't join in, though. She was too busy grappling with his cryptic revelation about his marriage and the turbulent emotions their conversation had churned up inside her.

"You two ready to grab lunch?" Brandon asked as he and Sara reached them.

Sara hooked an arm with one of Anamaría's. "After all this hard work, even I'm famished."

Anamaría looked at Sara, a silent *Are you okay?* passing between them. In recovery with an eating disorder she had privately struggled with since high school, Sara rarely brought up her lack of interest in food. She hugged Anamaría's arm tighter and gave her a reassuring nod.

"Any interest in Italian food at Salute?" Alejandro asked, adjusting his crutches under his armpits.

Anamaría grabbed his backpack for him, then the group began the trek back to their vehicles.

"Actually, a little bird named Sara told me that your parents own the best Cuban restaurant on the island." Brandon gave his signature head toss, shifting his bangs out of his eyes as they walked through the sand. "I haven't had decent Cuban food in ages. How 'bout we grab a bite there to celebrate a successful shoot?"

No one else probably saw it, but Anamaría didn't miss Alejandro's full-body wince. The absolute last place he'd go to celebrate was his dad's restaurant. According to Enrique, Ale hadn't even stepped foot in the place since his return.

Sara, who knew the condensed version of the Mirandas' familia saga, slid a nervous glance at Alejandro, then Anamaría, before suggesting, "Are you sure you don't want seafood? Fresh from the ocean?"

"If that's what you prefer, I don't mind," Brandon answered, confirming his easygoing personality.

They reached the sidewalk that wove around Higgs Beach, and Alejandro stopped in front of the restaurant's low fence to shake the sand off the rubber grippers on the bottoms of his crutches.

"Actually, you know how interested my mom is in your Instagram presence." He cut a quick glance at Anamaría, then back at his crutches as he stomped them on the walkway one last time. "Our moms are so nosy, I'm sure mine already knows all about Brandon and would love to meet him. I'm betting she'd love to hear what you two have planned together, don't you think?"

Sara laughed at his reasoning and Brandon chimed in with his approval.

Out on the road, two mopeds puttered by as Ale, Sara, and Brandon waited for Anamaría to respond. Sure, going to Miranda's might appease their mothers' inquisitive nature, but it also meant seeing his father on his own turf. The same turf Alejandro had been kicked out of the night before he left for good.

"Are you sure you don't need to head home and elevate your leg? I can fill the moms and the rest of your family in later," she asked, giving him a believable out while tiptoeing around the topic of his dad.

Alejandro surprised her by shaking his head at her suggestion. "Mami's been bugging me to come for lunch since I got back. Plus, Papi will be pleased to see you."

Uh-huh. She understood Alejandro's subtext. Victor Miranda would be happy to see *her*, just not his son. Which made it even more incomprehensible why Alejandro would agree to join them.

What the hell had he been thinking by agreeing to join Anamaría and the others for lunch at the one place he'd done everything he could to avoid since high school? Right up until he'd been banished from the premises by his father as a graduation present.

Elbow propped on the inside window ledge in Sara's RAV4, Alejandro cradled his forehead in his palm. This had the potential of turning into a shitshow.

Of epic proportions.

"You sure you're up for this?" Sara eyed him with worry as she waited for a van to pass them going east on Bertha, her left blinker flashing her intent to turn into Miranda's.

"Yeah, I'm fine," he mumbled.

She pulled into the parking lot that ran the length of the restaurant's side wall. Still painted the same tan shade it had always been.

Midway down the parking lot Alejandro sat up and leaned forward to peer through the front windshield. The paint job might still be the same, but apparently his dad had expanded, adding more indoor seating in the back of the building. When had that happened?

"Looks pretty crowded," Sara mused.

Barely eleven and the spots were already filling up. Good sign for business.

Bad sign for someone not interested in airing familia drama in a crowd of locals and tourists.

Which begged for a straight answer to the same *why* question that had echoed in his brain seconds after he'd convinced Anamaría this was a good idea.

¿Por qué? the voice of reason he too often ignored asked again.

He could take the easy way out and say it was to please his mother, who'd been harping on him to show his respect by visiting their beloved restaurant.

Or that he wanted to avoid the awkwardness of refusing Brandon's request to eat at the local hot spot his familia owned. But *awkward* would definitely describe the potential scene his papi might make when he spotted Alejandro.

¡Carajo! Alejandro dug two fingers at the spot between his eyebrows and rubbed at the dull ache intensifying with each taken parking spot Sara passed. Peeking at the side rearview mirror out his window, he watched Anamaría's Pilot following. Brandon's wide grin flashed, his hands gesturing with whatever story he was regaling her with.

That's why Alejandro was here.

Because he was and always would be a sucker for the girl who'd stolen, then broken his heart. Though she'd done so only because, he was slowly coming to understand, he had selfishly pushed her to dream his dreams, not her own.

The crushing weight of guilt pressed on Alejandro's chest.

All these years, he'd thought of himself as the one who had been rejected. Blaming her for the demise of their relationship. Channeling his anger and hurt and frustration into his career. Pushing the boundaries in search of something undefinable always just beyond his grasp.

He loved his job. He was fucking good at it. Brilliant, actually.

But this morning, with Anamaría as his main subject like in his early days, a weird, kind of carefree joy he hadn't felt in ages buoyed him. Reminded him why he had initially fallen in love with the unique view through his Canon lens.

Once she got over her initial nerves, Anamaría was a natural in front of the camera. Her charisma and charm was palpable.

The trust she placed in him by allowing herself to be vulnerable humbled him.

Today, he had soaked up her energy, allowing their emotional connection to feed his vision in a way he never let himself do with others. Not even with Morgan, who'd been more dear friend than wife. Something he should have admitted to Anamaría when she brought up his marriage out on the beach. Surprising the hell out of him.

He owed her a better explanation. Just not with others around to potentially interrupt or in the middle of wrapping up an important shoot that should be a boon for her business.

Which brought Alejandro back to why he was sitting in Sara's car, agreeing to enter the one place in Key West he'd rather avoid.

There was value in having a power player like Brandon Lawson in Anamaría's corner alongside Sara. Showing the guy a good time while he was here would benefit Anamaría. So, even if it meant walking into the lion's den, Alejandro would do it. For her.

"Here we go." Sara pulled between the white lines of a spot near the dumpster in back and cut the engine. Anamaría's SUV angled in beside them.

If luck was on his side, his mami's relief at seeing him would outweigh his dad's resentment. Big if.

A long sigh, weighty with his resignation, escaped before he could stop it.

"You and I don't have to go in," Sara offered, compassion pooling in her blue-green eyes. "You've been on your feet for a while. Anamaría and Brandon can stay, and I'll drive you home."

He shook his head, ignoring the dull throb in his leg that matched the one pounding behind his eyes.

Anamaría tapped her knuckle on his window, startling him. She grinned and opened his car door. "Brandon's grabbing your wheelchair while I help you—"

"I'm not using that thing here."

"It would be better—"

"No, it wouldn't." He already felt like a wounded pup, crawling back with his tail between his legs. No way was someone going to push him inside Miranda's when he could damn well walk.

She huffed out an irritated breath, one fist jammed on a cocked hip. "Ale, you were on your crutches the entire time we took the photos at Higgs Beach."

"And I'll be sitting inside the entire time we're here. So we're even," he countered.

"That's not funny." She scowled, her repetitive toe-tapping warning him that her irritation was edging toward pissed off. "Your injury and recovery are not a joke."

"Do you see me laughing?"

She growled. Like actually growled, as she shook her head. "Who is the professional medic here? And who needs to stop being so freaking contrary?"

Fire flashed in the specks of gold in her hazel eyes, and he realized she wasn't going to back down unless he gave her a good reason.

Alejandro turned to Sara, who watched their exchange with interest from the driver's seat. "Would you and Brandon please go inside and let my mother know we'll need a table for four?"

The woman he hoped might eventually become a friend, like her fiancé, looked from him to the doorway, where Anamaría now loomed.

Anamaría ducked into the small space between him and the car's dashboard. Her ponytail braid, fashioned with her deft fingers in between takes on the beach, swung down to bump against his thigh, mimicking the smack he felt certain she wanted to give him upside the head.

The white and deep purple AllFit windbreaker she wore over her matching sports bra had been zipped up halfway, drawing his attention to the swell of her breasts straining against the stretchy material. Her tropical shampoo mixing with the earthy scent of a morning spent in the Florida humidity tempted him to press his nose to her neck and breathe in her unique essence. Instead he teased his simmering desire for her by trailing his gaze past the sun-kissed bronze skin on her chest, to her full lips, aggravation-flushed cheeks, and gold-flecked eyes.

"AM?" Sara asked.

The two women stared at each other, apparently exchanging some kind of silent conversation, because Sara ultimately nodded, then pulled her keys out of the ignition.

"Fine, we'll head inside. You"—Sara's tone held a warning as she placed a cool hand on Alejandro's forearm—"thank you for earlier today. But remember, when it comes down to it, many of us here are team—"

"Navarro," he finished. "I know and respect that."

The secretive smile that had helped make Sara the sought-after social media maven she had become softened her no-nonsense expression. "And you." Sara pointed at Anamaría. "Give the guy a break; he did us both a huge favor."

"Yes, and I'm trying to return that favor by looking out for his obstinate ass," Anamaría complained.

Sara's light laughter trailed off as she slid out and closed her door. She motioned Brandon over and then led him down the walkway between the parking spots and the building toward the back entrance.

As soon as the pair disappeared inside, Anamaría backed out of Alejandro's front seat space, leaving her citrusy scent behind. He placed his right foot on the ground outside, then carefully lifted his left leg and swiveled to face the open door. Anamaría bent forward to help him, but he waved her off, placing his weight on his right leg and pushing off the door frame to stand.

"You are so hardheaded," she complained.

"Hello, pot, I'm kettle," he threw back.

The remark earned him a glare. He wiped the sheen of sweat from his brow, then finger-combed his hair back with a tired sigh. She was right, his leg hurt like a bitch. Rest would do him well, but he'd bite his tongue till it bled before admitting so. He would see this lunch through for Anamaría.

"Look, I get what you're trying to do," he told her.

"Oh really? You get it, but still won't listen to my medically trained advice?"

"Fine, you're right. I should get this damn leg elevated. Definitely take another over-the-counter pain pill, which I will once we get inside."

"Hold on a minute." Anamaría stuck a finger in her ear as if she were clearing it out. "Repeat that first part again, please? I think I misheard. I'm what?"

He hiked a brow with censure at her exaggerated dumbfounded expression. "Now who's being a smartass?"

"Takes one to know one." She tilted her head in a defiant slant, sending her braid swaying behind her. "Now, if I'm right, why the hell are you giving me such a hard time?"

He stalled for a few seconds, hating the need to share the ego-bruising truth. Unfortunately, her arched brow told him she wasn't going to let him off the hook.

"Coño," he muttered, scratching the scruff on his jaw. "Coming here isn't something I take lightly. You know that. So, I'll be damned if I'm going to face my dad and his inevitable hostility from a fucking baby stroller. Unable to stand up to him."

Both the fight and the laughter drained out of Anamaría. Compassion swept in to take their place, tipping her lips in a sad frown. "First, it's not a baby stroller. It's a—"

"I know what the hell it's called. Cut me some slack, okay?" He leaned back against the car for support.

"Fine, have it your way." Anamaría eyed him warily but didn't say anything about his leg when she finally spoke. No, she picked another, more difficult topic. "It's been two weeks almost. Have you and your dad not made any move to find common ground?"

Alejandro shook his head. "He won't. It has to come from me."

"And have you tried?"

He rubbed at the tired muscles along the back of his neck, playing it safe by giving her the easiest reason why he was here. Rather than the impossible one.

"Right now, I'm trying to be part of the Key West welcome

crew Sara requested when she gave me the lowdown on Brandon and his tie to AllFit."

"What?" Anamaría's face scrunched with a confused frown. "Sara asked— Ale, you don't have to do this. You've done enough already." She gestured behind him at the restaurant. The place that was more his papi's pride and joy than he would ever be. "This is a big ask I can't make."

"You didn't ask. Brandon did, the jerk."

Her lips twitched with a smile.

"Plus, this gets my mother off my back. She's been pushing me to give in and show respect for my dad by coming here. Between that and the two of you stressing out about my recovery." He slapped a hand to his forehead in exaggerated horror. "Carajo, you women and your nagging, me van a volver loco."

"Ha! *We're* driving *you* crazy. Does the term bird-hunting cliff diver ring a bell?" she teased, her grin breaking free to flash brightly.

She took a baby step toward him, reaching out to swat playfully at his sternum. Her hand lingered to caress his side. The light touch burned through his button-down as if she had brushed his bare skin.

Damn, he wanted her so badly, he ached with it. But he couldn't act on it. Doing so wouldn't be fair to her. What he had witnessed today confirmed what he had slowly begun to figure out, based on clues from Enrique, and her.

Anamaría may have waited to blossom into her own, but she had bloomed into a beautiful orchid, the symbol of strength and perfection that grew on the trunks of the palms and native trees around the Keys. She was a complex mix of her familia's deep roots, holding fast to the island's soil, and her burgeoning self-confidence, drawing him in with her vibrant personality.

He could appreciate the flower, but she wasn't his to pluck and take with him anymore. Thinking he could do so all those years ago had been his biggest mistake. Now he could help her flourish.

As if she read his thoughts, Anamaría surprised him by stepping closer and lifting up on her toes to press a kiss against his cheek. His eyes drifted closed as he savored the feel of her soft lips on his skin. When she started to ease away, his hands instinctively moved to her hips, loath to let her go.

Her palms splayed on his chest, she leaned in and gazed up at him. A warmth that reached the depths of his wounded soul shone in her expressive eyes.

"You might like everyone to think you're a badass," she said. "Climbing mountaintops, running with bulls, and all that craziness. But I know your secret."

Her last words were a husky whisper that had him ducking his head to hear her. The move brought her lips excruciatingly close to his. Desire swirled through him, pushing him to taste her sweetness. He refused to cross the line with her.

"In here"—her fingers patted his chest over his heart, and he was certain she had to feel its pace increase—"you're a softie. That's how you manage to take such beautifully moving pictures. No matter where you go, who you meet, or what you explore, you have a knack for capturing emotion in the amazing situations. Sharing it with those of us who admire your work."

No doubt about it, he knew he was a master behind his camera. His issues lay in an inability . . . more like an unwillingness . . . to connect with others once he set his Canon aside. Except for her. Yet even that small pleasure was destined to be short-lived because he would leave and she would stay.

"The thing is," she went on, moving infinitesimally closer until only a small space separated them. Her voice tipped lower still, as if she shared a secret for his ears alone. "Sometimes, you might need to peek out from behind your camera. Try connecting with those who are important to you. Try showing them why you see the world the way you do. You have a gift, Ale; don't use it as a buffer. Use it to unite, the way your stunning photographs do."

Her intuition slayed him. What she suggested sounded so easy. But when it came to his father, easy had never been a word that described their relationship.

"I don't— It's not . . ." He stumbled to a stop, uncertain exactly how to answer without potentially disappointing her. Something he definitely didn't want to do.

Her tempting mouth spread in a grin; then she surprised him again by cupping his cheek and stretching tall to press her lips against his in a kiss that was chaste and delicious but over before he had time to fully appreciate it. She winked impishly. "I think I've blown you away with my wisdom."

Rather than admit the truth in her claim, he took the easier route and hid behind her humor. "Actually, I'm relieved the truth has finally come out. You *are* a big fan of my work."

"Are you kidding me?" she cried, her forehead falling against his chest.

His heart swelled with affection, and he cupped the back of her head, thrilled to have her in his arms again. He tipped his head to press a kiss to her crown, but she smacked his chest with an open palm, none too gently, and pushed away from him.

"Un . . . believable!" she complained with an exasperated grimace. "After my thought-provoking advice, *that's* what you're going to focus on? ¡Ay, Dios, por favor, ayúdame! Men and their egos!"

Muttering another prayer for God's help under her breath, she dragged his crutches from the back seat, then held them out for him.

"I was kidding," he defended himself, covering her hands with his on the crutches. He tugged her closer, relieved when she willingly came. "I heard what you said, and I will admit that I'd like to try. But you know how hard it is with him."

She nodded. He released her to tuck the crutches under his armpits, and they walked in companionable silence toward the restaurant's back entrance. Anamaría grabbed the metal handle, pausing before she tugged it open.

"You sure you're okay going inside?"

Not really. He nodded anyway.

She eyed him warily. "I mean, when I said reach out to your papi, I didn't necessarily mean right this second."

"The longer I put it off, the more awkward it becomes. Besides, he likes you better. If we're together, maybe he'll at least let me finish my meal before he throws me out."

She smiled at his lame joke, but concern for him blanketed her beautiful face. Her reaction confirmed his decision to come inside with her. Despite the potential parental blowup.

"That is not going to happen," she promised.

"We shall see. Come on, let's get this over with."

Yes, showing up at Miranda's might invite the face-off with his father he'd been dreading. But this fragile new relationship he and Anamaría were forging, even with its faint undercurrent of unchecked need slowly simmering, deserved his attempt to face his dad, even knowing the man would never accept him. Never forgive him. But Anamaría might. That alone was worth it.

Chapter 13

Between the numerous hello hugs for her and welcome home hugs for him, along with the "¿Qué te pasó?" inquiries from a few of the old regulars that had Alejandro sharing his dive off the waterfall saga, Anamaría figured they'd eventually meet up with Sara and Brandon by dinnertime.

She smiled politely at Señora Gómez, a member of her mami and Señora Miranda's prayer group at St. Mary's, while Alejandro patiently thanked the older woman—again—for her continuing prayers. Concern pruned Señora Gómez's wrinkly face even more as she gently reprimanded him for causing his mami and abuela such worry.

As they stood practically on top of each other in the tiny space between the packed tables, Alejandro nudged Anamaría with his elbow. He ducked his head to slide her a bug-eyed, help-me stare, but she knew better than to cut off the older woman when she was mid-lecture.

"Papito, you need to visit your familia more often," Señora Gómez scolded, grasping one of Alejandro's hands between hers, the deep brown sunspots freckling her skin evidence of her years and time in the island sun. "We viejitas are not getting any younger."

"Who's a viejita?" he teased, drawing back slightly as if he were assessing her. "When I look at you, I don't see an old woman, I see one in her prime. A picture titled *Young Cubanita*." Fingers crooked, he swiped a hand through the air with a flourish, marking the label under the imaginary photograph.

The older woman's cackle rang out as she patted her tightly slicked-back hair and the little gray moño high on the back of her head. "Always a smooth talker, this one, ha, nena? No wonder he stole your heart again."

Anamaría winced. Alejandro's teasing grin faltered but rallied.

Before either one could clarify that they were not back together, the swinging door leading in and out of the kitchen pushed open. Ernesto strode out, arms swinging like a man on a pissed-off mission, based on his dark scowl. A black apron with the Miranda's name embroidered across the chest hung from his neck, the waist strings untied.

He jerked to a jaw-dropping stop when he spotted Alejandro.

The two brothers stared at each other in silence until the kitchen door pushed open behind Ernesto. Anamaría held her breath, anticipating the eruption if Victor Miranda joined them next.

Instead, Iona, the middle-aged single mom who'd been part of the Miranda's familia for decades, came barreling out, a tray laden with multiple plates balanced in her slender arms.

"Salte del medio," she grumbled.

Ernesto, visibly shell-shocked by his brother's presence here, dumbly stepped out of the way as she had asked.

The door swung in, then out, bumping into Ernesto's butt. The tap snapped Alejandro's younger brother out of his stupor. His quizzical glance slid from Alejandro to Anamaría, then back again.

"Hey, Ernesto," she jumped in, plastering a smile on her face. "Good to see you. Cómo está Cece?"

Ernesto wiped his hands on the apron as he strode over, giving her a hug and kiss on the cheek. The smell of cumin, peppers, and onion clung to him. It reminded her of the years she'd worked as a hostess and waitress at Miranda's because it meant she and Alejandro could spend more time together.

"I heard your New York trip went pretty awesome," Ernesto said, though his attention was already on his brother, who stood stiffly at her side. "Ale, this is a nice surprise."

Alejandro dipped his head in greeting. He pulled his hand out of Señora Gómez's but grabbed hold of his crutches, his fingers tightening around the rubberized grips, instead of shaking his brother's hand. Strange, because the two brothers usually got along as far as she knew.

Anamaría placed her palm on Alejandro's lower back in a show of support.

He flinched, then slowly relaxed. "I did a shoot for Anamaría at Higgs this morning. The guy who's working with her wanted Cuban food, and I couldn't really let him eat anything but the best, right?"

"Damn straight," Ernesto said, quickly ducking his head in apology for his language to Señora Gómez and her friends. "Perdóname."

"Está bien, hijo, we feel the same way." The older woman's smile squinted her eyes with pleasure.

"The place is packed," Alejandro said. "Business still going well, ha?"

"Yeah. New places pop up around town, but you can't beat the traditional good stuff." Ernesto clasped his older brother on the shoulder in a show of kinship Anamaría was happy to see. "It means a lot to have you stop in. Peak lunchtime might not be ideal. . . ." He eyed the kitchen door behind him, more than likely thinking about the looming unexpected father-son reunion and how badly that could go. Especially with the place packed.

Victor Miranda's unyielding personality when it came to carrying on his father's tradition and name through the restaurant and Alejandro's unwillingness to follow his father's old-school edicts had been fodder for post-mass Fellowship Hall whispering at St. Mary's, countless community gatherings, and private parties among friends since even before Ale had cut ties and run. Many local Cubans currently dining in Miranda's were aware of the Miranda patriarch's fraught history with his older son. Including Señora Gómez and her lunch companions, two elderly women equally as active in their church. Meaning, also equally active in the chisme sharing, even if the gossip might be well intentioned. Now all three ladies watched the interplay between the two brothers with keen curiosity.

Anamaría bit the inside of her cheek to stop herself from asking if they wanted some popcorn for the show. Snark rarely went over well with the elders in their comunidad. Experience, and enough whacks from her mami's fan, had drummed that lesson in her well.

"You know what? I'm sure our table's ready by now." Anamaría craned her neck to scan the dining area, relieved when Sara waved to her from a table in front of the big window facing Bertha Street. "We shouldn't keep Sara and Brandon waiting."

The usual round of cheek kisses ensued, Alejandro's a bit awkward as he tried maneuvering with his crutches amid a litany of "pobrecito" murmurs from the elderly women. *Poor thing* wasn't quite the phrase that came to mind when Anamaría thought about Alejandro's idiot move in El Yunque, but whatever.

"Dios los bendiga," the women chorused the typical good-bye blessing they had all grown up hearing.

Right now, Anamaría was hoping God's blessing would get them through lunch without Victor Miranda venturing out of the kitchen. With this crowd, the odds might be in their favor, since he typically stayed in the back ensuring everything ran smoothly during their busier hours. If he did step out for some reason, she hoped he came ready to break bread peacefully with his son.

Ernesto followed her and Alejandro through the sea of filled tables with their matte red laminate tops and aluminum edging. At the front, under the wide window that ran nearly half the length of the wall, Brandon and Sara sat at a table for six.

Her back to the dining room, Sara angled sideways to face Señora Miranda, who sat two seats over. Based on Sara's amused grin as she sucked on a paper straw in a glass of her usual lemon water, and Brandon's deer-in-the-headlights expression as he spoke to Alejandro's mom, Anamaría was guessing the infamous Cuban mami inquisition had commenced.

Coño, poor guy. No telling how long Señora Miranda had been grilling him.

A gray-haired gentleman in a peach guayabera and tan slacks reached for a copy of the *Key West Citizen* and his bill as he scooted away from a table on Anamaría's right. She paused for him to step ahead of her.

Alejandro bumped into her from behind, his chest colliding with her shoulder blades. She felt him wobbling on his crutches; then one of his hands gripped her waist to steady himself. Warmth spread across her belly at his touch.

"I hope you warned Brandon about my mother on your drive over." His low whisper tickled her ear, and a brushing of goosebumps shimmied across her shoulders.

"Honestly, it didn't even cross my mind. I was more worried about you and your dad and avoiding World War Three."

"Yeah, well, that's probably unavoidable," he grumbled. "Thanks, though."

She arched her neck to look up at him, only to find his angular jaw closer than she realized.

His earthy patchouli scent blended with the smell of spices and sautéed onions and peppers redolent in the restaurant's contained space, and somehow she knew she would always seek this special blend whenever she was here. Seek but wind up disappointed when she didn't encounter it because he was gone.

His gaze dropped to her mouth, then slowly slid up to meet hers again. Longing arced through her at the heat slow boiling in his eyes. Unfortunately, her rash kiss in the parking lot had done little to satiate her appetite for him as much as she had hoped it would.

Alejandro cupped her elbow. A move to draw her closer? Remind her of their whereabouts and the nosy audience watching? Señora Gómez's flip comment about him stealing Anamaría's heart again taunted her with the unavoidable truth. Whatever this was between them, Miranda's was not the place to delve into it. If she even should.

Turning back toward their table, she made a promise that history would not repeat itself. He would leave again, but this time she expected it and would be fine. More than fine. Staying busy chasing her own dream.

"Oye, hermano, that friend of yours looks like he's sweating through his workout clothes," Ernesto chimed in from the back of their caravan of three. "Mami must be in rare form. You better get over there and save him."

Anamaría squinted at the bright noon sun streaming through the wide window. It turned Brandon's blond hair a burnished gold and glinted off the silverware neatly laid out on the red laminate tabletop. Brandon swiped a hand over his forehead in a nervous gesture.

Knowing how intrusive the mamis' questioning could be, Anamaría hurried past the last few tables, intent on rescuing Brandon.

"—growing up near LA, I speak some Spanish, but— Hey, there you are!" Brandon's cheeks puffed out on a heavy breath when Anamaría reached their table.

He pushed back his chair to stand, gesturing to the open seats.

Poor guy. Even an elite athlete touted for his physical and mental stamina didn't stand a chance when up against a meddling mami digging for information. Anamaría and her brothers often joked about their mom, but her info-digging tactics with both of the men Anamaría had dated seriously after Alejandro had been relentless, CSI-worthy. Unfortunately for Brandon, Señora Miranda had similar powers of intimidation.

Señora Miranda's metal chair legs scraped across the gray linoleum as she scooted her black vinyl padded chair to the side so she could swivel and face them.

"¡Ay Dios mío, que sorpresa!" Her cry of surprise turned several heads their way. "Sara said you were coming, but I did not believe it. Ay, look at mis hijos. My boys. Together for a meal. Aquí." She clasped her hands at her chest. "A mami's prayers answered."

"Mami, por favor, don't make this into a thing, okay?" Alejandro warned, kissing her cheek. "It's lunch with friends. Eso es todo."

"There is no *that is all*. You are here. Finally." She stretched out her arms to clasp hands with her two boys.

"Not quite. I'm running to the ba—" Ernesto broke off and cleared a scratch from his throat. "Papi needs me to run an errand."

"Por favor, siéntate un ratito con us."

"You know I don't have a little time to sit down, Mami. We're slammed here, and I shouldn't even be leaving now, only they need, ugh . . . never mind. Sara, sorry I have to run. Hope you're doing good." The two of them exchanged a cheek press hello; then he held his hand out to shake Brandon's across the table. "Welcome to Miranda's. I'm Ernesto, Alejandro's younger, better-looking, obviously smarter brother. Seeing as how I'm not the one cascading off waterfalls in the rainforest."

"Get out of here, with this better-looking crap." Alejandro nudged his brother's shoulder.

"Ha, pero I don't see you arguing who's smarter!" Ernesto joked back.

The brothers' old camaraderie brought a breezy sense of peace to what Anamaría had worried would be a stressful meeting. Especially since Miranda's had in essence become Ernesto's turf, seeing as how he now stood in line to run the familia business. She hoped the forgiveness and understanding would eventually come from their father as well.

Señora Miranda's pleased grin rivaled Lulu's the last time Anamaría had taken the little girl to the panadería for a sweetbread treat. Maybe, just maybe, she could influence her husband while their oldest was home.

The two brothers exchanged a backslapping farewell hug, and Anamaría could have sworn she heard Ernesto murmur, "Good luck."

He waved good-bye to everyone and strode toward the entrance, reading something on his cell that had him frowning at the device. Whatever errand Señor Miranda had him running in the middle of the lunch rush, it had to be important. As soon as the glass door eased closed behind him, Alejandro sent her a quizzical look that told her he was thinking along the same something's-up line.

His mom didn't seem to have noticed anything, so Ale shook his head with a beats-me shrug. He sidestepped awkwardly around the table to take the chair on the end where he could extend his left leg while also keeping watch on the kitchen door in the back. No doubt standing guard for his father.

Anamaría took the seat between Sara and his mom, who lovingly patted Anamaría's thigh as she settled in her chair.

Señora Miranda handed Brandon one of the laminated menus wedged between the black napkin holder and the condiment tray. Like a proud second mami, she pointed out the healthy options Anamaría had championed: baked chicken breast with amarillo, the sweet yellow plantain pan sautéed in a light spritz of olive oil instead of deep fried; black beans and brown rice paired for the congrí; and picadillo made with ground turkey breast, the flavorful mix of meat, cumin, and other savory spices cooked with diced peppers and served with black beans and brown rice or on its own for those cutting carbs.

"See how smart she is. And she is working hard to help people everywhere eat and live healthier with her website. Have you seen it? We are so proud of her."

Anamaría's cheeks heated under the maternal praise. She leaned her head on Señora Miranda's shoulder with a fond smile, gazing in awe at the *AM Fitness* logo and web address on the new menus.

"Even though I'm the child she birthed and Anamaría is familia by choice, I guess you can see which one of us is my mom's favorite," Alejandro complained, drawing a laugh from Brandon and Sara and an "ay, por favor, que exagerado" from his mami.

He tapped a finger at an item on Brandon's menu. "Picadillo is Anamaría's comfort meal. Or . . . I guess, it used to be."

"Still is," she answered, touched that he remembered.

When Iona sidled over to take their order, Señora Miranda stepped away to assist the hostess-cashier in training. By the time she returned to their table, Iona was back with their meals.

"Wow, this all looks fantastic!" Brandon exclaimed.

"Here, you must taste a little of everything," Alejandro's mom insisted.

She had wisely asked for an empty dinner plate, onto which she promptly dished a small portion from each meal. Brandon's face lit with excitement as she spooned off some of Anamaría's ground turkey picadillo peppered with raisins and green olives, then a few bites of Alejandro's ropa vieja, and finally cut a few pieces of her bistec empanizado for their visitor. Anamaría doubted that Brandon normally ate breaded cubed steak, but he'd be glad he made the exception once he tasted Victor Miranda's recipe along with the brown rice, black beans, and sweet amarillo sides.

Sure enough, Brandon moaned like he'd tasted manna from heaven after his first taste of the ropa vieja.

"That's my favorite," Alejandro said, pointing his fork at the sample from his meal.

Sara held out a spoonful of her sopa de pollo, and Brandon leaned across the table to taste the savory chicken soup.

"Man, that's delicious." Brandon licked his lips, earning him a satisfied smile from the Miranda matriarch.

"My husband, he is a good cook, no?" she preened.

Brandon nodded and shoveled some picadillo in his mouth. Moments later, he gave Anamaría a thumbs-up at her menu selection and wiped his mouth with a napkin. "I don't think I can pick a favorite. Everything's incredible. Looks like I found my treat meal spot when I'm in town."

Satisfied that their guest had been properly introduced to the bounty of Miranda's kitchen, Alejandro's mom motioned for the rest of them to enjoy their meals. They ate in companionable silence for a few minutes; then the conversation turned to Brandon's first visit to the island, his hope to return for a longer visit, and the ways he and Anamaría might pair up for AllFit.

"And you will go to these big events together?" Alejandro's mom asked Anamaría.

"Well, we'll meet up there. When I can get off from the department or if an expo falls around my Kelly day, so I have the extra time off for travel. There's one mid-July I may attend. AllFit is also checking to see if I can do a cooking demo to promo my YouTube channel."

"Is that the one in London?" Brandon asked.

She nodded, looking forward to getting her first passport stamp.

"Great, I'm scheduled to be there for AllFit, too," Brandon said. "Afterward, I head to Costa Rica for an exercise and self-care retreat I'm coordinating. Alejandro, I thought you mentioned spending time there. Got any tips and must-see sites I should consider?"

The conversation turned to the six weeks Alejandro had spent in Costa Rica a few years ago and his annual trips back to visit the village he had photographed. Brandon mentioned the locations of several other retreats he had coordinated over the past year for clients, a new venture that allowed him to parlay his interest in travel with his fitness training.

"Maybe you could join me for a retreat sometime," Brandon suggested, motioning to Anamaría with his glass.

She nearly choked on her sip of water. Surprised by his invite to travel together when they'd only just met.

"I've had a mixed group with all three of the retreats so far. We could tag team workouts, and classes. Maybe you could offer a healthy cooking demo and nutritional meal planning. If we divvy up the logistics planning and share the financial arrangements, we'd each have time on our own to individually explore our location when the other takes the reins."

"Oh, that's a smart idea!" Sara scooted sideways to face Anamaría, who could practically feel Señora Miranda's over-protective radar sounding an internal alarm at the thought of Anamaría traveling to a foreign country with a man she barely knew.

She agreed with Sara, though: Brandon was capitalizing on a fabulous way to travel while earning money and building his business. There were plenty of healthy vacation packages touted on the internet these days.

Still, she could hear the concerns about Brandon's offer as if her own mami had joined them at the table to list them. With her three brothers joining in with their two cents. Papi would naturally wait to weigh in when she asked his opinion, because she typically did.

"Hey, if you two teamed up, I bet AllFit would even sponsor. If they don't already. Do they?" Sara threw the question at Brandon, her shrewd business mind that had most recently resulted in the launch of her own clothing line off and running with his suggestion. "They'd be crazy not to cash in on the promo op. If you two go with this."

"I had been waiting to crunch numbers. Gathering feedback and reviews from the first three retreats, but I mentioned it to them this past weekend when we were all in New York," he answered. He grabbed his drink and adjusted the paper straw for a sip. "We're negotiating."

"Yes!" Sara balled her fist and tapped the table beside her empty salad plate. "I think it's a perfect opportunity for you two."

"Maybe," Anamaría hedged. She didn't want to commit to anything without thinking through it. "Everything's still pretty new with AllFit. They might want to see the response from my sponsored posts before investing more in me."

Sara waved off Anamaría's argument, her blond hair dancing along her shoulders as she shook her head. "The response is going to be fabulous. I'm sure of it. You two have great energy together. And Alejandro got some incredible shots today. Right?"

She motioned toward him, inviting his agreement.

Alejandro's lips quirked in a cocky grin that had Anamaría giving him a playful eye roll because she knew what was coming. Sara had opened the door wide for an ego trip he couldn't help but take, as would most of her brothers.

He had the audacity to wink at her, and a delicious thrill sizzled through the secret spots in Anamaría's body. "Even though my mami tried to teach me it's not nice to brag, I have to say, in my hands, most subjects wind up looking incredible. But these two made it easy. So yes, I got some shots today that are pretty badass."

"Mi hijo, so humble," his mom lamented before taking a sip of her cortadito. The coffee and steamed milk's strong scent was a familiar one, reminiscent of Anamaría's childhood when she used to sit on her abuela's knee watching her win at dominoes.

"I can see why he and your baby brother get along so well," Sara said, joining the fun. "Both their own biggest fans."

"Ay verdad, nena." Señora Miranda reached across Anamaría to clink her coffee cup with Sara's water glass in solidarity of them speaking the truth, as the older woman lamented. Their shared laughter burst louder when Anamaría added her drink to the toast.

"Bro, these ladies are a force to be reckoned with. I'm with you, though, sure we got some sick pics at the beach." Brandon stretched a fist across the empty chair between him and Alejandro, who lifted his for a good-humored bump.

"Exactly," Alejandro agreed. "But, Mami, I'm only following your advice. You always said Ernesto and I should never lie."

Señora Miranda's *tsk* of disapproval had the rest of them chuckling.

"AM, you told me that you've always wanted to travel," Sara said, circling back to their topic. "This is the perfect way to make that happen."

"She's right. You two made a great team today." Alejandro's

agreement had Anamaría's surprised gaze flying up to meet his. He motioned between her and Brandon.

Was he serious? He couldn't possibly still be stuck on the idea of her and Brandon hooking up. That might be Alejandro's MO, but she had made it clear to him that she was not interested.

Alejandro dipped his head in the tiniest of encouraging nods. She squinted a glare, uncomfortable with his bizarre matchmaking. It was too weird. Too . . . wrong.

She wanted to be a big enough person to wish him well when he eventually left. But she highly doubted any scenario in which she would encourage Alejandro to be with another woman.

Equally as strange, for someone who constantly poked her toe . . . bueno, more like her whole body . . . into her kids' and those who were like her own kids' business, Señora Miranda remined uncharacteristically quiet. No opinions or unsolicited advice doled out.

The Cuban Inquisition had ended midway through the meal, a sign Brandon had made the first cut. His rave reviews about Miranda's had definitely earned him points. If he stuck around for long, there would be more questions, especially if the two of them pursued his retreat venture.

That was the blessing and curse of having mamis whose sun rose and set on their children. Something Anamaría never took for granted. As much as she might complain about it.

"If you're interested, let me know," Brandon told her. "Find out when you can get time off from the fire department. We'll pick a location we'd like to hit up and start working on details."

Picking up his lemon water, he leaned back against the padded vinyl chair, one arm hooked on the empty chair between him and Alejandro. "Or we could start smaller, make it a long weekend retreat here. I'm betting with our combined trainer experience, your nutritionist certification, and my contacts, we'd make a good business team."

Business team.

The phrase calmed her knee-jerk reservations about him getting any wrong ideas regarding the two of them. Sure, Brandon had flirted a little, but not once the whole morning had she gotten a creepy vibe. He genuinely came across as a good person. Not hyped up on his image or his name, which could have been the case given his social media popularity and stature in the physical fitness industry. Like Sara, he seemed to know how to work the angles and channels available to him in the right way.

A friendly business relationship between them would be ideal.

"Okay, let's find a common open date on our calendars and make something happen here in Key West," she answered.

Brandon's "now we're talking" and Sara's "fabulous idea" tumbled over each other. The two of them laughed, reaching across the red tabletop for a high five.

Anamaría watched the two of them excitedly talking, their conversation slowly dimming to white noise as she allowed the reality of recent events—earned from her efforts learning, working, and building the AM Fitness brand— to sink in.

Over the past few weeks she had gained an agent, signed a contract with her first sponsor, held her first official photo shoot, and agreed to partner in a new project that could allow her to combine one of her long-sidelined passions—international travel—with one of her professional goals—helping others learn healthier eating and living habits. Things with AM Fitness were suddenly racing ahead at warp speed.

The old Anamaría from a few years ago would have worried she was moving too fast.

Today, she wanted to stand on that balustrade railing at the pier like the proud woman in Alejandro's favorite picture and yell, *Bring it!*

When it came to AM Fitness, hell, her freaking life in general, for a while her speed had been molasses slow. It was past time to kick it in high gear.

Excited, she turned toward Alejandro, wanting to share her elation with him. Head bowed, he traced a finger through the sweat from his glass that had pooled on the table. He dragged his finger through the watery circle, completing it and going on to add a squiggly line on the bottom. He added another squiggly line next to the first one, and when he started on a third, she realized the figure was a jellyfish.

Nostalgia settled over her like a warm blanket as she recalled another watery creation of his, drawn on the hostess-cashier counter one hot summer evening after the dinner rush had died down and only a few stragglers stuck around.

Back then, he had stood behind her, his arms spread on either side of her, palms flattened on the counter. His water drawing had started with a large heart. A smaller one followed, embedded inside the first. Then he leaned close, his mouth hovering near her ear to whisper three precious words for the first time.

I love you.

Her heart fluttered at the memory. One of many shared firsts.

And today, they had shared another. Different from the others but important all the same. Their relationship was evolving. She wasn't quite sure how or where they'd wind up, but it had to be a healthier place than where they'd been the past decade.

The bell above the restaurant's front door jangled, and Alejandro glanced up from his water figure drawing, toward the entrance. His oh-shit expression came and went as fast as a pesky no-see-um biting her on the beach before she even realized the tiny bug was there.

He lifted a hand to greet whoever had arrived, but his tentative smile told her he was not thrilled to see them.

Chapter 14

Anamaría followed Alejandro's gaze to a man near the hostess-cashier counter, hooking a pair of Ray-Bans in the vee at the top of his tightfitting pale blue button-down. His shaggy, product-styled hair, dark gray skinny jeans, and matching suede Oxfords gave him a trendy vibe much younger than the mid-forties her patient assessment experience pegged him at.

The guy scanned the tables searching for someone, and as soon as he spotted Alejandro his mouth spread in a welcoming smile, a flash of straight white teeth in his darkly tanned skin.

Something niggled in her brain. A familiarity, like she knew this guy, but she couldn't quite place him. Maybe a call at the station or a—

"¡Alejandro, hola, que bueno verte!"

The man's deep voice exclaiming his pleasure at running into Alejandro clicked a memory into place in Anamaría's head. Marcelo, one of the owners of Bellísima. The gallery planning to host Alejandro's exhibit.

The exhibit that, as of yesterday, he hadn't mentioned to his mother. Certainly not his father. Now, should there be a break in the lunchtime crunch in the kitchen, Alejandro's papi might venture out to the dining area to greet customers. Then both his parents would learn about his upcoming show at Bellísima.

The savory picadillo, brown rice, and black beans she'd eaten sank in her belly like the *Salvación* anchor dropped overboard. The familia restaurant he had turned his back on to pursue the passion set to be recognized by the upcoming exhibit might not be the best place to make his announcement.

Alejandro shifted uncomfortably. "Marcelo, I didn't expect—"

"No, no, no, please don't try to stand." The gallery owner held up a hand, stopping Ale when he made to push back his chair to rise.

Sinking in his seat, Alejandro gestured around the table at their party. "Mi mamá, Elena Miranda, Anamaría Navarro, who you may already know through Enrique, Sara Vance, Luis's compro-metida, and Brandon Lawson, in town for some work with Ana-maría. Everyone, this is Marcelo López, co-owner of Bellísima, a private art gallery on Duval."

"Hola, welcome to paradise." Marcelo shook hands with Bran-don, then stepped around the table toward her. "Anamaría, the prettiest of the Navarros,"

She rose to return his hug. "Guilty as charged; nice to see you again, Marcelo. I think it's been a couple years."

"Es un placer." Señora Miranda extended her hand to take his, her eyelashes batting when Marcelo bowed low to kiss the back of hers.

"My pleasure as well." He winked, an obvious charmer, which probably served him well as an art dealer. "I see you are finishing up, so I won't keep you. Alejandro, I forwarded you an email from the consultant we discussed for your exhibition. Natalia's avail-able. Please let me know what you think."

"Will do, gracias. Enjoy your meal."

"I always do when I eat here. It is almost like my mami's cook-ing back home in the DR." Marcelo stepped aside, allowing two women in beach attire to pass by on their way to the cashier.

"Don't let my Victor hear that 'almost.' He will take it as a chal-lenge," Señora Miranda warned with a wily smile.

"¡Sí, señora, I will keep that in mind! I hope to see all of you at Bellísima for Alejandro's local debut in July." With a sharp two-finger salute, Marcelo started winding his way through the crowded seating area.

About midway through the main dining room he stopped at a table for two. A blond man around Marcelo's same age, casually dressed in skinny jeans and a distressed red tee with "I'm a dealer . . . of art!" emblazoned across the chest, half-rose to greet Marcelo with a kiss on the cheek. Once the couple sat, their clasped hands resting between them on the tabletop had Anamaría guessing the other man was Marcelo's husband, Logan, whom she had yet to meet.

Her baby brother was a big fan of the two gallery owners and the way the they highlighted local artists alongside more well-known names. By giving Alejandro a place to shine, they'd made a fan of her as well.

Logan waved their way, and Anamaría smiled in return, wiggling her fingers in a hello. She turned back to their table in time to catch Alejandro returning the greeting, too.

"Dime, de qué hablaba Marcelo?" Señora Miranda asked. She dipped her head at Brandon before repeating herself in English. "My apologies. What was Marcelo talking about, hijo? What is happening in July?"

Anamaría picked up her glass and took a healthy sip. A classic question avoidance move that often worked during Navarro familia dinner. She choked on her water when Alejandro did the same.

Sara nudged her with an elbow, a what's-up frown wrinkling her brow. The girl was learning how to pick up on SOS signals fast. A key skill as a Navarro sibling, especially when Mami was on a roll meddling or lecturing, or doing both at the same time.

Alejandro set his drink back on the table, taking great care to place it precisely over the sweat circle it had left. Another delay tactic if Anamaría had ever seen one.

"Well, querida Mami, I was thinking I'd share the news at home with you and Abuela, but I know you, and your inquisitive ways, and your propensity to keep needling until I divulge all my secrets—"

"Ay, here he goes again, que exagerado," his mother complained. She tugged a brown paper napkin from the dispenser and gave a moody swipe at the table.

"I love you, Mami, but I am not exaggerating. Am I?"

Alejandro turned to Anamaría, who was smart enough to mime zipping her lips shut.

"Chicken," he taunted.

She shrugged. No way was she jumping into this fray.

Sara hid her laugh behind a napkin pressed to her mouth. Brandon coughed into his fist.

Señora Miranda humphed, but her son's smart-aleck response didn't stop her prodding. "You still have not answered my question. ¿Por qué?"

"Because I think the answer will make *you* happy but maybe not . . . everyone." His last word, hesitantly spoken, grabbed his mom's attention.

Her hands stilled their table wiping. Lips pursed, eyes squinted with intent, face confession-time serious, she stared at her son. Anamaría knew that look well. It meant, no more hedging or joking. Game over. Señora Miranda expected the truth and nothing less from her son.

"Meaning," the older women firmly prodded.

"Meaning, on Friday, July third, Bellísima will be hosting an Alejandro Miranda exhibit."

Señora Miranda gasped. The balled-up napkin dropped from her hands as she reached across to cover Alejandro's with both of hers. "¡No! ¿De veras?"

He nodded. "Sí, it's true. Enrique introduced me to Marcelo and Logan, who are connecting me with an art consultant Marcelo knows from Chicago. She's going to help me select the pieces and display design and all the rest. And you—"

"Me?" His mom sat back, her arms falling limply on the table in her obvious surprise. "I can help?"

"I know this is something you've wanted for a long time, Mami. I was thinking you and Abuela might like to handle hiring and working with a caterer."

"Caterer, estás loco, nene. Miranda's will provide all of the food, por su puesto."

Alejandro's worried gaze cut to Anamaría's. Unlike his mami claimed, there was no "of course" when it came to Miranda's catering an event his papi would not approve of. But Anamaría also understood why Alejandro didn't want to discuss his father in front of Sara and Brandon.

"You can go over those details with Marcelo and Logan," Anamaría suggested. "No need to worry about it right now."

"I will take care of the food. And your father." The flat palm Señora Miranda slapped on the tabletop punctuated her sentence like an exclamation point demanding no argument.

"Mami, I don't want any stress for you or anyone else in the familia. That's not why I agreed to do this."

"That evening will be about how proud we are to celebrate your beautiful talent, hijo. Te lo prometo."

Anamaría wrapped her arms around Señora Miranda in a loose hug, silently vowing to help her keep that promise.

"Gracias, Mami." Alejandro reached for his crutches where they leaned against the wide window behind him. "If everyone will excuse me, I'd like to say hello to Logan on my way to the restroom. Then, my leg is telling me it's time to get home and elevate it."

Brandon shuffled the remaining plates and glasses around, searching the table's surface for something. "I don't think Iona brought the bill yet, did she?"

"Your lunch is on Miranda's. Bienvenido, welcome," Señora Miranda told him. "Maybe you will mention us on your social media, no? Like Sara and Anamaría?"

"You got it." Brandon grinned. "And I will definitely be back the next time I'm in town."

A few minutes later Anamaría saw Alejandro head down to

the back hallway where the restrooms and office were located. As soon as he disappeared into the men's room, Ernesto strode through the front entrance. The same annoyed scowl he had left with earlier remained in place.

Anamaría swiveled in her chair, tracking his determined footsteps toward the back. Victor Miranda pushed the swinging kitchen door out of his way with a beefy hand and stormed out. He followed his younger son into the back office without bothering to greet the locals like he normally would.

Tension seized Anamaría's in its grip. Whatever was going down between those two did not look good. Señora Miranda hadn't noticed her younger son's entrance, but if Victor ran into their elder son right now—

As if on cue, Alejandro exited the restroom. Rather than heading back to their table, he step-swung on his crutches, moving closer to the office. Blatantly eavesdropping on whatever was happening behind the closed office door.

In the strange way life's lessons filter through your brain at random moments, the advice one of their middle school catechism teachers gave their class when she and Alejandro had been preparing for confirmation whispered in her head, *Eavesdroppers rarely hear anything good about themselves.*

Down the darkened hallway, Alejandro hunched against the wall, his head lolling to the side. Apparently, he was learning first-hand the veracity behind those old words of caution.

"Hey, guys, I'm thinking I should go ahead and take Alejandro home." Her chair scraped against the gray linoleum as she pushed it back to stand. "Do a quick check of his vitals and pin sites. Make sure he didn't overdo it today. Brandon, would you mind if Sara dropped you off at your hotel instead?"

"No problem," Brandon said.

"I need to head downtown anyway," Sara chimed in

"Mami is home watching Lulu while Cece goes to the doctor. If you want me—"

Señora Miranda broke off when the hostess motioned for her

attention, then jabbed a finger at the old school cash register with a confused expression. The older woman mumbled something about Gen Z and millennials and technology, then hugged them all good-bye, asking Anamaría to please text her an update once Alejandro was settled at home.

"Here, give me your keys and we'll transfer his camera bag and wheelchair to the back of your car," Brandon offered.

"Thank you." Anamaría followed them to the back entrance, where she waited for Brandon to return her keys, the whole time praying all hell didn't break loose before she could get Alejandro out of there.

"I do not want your mother to know about this, me entiendes?"

Standing outside the Miranda's office door, Alejandro shook his head as if his papi had asked him if he understood his edict. It didn't make any sense at all.

"Papi, she's not going to like being kept out of this." Ernesto's worried plea had Alejandro straining to hear better through the thin walls. "The insurance adjuster said there's nothing they can do. It's up to the bank, and we don't have enough equity in this property. Let me talk with CeCe about a second mortgage on our place."

"You will not jeopardize your familia's home because of my error in judgment."

Alejandro drew back in surprise at his father's revelation.

"Fine," Ernesto shot back. "Then let's ask Ale. He may be able to give us a loan to help—"

A loud slam reverberated from inside the office, cutting off whatever Ernesto meant to say next.

"Your brother has nothing to do with our restaurant. He and his money are not welcome here."

Alejandro jolted at the bitterness in his father's voice. The words, while not unexpected, stung worse than the time he'd swum through a swarm of jellyfish. Feeling as burned and raw as he had back then, Alejandro sagged against the wall.

He could hear his brother and father arguing, but his will to listen evaporated.

Suddenly the office door flung open and his father stormed out. Alejandro straightened away from the wall. Shoulders stiff, head high, he braced himself to face the inevitable firing squad of his father's verbal onslaught.

Victor drew to a halt when he spotted his son. Body rigid with anger, a low growl burst from his papi's throat before he demanded, "Qué haces aquí."

Alejandro squinted into the dappled sunlight streaming through the glass door to the outside patio seating area at the end of the hall behind his father. The gloomy darkness matched the thunderous scowl stamped on his papi's jowled face.

"Anamaría has a business contact in town. We brought him for lunch."

The disbelieving *humph* his father answered with grated. Why the hell the man would doubt even a simple explanation spoke of his irrational mind-set. Underscored why Alejandro never bothered trying to reason with him. Because in Victor Miranda's mind, there was only his way, or the wrong way.

"Why are you listening where you should not be? What did you hear?" his old man demanded.

"Nothing. Or not enough to make any sense of it. But Ernesto is right. If it's financial help you need, I can provide it."

"Ha!" his father scoffed. "Why would Miranda's, why would I, depend on you for assistance? Te fuiste, y nunca miraste pa' tras."

His father spit out the unfair accusation that Ale had left and never looked back as if it had been of his own accord, and the injustice unleashed the rebuttal Alejandro had uttered in every argument he had held in his head with his old man over the years. "I never came back because that's what you told me to do. It is not the choice I wanted to make. But the one you forced on me."

"No, no lo acepto. Uh-uh. I will not accept your blame." His father's scowl deepened when Alejandro shook his head. "You are the one who spit on your abuelo's legacy. ¿Qué fue lo que dijiste? Tell me again. What was it you said?"

No matter how much Alejandro wanted to defend himself, nothing would make right the hateful insult he had yelled that night. He couldn't take it back. No matter how badly he wished.

"Do you not remember? Porque I do. This is not enough for you." His father flung his arm out toward the Miranda's dining area, barely missing one of Alejandro's crutches with his wild gesture as he brought his open palm back to pound against his chest with a heavy thud. "Everything I have built is not good enough for you."

"That's not true. It never was. Papi, I only wanted—"

"Eh!" His father held up a hand to silence him. The nicks and calluses and scars on his palm and fingers were testaments to the hours and years he had labored as the head chef in their beloved neighborhood restaurant. Underneath his black apron with *Miranda's* embroidered across the front, his father's burly chest rose and fell with each labored breath.

"You made yourself very clear, Alejandro. Miranda's is of no importance to you." His father bent toward him, his eyes dark pools of anger. "Our familia is of no importance to you. So, vete."

Alejandro flinched, the slap of his father's words a sharp sting across his face.

Despite telling *him* to leave, his father narrowed his eyes in a steely glare, then stomped away with another feral growl.

The fight drained out of Alejandro, and he sagged against the wall again, head tipped to lean on the doorjamb. One of his crutches clattered to the linoleum floor. He ignored it.

Regret and anguish burned in his throat. His father's contempt confirmed what Alejandro had known all these years. Even if he wanted to, there was no way he could come back to Key West, make it his home base in between jobs as Atlanta was now.

His father would never forgive him. His familia would forever be fractured.

* * *

"Alejandro, you okay?"

His eyes closed, he heard Anamaría's concerned voice call to Alejandro from the dark place his papi's harsh dismissal had sent him.

Damn that man for still being able to hit where it hurt. Wounding him with contempt and disdain. Even when Alejandro knew the shots were coming.

Our familia is of no importance to you. So, vete.

If he could easily leave like his father had ordered, he would.

But his injury physically prevented that.

His professionalism required he honor the contract with Marcelo, Logan, and Bellísima.

More important, he wasn't ready to say good-bye to Anamaría. Not when they were just starting to find footing in this new . . . friendship of sorts they were forging.

At least until after the exhibit's opening weekend, he was anchored here, intent on withstanding the buffeting storm winds his father blew.

Ernesto stepped out of the office at the same time Anamaría reached Alejandro's side.

"Hey, here you go." She bent to grab his crutch, the tail of her long braid nearly sweeping the floor until she pushed it back over her shoulder. "I guess dropping it is better than throttling your dad with it. So, yay you for self-restraint."

He lifted his left arm when she moved to tuck his crutch under his pit. His lips quirked at her lame joke. "Small blessings."

Her empathetic smile, the hand she kept on his waist after he had adjusted the crutches and stood fine on his own, they seared his heart with a yearning for the comfort he knew he would find with her alone.

"Papi shouldn't have said what he did," Ernesto offered. "He's wrong, Ale. We all know it."

"I don't. Maybe I should have hired a home health provider back in Atlanta instead of poking the bear by letting Mami guilt me into coming ho—" He rubbed his nape, massaging the muscles bunching in protest. "Into coming back."

"No, you were right the first time. Coming *home*," Anamaría stressed. "That's what this island is."

Ernesto cupped Alejandro's shoulder. "He'll change his mind. Right now, he's stressed about the insurance mix-up and the bank giving fits about a loan. Pero we'll figure it out. We always have in the past. And he'll back off. I'll work on him."

Unlike his little brother, skepticism colored Alejandro's perspective. "Sounded to me like you've been hitting a wall trying to talk sense into him. He never listens to anyone."

"Like I said, we'll handle the bank. Just don't let him push you away again. I like having you back." Ernesto squeezed his shoulder in a reassuring grip.

The hopeful expression on his brother's face reminded Alejandro of when they were kids and Ernesto begged to be included with the older boys' fun. Now his baby brother dealt with solving their familia's problems, while Alejandro fled them.

"I gotta run to the kitchen, wrap up the lunch rush, and start prep for dinner so I can get home to Cece and Lulu. But I'll see you at Mami and Papi's later. Okay?"

Anamaría's advice out in the parking lot before lunch played through Alejandro's mind. *Peek out from behind your camera. Try connecting with those who are important to you.*

Like his little brother.

"Yeah, sure, where the hell else would I be with this bum leg." Ernesto's grin had Alejandro answering with a smirk of his own. He nudged his head toward the kitchen on the other side of the wall where they stood. "Go on. Besides Mami, you might be the only one to keep him from biting off someone's head in there. Save the staff. I'm fine."

Ernesto dropped a peck good-bye on Anamaría's cheek, then disappeared around the hall corner.

Once she and Alejandro were alone, instead of backing away, Anamaría stepped closer and put her other hand on his waist. The warmth of her palm spread across his stomach, and damn if his crotch didn't perk up. Craving a much more intimate touch from her.

"What do you say the two of us get out of here together?" she whispered.

Damn, he didn't know what she had in mind by her offer, but he sure as hell knew what his body wanted. It ached to be with hers. There was no use denying it, at least not to himself. But that need had led him to selfishly hurt her in the past. He couldn't let that happen again.

Lust urged him to drag her body against his, taste the sweetness of her lips and tongue. Instead, he forced himself to rein in his lust, reaching up to softly trace her jawline with his fingertips. The light streaming in from the patio door danced across her beautiful face creating a mix of shadow and light. Her eyes fluttered closed and he let himself explore the face he saw in his dreams. High cheekbones, straight nose, arched black brows, and lush lips. Details emblazoned on his mind. And in his heart.

Touching her was delight and torture, leading him to pull away before he did something foolish. Something he couldn't take back that would ruin the tentative relationship they had started rebuilding.

Anamaría's inquisitive eyes peered up at him intently. Assessing him like one of her patients on a call.

"I know he gets to you," she said softly.

"Whatever. It is what it is," he lied.

"You can't fool me."

He frowned.

"Or scare me with that mean scowl."

"Is that so?"

She tipped her chin up with confidence. "Uh-huh."

The flash of white as she grinned drew his gaze to her wide mouth. His blood pulsed with the desire to kiss her.

"Your dad's not always an easy person to love," she said. "He's demanding and set in his ways."

"Try *hardheaded. Intractable. Inflexible.*" He stopped. Hiked a brow. "Should I go on?"

She tipped her head and lifted a shoulder toward it. "If it makes you feel better."

"This . . ." Gently, he grasped her chin between his thumb and forefinger. "Being with you. Remembering the good times here, instead of the battles I fought with him. That makes me feel better."

It would be so easy to dip down and press his lips to hers. See if she still preferred the same cherry ChapStick.

"It can't be easy taking his rejection, when what you want is his acceptance," she murmured.

Coño, how could she see what he felt for his father, yet not know what lay in his heart when it came to her?

Unable to answer the great conundrum of his life, Alejandro lowered his forehead to hers. Seeking some kind of connection with her. Desperate to soak up her empathy and understanding. Unable to avoid the distressing reality that he couldn't offer her what she deserved in a partner.

His father had just confirmed that ugly reality.

"Come on, let's go," she said.

"The others—"

"Sara took Brandon back to his hotel. Your mom's behind the hostess counter helping the new girl. She said your abuela's watching Lulu, so you won't be home alone if you need anything."

He grimaced. Spending time with his niece was usually a treat, but after the confrontation with his dad, he needed to decompress. Not put on a happy face for sweet, impressionable Lulu.

"Or you could come hang out at my place for a bit." Anamaria's fingers flexed on his waist, and he caught the flash of surprise in her hazel eyes. As if her invite had slipped out unintentionally. Yet she didn't take it back. "We can, um, use my Apple TV to view your photographs on a big screen. Maybe go ahead and decide on our favorites, while you elevate your leg."

Her place.

Those two simple words tempted him like a siren's call luring a ship captain to wreck and ruin against the jagged ocean reef.

He thought about the hangouts and hideaways they'd found as teens when they wanted the privacy they couldn't find living with their parents. Back when they had talked about getting a place together someday.

Did he want to see the space she'd made her own? Where she ate and slept and watched the romantic comedies she used to love and read her favorite books and lounged in comfy pajamas . . . or out of them.

Hell yeah.

Stepping back, she hooked a hand on one of his crutch bars. "What do you say? My place?"

It wasn't a coy offer. There was no sexual innuendo in her invitation. But fuck if his blood didn't thrum through his veins, his body going hard like she'd invited him over to share a private party for two.

"I'm in."

Her smile widened at his answer. She tapped her hand on his crutch bar, then started backpedaling toward the main dining room and the side back entrance.

Someone stepped into the hallway just as the clouds must have shifted outside, sending a bright stream of sunlight through the glass door. Alejandro squinted, momentarily blinded.

"Come on, let's go— Oh! Excuse me! I didn't mean to bump into— Papi!" Anamaría's cry had Alejandro blinking to clear the spots from his eyes.

Dread swooped over him like a black crow warning of bad luck when he realized that it was, indeed, her father. Shit, this place was like a messed-up familia reunion reality TV show. Who the hell else was going to pop up next? Her mom?

The very real possibility of that happening had his lunch threatening to make a gross reappearance.

"Anamaría. Alejandro." Her father's tone managed to convey both interest and warning.

Alejandro ducked his head in respect.

"This is a nice surprise, Papi," Anamaría said.

Nice was not the word Alejandro would have used, but he wisely kept quiet as Anamaría stretched onto her toes to give her papi a cheek kiss.

The Navarro patriarch might have aged in the past twelve years, his hair now more salt than pepper, but the steely gravity in his voice had not rusted over time. The tall, broad-shouldered physique he had passed along to his sons remained equally as intimidating as Alejandro remembered. The older man's piercing eagle eyes that missed almost nothing on and off the job might have a few more lines arcing around them, but they were still sharp. The authoritative yet calm demeanor that had served him well as a Watch Commander with the city's fire department and with a houseful of rambunctious kids like his own hadn't changed either.

Whereas Alejandro's father's booming voice could silence a room, one stern look from José Ramón Navarro put a quick halt to any misbehavior. The man exuded patience, respect, and a take-no-shit attitude with the perfect balance of compassion. The type of parent whose quiet disapproval weighed more heavily on you than the blustery outbursts Alejandro's father preferred. Señor Navarro listened when you talked, but never refrained from telling you the hard truth.

Right now, his stoic expression warned of the hard truth that Alejandro better not be doing anything to hurt the man's precious Princesa again.

"I was wondering when we would get around to seeing each other, Alejandro. Welcome home."

"Gracias," Alejandro answered, feeling every bit the same inexperienced teen anxious to earn Señor Navarro's approval that he'd been the last time the two men had seen each other.

Anamaría's dad shifted his gaze to his daughter. "¿Todo bien aquí?"

"Sí, all good. Alejandro actually saved my first AllFit shoot this

morning when the photographer from Miami couldn't make it."
She twisted her torso to send Alejandro a frazzled, I-can't-believe-
this look reminiscent of the time they'd gotten caught sneaking
off her papi's boat in her backyard after curfew.

"Happy to help," Alejandro said.

Her crazy-eyed look relaxed before she turned back to her dad.

"The others wanted Cuban food, so we brought them here,"
she explained. "We're on our way out now."

"Muy bien." Señor Navarro pressed his back against the wall,
making room for Anamaría and Alejandro to pass by. "¿Llama a
tu mamá, okay?"

"Yes, I'll call her this afternoon." The adolescent moodiness
his request that she touch base with her mom used to elicit when
they were teens had matured into adult acceptance of the inevitable. "Although I'm sure Ale's mom has already texted Mami and
filled her in on our lunch here."

Señor Navarro's laugh loosened some of the tension knotting
Alejandro's neck at running into him. As they drew even, Señor
Navarro stuck out his hand to shake, his firm grip tightening
enough to snare Alejandro's attention.

He braced himself for the condemnation, at the very least the
censure, he expected from the man who was one of his father's
closest friends, not to mention for the way Alejandro had hurt the
older man's daughter.

Instead, he found empathy on Señor Navarro's age-lined face
and in his sharp eyes.

"Your familia has missed you, Ale." He sandwiched Alejandro's hand in between both of his. "I always try to remember the
advice my father gave me once. A man's pride in his work is important, unless it leads to his downfall. Perhaps my papi's words will
help you, at some point."

"Gracias," Alejandro replied.

He tried to consider the lesson and how he could apply it to his
life. But with his father having just thrown his offer of financial
assistance back in his face, he had a hard time not applying the

excessive-pride lesson to his papi. Probably not the message Señor Navarro expected him to gather from the advice.

"Con cuidado." Her dad's grip tightened. He slid his gaze to his daughter, waiting by the side door, nibbling her bottom lip nervously.

Be careful. But what Alejandro assumed the older man really meant was: *Don't hurt her.*

Señor Navarro didn't have to worry. Alejandro would dive off another waterfall and bust up his other leg before knowingly hurting Anamaría again. If he had his way, he'd leave here after the July exhibit with the two of them amicably wishing each other well, supportive of their separate dreams. From a distance.

"Understood," he answered, relieved when the hard line of Señor Navarro's lips relaxed, and he released his hold on Alejandro's hand.

Anamaría waved good-bye once more as she held the door open for Alejandro. Without a word, he step-swung passed her and out into the hot afternoon.

Once they were outside, Anamaría stopped about halfway down the sand-dusted sidewalk, halting him with an insistent "Wait!"

"What now?" he complained.

Practically everything he'd been avoiding since his return had already happened in the couple of hours they'd spent at Miranda's.

"Smell that?" She sucked in an audible breath.

He frowned. His gaze scanned the parking lot as he took a whiff of air. Onions, peppers, fried food . . . a sulfury-salty hint of the nearby ocean. Nothing out of the ordinary.

"It's the smell of freedom from parental oversight!" she exclaimed.

Arms spread at her sides, face tipped toward the sun with a wide smile, she took another deep breath that raised her chest, calling his attention to the swell of her breasts above the seam of her exercise bra. Head back, she exposed the smooth column of her throat. The desire to press his face to her supple skin and breathe in her scent and taste her delectable lips nearly knocked him to his knees.

Crap, less than two minutes ago and no more than thirty feet away from here, her father had flat-out laid down the law: *Hands off.*

And here Alejandro stood, already thinking about tracing his tongue along the hollow at the base of her throat, drawing a wet trail to her cleavage . . . lower.

Burying himself inside her luscious body.

He tried shaking off the carnal images that had only been wishful thinking when he was miles away, alone in his room or his tent or his town house. Thoughts that inevitably led to his cock responding in ways he couldn't control. Or hide.

"Come on!" Her cry snapped him out of his delusional state to find her sashaying toward her Pilot, her seductive hips swaying from side to side with her quick steps. "Hurry up! I feel like, if we don't get out of here soon, my mom might show up next!"

He laughed because he'd had a similar thought inside but hadn't divulged it. A remnant of when they were kids, complaining about their parents, mostly their moms, having eyes and ears all over the island.

This new place in their relationship might still be tenuous and fresh, and he'd have to figure out how to squelch his libidinous thoughts about her, but he planned on enjoying their time together for as long as he was here.

Starting right now.

Chapter 15

Okay, so inviting Alejandro home with her may not have been the brightest idea. Anamaría bit her lip as she slowed for the red light at the intersection of Flagler and Kennedy. Ahead on the left, Station 3 had its bay doors up, the engine parked inside. Not a soul in sight. Good for them; it looked like they were having a quiet moment during their shift.

Those times were golden for training, workouts, Ping-Pong matches, or relaxing. The latter of which she did not envision happening once Alejandro stepped foot inside her town house.

She slanted a glance at him out of the corner of her eye.

Eyes closed, right arm crooked across his forehead, he reclined beside her in the front passenger seat. Before leaving Miranda's he had pushed the seat as far back as it would go, assuring her his leg would be fine for the short trip to her place in Stock Island.

"Headache?" she asked softly, relieved he'd taken her suggestion to at least lie back and stretch out his leg on their short drive.

"Slight. Hoping you've got some naproxen at your place." His left eye peeked open at his request.

"If you ask nicely."

A corner of his mouth quirked. Then he closed his eye again and resumed his napping impersonation.

The driver stopped in the right lane waved to get Anamaría's attention. She waved back, recognizing an old high school friend, now married with a kindergartener and first grader whose classes Anamaría had visited for a fire safety talk.

Suzy had been a year ahead of Alejandro and Anamaría. She had graduated, split up with her boyfriend, Jerry, and headed off to the University of Florida. Four years later, degree in hand, she came home, started working for the bank, and reconnected with her high school sweetheart.

A wedding and two kids later, the former Key West High Key Club president sat in a maroon minivan with a child's booster seat in the back, grinning and waving, looking pleased with her life. While Anamaría sat next to the only man she had ever loved, stuck between keeping him at arm's length in an act of self-preservation and feeling out this new whatever they might have as adults.

The light changed to green, and Suzy pulled away with another wiggle of her fingers and a peppy smile. Anamaría eased her foot from the brake to the gas pedal, continuing down Flagler. Her mind meandered over ideas, memories, what-ifs, and what might still bes. While Alejandro dozed beside her, she made the short drive out of Key West, over Cow Key Channel into Stock Island. Each mile closer to her house, her jitters kicked up a notch.

Sooner than she was ready, she made the right turn into the small subdivision where her town house was located. The U-shaped road started and ended on Maloney Avenue, with twenty raised, two-story pale-pink-siding town houses connected in pairs. Two buildings down on the left awaited Anamaría's proudest purchase of her life. The day she had signed the papers and been handed the keys to her own piece of property was the day she truly felt like she'd become an adult.

She parked in her spot directly in front of her town house, with its wooden steps and white railing leading to the first floor porch where potted ferns greeted visitors. As she gazed at her home, she couldn't help but recall the places she and Alejandro had talked about buying when they finally moved in together. Old Town, Midtown, up the Keys . . . as long as it was just the two of them, it hadn't mattered.

Wishful, adolescent dreams spun from sugar. Easily dissolved and forgotten.

Or so she told herself.

"This you?" Alejandro raised his seat backrest to sit up. Rubbing at his eyes, he ducked to peer at her town house through the front windshield.

A large palm tree played sentinel in the tiny yard between her building and the one to its right. The arcing fronds rustled in the humid breeze, casting dancing shadows on the concrete sidewalk and patch of grass. Several short plantain trees marched down the center of the grassy area between the two units to the backyard where a sprawling geiger tree, its large dark green leaves and deep orange flowers clustered on the ends of its branches, held court.

"Yep, it's all mine," she answered.

"I like it. The neighborhood has a welcoming feel."

"Thanks. It also has a *mortgage* feel but seeing that deduction from my bank account each month actually makes me proud. And, when you're done hobbling up the stairs"—she stepped out of her vehicle, then grabbed their backpacks and his crutches from the back seat—"I bet you'll be thankful you came home to your parents' place to recuperate instead of hiring someone to help in your Atlanta town house."

Actually, she'd give him halfway up the steps before his first curse.

With both their backpacks flung over one of her shoulders, she followed behind him, ready to catch him should he lose his balance. Added bonus, the view of his butt in his faded black cargo shorts.

By the time he made it to her front porch, the island humidity and heat, along with the exertion of traversing the stairs relying on his right leg alone, had left their mark. A sheen of sweat coated his face and a dark circle plastered his button-down to his back between his shoulder blades. He swiped at his forehead with the back of a hand and muttered the next in a line of *shits*, *damns*, and *carajos*.

Anamaría unclipped her keys from the notch on her bag as she moved toward the front door.

"Here, let me get out of your way." Alejandro edged backward to give her more space. His right crutch banged against the clay pot filled with bright pink geraniums.

"Shit, sorry!" he muttered, adjusting to his left only to smack a pot of orange Gerbera daisies with his other crutch.

"Carajo, I didn't mean to . . ." He shuffled awkwardly on his right foot, his head swiveling from side to side in search of a place to set his crutches safely down between the smattering of potted plants scattered around her entry and along the base of the white wooden porch railing. In his unwieldy search, he wound up losing his balance and pitching forward.

"Oh, cra—!" Anamaría grunted, bumping her forehead against his shoulder.

Her keys plunked onto the wooden floorboards as her arms slipped around his midsection to stop him from landing face first among her potted garden. His forearm smacked the doorframe in his own attempt to catch himself, but momentum careened him forward and she wound up sandwiched between her front door and him, her face squashed against his chest. A button on his shirt poked her cheek. Her nose pressed into the skin exposed by the vee of his shirt.

"Ay, we have *got* to stop winding up like this on front porches," she muttered, her voice muffled.

Alejandro laughed, the sound rumbling from his chest into her ear. The faint smell of his cologne mixed with his body heat and suddenly all she could think about was nuzzling him with her nose. Kissing her way up his chest and neck to his lips. Letting her hands roam the curves and dips of his broad chest and back.

But despite her raging hormones where he was concerned, she wasn't sure if she wanted to mess up their friendly truce by adding sex to the mix. Did she?

No.

Yes.

No?

Hell, maybe.

"I swear I am a lot more coordinated than these annoying crutches make me appear," he groused.

"Well, the jury's still deliberating that one, based on the evidence of your free fall in the rainforest, not to mention this is the second time I've rescued you from falling," she teased, relying on humor to mask the uncertainty plaguing her.

His chuckle sent a puff of warm breath whispering across her forehead.

She peeked up at him. The light blue sky with its cotton ball clouds was the perfect frame for his dark hair and bronze skin. His prickly scruff gave him a roguish appeal, like he needed more help in the appeal department anyway. The eyes she knew almost as well as her own stared intently down at her, awareness heating their depths.

She wanted to give in to her lustful thoughts. She wanted to push him away before she got hurt again. She wanted to drag him inside and have wild, crazy makeup sex. Bueno, as wild as a man with a fractured tibia shaft could safely have, but she didn't mind being inventive.

And then . . . then, what?

The question whispered from the logical side of her brain. The one wisely working to shut down the wanton parts of her body screaming for his attention.

And then what?

As if he somehow saw the inner battle she fought reflected on her face, Alejandro splayed a hand on the doorframe, then straightened his elbow, lifting his weight off her.

Anamaría shifted out from under him, instantly missing his

warmth. Struggling with how to squash the swarm of desire building inside her for this man whose dispute with his father, and his own wanderlust, compelled him to leave again.

Dios mío, what was she doing bringing him here? To her home. The one place on the island that didn't have his mark. The one place devoid of any memories of them together.

Once he walked through this door, that would no longer be true. She'd have nowhere to go that didn't remind her of him.

"Sorry about that," he mumbled, giving her smattering of flower pots the stink eye. "What's with all these plants, anyway? You opening up a garden shop as a second side hustle or something?"

"Not funny," she answered, crouching down to pick up her key ring.

She rose and thumbed through her keys in search of the one for her house, her stomach clenched with unease. Her hand trembled as she slid the key in the lock. Of course, the temperamental thing stuck. She'd been meaning to spray a little WD-40 in the keyhole but kept putting the chore off for later. Sucking her teeth with irritation, she grabbed the knob with her left hand, jiggled the key with her right, bending over to get a better look.

"Here, let me try." Alejandro stepped closer and his hip bumped her butt.

She jerked to a stand as if he'd prodded her with a hot poker.

"You okay?" he asked.

Her heart pounding, she spun around to face him. "You really want to know?"

"Wouldn't have asked if I didn't."

His confused frown left her wondering if she might be the only person standing here with one foot stuck in the past and the other in the present.

Overhead, a military jet from the nearby Boca Chica naval air base roared by, leaving a wispy white contrail across the blue sky. She watched it dissipate, wishing her feelings for him would fade away so easily. Hurt by the thought that his for her actually had.

The mix of desire and despair overwhelmed her and she let her eyes drift closed, blocking out his ruggedly handsome face.

"Hey, what's going on? Talk to me." Alejandro's fingers lightly caressed her jawline, then softly tucked loose strands of hair behind her ear.

The concern in his voice paired with the intimacy of his touch, reached inside her soul to push her over the edge of reason.

"Coño, I'm frustrated! Okay?"

He blinked several times, clearly dumbfounded by her outburst.

She huffed her annoyance and swatted his chest. "I'm frustrated with you for being so hardheaded. With your dad for being such a hard-ass. And with myself for still wanting you so damn badly I can't even unlock my fucking door."

Her words were like a grenade dropped on the porch floor. Shocking them both. Several tense seconds ticked by. His jaw muscles tightened, his piercing eyes locked on hers. She licked her bottom lip nervously, then tugged it between her teeth to avoid spewing another embarrassing revelation. His hungry gaze dropped to her mouth and all she could think about was her all-consuming need to feel his lips. On hers. Now.

"Ale," she whispered, his name more a longing-filled sigh that lit the fuse of their desire.

His crutches clattered to the floor as he pulled her against him. His firm lips covered hers, and she willingly opened for him, wanting, needing, to taste him.

His tongue brushed hers, slow and languid, stroking and tangling, and she moaned with pleasure. He tasted like sin and sweetness with a hint of the lime he'd squeezed in his water at the restaurant.

He cupped her face, angling her head to deepen the kiss. Her hands trailed down his chest, exploring the changes in his physique, desire building at her core. Reaching his waist, her fingers hooked on his belt loops, tugging their lower bodies flush. Desperate to satisfy this need to be one with him again.

His lips broke from hers to trail a line of heated kisses up her jaw. He nibbled on her earlobe, sucking it into his mouth, then blowing a soft breath in her ear. His hands spanned her rib cage, his thumbs gently grazing the underside of her breasts. Lust shot through her, making her clit throb for his touch, and she arched backward, bumping her head on the door. Her pelvis thrust against him, her body seeking his, reveling in the hard length of his erection.

A car door slammed in the parking lot below.

Alejandro pressed his forehead to hers, their heavy breaths mingling in the small space between.

"Unless we wanna put on a show for your neighbors, we should get inside." He rocked his pelvis against hers imitating the act they both craved. His thumbs swept over the underside of her breasts again and her nipples pebbled, anxious for his attention.

The sound of female voices trickled through Anamaría's lust-filled brain. The fact that she and Alejandro stood on her front porch, their intimacy in full view of anyone on the street or parking lot, slowly registered. Along with the voice of sanity determined to squelch her fun.

Letting him inside would mean giving in to her craving for him. While also knowing her heart would have to let him go, eventually.

Could she do that?

"Hey, it's okay if we put on the brakes." Alejandro rubbed his knuckle across her chin, circling the little mole below the right side of her mouth. The one he used to like to—he dipped down and pressed a chaste kiss on her mole. The sweetness of his move, the reminder of how incredible he used to make her feel . . . how incredible he had made her feel right now . . . tipped her over the edge.

"We can back off," he continued. "Stay . . . I don't know . . . whatever we are. Friends. If that's what you want."

Friends.

It was better than the nothing they'd had for almost twelve years.

Was that enough? Is that all she wanted?

They had parted terribly as kids years ago. Neither able nor ready to admit the fact that forever wasn't for them.

Now they were adults. Could they find a better way?

Enjoy being together during whatever time they had. Saying good-bye without the heartache and acrimony.

No more what-ifs. No more what might have beens.

Only right here. Right now. Eyes wide open. Grabbing what they desired and deserved.

Anamaría slid her hand down his forearm to hook their fingers. "I don't want to put the brakes on."

He stared at their joined hands for several breath-stealing seconds before he glanced up at her, hope swimming in his eyes as he studied her.

"I have an idea," she said. "A really *good* idea."

The roguish grin of his that curled her toes and sent tingles to secret places flashed. "I'm listening."

"You and I. We have some . . . some unfinished business. What if we simply enjoy our time together? And when you leave, this time, no hard feelings. No regrets."

Her heart pounded in her chest at her bold offer.

Alejandro's intent gaze searched hers. "Are you sure? The last thing I want is to hurt you."

Bueno, she didn't want that, either.

But what good would come from denying herself? Maybe what she needed in order to finally move on was closure. The healthy kind of closure. On equal terms.

Stepping toward him, she brought their joined hands to her chest.

"We didn't get things right the first go-round. This time, we can. I know what I want, so I'll be fine. What about you?"

Desire flared in his dark eyes. "Princesa, I screwed it up before. But there's never been any doubt about what I want. You." He ducked down to steal a kiss, speaking his next words against her lips. "If you'd hurry up and open this damn door, I'll show you how fine I can be, too."

"Ay, that ego of yours. It just might get you into trouble."

"The best kind of trouble. Now, are you going to let me in, or are we gonna keep scandalizing your neighbors?"

Like one of his late-night fantasies come to life, Anamaría pushed her front door open, reached down to grab his crutches, and handed them to him. As soon he was situated, she stepped backward into her town house and crooked a finger for him to follow.

Alejandro didn't need to be asked twice.

He step-swung inside, desire for her fueling him.

"Welcome to my humble abode," she said, spreading an arm out to encompass the first floor, with a little wave at the stairs along the left side heading up to the second level.

He let his gaze roam around the long, open space that comprised the kitchen, dining, and living areas, ending with a wide window and door to what looked like another small porch on the back.

"Two bedrooms, two and a half baths, almost twelve hundred square feet that are all mine." The pride in her voice reminded him of the way he'd felt during his first exhibit. Man, how he wished she would have been there.

Now she was offering them a chance to have what they'd dreamed about as teens. For a little while at least. Which was way the hell better than the fat fucking nothing they'd had all these years.

"I like it," he mused.

His gaze trailed around the main floor, landing on the little touches that spoke of her. The collage of family pictures stuck to the white refrigerator-freezer. The NutriBullet on the gray Formica counter, used in the smoothie recipe videos he'd watched on her website. A pair of black Kinos and tan pair of chanclas set neatly by the door exactly like at her parents', the slip-on sandals ready for a quick trip outside to take out the trash or grab a forgotten item in the car.

Or meet up with your boyfriend when he swung by for a midnight rendezvous after the parents were asleep. Not that she had to worry about that anymore. But the shared memory made him smile. And grow hard anticipating their uninterrupted fun ahead.

He moved deeper into the house, past a light oak breakfast table for four with navy accents, the same color as the textured, woven fabric of a sofa sectional with a chaise on the far end. The perfect place to stretch out and elevate his leg. Or continue what they had started on her porch.

Hoofing it like an invalid with one good leg up the stairs to her bedroom was not the kind of foreplay he had in mind. But if— shit, he was hoping for more like *when*—Anamaría gave him the "go" signal, he planned to let her take the lead. He'd scale those stairs if need be.

"Do you want something to drink? Water, Gatorade?" She opened the fridge and scanned the inside while she asked.

"I'm good, thanks." Good getting a feel for her sanctuary. Committing it all to memory so he could picture her here when he was alone, missing her.

There weren't many knickknacks or dust collectors as she used to call the figures and mementos her mom kept around their house, but enough touches to make the place homey. A few family photographs in black frames were arranged along the stair wall where the door to a half bath stood slightly ajar. In the living room area, he spotted a *Women's Health* magazine and a MacBook Pro laptop, its shiny blue protective case decorated with an AM Fitness sticker, both resting on a small black coffee table.

He perused the framed candid photos of her and her family, soaking up the events and moments he wasn't a part of because he hadn't been there.

"Whose birthday was this?" he asked, pointing to one of her

and her brothers gathered around the dinner table, a cake with candles in the center.

"Luis's. Three years ago, pre-Sara." She held up a framed photo on the entertainment stand next to what looked like a fifty-inch TV. "These two handfuls are José and Ramón, Carlos and Gina's boys, at the beach with Lulu and me. Here's one after the mass celebrating Mami and Papi's thirty-fifth anniversary earlier this year."

The peek into her world proved bittersweet. Images of the fulfilling life she led without him, but instead with those he could count on to make sure she was okay when he was gone.

"I take it Mallory Square's still one of your favorite hangout spots?" He gestured toward the large print of the Sunset Celebration ritual popular with locals and tourists alike.

"Uh-huh. The energetic hum of life juxtaposed with the calm inevitability of the setting sun."

Kind of how he felt with her—alive with emotion and yet, at peace.

His attention caught on two vivid original paintings. One of Higgs Beach at sunrise and the other of a fishing boat much like her papi's, the *Salvación*, out on the open ocean. Both took up the short wall that butted up against the angling stairs. The initials *EN* were slashed in the bottom right corner of each painting, identifying them as Enrique's work.

"I'm surprised you have these. I thought he wasn't selling or even displaying his pieces anymore," Alejandro said, awed by her brother's talent.

Anamaría joined him in front of the paintings. "He only gifts them now. And even that's not too often. It's such a shame because he's so freaking talented."

"I'm going to get that story out of him sometime. Right now though, there are more important things that have my attention." He tucked a few loose strands of hair behind her ear, let his touch linger over her jaw.

"The place feels like you," he said, taking in the potted ferns and exercise bike angled so she could watch the television, probably the romantic comedies she had dragged him to all the time. "It's comfortable. Homey."

"Thank you, I think?" Her nose scrunched in a cute grimace. "Not sure many women like being described as homey or comfortable, but my house thanks you for the compliment."

He chuckled as he leaned his crutches against the sofa, then sank onto the top of the back cushion.

"How about gorgeous?" he suggested.

She tapped her chin, her brow furrowed in an exaggerated frown, as if she were considering his response.

"Sexy as hell?" he tried again.

Her naughty grin had his blood pulsing to his crotch, his body ready and willing for whatever sinful ideas had her eyes lighting with mischief.

"Killing me with how far away you are?" The truth in his words stole the banter from his voice, leaving it a raw, need-filled plea he should have been ashamed to reveal. Instead, he held his palm out to her, a silent request for her to join him.

"Well, when you put it like that." Her teasing smile widened, and she moved toward him.

He caught her nervous swallow. Noted the way her fingers flexed, relaxed, then flexed again at her sides. Yet her gaze never wavered from his.

"Are we crazy for doing this? For wanting this?" She placed a hand on his shoulder, stepping closer to stand in between his legs. "For taking what we can have now and saying good-bye in a better way when the time comes?"

The uncertainty marring her brow tugged at his need to make her feel safe.

"Hey." He took her other hand in his. Softly caressed the back of hers with his thumb. "If you're unsure about this . . . if you have any doubts . . . we backpedal. I'll hang out, rest my leg on your comfy chaise." He tipped his head to the extended couch behind them. "We can check out today's pictures like we planned. But this, us—"

Lifting their joined hands, he pressed a kiss to her knuckles. "It only happens if we both want it." He kissed the back of her hand again, his gaze holding hers intently. "I know I do. But that's not enough. And it's absolutely okay if you want, or need, to hit pause."

Her eyes searched his intently, as if the answers she sought would be found there. He channeled his love for her, needing to reassure her of his commitment to doing what was right for her this time around. To put her first, like he should have done before, instead of pushing her to follow him, then letting their relationship end in a ball of flames that had left them both destroyed.

"The smart decision might be to pause," she murmured.

For a heart-stopping second, he thought it was game over. Back to tentative friends. Retreat to their separate corners, alone.

Then her delectable mouth curved in a sweet smile. Pulling her hands from his light grip, she grasped his shoulders and edged deeper into the space between his legs, until their torsos nearly touched and her hips brushed his inner thighs.

"Then again, smartest doesn't always equate to the most fun." A playful spark ignited the gold flecks in her hazel eyes seconds before her eyes drifted closed and she kissed him.

Desire, swift and hot, scorched through him. He grabbed her waist, pulling her hips flush with his. She came willingly, adjusting her stance to avoid his injured leg. Her tongue swept across his lips, seeking entrance. He opened, savoring the taste of the mint she had popped into her mouth on the drive home. Their tongues tangled and stroked each other. She moaned her pleasure, one hand spearing through his hair along his nape, encouraging him. Their kiss was hot and frenzied and still not enough.

Suddenly she pulled back, her fingers reaching for the buttons on his shirt, making quick work of them. His elbow bumped his crutches, and they clattered onto the mottled gray and white tile floor.

Never one to be idle, he grasped the zipper on her windbreaker. The damn thing caught in the white material and he had to raise, then carefully lower it a couple times, revving his anticipation of divesting her of the barrier between her skin and his lips. Her cleavage beckoned, and he bent to kiss her warm skin.

"Off, now," she demanded, pushing his unbuttoned shirt over his shoulders. He released her long enough to shrug off his button-down and tug his white T-shirt over his head. He emerged to find her white and purple windbreaker in a puddle on the floor. His shirts soon joined it.

Her hands explored his pecs, fingers teasing across his collarbones and shoulders, down to his biceps, then back again, leaving a trail of pin-prickly awareness that heightened his desire for her. She ducked down to place a kiss over his heart, the tip of her tongue sneaking out to taste him. Her throaty *mmmm* had his dick hardening.

Lust drove him and he reached for her. Hands spanning her hips, he ran his thumbs along the elastic waistband of her black leggings. He traced her obliques, spread his palms across her rib cage. His blood pulsed as she trembled with his caress. Anxious to touch more of her, he slid his hands to cup her ass, drawing her flush against him, letting her feel his reaction to her.

She gasped, her eyes flashing with wanton desire. Then she bent to nip his neck with her teeth, nibbling her way to his ear where she licked, then blew on the sensitive lobe.

"You smell delicious," she murmured, nuzzling his ear with her nose.

He growled low in his throat, his erection throbbing for her. His fingers kneaded the round curve of her butt, reveling at the feel of her shapely curves in his palms. Still, it wasn't enough; he needed more of her. Craved more of her.

She sealed his lips with hers, their kiss fevered. Demanding. Her giving and taking as fiercely as he did. Tongues twisting, teasing. Hands roving over each other, reacquainting themselves with curves and dips and planes. Their motions frantic and hungry, as if she felt his same need to make up for the last twelve years of separation.

He filled his palms with her lush breasts, rubbing his fingers over her nipples through the purple Lycra bra, the taut pebbles heightening his driving need to taste them.

She did her own exploring, fingers and mouth and tongue roaming over his torso, her hands skirting around to massage the muscles along his back. Her short nails skimmed down his spine, sweeping around to tease his sensitive nipples. His erection strained in his shorts, begging for her attention.

"I missed you," she whispered, burying her face in his neck, her warm breath heating his skin.

He cradled her in his arms, relief seeping over him and soothing his fear of her rejection. Something he continually experienced with his father. What he thought she had done in the past.

Only now he knew differently.

"I've missed you, too," he said, knowing he had already told her so the other day when the words had slipped out unbidden, torn from his soul like a Band-Aid ripped off of an unhealed wound.

Now he readily admitted them. The rush of gratification that came from voicing a truth he had denied as a matter of pride washed over him like a cleansing wave, and he couldn't stop himself from repeating the heartfelt confession. "Dios, how I missed you."

He felt her smile against his neck, followed by a sweet kiss where his pulse beat rapidly. Another press of her lips on the curve of his jawbone. Another on his chin. A chaste trail to his lips, where she sucked his bottom lip into her warm mouth in a decidedly unchaste move that had lust throbbing in his shorts.

Growling low in his throat, he devoured her mouth, invading it with his tongue just as she had invaded his heart. Her hands dived into his hair again, massaging his scalp while her lips teased his and her pelvis undulated against him in a motion natural and raw.

When they finally broke apart, their heavy breaths mingling, they stared at each other. Him dazed by the reality of being here with her again. She was as sexy and sweet and loveable as he'd always pictured in his dreams.

"Now that we've established that we both missed each other, what are we going to do about it?" Her gaze slid to the chaise section of the couch.

Alejandro straightened, and she wrapped an arm around his waist to help him hop around the piece of furniture. Once he sat down, leaving his left leg dangling off to the side of the cushion and out of the way, she gently pushed on his shoulders, encouraging him to lie back.

"Wanna play doctor with me?" she suggested, waggling her eyebrows playfully.

A laugh burst from him at her unexpected but welcome question.

She paused, fingers on the button of his shorts, actually waiting for him to give her the okay. As if the erection straining for release wasn't enough of a sign that he was *more* than okay with her ministrations.

He brushed her fingers aside and quickly unbuttoned his cargo shorts in answer.

She helped him elevate his hips to tug down the material; then he extracted his right leg, leaving the shorts to dangle from his other thigh. Her ponytail braid slipped over her shoulder, the ends tickling his stomach when she bent to kiss his knee above the top ring.

"You okay?" she asked softly, glancing up at him from under her lashes.

"Never better."

He brushed his fingers along the juncture of her neck and shoulder, marveling at her soft skin.

"We have to be careful," she told him. Her gaze cut down to his injured leg again before coming back up to meet his.

"It's fine. I'm good. Or I will be as soon as you stop worrying and get back to playing doctor. I'm waiting for my house call." He pressed his wrist to his forehead and grimaced as if in torment.

"Hey, Doc, I think I have a fever. You really need to check me out."

She laughed at his antics but quickly sobered. "You tell me if something hurts. If you're uncomfortable or—"

"Anamaría, I'm good. *We're* good." He caressed her forearm hoping to soothe her fears. Acknowledging, privately, that her concern for his well-being touched him in a place no one else had ever been able to reach.

"I promise," he assured her when that tiny worry groove appeared between her brows. "But I can assure you I'll be a helluva lot better when there's a little less talk and a lot more action."

He winked and she dropped her head back to groan up at the ceiling. "Ay Dios mío, that was so cheesy."

But the worry eased from her beautiful face and the tension relaxed from her shoulders when she glanced down at him again.

"Come here." He beckoned her with a jerk of his head. Wanting her closer.

Instead, she surprised him by crossing her arms and deftly peeling off her sports bra. The scrap of material landed on the tile floor as she grinned and straddled him.

Damn, she was hot.

He cupped her breasts in his palms, moving them in slow, languid circles. Her eyelids drifted closed as a moan of pleasure escaped her kiss-swollen lips. She put her hands over his, guiding his fingers to play with her nipples. Showing him what she liked. His erection pulsed with need. She ground against him, bold and confident. Something neither of them had been in their youthful explorations together.

He marveled at this new side of her. Silently promised to cherish her the way she deserved. A sense of rightness, of finally being whole again, seeped into the dark, lonely recesses of his heart.

"Ay, Princesa, me vuelves loco," he murmured, certain if he didn't get inside her soon, she would indeed drive him crazy.

He stretched up to lap at the curve of her breast with his tongue, desperate to satisfy his longing to taste her. It wasn't enough.

"I don't know about you, Doc," he told her as he trailed his tongue from one of her breasts to the other. "But this patient is ready and willing to undergo a full body work up."

She laughed, a rich, throaty sound that was sweet music to his lonely soul. "Ay, papito, show me where it hurts, and I'll kiss it all better."

Chapter 16

Seated next to Luis at the round kitchen table in the nook overlooking their mami and papi's backyard and canal, Anamaría handed her brother the salad bowl. He dug in, refilling his plate with more of the fresh spinach leaves and mix of raw veggies she insisted her mom add to their regular dinner menu.

Outside, the early-evening sky held a loose grasp on the day's orange sherbet and cherry red sunset colors while the night's dark blue and violets descended. Lights flickered on in their neighbors' homes up and down the canal. The yellowish glows shone out of windows and off screened-in porches to shimmer on the surface of the deep water.

Tonight, she and Luis were the only two siblings in attendance because José's T-ball team had practice, which meant Carlos and Enrique were at the baseball field coaching, while little Ramón tagged along picking up pointers and serving as batboy. Sara had driven up to Miami for meetings about her clothing line and South Beach boutique, while Gina relished a few hours of well-earned solitude at home.

But come this weekend, the Navarros would all be seated around the larger dining room table, breaking bread, catching up, and granting their matriarch's wish to have all her children and grandchildren together at least once a week, outside of mass. Anamaría readily admitted their weekly meals were something she and the rest of her familia looked forward to as well.

"Ay, nena!" her mom exclaimed, scooping up a bite of mashed potatoes with her fork. "I cannot believe how many new peoplers you have since those pictures Alejandro took for you y ese nene. ¿Cuando fue eso, ha? Two, three weeks ago now?"

Anamaría shared a grin with her brother. "Sí, it was a little over two weeks ago. Pero they're called 'followers,' Mami. Not 'peoplers.'"

Lydia waved off the correction like a pesky mosquito, the faint lines crossing her brow deepening with a *whatever* frown she would have told little José was rude to make. "Gente, people, followers. You know what I mean. Anyway, today I joined Elena for lunch at Miranda's and she showed me the Instagram app. She's one of your people—ay, followers, sí? And Sara's, too. It's very nice of you to help Elena with her Instagram wall."

Instagram feed.

Anamaría silently made the correction, her exasperated gaze meeting Luis's. Wise man that he was, her brother shoveled more pork roast in his mouth. His way of telling her not to bother, it was a hopeless endeavor, trying to teach their mami about social media apps. Luis, who preferred his privacy and chose to stay off social media, leaving that domain to his successful fiancée, knew there was a good reason why their mami didn't own an Instagram or Twitter account.

Lydia Quintana de Navarro could successfully chair the committee for a St. Mary's event hundreds would attend. Had done so for years. She'd managed their familia budget and household, raised four fantastic kids—as she was fond of saying—and mentored countless others in the church teen program.

But when it came to technology, *challenged* did not even begin to describe their mami. She struggled mightily to find her way around her personal profile on The Facebook, as she referred to it.

And even with that single social media account, there were times one or more of the Navarro siblings cringed when they read a comment their mami made on a familia member's or friend's post. Nothing like waving the digital chancla at someone in front of their thousands of "friends."

No need to increase the number of potential recipients of her well-intentioned, if boundary-pushing, advice by giving her access to a Twitter or Instagram handle, too.

"Ale's pictures were amazing. And really, boosting AM Fitness's reach to better promote the AllFit brand has been a group effort," Anamaría explained, cutting a piece of the pork roast next to the large helping of salad on her plate. "Brandon, Sara, and AllFit have posted different images from the photo shoot with Alejandro on their social media platforms, tagging me and encouraging their followers to find me. And with Brandon sharing a teaser about the Key West retreat we're planning together, things have really taken off."

She speared the pork with her fork, nonplussed by the bullet train her side hustle had boarded. Astounded by the huge jump in followers, views, and subscribers on her YouTube channel, plus the requests for information about her online personal training programs. Now she was looking into the logistics of creating a monthly subscription service for nutrition and training clients. The passive income potential could really skyrocket, boosting her monthly budget.

Brandon had mentioned the idea to her during a retreat-planning call, and Alejandro was giving her a few key photography and videography tips to improve her posts.

She grinned thinking about the photo shoot she and Alejandro had started in her home gym in the storage space beneath her town house. Started but not finished because they had gotten a little distracted. And disheveled.

His *Damn, girl, you look hot*, murmured under his breath, but loud enough for her to hear as she'd lain back on the padded bench, had drawn her attention. She'd swiveled her head to where he sat on a black metal barstool, his Canon at the ready. Her tongue made a slow swipe of her lower lip and his camera wobbled. A blazing heat that matched the one burning inside her flared in his espresso-colored eyes as he peered over the top of his Canon, and she had nearly dropped the twenty-pound free weights she held above her chest.

Her body had instantly responded to the lust he didn't even try to hide from his face. Her breasts grew heavy, their sensitive tips straining against the tight sports bra material. Need pulsed between her legs, swift and urgent. Her weights had clunked to the padded floor, and he'd set the camera aside, his intense gaze never leaving hers. Together they'd maneuvered him to the bench, his shirt and her exercise bra off before his back hit the black padding, her mouth devouring his.

So far over the past two weeks they had christened her sofa, the kitchen table, both the master and guest beds, and for old time's sake, she had laid the back seats flat in her Pilot so they could make out in a car like they had as teens. Given his injury, there'd been a need for dexterity and creative thinking, but they'd been up to the challenge.

Adding her home gym to their secret list when he'd come home with her after the Zumba class at St. Mary's earlier today meant she'd never be able to work out down there again without picturing Alejandro's lean, sculpted body stretched along the weight bench, naked and gloriously ready for hers.

Dios mío, the man might be a genius behind the camera, but in front of it? His hands, his fingers, his lips . . . they did dangerous, wicked, amazing things to her body.

"Verdad, nena?" her mom asked, the question unwittingly dispelling Anamaría's delectable daydreams.

"Right about what?" she asked. "Sorry, I zoned out thinking about Alejandro. I mean, thinking about something he, um, suggested for my home gym."

Her face flamed and she reached for her glass of lemon water.

Her mom smiled, that see-Mami-knows-best smirk that usually preceded her "te lo dije."

She had no idea what her mom thought she had "told her," but it certainly wasn't to engage in this no-strings fling with the man Anamaría had never completely gotten over, all in the guise of finally having closure.

She would. Have closure, that is. As long as she didn't let herself get sucked into considering those pesky what-ifs again. There were none. Only an amicable separation after his exhibit in six or so weeks, when they would go their separate ways.

"You know me," Luis said. "I only see your posts and stuff when I'm looking over Sara's shoulder or she sends me a screen shot of something. But she's been impressed with the way everything's played out so far for you."

He nabbed another slice of Cuban bread from the towel-covered bowl in the center of the table, using it to mop up the juice from his pork roast. Oh, the empty carbs her brothers ate, despite her nagging.

"She thinks you and Brandon teaming up is golden, for both of you," Luis said after swallowing a hefty bite of bread. "And you know she wouldn't say that lightly."

"We're very proud of you, nena." Her papi nodded from his seat in front of the backyard window. The lights from the Sellers' house across the canal shone through the wide kitchen window, hovering like fireflies around her papi's head. "You have worked hard on your business for many years. Growing in smart ways. I think you are ready. It's good to see you no longer letting anything, or anyone, hold you back."

For a man who rarely doled out advice without being asked, this was the second time since she'd arrived about an hour ago that he'd made a comment she swore was riddled with subtext. She studied him, searching for some clue, a hint of what he might be implying. His typically calm, judicious demeanor remained unchanged, which made it even more difficult for her to tell.

Maybe she was reading into things. Catholic guilt, instilled throughout elementary school at St. Mary's and from years living under her devout parents' roof, was alive and thriving inside her. Her extracurricular activities with Alejandro lately fed it.

While her mami loudly proclaimed her absolute joy that Anamaría and Alejandro were spending time together, Anamaría was lying, telling her meddling mami that Alejandro and she were simply trying to rebuild their original friendship. Facilitated by working together on her videos and photography, while she watched over his recovery exercises and occasionally chauffeured him to and from Bellísima for exhibit planning.

The two of them were being painstakingly careful to keep things platonic when they were out in public. Not wanting to provide fodder for gossip that would inevitably find its way to one of their mothers.

But when they were behind closed doors . . . Oooh, that was a whole different story. One she relished rereading with him every day. And night. Of course, sneaking around meant they had yet to spend an entire night together. To do so would require explaining his absence to his mom and abuela the next morning. Talk about a Cuban mami inquisition to be avoided at all costs.

Anamaría's Apple watch vibrated with an incoming text. Alejandro's name flashed on the tiny screen followed by his message: *SOS!*

She frowned and raised her wrist to reread his call for help.

"Excuse me." She pushed back from the table, rushing to explain before her parents reminded her of the no phones during dinner rule. "Alejandro just texted me an SOS."

Papi and Luis straightened in their chairs, eyes alert, as if dispatch had sent a Tone Out sounding through their dining room, alerting them to a 911 call.

"Did he provide any details?" Papi asked, his question delivered in his firm Watch Commander voice.

She shook her head as she stood.

"Go grab your phone, nena, and call him back!" her mother

cried, waving her crumpled napkin in the air as she shooed Anamaría away. "Or tap your watch. Whatever it is you do when I see you speaking into your wrist like one of those Star Trek movies."

Luis's mouth twitched at their mami's non–tech savvy order, although, much like their papi, Anamaría's brother's body language shouted alert, ready to race to help if needed.

Not wanting to call Ale on speakerphone via her watch, Anamaría hurried into the adjacent living room where she'd left her backpack. No surprise, her mami followed behind her. The anxious frown and the napkin twisted to shreds in her mami's hand kept Anamaría from grumbling a request for privacy.

Alejandro picked up on the first ring. "Cece's in labor."

She gasped, then turned, wide-eyed, to her mom.

¿Qué pasa? she mouthed.

Alejandro continued speaking on the other end, so Anamaría held up a finger to stop her mom from repeating her *What's happening?*

"My dad's holding down the dinner rush, but there's some kind of office party, so it's crazy at Miranda's," Alejandro continued, the words tumbling out of him in a rush of frazzled panic. "Ernesto's driving Cece to the hospital, but apparently she needs my mom there, too. Something about Mami being an ab-abduedla? I don't know what the hell she meant."

"A birthing doula," Anamaría explained. "With Lulu's labor and delivery, your mom provided emotional and physical support to Cece, similar to what's provided by a person known as a doula."

Cece's in labor? Anamaría's mami mouthed.

Anamaría nodded as Ale kept talking, the anxiety and stress of someone who had never experienced the wonder of childbirth before evident.

"Sure, doula, that sounds right. The problem is, Abuela's not over the flu yet, so they don't want her watching Lulu and getting her sick before the new baby arrives. My mom can drop me at Ernesto's to babysit, but alone I'm not sure—"

"I'll be right over," Anamaría told him.

His "Thank God!" on a whoosh of breath sounded through the cell's speaker before he asked, "Are you sure?"

As if Ale had asked her the question, Anamaría's mom gave an exaggerated nod. She made a quick sign of the cross, then clasped her hands, her lips moving in a prayer for Cece and her unborn child.

"Of course I'm sure." Anamaría dug her keys out of her bag as she headed for the front door. "I'm still up in Big Coppitt at my parents', so it'll take me a little longer to get to Midtown. Let Lulu know not to worry, her favorite babysitter is on her way."

His raspy chuckle was a good sign that the poor guy wasn't totally freaking out.

"I've got a little over six weeks of spoiling her to knock you out of that number one spot. You better watch out." The playful challenge erased the nervousness that had tinged his voice moments ago. It also reminded her of the clock ticking down their time together.

Moments later, her papi followed Anamaría down the wooden front steps to her SUV. The motion sensor light mounted on one of the front pillars that raised their house per hurricane safety building codes illuminated them, casting long shadows over the driveway. The familiar scent of the full bougainvillea vines trailing up the stair railing sweetened the humidity-laden air.

Her papi opened the door for her, giving her cheek a kiss before she slid behind the wheel. Instead of backing away to wave good-bye, he stood in the door opening. "You know I usually leave the meddling to your mamá. Pero ahora—but right now, I can't hold my silence, Princesa."

Anamaría frowned at his serious tone. "What is it?"

"Back then, after my heart attack, cuando te quedaste aquí." He rubbed a hand over the center of his chest, where the scar from his open-heart surgery marked him, before repeating himself. "When you stayed here, I worried that at first it was because of me. And then—"

"Papi, I stayed because it's where I needed to be. It was the right decision."

"At the time." He nodded slowly. His face set in the solemn, pensive expression that meant he was considering the right words of advice to offer. "Later, in the years since, I have occasionally wondered if it may have become the safe decision instead. Keeping you from something else."

She sucked in a quick breath, shocked by his perception. Wondering how long he had known a truth she'd only come to terms with in the last few years.

He cupped her shoulder with a large yet gentle hand. "I have always told you, nena, anything is possible with hard work and passion. Right?"

She nodded dumbly.

"That goes for *all* aspects of your life, not only your job, Princesa. Remember that. And perhaps you want to share my advice with someone you have been spending quite a bit more time with lately, ha?"

"Oh, Papi, we're not . . ." She fumbled for words, unwilling to lie to her father. Absolutely certain she didn't want to discuss the friends-with-benefits arrangement that could very well wind up biting her in the ass, either. Talk about an uncomfortable father-daughter topic.

"It's not what you think," she finally said.

He gave her shoulder a comforting squeeze. "There is no need for you to explain anything, Anamaría. To me or your mother. Simplemente, un consejo."

Simple advice, huh? When it packed a wallop of truth like his did, *simple* was an understatement.

"Gracias, Papi. Te quiero."

He repeated her *I love you* as he gave her another quick adiós peck on her cheek and a *Dios te bendiga* blessing. After closing her car door, he tapped the hood, signaling the all-clear for her to back out of the driveway.

There was nothing simple about her and Alejandro's situation either. Papi's claims about her past decisions were only partially true.

Her decision to stay in Key West wasn't a *safe* one. Being close to her familia, actively involved in each other's lives, even when she complained about wanting her space. That was part of who she was as a person.

The safe choice? If she was honest with herself, it was staying at the fire department. Continuing to work toward her pension alongside her brothers and father, choosing not to pursue the more iffy career path of nutrition and training full-time. Not turning her back on their Navarro familia legacy, like Alejandro had.

She immediately halted that line of thinking. It wasn't fair to him.

Their situations were different. Her entire familia would give their blessing if she chose her own route. His father had not.

But even if the rift between him and his father was healed, she had no idea whether or not Alejandro would choose to make Key West his home base. He had always felt confined here, living under what they had joked was their mamis' microscope.

Just as it hadn't been fair of him to ask her to leave for good all those years ago, it was unfair for her to ask him to stay now.

As she drove down the Overseas Highway, past the U.S. Naval Air Station at Boca Chica, she thought about her dad's advice.

Anything is possible with hard work and passion.

In her case, those wise words were best applied to AM Fitness.

They might encourage Alejandro to work at reconnecting with his father. She could pass them along and see.

But as for her and Alejandro, no amount of "hard work" would change the fact that her close ties to their island weren't ones she was willing to cut, while he'd shown no signs of wanting to drop anchor here in between jobs.

They'd come full circle to where they'd been twelve years ago. Only now they were mature adults planning for their eventual separation.

Planning, while also dreading.

* * *

"One more story, por favor?" Lulu begged. Her purple sheet and comforter tucked under her chin, the little tyke peered up at Anamaría with big, pleading eyes.

How could anyone resist such cuteness?

On the other side of the twin mattress, the three books they'd already read resting on his lap, Alejandro smirked. He probably knew she was about to cave. But really, why deny a child's love of books, especially in this day and age of electronics?

"Okay, one more, and then"—Anamaría tapped Lulu's nose playfully—"bedtime. And when you wake up in the morning, we'll have news about your new baby brother or sister!"

Lulu's face lit with excitement. "'N'-'n'-'n' I can see da baby. 'N' holded da baby. 'N' hug da baby! 'N' wuv da baby!"

With each new item on her list of things she planned to do with her new sibling, Lulu's excitement grew. Her eyes widened. Her engaging grin plumped her round cheeks, turning her into the exact opposite of a sleepy child ready for bed.

Anamaría shared a raised-brow, uh-oh glance with Alejandro. They'd been in the throes of Lulu's nighttime ritual for almost forty-five minutes. This after the little bugger had convinced her uncle to give her an extra serving of chocolate ice cream. Second dessert, they had called it while mugging for Anamaría's cell phone camera with matching chocolate mustaches.

With Lulu, he turned into such a gooey pushover. An endearing quality that inevitably stirred Anamaría's imagination into picturing him with a child of his own. Of their own.

Dangerous musings that had no place in their here and now.

"'N' I can—"

"But first," Alejandro interrupted his niece, tucking the edge of her lilac-colored blanket around her tiny shoulder, "you have to go to bed and get some rest. Or you'll be too tired to hold the baby tomorrow."

He combed his fingers through his niece's dark curls, the tender gesture matching the expression softening the chiseled angles of his face.

Anamaría's heart melted a little more as she watched his sweet interactions with Lulu. Earlier, Alejandro and his niece had sat at the round kitchen table, heads angled close, sharing crayons as they worked on a page in her Wonder Woman coloring book together. Later, Alejandro had sprawled patiently on the floor, his healing leg propped up on a decorative throw pillow, while Lulu had carefully clipped every barrette in her plastic box on top of his head.

In high school, those selfies of him and Lulu might have been useful bribery footage. Few teen boys wanted a pic of them playing hair salon on the internet.

Adult Alejandro, all six foot plus of gorgeous, mushy-hearted maleness of him, had already posted a photo to his Instagram Stories with the caption "This tío is #blessed!"

"We'll read one more," he told Lulu, bending to place a goodnight kiss on her forehead. "Then sleep time. Deal?"

The tip of her chin disappeared under the blanket's edge with her nod.

Alejandro smiled, the tenderness spreading warmth through Anamaría's chest. He brushed a curl off Lulu's forehead with his thumb, then ducked low and whispered to her, "Te quiero."

"I wuv you, too, Tío Ale," Lulu said, her high-pitched voice solemnly sweet. Her hair rustled against her sheets when she turned her head to look at Anamaría. "Quiero leer *Alma*."

"Oooh, you want to read *Alma*? Good choice!" The story about a little girl who complains that her name is way too long but then in learning the story behind each of her namesakes comes to see that one day she will have her own story to tell was also one of Anamaría's favorites. She held up the two versions of the child's beloved book. "In English or Spanish?"

"Both," Lulu suggested.

Anamaría and Alejandro laughed.

"Your tío Ale said one book, but nice try." Anamaría wagged her finger at Lulu, who giggled in response. "Let's read in Spanish."

Alejandro shifted to lie down beside his niece. Lulu snuggled closer to him, and damn if seeing the two of them nestled together didn't send a pang of yearning for the dream that would never be searing deep in Anamaría's soul.

Rubbing at the anguish deep in her chest, she prayed that it would crest, then eventually fade away like the concentric circles that formed when a fish jumped in the ocean.

But when Lulu's and Alejandro's similar eyes gazed up at her expectantly, she realized with sudden clarity that this dream would probably never go away. She'd simply have to learn to live with its loss.

"I's weady," Lulu singsonged.

Overcome with love for this precious little girl and the man who would always own her heart, Anamaría opened the beloved children's book and began reading.

An hour later, she and Ale lounged on the leather sofa in the living room of Cece and Ernesto's modest two-and-one home on Seidenberg Avenue. An Amazon rainforest documentary played on the thin television mounted on the wall in front of them. Ale reclined on the buttery yellow leather cushion beside her, a muscular arm draped over her shoulders. Her head nestled in the comfortable crook of his arm, one hand at home on his chest.

"So, the art consultant from Chicago you and Marcelo have been working with arrives . . . when?" she asked Alejandro.

They'd been going over their respective schedules, hers busier than normal now that everything with Brandon and AllFit was speed racing.

"Let me check again. I skimmed the message quickly while you were bathing Lulu." He pressed a kiss where her hairline met the top of her forehead and thumbed through email on his cell.

She closed her eyes, the contentment of them simply being here together, doing absolutely nothing other than enjoying each other's company flooding over her.

"Looks like Natalia gets here the second week in June and plans to stay for . . . a few days," he summarized as he scanned the email. "Then she'll return on the . . . where is . . . oh, here. On Monday before we open that Friday, July third."

"I hope I can meet her. It'll depend on how my training schedule shakes out." Anamaría circled a clear button on his shirt with her fingertip, then traced the material's wavy pattern of small blue and white lines with her nail, following them as they undulated over his pecs.

"Mmm, that feels good," he murmured.

Dropping the cell phone on his lap, he nudged her chin up with a knuckle, then ducked down to brush her lips with his in a featherlight caress. Once. Twice.

Her hand fisted in his shirt, pulling him toward her as desire simmered to a low boil inside her. His mouth opened over hers and their tongues brushed. Languidly twisting and savoring and seeking each other. Mimicking the act her body craved.

He sucked her lower lip in his mouth, nipping it with his teeth. She moaned her pleasure. Her hand slid down his chest, desire driving her to find his hard length straining behind the zipper of his khaki cargo shorts. Brazenly she stroked him, reveling when his hips bucked, pushing his erection against her palm.

"God, I want you," he groaned.

Cradling her nape with his left hand, he devoured her mouth again. The muted sounds of the narrator droned through the room, intermingled with their moans and sighs and murmurs of affection. His palms kneaded her breasts, his fingers teasing her nipples into hard nubs straining for more of his attention.

She broke their kiss on a gasp, desire threatening to consume her.

Alejandro placed a soft peck on the mole beneath the right edge of her mouth, moving to drop another on the ridge of her jaw. Another at the juncture of her neck below her ear. He laved her lobe with his tongue before sucking it into his mouth. His teeth nipped at the sensitive lobe at the same time his hands languidly massaged her breasts and she grew wet with need.

A wild animal screeched in the documentary, startling her. The light flashing on the TV screen brightened, and she was reminded of where they were. That Lulu dozed in her room down the short hall and could wander out here at any moment.

"We should probably . . . oooh."

Alejandro blew in her ear again, robbing her of the ability to form words.

The rush of warm air sent a thrill shimmying an erotic trail down to her breasts. Her nipples pebbled in response, anxious for his touch. Rational thought fled, heading out the back door in her brain.

"Might wake up," she murmured.

"Hmm?"

His teeth nipped at her jaw and she angled her head, giving him better access to pleasure her.

Somehow a thought wormed its way back into her head. "Lulu . . . awake."

He froze; then, with a horrified expression, Alejandro stretched up to peer over the back of the sofa toward the hallway. "Lulu? Are you out here?"

A bird's trill answered on the television.

Laughter bubbled up in Anamaría's throat. Alejandro collapsed against her, groaning and burying his face in her neck. The day's scruff on his jaw scratched her skin heightening her awareness of him. The softness of his hair tickled her jaw as the hard angles and planes of his body melded with hers. His woody patchouli and spice scent invading her senses with its intoxicating allure.

He released a shaky breath and drew back to stare down at her. His face flushed with passion, his lips wet from their kisses, he looked sexily tousled and horny. Exactly how she felt.

"Coño, this is like high school all over again," he complained. "Us making out on the living room sofa, in danger of getting caught by familia walking in."

She chuckled. "Truth."

He grinned back at her, all boyish charm and manly magnetism that had her heart tripping over itself.

"So, your exhibit as a whole? It's going well?" she murmured, trying to pick up the thread of conversation they had dropped when they'd gotten deliciously distracted.

Gently, he tucked a lock of hair from her ponytail behind her ear. "It's coming together, thanks to Marcelo and Natalia."

"He sure sings her praises, doesn't he? She must be pretty great at her job," Anamaría said.

Ale nodded. His gaze strayed to the television where a brightly colored bird, its wings spread in flight, glided above the splendor of the rainforest canopy.

"The two of them grew up in the same neighborhood in Chicago," he explained. "Seems like people there are as tight as many of us locals here. She has a good eye. You can tell by the photographs she recommends, those she nixes. Her vision for showcasing specific ones is strong, vivid. I really like working with her."

Much like his niece when she had rattled off the fun she planned to have with her new sibling, Alejandro's face lit with excitement when he talked about this new art consultant.

Jealousy flared inside Anamaría.

Adamantly, she stomped it out like the embers of an illegal fire on the beach. She had no idea what this Natalia looked like, so she had no business picturing her like his ex—tall, statuesque, beautiful. Even if Natalia wound up matching that description, it didn't matter. Jealousy had no role in Anamaría and Alejandro's relationship.

In fact, they were both making progress with their respective, also separate, goals.

His recovery was going well. This week, he had relied on the crutches more often than the wheelchair. According to his orthopedist, barring any strange setback, he might be ready to have the Ilizarov fixator rings and wires removed the week of his show's opening. That meant he'd be free to leave shortly after.

And she . . . she'd been offered a chance to attend two AllFit-sponsored marathon races over eight days in Europe. Anamaría and Brandon were set to work the company's booth at the expo, with her having two hour-long cooking demonstrations. Her Captain at the fire station had already approved her request to swap Kelly days and tack on another day of leave. As soon as she'd gotten word, she'd driven to the Miami Passport Agency to apply for an expedited passport.

Come the second weekend in July, she'd be in Barcelona. Alejandro would be back home in Atlanta, or, if his agent had his way, already off on his next shoot.

She reminded herself that she'd gone into their temporary arrangement with her eyes wide open. The problem was, her heart had remained in the picture. Filled with love for him.

Oh, she wouldn't go back on her no-strings promise. Wouldn't let him know that while the anger and disillusion of their first breakup would be missing from their second, there would still be anguish. For her anyway. But she'd get through it. She would not ask him to stay, but she could love him from afar while they pursued their dreams on their own.

"It's good to hear you're happy with Natalia's vision for your pieces. They deserve the best," Anamaría told him.

"She's come up with the layout for where each piece will be placed inside Bellísima. Although there's a special section I've been thinking about adding. It has the potential to really resonate with longtime Conchs." He paused, a strange nervousness creeping into his voice as he sat up.

Anamaría shifted, crooking her left knee between them to face him. "But?"

"But I haven't shown anyone these photographs because they're—they're kind of personal."

"Okay, now I'm intrigued." Anamaría started to make a joke about him snapping illicit pics of himself to ease the uncertainty she sensed in him, but the raw vulnerability stamping his angular features stopped her. She cupped his jaw, seeking to help soothe whatever worried him. "These photographs sound important, Ale. What does Natalia think about them?"

"She doesn't know."

"What?" Anamaría drew back in surprise. "You just said she's great to work with and has a fantastic eye for selecting the right images. Why are you holding these back from her?"

He wove a hand through his hair, sliding it down to cup the back of his head with his palm. "Because I took them when I was in Cuba for a commercial shoot and spent a day on my own. Retracing my parents' and abuelos' steps. Visiting familia I'd never met before."

Anamaría sucked in a surprised breath. "Does your mother know? I'm sure she'd love to see the—"

"No. And neither does my father." He scrubbed a hand over his face in obvious discomfort. "Part of me thinks I should show the photographs. That Mami and Abuela, your parents, those older-generation Conchs who will hopefully come see the exhibition, might feel a connection to their birth home, the Cuba they left behind . . . I think . . . hell, I hope . . ."

With a heavy sigh that puffed out his cheeks, he collapsed back onto the sofa and stared up at the ceiling.

"You hope what?" Anamaría prodded.

He swiveled his head to look at her. In the muted light from the television, the butter yellow leather cushion was a stark contrast to his tanned complexion. His umber eyes brimmed with uncertainty. Something she'd never seen when it came to his photography.

"God, I don't want to make a mistake," he said, the admission gruff with unease.

"You can't make a mistake when it comes to your work, Ale. Every image of yours I've ever seen is breathtaking." She pressed a hand over his heart and leaned closer, willing him to see the sincerity in her eyes. "I'm sure your Cuba photographs are the same. Would you like to share them with me, maybe I can help you decide?"

His throat worked with his swallow, and Anamaría held her breath, wanting him to trust her.

Leaning forward, he snagged his iPad from the low coffee table and pressed the side button to bring the contraption to life. After several swipes and taps of the screen, a folder opened to reveal a list of images. He clicked on one she recognized from a faded picture framed on the cashier counter at the restaurant, the original Miranda's in Cuba. His photograph showed the building as it was today, run-down and graffittied, but still standing. A tangible reminder of the man who had sacrificed much for his familia to have the blessings they cherished today.

Alejandro continued scrolling through the images on his screen, stopping on particular ones that caught his eye. Much like Lulu enjoyed doing when he allowed her to play with his iPad.

"Wow! I may not be a trained art consultant, but Ale, these are gorgeous. I say, follow your gut; add them to your exhibit if there's still time. Thank you for sharing them with me. For trusting me."

"You're the first," he admitted, his voice gruff with emotion.

She tore her gaze away from the image of a dilapidated, dried-up fountain in the middle of a park, surrounded by a promenade circle, its intricate tiles weathered and cracked with time and age.

"I am?" she asked, touched by his gift to her.

A chagrined smile curved his lips, giving him a boyish charm. Unable to resist, she stretched up to kiss his cheek.

He hugged her close, his arms tightening deliciously around her. She squeezed him back, her love for him taking hold, making her loath to release him.

"I want these photographs to be a bridge," he told her, when they broke apart. "Not completely demolish one that's barely hanging on like the Old Seven Mile Bridge up the Keys."

Or the one separating him and his father.

"He's still barely speaking to you?" she asked.

"Yeah." He sagged deeper into the sofa cushions as if the single-syllable word was too much for him to carry.

"Opening Night, any chance he'll come?" She pitched her voice low, afraid her question and the dismal answer she anticipated would cause him more grief.

"Doubtful." The self-deprecating tug at the corners of his

mouth, the sadness now shadowing his eyes, made her ache for him.

Leaning her forearms on his chest, she cupped his face with her hands, seeking to comfort him. "Those pictures, your exhibit, they are not a mistake. I'm sure of it. Everyone is going to love *all* your photographs. And your dad? He'll come around; you'll see."

Skepticism flashed across his face.

She hated seeing him so hurt. Hated that she didn't know how to help.

"I think you should show Natalia these photographs, Ale." She grasped the edge of his iPad. "They could be the pièce de résistance to your show."

He rubbed a hand over his jaw, considering. His earlier unease beginning to dissipate. "I really want to add them to the show."

"Then do it. I am one hundred percent behind you."

A seductive, naughty smile curved his lips. "Behind me, and under, and on top of me. All my favorite positions when it comes to you."

She snorted a laugh and shook her head. "Leave it to you to turn a serious conversation into something sexual."

He ducked his head to nip at her lips with his, trailing his mouth to her ear. His warm breath sent chills chasing across her shoulders as he whispered, "But you love it, don't you?"

She let her eyes flutter closed, afraid he might see the truth she would have to find a way to deal with later. Yes, she did love him. That's why she planned to soak up every possible minute with him, committing them all to memory, so she could savor them later when she was alone but kicking ass with AM Fitness.

He nuzzled the shell of her ear with his nose, slowly turning up the heat on her constantly simmering desire.

"I think we've talked about work stuff enough already," he murmured, pulling back to take one of her hands in his. Lifting it slowly, he pressed a kiss in the center of her palm, gently closing her hand as if wanting her to hold tight to his kiss. Treasure it when he was gone. The tender gesture sent a pang of longing straight to her heart.

"I agree. There are far more fun activities we should be enjoying," she said.

He flashed a sexy smile as his mouth strayed from her palm to her wrist where his tongue licked across her pulse point. White-hot heat shot up her arm, electrifying her nerve endings.

His mouth strayed higher, liquid fire scorching her skin as the tip of his tongue slipped out to taste her forearm. The juncture of her elbow. Her biceps.

Her core pulsed with lust, desperate for his touch, craving his tongue in secret places that throbbed with need. She slid her hand under his shirt, reveling at his sharp intake of breath as her fingers splayed across his abs.

"What do you say?" he murmured against her skin. "Any chance I'll get to second base before someone from our familias catches us?"

She chuckled, charmed by his humor.

He spanned her rib cage with a palm, his thumb languidly stroking the underside of her breast. Her nipples tightened in response.

"Oh, yes," she murmured. "The odds are definitely in your favor."

Arching her back, she splayed a hand on the cushion behind her for support. He took her invitation, cupping her breasts with both hands, and she gave herself to the carnal ministrations her body longed for.

His mouth and tongue joined the fun, concentrating their sensual assault on her cleavage spilling from the scoop neckline of her formfitting tank.

A low thrum of pleasure hummed in her throat. Needing to feel him, she snuck her left hand under his shirt to explore the firm muscles along his back and shoulders. Her fingers at his nape encouraging him with slight pressure.

"You are so fucking sexy," he groaned.

His teeth grazed her nipple and she gasped, her hips bucking.

"Sí, más," she rasped, needing more and not ashamed to let him know.

His cell phone vibrated on his lap where he'd dropped it earlier.

"You have got to be kidding me," she groaned. "Un-freaking-believable."

Alejandro buried his face in her chest, his strangled laugh shaking his shoulders.

She reached for his phone, wedged between his shorts' waistband and tented zipper, proof of his matching desire for them to move way past second base.

His brother's text illuminated the screen, and she squealed with excitement as she read aloud, "'It's a boy!'"

"Well, there you go," Alejandro said, grasping her waist and tugging her onto his lap. "I think this calls for a little adult celebrating. Don't you?"

Chapter 17

"You've been holding out on me."

Surprised at the accusation, Alejandro halted in the doorway of Bellísima's office.

He frowned at Natalia, her petite figure in black, slim-fitting slacks and a silky sleeveless orange blouse, dwarfed by the over-sized vintage channel-back accent chair with its textured pink velvet upholstery. It was one of several signature pieces Marcelo and Logan had collected and sprinkled throughout the gallery, including this small office at the back of the building.

After walking through the gallery visualizing her plan for the various sections of his display, Natalia and Alejandro had settled in here to continue weeding out the final selections while the two gallery owners ran out to grab lunch for them all.

"I'm not following you," Alejandro said, in response to her vague declaration.

Feet curled under her, the savvy art consultant didn't even bother glancing up. At some point since he had stepped out to take a call from Ernesto, Natalia had made herself comfortable. Her straight dark brown hair was now pulled back into a no-nonsense chignon low on her nape. Her stylish, but sensibly low, black pointy-toed heels sat on the floor in front of the vintage chair.

All business, she continued scrolling through whatever held her attention on his iPad. The occasional "hmm" her only communication.

Step-swinging on his crutches, he headed toward the antique mahogany desk, another beautiful piece of furniture that spoke of Marcelo's and Logan's refined taste and superior eyes. It went with the vivid oil painting that took up a significant portion of the inside wall the desk faced. Alejandro hadn't missed the *EN* scrawled in the bottom right corner, but he would have recognized the dramatic colors and textures, the bold strokes a mix of knife and brush, that stamped the artwork as one of Enrique's anyway.

One of the few pieces hanging in a location other than one of his familia members' homes.

"That exquisite piece grabs my attention every time I walk in here, too," Natalia mused, although she had yet to glance up from his iPad screen.

"He's so talented. Shame he's not producing work like that anymore. At least, he hasn't said anything to me about any new paintings."

Her chin came up, her expertly shaped brows angling together. "You know him?"

Alejandro blinked, taken aback by the intensity of her abrupt question. Leaning his crutches against the desk, he tucked his hands in the pockets of his navy twill shorts. "Uh, yeah. He's my—"

Crap, the words *girlfriend's brother* nearly slipped out, unchecked. He fisted his hands, pushing away his frustration. No need to put labels on Anamaría and himself.

"He's my best friend on the island," Alejandro amended.

"Oh really." Natalia's hazel green eyes widened, a smug smirk twisting her red lips. "Interesting. So, you could introduce me to this reluctant, incredibly talented artist that Marcelo and Logan swear cannot be convinced to paint on commission. No matter the offer."

He noticed she hadn't asked him a question. Rather, made a suggestion as if she were simply giving Alejandro an opportunity to do something for her. She was wily, this one.

"I would, if I could, but I can't," he answered, purposefully leaving her hanging with his infantile response.

If she was interested in E's artwork, maybe Natalia would be the one to find out why he'd up and left a promising art career in Miami to come home and relegate his talent to painting mementos most tourists took home only to get rid of in a garage sale a few years later. E's work deserved better than that.

"Why not?" she challenged, unperturbed.

"Because."

With her head cocked, arms crossed, her pursed lips had no need to move. Alejandro heard her annoyed *yeah, right,* loud and clear.

"Because he's a local firefighter out of town for two weeks at the fire college in Ocala. That's North Central Florida," he clarified. "But he will be here for the opening. So—"

"So, you will be a wise, considerate friend and introduce him to the woman who can brighten his future." Natalia's satisfied grin drew an anticipatory smile of his own.

"We shall see."

"Yes, we shall." With that, she went back to perusing whatever had precipitated her accusation when he had first walked in.

Alejandro shuffled through the sheets of paper on the desktop. Perusing the different layout renderings Natalia had sketched before her arrival yesterday. He spread them out over the marbleized green and brown surface to examine each area individually.

"That still doesn't get you off the hook," she warned him. "Like I said, you've been holding back."

"Care to elaborate?" he prodded.

"Her."

His *Excuse me?* wilted on his tongue when Natalie turned his iPad around to show him what had her so enthralled.

Shit. His stomach dropped as he realized what she had found.

Anamaría's face stared back at him in black and white. Her silky, nearly waist-length hair loosely fanning over her shoulders. The top three buttons of his white shirt left undone, the loose material teasing him with a peek of her black lace bra and the curve of her delectable cleavage. The gray headboard in her master bedroom filling the background.

Those details paled in comparison when you stared into her expressive hazel eyes. Wondered at the smile tickling the faintly curved edges of her mouth.

Natalia slid her finger across the screen to bring up the next picture.

Anamaría. Same location, same setup.

This time, her head was tipped back in laughter, her hair mussed, cascading down her back in dark, silky waves, wispy strands falling across half her face. Pure joy exuded from her pores, flashed in the sly glance out of the corner of her eyes. Her beauty mark teased him, reminding him of the times he'd kissed it, traced it with his fingertip.

He'd been scrolling through the pictures earlier and neglected to close the file titled "Her" that normally would have required a password to access.

A title that made absolute sense because there would only ever be one *her* for him.

A title that no one questioned on the off chance they were looking over his shoulder as he searched for a file.

A title he may want to consider changing to "Keep Your Mitts Off."

Or "Stay the Hell Away."

Or, even better, "Mine."

"How come I haven't seen any of these photographs?" Natalia asked, one brow arched in a confident challenge.

This might only be the second time they'd met in person, but they had exchanged enough emails and conference calls over the past six weeks that Alejandro knew she wouldn't back down until she had an answer that satisfied her.

Dropping the paper with the rendering marked *Mi Cuba*, he sank down into the black leather high-back desk chair, considering how best to pacify her interest. Without opening a can of worms he refused to fish with.

"Those are not for display," he answered.

"Unacceptable."

"Nonnegotiable," he countered.

Her lips curved in a smug smile. "Word to the wise: When you wave a red flag like that in front of me, telling me something's impossible, it only makes me dig in, even more determined to do it."

Natalia's physical stature might be a petite five feet two inches, but while working with her Alejandro had realized that her personality was large enough to fill the body of a seven-foot-plus professional basketball player. Large, commandeering, able to get the job done—well.

"Tell me your concerns," she directed, her posture deceptively relaxed. "And I will allay them. That way we can move on with my brilliant idea."

If he weren't so freaked out by her suggestion, he would better appreciate her cockiness. She was good. But what she asked of him? No way.

Elbows propped on the chair armrests, Alejandro steepled his hands in front of him, considering how best to outmaneuver an outmaneuver-er like Natalia.

"Those are personal. The subject . . . she's . . ."

He pressed his fingers to his lips, unable to voice the priceless value of the photographs without revealing more about himself than he cared to in this professional setting.

"She's personal. She means something. To me."

When they went their separate ways, those photographs and

his memories were all he would have of Anamaría. Intimate touchstones from moments the two of them had shared together. His connection to the world, the woman, he couldn't have.

Natalia stared at him for several seconds, her expression pensive. Then she turned the iPad around so she could view the screen again. Setting the device on her lap, she methodically scrolled through his collection. It was a mix of oldies from his and Anamaría's youth and more recent ones since he'd been back home.

"This one," Natalia said firmly. "*This* is the featured image for the People of the World collection."

He sat forward in the leather seat, leaning across the mahogany desk to get a look at the iPad. Natalia lifted the far side, angling it for him to see better.

It was Anamaría, of course.

Walking in the Gay Pride Parade this past Sunday. Head high, shoulders tall, her long braid twisted on top of her head like a crown. The black short-shorts she wore showcasing her gorgeous legs and the white block letters on her purple tee announcing the City of Key West's official philosophy: "One Human Family."

In her left hand she waved a rainbow flag, the ocean breeze pulling it taut in the exact moment his Canon clicked. Her right hand tightly clasped that of Ormond Jones, her Red shift partner at the station.

The affable Black man who rode with her in the ambulance, or the Box as they affectionately called it, was 250 pounds of broad-shouldered pure muscle fueled by a good-hearted dedication to the people he served and having his shift partner's back, on and off the job. That alone made Alejandro his fan.

On the other side of Anamaría's partner, strode Jones's husband, Eddie, a math teacher and track coach at Key West High. Hands interlocked, the camera had caught a moment when both men looked at each other, joy evident in their broad smiles, love shining in their glistening eyes. As she marched alongside her friends, Anamaría's tanned cheeks plumped with her Cheshire cat beam, proudly part of a human chain proclaiming solidarity and the need for social justice.

Above their heads, a blur in the background with the camera's focus on Anamaría and the two men, a mix of Pride flags waved in the breeze and a bystander held aloft a poster with the word *LOVE* scrawled in rainbow letters.

Love, respect, friendship, familia—

They swirled around and from them. Visible in Anamaría's, Jones's, and Eddie's physical and emotional connections. From their linked hands to their shared smiles. The confident jut of her chin that said, *I hear you.* Jones and Eddie's adoring expressions that said, *Lean on me; I got you.* The conglomeration of people, signs, and flags sending the clear message *We're all in this together.*

Staring at the photograph, Alejandro heard her deep, throaty laughter. Felt the love shining from her golden hazel eyes.

Natalia was right. It was the epitome of his exhibition, his brand. But Anamaría's pictures were different from the others. He saw it. Sensed it.

Putting her on display was like cutting open his chest for the world to see. He couldn't do that. Couldn't lay himself bare before the eyes of his familia, their comunidad, complete strangers. He needed to leave with at least a little bit of his pride still intact. It was all he would have.

That and his talent.

Because he *would* leave. No matter how amazing his time with her had been, and despite a few ideas he had considered that might allow him to stay in Key West while working, it had become distressingly obvious at his parents' house that him being here could very well destroy their relationship.

The memory of the argument between his parents he overheard a couple weeks ago was like an ice pick to his chest. Alejandro had left his room for a late-night glass of water when he came across his parents squared off like two prizefighters in the kitchen.

"¡Es nuestro hijo, Victor!" his mother had whisper yelled, reminding Alejandro of the times she had reprimanded him or Ernesto in the middle of mass.

It hadn't taken him long to figure out this argument between his parents was not a minor one. Nor, it turns out, had it been their first since his return.

"I know he is our son," his father had grumbled.

"Pues, tienes que apoyarlo," his mom had insisted, as if simply telling her husband he had to support his son would be enough to convince him to change his ways. "¿Qué te pasa?"

"What is wrong with me?" his father had sneered. "More like, what is wrong with *him*, ingrato. He is too good to dirty his hands in my kitchen or serve those who come to our restaurant for food, laughter, and familiar faces? Que se vaya."

His mother's gasp almost had Alejandro hurrying around the partial wall separating them to ensure she was okay.

"Con cuidado, Victor. Be very careful. If you tell my son to go again, you will have to go, too."

"Elena!" His father's shocked voice had matched the trembling shock vibrating through Alejandro at his mother's ultimatum.

Alejandro had stumbled back to his room dazed and dejected. He had heard his parents argue in the past. Hell, all kids did at one time or another. But this, a threat to kick his father out, that had never happened.

Alejandro had made many mistakes in his life, but he refused to be the wedge that drove his parents apart.

As it stood now, his mami was nearing two weeks of minimal conversation with his papi because of their fight over his refusal to attend Alejandro's opening night.

A miserable development Alejandro had not shared with Anamaría because he was too ashamed that his presence had created a rift in his parents', until now, solid thirty-five-year marriage.

No, Key West was too small for him and his papi to coexist. It could irrevocably fracture their familia if he did.

But Anamaría couldn't go with him. He wouldn't be selfish and ask her to.

Time and time again, he'd seen or heard evidence about how she thrived here. How she helped others thrive.

The fitness programs she regularly organized for firefighters, their families, and the community. Classroom visits in her gear to talk about fire safety. Free healthy cooking and Zumba classes at St. Mary's. Races and other events she volunteered with, raising money for local charities and organizations.

They shared one common truth he hadn't understood in his youth and could no longer discount: Like the mangrove forests growing in the salty waters of the Florida Keys, Anamaría's roots were complex, protective, life-giving, and strong. She was fully anchored here.

While he . . . he thrived on the adventure and experiences his profession provided. For a brief time, he'd started to wonder if he could make Key West his home base. Returning to Anamaría in between gigs. Spending time with familia.

But after overhearing his parents, he knew he had to go.

Dejected, Alejandro collapsed into the leather desk chair. The vivid image of Anamaría at the parade, marching for love, was barely visible to him from this angle. Leaning his head on the top edge of the soft seat back, he closed his eyes, blocking her photograph out completely.

"This one is going into the exhibit precisely *because* it is so personal," Natalia announced with finality.

"No, it's not," he muttered, forcing himself to keep his frustration on a tight leash.

Natalia didn't know what she was wading into here. This wasn't the warm, gentle waves lapping the Higgs Beach shoreline. More like dark, cold, shark-infested waters.

A bone-weary sigh pushed through his lips.

He heard rustling, the slide of material, and figured she was unfolding herself from the comfortable channel-back accent chair. A light clunk on the desktop alerted him that she had approached.

"I get that we don't know each other personally. Yet," she qualified, her tone calm and matter-of-fact. "But I do believe that, based on our work together thus far, I have earned your professional respect. And, I hope, a measure of your trust."

Fuck, she wasn't going to let this go.

His gut tightened. She was right. He did respect her as a professional. Down to the most minute detail thus far, she was batting a thousand for his exhibit.

But he wasn't able to go where she pushed him to go.

"You're freaking amazing behind a camera," Natalia went on. "Your talent is undeniable. And yet, these photographs." Her finger jabbed the table. "Every single one with *her*. Whomever she is. They're real and raw and fucking brilliant. Whatever you tapped into when you took those personal shots in Cuba. That's here. Amplified. Trust your talent, Alejandro. Damn it, trust mine!"

When he lowered his hands from his face, Natalia loomed over the desk. Her hands splayed on its surface. Her face mutinous.

"I do trust you," he answered. That was the easy part in this whole scary scenario.

"Okay, that's good." She straightened, spinning on the ball of her bare foot to pace toward the wall facing the desk, with E's painting.

"So what's the problem then?" she pressed. "Is she an ex and she might show up with her new lover? Or, shit, her husband?"

"No. We're actually friends."

"Ha!" She spun around, her chignon jarring loose. "You are so more than friends. But"—she held up a hand as if to stop an argument he planned to give, which he didn't—"that's for you and her to figure out, not me."

He shook his head. "There's nothing to figure out. She lives here. I don't."

"But you're *from* here. You have familia here. ¿Cual es el problema?"

"Part of the problem is, my job takes me all over. However, that also happens to be an aspect that appeals to me about my job."

"Is this why you were picking my brain about a coffee table book of your photographs? An idea I've already said is genius. Or why Marcelo has been talking about you putting together a Keys Life exhibition?"

"Yes. And yes. But those are both moot points now." He heaved a sigh and rubbed a hand over his face, massaging his left eye and socket where a jackhammering headache throbbed. "Even staying part-time isn't going to work. There's an issue with my family that makes it impossible."

"Time-out!" She speared her hands together to form the letter *T* as if she were an NBA referee stopping play on the basketball court. "As much as I happen to like you as a person, I do not have the patience to become your relationship or life counselor. I'm too blunt. Trust me, I'd suck at it."

"Really? I hadn't noticed."

She gave him a droll look. "The thing is, Marcelo and Logan hired me to do a job. And I'm going to do a kick-ass one that blows the roof off this joint because you allow us to showcase the best of the best. Didn't you say you're willing to sell some prints to put toward your family's restaurant?"

"Hers will not be for purchase." He placed his open palm protectively over Anamaría's image on the iPad screen.

A triumphant gleam flashed in Natalia's eyes, and he realized what he'd just said.

"No, they won't be for sale," she agreed. "But at least one will be shown. Respectfully. Artfully."

Head bowed as he stared down at Anamaría peeking through his splayed fingers is the screen, Alejandro nodded, trusting Natalia's word as much as her experienced eye.

Many of his pictures of Anamaría *were* exhibit caliber. It was crazy for him to be afraid of showing his best work because of what it might reveal. Maybe it was time for him to stop hiding behind his camera.

He sucked in a deep breath.

Never in his life had he held back when it came to his art. Hell, that's how he wound up fracturing his tibia in the first place. Why start now?

Meeting Natalia's gaze, he slapped his hands together and rubbed them briskly.

"Go big, or go home," he said.

Natalia grinned as she pumped her fist in the air. "That's what I like to hear!"

His problem: he wanted to do both, go big *and* go home.

If he could reach his papi, big *if*, Alejandro just might get both.

Chapter 18

"You look fine; what's with all the primping?" Enrique asked.

Anamaría scowled at her little brother, who responded maturely by giving her a bug-eyed "whatcha looking at me for" glare.

Ignoring him, she flipped down the sun visor in his SUV to inspect her makeup in the lighted mirror.

"This is a special night," she told him, using a ring finger to lightly rub at a mascara smear under her right eye. "The least you could have done was dress up."

She flicked a glance at his typical slender-fit black jeans and tight black tee, its short sleeves cuffed to show off his muscular biceps. At least, they weren't ripped jeans.

"What are you talking about? I put on a pair of dress shoes." Raising his left knee between the steering wheel and the gray leather door interior, he gestured to his black lace-up Oxford sneakers. "See?"

"Real nice. Your best friend's finally having his first gallery opening night here, but God forbid you put on a pair of slacks. Or maybe a sports coat?"

Enrique blew out a breath between his lips. "Look, Mami, quit your nagging and finish touching up your lipstick or whatever you gotta do so we can go already. You're the one who said she didn't want to be late."

Leaning back in his seat, Enrique checked his watch, adjusting the black leather strap more comfortably on his left wrist.

She didn't say anything, but Anamaría noticed that her little brother had gotten a trim today. His jet-black hair, cut tight on the sides, left longer and naturally wavy on the top, was even styled with a bit of product. No way he'd readily admit that he'd done his own primping before leaving his place.

Giving Enrique a hard time was mostly to keep her mind off the swarm of bees in her belly. And silence the ticking clock in her head.

Reaching for her trusty backpack between the two front seats, her hands met with her small envelope purse instead. *Small* being the operative word. It was a wonder how some women relied on a purse this tiny on a regular basis. Where the heck did they put Band-Aids and antibiotic ointment? A protein bar or hand sanitizer?

After only adding some cash, her ID and credit card, plus her cell phone, she barely had room for her plum lip stain. Not that she would share her grumbling disbelief with her brother. He'd only give her a hard time about it. Instead, she wiggled her evening bag at him playfully.

"See, this is what it means to be an adult, dressing appropriately for an occasion," she teased.

He shook his head. "Yeah, not happening. It clashes with my outfit."

"Wise guy." She smacked his thigh playfully with her bag.

"Oye, watch it!" he complained.

Removing her plum lip stain, she tugged the lid off, then stretched up to peer at her reflection in the mirror, moueing her lips.

"Remind me again why I agreed to drive with you?" Her brother pressed his fingertips to his forehead as if he were trying to divine a secret message. "And how that wound up being me driving from my house, a few blocks from here, all the way to Stock Island to pick your ass up?"

"Excuse you." She pointed her lip stain at him. "My *fine* ass, thank you very much."

"So modest. What would Mami say if she heard you?"

"Says the guy wearing his shirt a size too small so he can show off his hot bod."

Enrique flashed the cocky half smirk that had had most women, young and old, single and married, fawning at his feet from the moment his voice changed and his muscles started developing. "Hey, when you got the goods—"

"Ay. Dios. Mío." Capping her lip stain, she dropped it inside her minuscule purse, then gave her brother a duck-mouthed, child-please stare. "Whatever you do, promise me, you will not present this"—she waved a hand in the air from his head to his seat cushion as if to encompass all of him—"machismo or whatever you're playing at to Natalia Peréz when we get inside. Alejandro's really impressed with her, and she sounds like a good professional contact for him. I've met her once, briefly, but I would like *us* to impress her so it reflects well on him."

Enrique's playful grin disintegrated, and he reached across the center console to cover her left hand where it lay on her chiffon dress skirt.

"Look, I know you have Vanessa and now Sara to talk about all your girl shit, uh, stuff, with, and Luis is the listener out of all of us, but if you need to . . . I don't know . . ." Brow furrowed, he shook his head. His obvious discomfort at the touchy-feely "stuff" juxtaposed with his need to be supportive had her bad-boy brother endearingly at a loss for words. "Vent or . . . whatever."

Touched by his gesture, Anamaría threw him a lifeline. "Or take a few jabs at a punching bag together?"

"Yeah. That's more my speed." He winked but also squeezed her hand a little tighter, his face serious. "I don't know exactly what's been going on with you and Ale, and you don't have to tell me. But just so you know, I warned him when he first got here. If he hurts you again, I will hunt him down like a dog."

Sappy tears pricked her eyes. "You'd do that for me?"

"Princesa, we all know you could probably kick his ass yourself. But please, remember my ego, and just go with me on this."

Her more often wise-guy brother was being so sweet, she let him get away with using her dreaded nickname.

"You'll be happy to know he won't be breaking my heart this time." She forced herself to smile, better to start practicing now, as she uttered the lie she'd soon be telling everyone. Just like she had been telling herself for weeks.

"Yes, we've been spending a lot of time together, but we're both clear that Alejandro and I will part as friends when he leaves again, or when I leave for Europe on Wednesday. No hard feelings."

Enrique squinted at her in the shadowed front seat. Doubt shone in his dark eyes, but thankfully he didn't argue with her.

Down the length of Whitehead Street, city lights started to blink on as dusk neared. A rap sounded on her passenger side window, startling her. She jerked away from the door and swung around to glare at the interloper.

Luis stood on the sidewalk, his big hands buried in the pockets of his black slacks. He ducked his chin at her in greeting, as if not realizing he had just scared the bejesus out of her.

Beside him, Sara's tall, runner's figure had been poured into a bright orange fitted sheath dress that hit her mid-thigh. She sent Anamaría a wiggle-fingers wave, then tilted her head toward the intersection of Fleming and Whitehead a little farther down the sidewalk as if to ask, "Ready to go?"

"Okay, let's get this party started," Anamaría said to Enrique.

He stared at her for a couple beats, his gaze intent, searching for a truth she didn't want to share. Finally, he nodded and reached for his door handle.

Relieved, Anamaría did the same, grasping Luis's hand when he held it out to assist her from the car. The usual hello hugs commenced, and by the time she and Sara had finished complimenting their outfits Enrique had joined them on the sidewalk. She ducked to avoid a low-hanging branch from the flamboyán tree near Enrique's vehicle, surprised to see he had slipped on a black blazer.

She shot him an "are you kidding me" glare for pulling her leg the entire time she'd been grilling him about being underdressed.

He grinned, crooking his arm for her to loop hers through.

The four of them chatted as they strolled down Whitehead, making a right onto Fleming and heading toward the gallery on Duval Street a short block away.

Fourth of July meant tourists flocked to the island joining locals ready to kick off a long weekend of revelry and fireworks. At 6:50 in the evening, sunset was still about an hour and a half away, but as shadows lengthened along the busy streets, people headed west toward Mallory Square. The famed sunset festival would have kicked off already with street performers wowing the crowd, vendors hawking their beach-themed wares, and the breathtaking open ocean view of Mother Nature's nightly artwork.

Despite the allure of an island sunset several blocks away plenty of people meandered the downtown streets, popping in and out of the various T-shirt shops and stores, grabbing a bite to eat at the smorgasbord of restaurants, or enjoying a TGIF happy hour at any number of downtown watering holes.

On the corner of Duval and Fleming, Anamaría spotted Bellísima in the one-story building with soft yellow siding and white-trimmed windows housing a row of businesses on the opposite side of the street. The gallery's glass door was already propped open, although the event didn't officially start for ten more minutes, and a middle-aged couple headed inside.

As they neared the entrance, Anamaría caught site of a two-by-three foot painting canvas propped on a wooden easel in the wide front window. Swooping calligraphy brushstrokes in red paint announced: "Award-winning Local Photographer Alejandro Miranda's Window to the World Exhibit."

Next to the painted sign, propped on another wooden art easel, sat an eleven-by-seventeen publicity photo of Alejandro. The full-face shot had been taken mid-laugh, joy plumping his cheeks, his eyes glinting with humor. Behind him, a cobblestone path led between two brick buildings. Sunlight glistened through the narrow pathway, practically beckoning him to follow, see where it might lead.

Anamaría paused in front of the gallery's window, staring at Alejandro's image, moved by the happiness captured in that moment. Knowing him and his sense of adventure, always in search of his next great photograph, he would have snapped his picture, then turned to head up the narrow alley. Away from her.

"You ready to go in?" Sara asked. She wrapped an arm around Anamaría's shoulder, drawing her attention away from the publicity photo.

She read Sara's real question, *You gonna be okay?*, in the pinched look around her friend's blue-green eyes.

"Carlos texted about twenty minutes ago," Luis said. "He, Gina, and the boys are already inside. I guess Alejandro invited them to come early, so he could show the boys around before things get busy."

Anamaría nodded, knowing the details already. Ale had asked her if she'd like to join them, but she had a special client in town for the weekend and couldn't late-cancel on the woman. Plus, heading into Bellísima determined to be happy for Alejandro's success, without revealing the sorrow eating away at her soul would be a helluva lot easier if she walked in surrounded by reinforcements. Sara and two of her brothers.

"After you, beautiful," Luis told Sara. He swept an arm toward the entrance for his fiancée to precede him.

"Why, thank you," Anamaría joked, as she followed Sara inside.

Luis shot her a wink as she passed; then he slid in ahead of Enrique, who murmured, "Age before beauty."

The familiar adolescent dig had her smiling, and a measure of the tension knotting her belly eased.

Inside, Marcelo and Logan greeted them warmly. The couple handed out half-page layout maps and explained how the various collections were spread throughout the gallery. Having heard the details from Ale already, she listened with half an ear and peered around the early arrivals, noting several of their high school classmates and a group of older women from St. Mary's. She caught sight of Gina and Carlos deeper into the open space, their boys standing in front of another photograph farther away. But she didn't see—

Alejandro.

Her pulse raced when she spotted him, looking all panty-melting gorgeous in a tailored suit while talking to Natalia near the office door at the back of the gallery.

With Anamaría's schedule busier than usual lately and Alejandro's all-consuming preparations leading up to tonight, the two of them hadn't spent as much time together this past week. When they had, Natalia's name had peppered many of his sentences.

During their brief introduction, Anamaría had been drawn to the other woman's confident personality. The petite brunette was professional, no-nonsense, and strikingly beautiful. Definitely a memorable combination.

While Anamaría knew nothing was going on between Ale and the engaging art consultant, she couldn't help but envy the time the woman had spent with him. Especially with that damn ticking clock counting down the days, hours, minutes Anamaría had left with him.

As he spoke, Ale swiveled to face the gallery, a single crutch tucked under his left shoulder. The Ilizarov external fixator rings and pins had been removed earlier that week, so he'd graduated to a CAM boot and one crutch for added support. He'd been so restless and impatient for that moment to arrive. Complaining about the limitations, especially when it came to their fun and games. She had been equally as anxious for their removal, even though it meant he was one step closer to being ready to leave.

Tonight, he had ditched the CAM boot rather than wearing it over the slim-fit charcoal suit pants that hugged his hips and thighs and narrowed down his legs. A crisp white button-down left open at the collar and a charcoal single-breasted jacket spanned his broad shoulders, while a pair of black brogues capped off his devastatingly dashing ensemble. His head tipped back on a laugh and her breath caught at the sight of him relaxed and happy, in his element. She wanted that for him. Had secretly prayed he could finally find that here.

Beside him, Natalia's smile widened, her hands motioning along with her words. Several men nearby eyed her, and Anamaría figured the combination of Natalia's animated personality and trendy vibe was hard for them to resist. The art consultant's outfit tonight was pretty spectacular. Her black lace palazzo pants with matching black undershorts left her shapely bronze legs in peekaboo view, and a bloodred figure-skimming sleeveless halter top tucked into the waist of her pants, the color matching the slash of red on her lips.

Together Alejandro and Natalia moved into the open gallery area, pausing to talk to an older couple Anamaría recognized from the Miranda's neighborhood. His abuela and Señora Miranda should be here already having arrived earlier to help set up the catering. Someone else from Miranda's would work the event so his mom could enjoy herself, though knowing her, she'd check in with her employees.

Ernesto and Cece, sans their little ones, walked around the partial wall in the center of the gallery. With the new baby boy at home, Alejandro's brother and sister-in-law wouldn't stay long, but Anamaría's heart swelled with joy for Ale as he and his brother exchanged a back-thumping hug. Ernesto pointed at something Anamaría couldn't see through the growing crowd, and the brothers stepped in tandem toward another partial wall that created a little nook off to the left. Alejandro's lips moved, his hand releasing the crutch grip as he gestured toward whichever photograph they discussed.

"You want to go say hello or start making our way around the exhibit?" Sara asked. She looped an arm around Anamaría's waist, apparently taking her job of sticking close for moral support seriously. "Oh, my goodness, look at that one. It's amazing."

Sara pointed at a stunning photograph of two nuns dressed in full light blue and white habits, about to join a mass of people who created a long line trailing into the distance. If Anamaría remembered correctly, Ale said he'd taken that one in Portugal, while participating in a pilgrimage to Fátima.

"You just got back from New York, so you and my brother deserve a date night. Go wander. Enjoy yourselves," Anamaría answered. She leaned close to her soon-to-be sister-in-law and whispered, "I'll be okay."

"Are you sure?" Sara waited for Anamaría's nod; then she and Luis linked hands and moved into the Cultures around the Globe area.

Iona ambled by, and Enrique snagged two glasses of bubbly from the tray Miranda's longtime waitress held aloft. Pride for Alejandro swept through Anamaría at Iona's awed praise for his work. The older woman encouraged them to check out the savory appetizers, then headed off to serve other guests.

"Who the hell is she?" Enrique whistled softly. "Coño, Alejandro's been holding out on me."

She followed her brother's intent stare toward the back of the room. "Pick your jaw up off the floor, hermanito. That's Natalia."

"The art consultant from Chicago?" Surprised interest widened his eyes at the same time a sly grin curved his lips. "Hell, I woulda stopped by as soon as I got back from my training if I had known she was—"

"Thank goodness you've been out of town then," Anamaría interrupted, her gaze trained on Natalia, now deep in conversation with a portly middle-aged gentleman Anamaría didn't recognize.

Alejandro hugged his brother again and kissed Cece's cheek, leaving them in the Nature and Wildlife area to join Natalia and the other man.

"Come on. We're going in." Enrique placed a hand on the small of Anamaría's back and downed a hefty swig of his Prosecco. "I need an introduction."

"She is *not* a random hookup, E," Anamaría warned her playboy brother. "Please don't muddy things for Ale. Like I told you, Natalia has great contacts that could lead to something good for him."

"Cut me some slack. I just want to meet her. Maybe she'd like a private tour of our intimate little island." Enrique waggled his eyebrows like the lecherous fool he could be.

Anamaría squinted at him in warning. His wolfish grin widened.

She would have punched him in the arm, but they stepped apart to allow an old man in a cream guayabera and dark brown slacks to pass between them. Stooped low over his cane, he clutched the layout map in his hand, his thumb crooked over the section marked *Mi Cuba*. Removing a white handkerchief from his shirt pocket, he swiped at his eyes and swayed slightly to his right.

Enrique cupped the older gentleman's elbow to steady him.

"¿Está bien?" E asked, pitching his voice lower to give the man a measure of privacy now that the gallery had begun filling up.

"Sí, I am fine. Gracias," the gentleman answered. "Lágrimas de alegría."

Tears of joy?

Anamaría shared a confused glance with Enrique.

"Be sure to visit Mi Cuba," the older gentleman recommended. He set a trembling hand over his heart, his wrinkled face softening with nostalgia. "Recuerdos de mi isla. Tan bellos."

With a dip of his head, he continued toward the front door, repeating his last words, "so beautiful," and murmuring about the "memories of his island."

The man's heartfelt reaction confirmed that Anamaría had

been right by encouraging Alejandro to showcase his secret photographs, despite his unease about his father's reaction.

Excited to share the older man's praise with Alejandro, Anamaría elbowed her brother, signaling her intent to move on.

"There you are!" Ale cried, waving his hand high above the crowd when he spotted her.

She grinned back, a blush rising in her cheeks as his gaze slowly traveled over her. The extra time blowing out her long hair and creating a natural look with her eye shadow, plus the price of a new cocktail dress, was well worth it when she caught the unbridled desire in his eyes.

He winked, and her stomach flip-flopped as she recalled him peeking up at her from under the bed sheet with that same naughty expression. He spread his palm up and let his gaze quickly dart about the space as if inviting her to look around with him before his gaze came back to rest on her, his face alight with wonder.

You did it! she mouthed, grinning like a fool, giddy with glee that his youthful dream was now a reality. Her heart singing with elation over sharing this momentous occasion with him.

The portly man in the cream business suit who'd been speaking with Natalia had already started edging away by the time Anamaría and Enrique reached them.

"Let me know which offer you want me to book first. As your agent, I say Napa. But it's your call. Great job here, you two." He circled a pudgy finger in the air, indicating the showcase. "I'm out. Shoot me a message."

"I will. Hold on a sec, Robert." Alejandro clasped the guy's shoulder while turning to include Anamaría and Enrique in their circle. "Let me introduce you to my . . . uh, to two friends of mine. Anamaría Navarro and her brother, Enrique, one of my old partners in crime growing up."

As she shook hands with Alejandro's agent, Anamaría prayed her polite hello smile didn't mimic her wavering heart at Alejandro's stumbling introduction.

Had he started to say something else? Call her something else?

Or had he simply realized that their relationship, as it stood now, didn't really have a label suitable in a professional setting?

Friends with benefits? Temporary lovers?

Or what was the latest term she'd heard from a rookie at the station? *Situation-ship.*

She bit the inside of her lip to stop a denial from slipping out.

None of those options were ideal.

Then again, this countdown to the end wasn't, either.

With a final farewell and a "pleasure meeting you," his agent departed. Alejandro swung-stepped closer to her and cupped her elbow. A tiny spark tingled at the innocent touch paired with his not so innocent smile.

"You look incredible." His appreciative gaze traveled slowly down her body like a lover's caress, pausing at her dress's deep V-cut neckline that left her no option but to go braless, down her swirly pleated skirt to her newly painted toenails. Their shade of red one of her favorites mostly because of its plucky name, Tell Me About It Stud.

"Thank you," she murmured.

"And your hair," he mused, his voice hushed as if he spoke the words aloud without realizing it.

She'd left her hair loose tonight. Something she didn't do too often, especially in the summer with the high heat and humidity.

But the other evening, lying in her bed, both of them hot and sweaty and sated, he'd mentioned how much he liked it when she wore her hair down. How he loved running his fingers through the silky strands. As he did now.

Gently, he brushed her hair off her shoulder, warmth spreading over her skin at his light touch. The back of his fingers strayed along her collarbone, then followed the thin spaghetti strap that held up her dress. The scrap of material stretched past the side of her neck, his roving fingertips tracing the edge where the material met her skin.

Leaning in, he pressed a chaste kiss to her cheek in the casual hello shared by most in their comunidad. But his fingers continued tracing the dress strap to where it crisscrossed with the other one in the center of her back. His splayed hand scorched her bare skin, stoking the fire of desire that constantly simmered inside her when she was with him.

Pulse sparking, she placed a hand on his chest, longing to grab his lapel and pull him in for a tongue-tangling kiss the likes of which might scandalize their mamis. Then again, knowing them, maybe not.

If they were somewhere private, she would be in his arms by now. His mouth plundering hers. Her hands frantically working to undo the buttons on his shirt, anxious to explore the curves of his chest, the muscles rippling along his back. Dipping lower to revel at his body's reaction to hers.

Instead, he eased away, his large hand slipping to the small of her back, leaving a trail of heat and need pulsing through her.

"And what about me?" Enrique complained, clasping Ale's outstretched hand and stepping in for a bro's shoulder bump.

"I have a feeling you're pretty confident about how good you look," Natalia drawled, stepping around the guys to press her cheek against Anamaría's in greeting.

"You've certainly got that right," Anamaría said with a laugh.

"Is this the friend you mentioned, Alejandro?" Natalia asked, facing Enrique.

At six foot four he towered over the petite woman, but she didn't seem the least bit awed by her brother's charisma. In fact, red lips quirked, head tilted at a saucy angle, Natalia eyed Enrique as if she were studying a new painting, deciding whether it deserved her consideration. Anamaría bit back a grin. This was more than likely a first for her Lothario-impersonating brother, who was used to swoony sighs from most women.

"Shame we haven't met sooner." Thumbs hooked in his front jeans pockets, Enrique arched a rakish brow, his brown eyes sparking with interest. And challenge. His lips twisted in his trademark cocky smirk.

No way, Anamaría nearly groaned out loud. Had the nitwit already forgotten her warning that Natalia was off-limits when it came to his cat-and-mouse game?

She glanced at Alejandro thinking he'd prefer to pull the plug on the sexually charged sparks flying between E and Natalia. Surprisingly, Alejandro's smirk mirrored her brother's.

Ale crooked a finger at her and tipped his head to the side. "Come, I have a surprise I want to show you."

She hesitated, but neither Enrique nor Natalia seemed to notice anyone else around them. "I'll catch up with you later, E, okay?"

Her brother didn't even answer.

"What the hell is going on back there?" she asked as soon as she and Alejandro had moved out of earshot.

"It's either going to be World War Three or they'll make their own fireworks while Natalia's in Key West. I'm not exactly sure which."

"Yeah, it's that first one I'm worried about."

"He's a big boy. And believe me, Natalia can hold her own," Ale assured her.

They reached the end of the support wall that divided the gallery into two sides, and he gently clasped her upper arm, drawing her to a halt. "Close your eyes."

"What?"

His thumb rubbed her arm lightly, the friction raising goosebumps across her skin. "Just humor me, por favor."

She frowned her confusion, but the hopeful plea in his dark eyes convinced her to go along with him.

"Fine, but only because you asked nicely."

Once her eyes were closed, her other senses heightened. The murmur of people milling about and Little José's giggle somewhere off to her right seemed louder. The scent of Alejandro's seductive aftershave mixed with the fried empanadas, plantains, and croquetas from Miranda's was more pronounced. The warmth of his light grip on her arm as he guided her forward a couple paces seeped down her arm.

Then his fingers moved to her shoulder, softly turning her to the right. The metallic squeak of his crutch hinted at his move-ment seconds before the material of his suit jacket brushed against her bare shoulder blades. She shivered, her body tingling with awareness.

"So, remember when you signed that release form giving me permission to display a picture of you?"

She gasped. "Dios mío, you promised to show me first."

Her eyes fluttered and he quickly covered them with his hand. "Ah-ah-ah! Not yet."

"Alejandro," she drew out his name in a soft warning, suddenly nervous about what she would find hanging on the gallery wall.

He was constantly snapping pictures when they were together. That was nothing new. But there'd been that one afternoon a week or so ago when they had goofed around in her master bed-room, him clicking away like he used to when they were younger. Only these pics had gotten a little racy. Oh, she'd remained mostly clothed, but no way in hell did she want her papi walking in here to find a blown-up photograph of her in nothing but black lace panties and Alejandro's button-down.

"Actually, I promised I wouldn't share anything inappropri-ate," he qualified.

An embarrassed flush crawled up her face, heating her cheeks.

"*My* idea of inappropriate. Not yours," she specified.

He chuckled, then said thank you to someone who walked by offering their praise. She couldn't place the voice.

"You have my word," he said softly, bending so close his chest pressed against her back. Instinctively she leaned against him, seeking the intimacy she had missed the past few days. His minty breath warmed the side of her face, as he continued. "This pho-tograph is the opposite of inappropriate. It exudes joy, respect, comunidad, belonging, and love. Definitely love. It's one of my favorite photographs because it represents everything that makes you absolutely perfect."

"Ale." His name whispered out on a breath, his declaration leaving her overwhelmed by his honesty.

She reached out blindly, needing a connection with him. His fingers caught hers, lacing together until they were palm to palm.

He raised their joined hands to press a kiss on her knuckles, and her chest tightened with longing.

"Are you ready?" he whispered.

"Yes."

Chapter 19

Having passed the fat-burning zone back when he first covered her eyes, Anamaría's heart rate triple-timed as he uncovered her eyes and they fluttered open.

She gasped, shock snatching the breath from her.

In the center of the pale wall in front of her, as the main highlight of the People of the World section, hung a poster-sized color photograph of her, Jones, and Eddie walking hand in hand at the Gay Pride Parade last weekend. Smaller photographs of people celebrating, mourning, working, performing, and going about their daily lives across the globe dotted the rest of the wall, completing the display, but the larger photograph of her with her partner and his husband lured passersby to the collection.

Unable to resist, she edged closer, eyes drawn to the image.

Her gaze flitted across the expanse, taking in every detail. From their linked hands, to the absolute joy on the men's faces as they gazed at each other and her wide openmouthed grin, to the regal crown braid she'd woven in her hair and the sun's glare off Jones's dark bald head, to the rainbow letters in the *LOVE* posters other marchers held high in the background. Some details in sharp focus, others a mesmerizing blur of colors. All parts of one impactful, breathtaking piece.

The small label under the bottom right corner, written in a neat script, read: "Love Is Love; not for sale."

"What do you think?" Alejandro asked, his tone insistent and hesitant and hopeful at the same time. As if he felt compelled to know yet was afraid of her answer.

"It's incredible." The words rushed out of her on a wave of heartfelt wonder. "Jones and Eddie are going to flip when they see this. It's . . . it's—"

Overcome with elation, she spun to face him. Her chiffon skirt billowed out in a wide circle, wrapping around his charcoal dress pants.

"I love it, Ale," she gushed. She grabbed his lapels to tug him in for a real kiss, not the friendly chaste kind they had exchanged when she arrived.

Alejandro's smile broadened. "Good, because I lov—"

"There you are!" Her mami's exuberant cry cut Alejandro off.

Cursing her mom's terrible timing, Anamaría smoothed his lapel and turned to greet her parents, all the while wondering if Alejandro might have been about to say the words neither one of them had said to the other in years.

Arms outstretched for a hug, her mami rushed toward them. "Ay, Alejandro, your work is magnificent. We are so proud of you, aren't we, José."

Anamaría's papi kissed her cheek, then clamped his hand on Alejandro's shoulder. "Yes, we are. Very proud. And this"—her papi jutted his chin at the parade photo—"this one is your best, verdad?"

"Ay, Papi, we all know you're biased. Pero I love you." Anamaría hugged her mom, already forgiving the interruption in the face of her resounding approval of Ale's photographs.

"Have you made it to the back of the gallery yet?" she asked, knowing that's where they would find the Mi Cuba collection in a semiprivate viewing area.

"No, little José and Ramón held us up with the animals," her mami answered. "Alejandro, por favor, tell me you use one of those zooming-in cameras when you are out there con los leones y los elefantes."

Alejandro chuckled, assuring her he was always safe when shooting animals in the wild. He motioned to the gallery's far back corner across from the office. "Ven, I would like to show you what I hope will be your second-favorite area, after this one, of course."

Her papi clapped him on the shoulder again. "You are learning, hijo. There is hope for your generation after all."

When they reached the private viewing area, they found Alejandro's mom standing a few feet away from the black curtain hanging in front of the room's opening.

Señora Miranda's red-rimmed eyes and splotchy face had them all quickening their pace to reach her.

"¿Mami, qué te pasa?" Alejandro handed his crutch to Anamaría's dad, then wrapped his arms around his mother.

She sniffled, tears welling in her eyes.

"What's wrong?" he repeated, pulling back to gaze down at her. "Did you and Papi fight again?"

Again? Anamaría frowned. What did he mean by that? She looked to her mami, who shook her head, indicating she was in the dark, as well.

"No, no, hijo, I blame *you* for mis lágrimas," his mami said on a sniffle as she wiped the tears she, for some reason, attributed to him. "These I shed with pride." Cupping his face with both hands, she gave him a watery smile. "What you have done here, what you have gifted our familia and our generation with inside this room . . ." Her voice broke and she finished on a raspy whisper. "Gracias, hijo."

Alejandro hugged her tightly, his worried expression melting into relief.

Knowing how badly Alejandro had feared his mother's reaction to these specific photographs, how much her words must mean to him, Anamaría gently rubbed the area between his shoulder blades, offering support.

"Where's Abuela?" he asked.

"She was feeling a little tired. Marcelo took her to his office to rest in the quiet. We can show her this room once the crowd has left, okay?"

He nodded, but Anamaría caught his gaze flitting to the office door, a tiny groove marring the space between his brows with his frown.

The curtain blocking the private viewing area's entrance brushed aside and two teenaged girls exited. Señora Miranda grasped the material to hold it open, and the teens shuffled past, one leaning toward the other with a murmured, "That was pretty cool." Then, her round face beaming with pride, Alejandro's mom invited Anamaría and her parents into the private viewing area.

Just as the curtain fluttered closed behind them, Natalia poked her head inside.

"Excuse me for interrupting." Her sharp gaze politely paused on each of them before stopping with Alejandro. "There's a gentleman interested in purchasing a piece in the Nature and Wildlife collection, but he'd like to speak with you first."

"Vete, hijo. Go on!" His mami shooed him with a flick of her wrist. "José, Lydia, and I will reminisce about our Cuba while I share our familia historia through your fotografía maravillosa. Go take care of your business. We will be here waiting for you."

She gave him another watery, pride-filled smile before clasping Anamaría's mami's hand and leading her best friend toward the far corner. Seconds later, the two moms were gushing over a picture taken along the Malecón in Havana. Her father's deep voice joined theirs with his own awed exclamation.

Beside her, Alejandro cupped her elbow, an apology shadowing his dark eyes. "I'm sorry. I'll be back as soon as I can."

She ran her fingers down his lapel, as close to a caress as she would allow herself in front of their parents but still wanting to soothe his worry.

"Why are you apologizing? This is fantastic, Ale. Plus, the more pieces you sell, the more you'll be able to help your . . . um . . . those who are in need." She picked her way around the words, speaking in code since Ernesto had admitted that their mom was still not aware of the issues Miranda's was facing with the bank and their previous insurance policy lapsing.

"Thank you." He pivoted on his good leg and took a swing step away, then suddenly turned back to her. "All the work and planning and preparing for tonight, while dealing with the tension at home, I wouldn't have made it through without you."

Reaching out, he snagged a lock of her hair, then let it sift through his fingers. "I want you to know—"

"Alejandro, the buyer doesn't have much time," Natalia called. Her arched brows wrinkled her forehead as she mouthed, *Sorry*, to Anamaría.

Anamaría waved off the apology with an understanding smile. The woman was doing her job. And doing it well by the sound of things.

With a muttered, "I'll try to hurry," Alejandro strode from the viewing area, leaving the curtain fluttering behind him.

Twenty minutes later, Anamaría still waited by the entry as her parents and Señora Miranda stood, mesmerized, staring at the grouping of images titled Mi Familia. Three smaller pictures hung on both sides of and above a larger one. The courtyard fountain photograph Anamaría had seen the first night Alejandro shared his Cuba pictures with her hung on top. The one on the right featured a modest cream stucco church with a wooden steeple rising into a soft blue sky dusted with wispy clouds. In the last of the trio, two older women in worn batas that hugged their round bellies stood side by side, their arms laden with mangos from a sprawling tree behind them as they mugged for Alejandro's camera, smiles wide and friendly.

But the pièce de résistance holding center stage, the one that had Señora Miranda's hand covering her trembling lips, was the large photograph of a dilapidated one-story corner building, its windows pieces of jagged glass or boarded-up completely, red graffiti decorating the planks. Its wooden sign tilted and weather-beaten, a faded capital *M* in a flourishing script its only identifier.

"Ay Dios mío!" Anamaría's mami gasped. She pressed a hand to her chest, her fingers worrying the crucifix dangling from her gold chain. "¿Esto es Miranda's? ¿La original?"

"Sí, it is," Señora Miranda answered, nostalgia tingeing her words. "Victor's parents courted while strolling around that fountain. This church is where they were married, where Victor and his brother were baptized. And these . . ." Her fingers hovered over the image of the two women. "Victor's primas. Cousins he has not seen in person since he left. These pictures . . . son fantásticos."

A yearning for old times, for familia they hadn't hugged in decades, weighed on her words. At the same time, it was clear that pride in her son's masterful work bolstered her spirit.

"Has Victor seen these?" Anamaría's dad asked.

Señora Miranda's smile faded as she shook her head.

"He didn't walk through the display when he brought the food?" Anamaría's papi asked, his fierce frown broadcasting his displeasure when Señora Miranda shook her head again.

"Victor cooked, porque I threatened him with—bueno, that does not matter. He cooked the food, pero staff helped me with everything. El cabezón refuses to listen to me. ¡Ya casi estoy harta de él!"

Anamaría flinched at the harsh, angry words. It wasn't unusual for Señora Miranda to call her husband hardheaded. *El cabezón* had always been more of an endearment in the past. Everyone knew Victor Miranda's stubborn streak wasn't a mere mile wide, more like almost the ninety miles that separated Key West from his beloved Cuba.

But *casi estoy harta de él*?

For Alejandro's mom to say she had almost had enough of her husband, with such finality and anger . . . what the hell had been going on between the Mirandas? And why hadn't Alejandro said anything to Anamaría about it?

Anamaría's mom wrapped an arm around her friend's shoulder. Her dad stepped away from the two women, his mouth set in a thin line, his expression foreboding. That look often meant trouble for her or one of her siblings, typically Enrique when they were kids.

Her papi pulled his phone from his pocket and stared down at the device, though she didn't think she had heard his cell vibrate. His thumb swiped the screen, tapped a few times; then he lifted the phone to his right ear to listen to a message.

"Lydia, a situation has come up. I will be back as soon as I can." He kissed her mom's cheek, dipped his head in deference to Señora Miranda, then gave Anamaría a grim nod before ducking around the curtain.

She stared at the undulating material for several seconds, surprised by his abrupt departure.

When she turned back to the mamis, hers had guided Señora Miranda over to peer at the photographs commemorating Operación Pedro Pan. The images honored those who had come to the United States as children through the operation's efforts. Alejandro had visited with a handful in their homes or workplaces, snapping their photographs as they held aged pictures from their childhood. Some had even shared handwritten messages about their experiences, which were framed as part of the display.

Heads angled close together, the two moms were soon engaged in a serious discussion about Cuban history and how their familias had been affected. Wanting to give the two of them some privacy, Anamaría excused herself to make a trip to the ladies' room, thinking she'd also check on Alejandro's abuela.

She reached for the curtain, the silky black material slipping through her fingers when she heard Alejandro on the other side.

"Again, I appreciate you giving my idea consideration, Marcelo. I know projects like the one we discussed, when done well, require I commit to being in one location, being *here*, for at least six months."

Anamaría blinked with surprise. Joy coalesced with shock at

Alejandro's words, rooting her feet to their spot. Questions bombarded her mind in rapid-fire succession.

Could Alejandro really be considering staying in Key West? Giving himself more opportunity to make amends with his father? Giving her and him more time together?

"Which is why I have to pass. I still think you should pursue it, Marcelo. It's a good idea. Only not for me. I can't stay here."

Wait? He was turning it down?

Like a plug pulled from one of her nephew's blow-up water floats, the breath she held gushed out of Anamaría, leaving her deflated and empty.

"Are you sure?" Marcelo asked, his obvious disappointment a fraction of the searing disappointment seeping through Anamaría, scalding her heart.

"Positive," Alejandro answered. "Too much missed opportunity out there. And, as I mentioned, it's not a good idea for me to stick around here."

Marcelo said something else, but his voice was muted by the blood whooshing in Anamaría's ears. She clamped her lips together to smother a whimper of pain as her heart shattered, splintery shards slicing her chest.

It's not a good idea for me to stick around here.

Dios mío, if she needed any more proof that her feelings for him were one-sided and she should keep singing the friends-with-benefits song they had agreed on, now she had it.

He'd been given an opportunity to stay in Key West while still pursuing his photography. A chance to be with her. But he was turning down Marcelo's offer. Encouraging the gallery owner to look for someone else.

Alejandro would always be lured by the adventure he sought in faraway places. The call of something bigger awaiting him far from their island held more appeal than those he left behind. Than her.

She'd known that all along. It was her breaking their pact this time, not him.

She'd been a fool. Tricking herself into thinking all she desired was closure, a chance to make a clean break, when she had been secretly hoping he would decide to stay this time. Drop his anchor for good and make Key West, instead of Atlanta, his home base.

If Alejandro stayed, together they could work at changing his dad's mind. Continue giving him opportunities like tonight to see how Alejandro's work held value. How his talent honored and paid tribute to their familia and their culture's legacy.

But running away, choosing to leave not because he had to but because he wanted to, would only maintain the rift between father and son with no way to move past it.

"Bueno, I say we wait until the time is right for you. Whenever you are ready, we will be too," Marcelo said on the other side of the curtain.

"I appreciate it," Alejandro responded. "But I won't change my mind. I can't. If you'll excuse me, I should check on my mother."

Coño, he was coming inside.

Anamaría swiped at a tear she hadn't even realized had trailed down her cheek. She needed to get out of here, pull herself together, or she'd risk revealing her true feelings for Ale. Something she absolutely refused to do.

Her world might feel like it was crumbling around her again, but this time she wasn't an insecure teen uncertain about the direction of her life. This time, she had AM Fitness and her partnership with AllFit to concentrate on, to keep her focused on anything other than devasted dreams.

One hand pressed to her belly in a desperate attempt to calm the hornets swarming inside her, she brushed aside the filmy curtain and stepped into the shadowy hallway.

Alejandro blinked his surprise when he saw her, but quickly recovered and flashed his sexy grin.

The hornets in her stomach buzzed, stingers ready to do their damage to her already wounded soul.

"Hi, I was just about to come find—"

"Our moms are giving each other a history lesson," she interrupted.

Unable to meet his gaze, afraid he'd see the disillusionment in her eyes, she gazed past his shoulder, searching the crowd for her brothers or Gina and Sara. Damn it, they were supposed to be her lifelines in times of need. And this was definitely a freaking time of need.

"Everything okay?" Alejandro shuffled closer.

His warm palm caressed her arm and she edged away, her chest aching. He frowned, head tilted in question.

"I think my papi got a text from the station. He stepped outside to deal with whatever's going on," she told Alejandro, thankful for the out her dad had inadvertently given her. "I'm going to see if he needs my assistance."

Head high, insides trembling, she edged around Alejandro, intent on leaving before the inevitable foolish tears fell. Determined to save face in front of everyone, especially him. Her heart might be broken, but she had survived a broken heart before. She would again.

"Anamaría? Wait!" he called.

Heads swiveled their way at his cry, and her footsteps faltered. Turning to face him, she forced a smile to her stiff lips.

"You did good, Ale. Tonight's a success." She gestured around the open gallery with her silly gold clutch. "Everyone's proud of you."

"What's going on?" he pressed. His crutch squeaked as he leaned on it to step toward her.

She shook her head and backed away. "Nothing. I just want to make sure everything's okay with Papi. But you should go touch base with your mom. I didn't get a chance to check on your abuela, but she's going to love your Cuba section. You were right; it resonates with their generations, in a good way. Go, be with them. I'll . . . I'll catch you later."

"Ana—"

"Enjoy this." Arms spread at her sides, she twisted to indicate the friends and familia who had come to the gallery in support of the local celebrity. He had succeeded in achieving his dream. On his own.

Now it was her turn. On Wednesday she was leaving for Europe. Maybe twelve years later than anticipated. And with a different guy at her side, one who was only a friend. But she was done living in the past. Done waiting for someone else to make his decision and hope he included her. Done holding *herself* back.

"You've earned it, Alejandro. I'm happy for you." Her voice caught at the end, and she clamped her mouth closed. Willing herself not to fall apart. Not yet.

Without waiting for his response, she spun away, weaving through the crowd and moving quickly toward the front. Her heart bid her to take one last look at him. Her head kept her gaze focused on the main entrance and escape.

This was Alejandro's world.

Beyond that door up ahead, she had her own world to conquer. A business to grow. And a heart to mend.

Something was wrong; Alejandro was certain of it.

Anamaría had raced out of the gallery like the hounds of hell were chasing her. And now she wasn't answering her phone.

After she went looking for her dad, Alejandro had brought his abuela to meet up with his mami and Señora Navarro, answering their deluge of questions about his trip to Cuba and reconnecting with their relatives there. His mami had cried again when he talked about finding the original Miranda's and what it had been like imagining his abuelo, a man he had never known other than through pictures and stories, tirelessly cooking for customers. A man reminiscent of his own dad. Broad shouldered and robust, with a dark slash for a mustache, known for barking orders to those working alongside him in his kitchen, willing to work harder than anyone else, intent on making a good, honest living to support his familia.

Had he known his boys' favorite foods and brought them home

when he closed the restaurant for the night, even when he was at odds with them, like Alejandro's papi did?

Would Alejandro's abuelo have been proud of him and his work, even when his father was not?

Alejandro rubbed the ache in his chest wrought by the question that had haunted him all these years.

Seeing his familia's emotional reactions to his photographs, hearing similar praise and awe from others throughout the gallery filled him with a sense of gratitude. And naturally, a measure of pride.

But none of that mattered if Anamaría wasn't here to celebrate and share the moment with him. He'd even settle for an *I told you so* from her, as long as she was by his side, flashing her cheeky grin, making tonight, making every night, complete.

Fuck, why did it take the fear of a problem between them to make him realize the truth?

He didn't want to leave her for good. He wanted to be with her, love her.

He simply hadn't figured out how yet.

"Are you sure Enrique didn't say anything to you?" he asked Natalia as he followed her into Bellísima's office to finalize the sale of another piece. The woman was a freaking rock star when it came to matching artwork with prospective buyers, then closing deals.

When he had told her he planned to sell some of his photographs to help Miranda's, she'd simply said, "Leave it to me. I'll get you top dollar, so you can ease your brother's and father's worries."

That's exactly what she'd done tonight.

"Like I said the first, oh, I don't know . . . What are we at, fifty-seven times now? I lost count." Natalia heaved an exaggerated sigh and widened her eyes at him in a classic "you are driving me crazy" glare. "Your talented friend and I didn't talk too long. Enrique clearly wasn't ready to debate the value of sharing your God-given talents professionally versus hoarding them to yourself or, worse, applying them to vacation mementos that tourists impulse buy and later toss in the garage sale pile."

Her red lips twisted with derision, indicating her distaste for Enrique's waste of his talent. A sentiment Alejandro normally agreed with but didn't care to discuss at the moment.

"The last time I saw your obstinate friend, he and your muse were slipping out the front door." Natalia hitched a shoulder, her expression twisted in a surprising show of sympathy he didn't expect from the no-nonsense business woman.

He wasn't looking for sympathy though. What he wanted was answers.

There were two people still in the gallery who you could always count on to know more about the comings and goings-on of their offspring than said offspring would like. Tonight, their meddling mamis just might come in handy.

Swiveling on his good leg, Alejandro step-swung toward the office door. "FYI, when I find out where Anamaría is, I'm outta here."

"Wait!"

He stopped, not because of Natalia's blunt command, but because she'd proven herself to be more than just the art consultant Bellísima had hired, becoming a professional peer he admired and hoped to work with again in the future. Even more, a friend he'd look up the next time he visited the Windy City.

"What?" he asked, glancing over his shoulder.

When she set down her pen and splayed her hands on the mahogany desktop, he figured he was getting ready to hear another one of her astute observations. Many of which he typically found himself agreeing with.

"Look, I don't know all the details and I especially don't need any of the mushy ones," she told him matter-of-factly. "But when I look at your photographs with her, I am *blown away*. Emotionally, artistically. When you talk about her, you're like some guy in one of those romantic comedies my girlfriends have given up trying to convince me to watch with them."

The kind Anamaría had always dragged him to when they were kids. The kind they had started watching at her place last Friday. Until Movie Night turned into Make Out Night on her couch. In her bedroom. Later, in her shower.

"So." Natalia pushed the leather office chair back and stood. Not that doing so increased her height by much. Although the intensity of her piercing stare could cut anyone down to size when she wanted. "I'm not sure I believe in all that happily-ever-after crap, but if you feel that way about her . . . and have since freaking high school, that's either pathetic or as real as it gets. Por favor, no seas estúpido, do something about it."

Coño, she had that arched-brow, you-know-I'm-right expression down to perfection.

Don't be stupid. Do something about it.

Once again, he found himself unable to argue with her observation.

That meant he had to find Anamaría, make sure she was okay, and finally admit the truth. While he hated the rift between his parents, his father's inability to accept him could no longer force Alejandro to put distance between him and the woman he loved.

"You're right," he told Natalia,

"Of course, I am." She grinned and sank onto the desk chair, her attention moving to the paperwork detailing the evening's sales figures "Fine, go on, get out of here. I'll stay and be my usual brilliant self. You can thank me later."

Alejandro pulled open the office door at the same time the black curtain covering the entrance to the Mi Cuba display across the hallway fluttered aside. His father loomed in the opening, and Alejandro reared back in surprised shock.

They froze and stared at each other in silence.

A son's keen disappointment and resulting anger flooded Alejandro's chest. Why was his papi here? The man had made it glaringly clear to everyone in their familia, and more than likely a few neighbors who overheard him bellowing, that he would set foot in Bellísima the day he added hot dogs to the menu at Miranda's.

Translation: never.

"Victor, salte del medio."

Despite his wife's bid for him to move out of the way, Alejandro's dad stayed rooted to his spot, and she wound up squeezing past him. As soon as his mom spotted Alejandro in the office doorway, she joined them in the game of freeze tag.

Do something about it.

Natalia's no-nonsense advice played back in his mind.

The only "something" Alejandro had done in this battle of wills with his father was leave. His home. His familia. The woman he would always crave and need.

Not anymore.

Alejandro closed the office door, giving him and his parents more privacy. "Hola, Papi, I appreciate you coming."

His mouth a grim line, his dad dipped his head, accepting Alejandro's olive branch. "Sí, pues, I am grateful to have a friend who does not take no for an answer."

He jabbed a beefy hand toward Anamaría's parents, who stood at the end of the short hallway near the Cultures around the Globe collection. Lydia Navarro looked on, her face creased with motherly concern. Her husband exuded his usual air of quiet authority and calm acceptance, the latter something Alejandro had always wanted from his own father.

An indecipherable look passed between the two older men; then Anamaría's dad put his arm around his wife and led her away.

"I'm surprised—"

"I want to—"

Alejandro and his father spoke in unison, each breaking off and gesturing for the other to go first. A strained silence fell between them.

Alejandro crooked a finger and tugged at his shirt collar, the fastened top button suddenly making him feel constricted and hot.

He cleared his throat and motioned to the dark curtained area. "If the Mi Cuba space is empty, why don't we step back inside? The art consultant is finishing some business in the office."

"Elena, por favor, give us a few minutes to speak alone."

Alejandro's mami's worried gaze skipped back and forth between him and her husband.

"I will not cause a scene," his old man grumbled.

"¿Me lo prometes?"

"Sí, vieja, I promise." Gently, he cupped his wife's shoulder, lips curved below his mustache in the first smile Alejandro had seen from his father in weeks. "Our son and I have an overdue conversation. Déjanos."

After patting Alejandro's cheek with a murmured *I'm proud of you, hijo*, his mami did as requested, leaving them and hurrying down the hall to join their friends.

Alejandro followed his father inside the private room. There, surrounded by the photographs that had felt like Alejandro's one true connection to his abuelo's legacy, the weight of familia responsibility settled on his shoulders.

His father's footsteps slowed in front of the Operación Pedro Pan cluster before he crossed to the group commemorating their familia's ties to the beloved island many had fled.

Alejandro's heart hammered in his chest. His papi had accused him of turning his back on his familia, the legacy his abuelo had sacrificed so much for. Would his father view Alejandro's photographs as irreverent? Or as the homage a grateful grandson intended them to be?

Apprehension tightening his gut, Alejandro waited respectfully for his father to take the lead. Seconds ticked by like a bomb counting down to detonation.

"I have not seen this building since I was four years old," his father said in a gruff whisper. He cleared his throat before continuing. "The night before your tío Juan and I had to leave."

"I know." Alejandro had heard the story countless times over the years. It'd been a gauntlet thrown at his feet during their epic fight. Foolishly, Alejandro had reacted by cursing the restaurant, goading his father, who responded by ordering him to leave and never come back.

The bitter taste of shame rose in Alejandro's throat at the memory.

"These photographs." His papi's work-roughened hand pointed toward the original Miranda's, then looped in a circle indicating the smaller images surrounding it. "Todas son—"

His deep, gravelly voice shook, then cracked before he broke off, leaving Alejandro wondering, *They are all what?*

Not within his right to claim as part of his history? Not after disavowing it?

Regret burned in a hot flush down the back of Alejandro's neck as the words he'd yelled at his father all those years ago played through his head, ringing a death knell for their relationship.

I want more than this place!

Dios, if he could only take back those words.

Exert his independence without demeaning those who had sacrificed for him to have the very options laid out before him.

His father stared at their familia photographs, shoulders slack, his throat working to swallow words or emotions Alejandro could only guess his papi didn't want to share. That left it up to him to take the first steps to bridge the distance between them. He had to try because whether he succeeded or not, he wasn't leaving again. At least not for good.

"My presence has caused problems for you and Mami. For that, I am truly sorry, Papi. That has never been my intent." Standing shoulder to shoulder, he caught his father's shift and interested glance his way. Bolstered, Alejandro continued. "What you two have together, it's beautiful. I admire and, hell, even envy, your relationship. I don't want to be a problem for you two, but Papi, I can't stay away anymore. I don't want to."

"I don't want that, either. None of us do, hijo," his father said, his voice thick with emotion. Turning back to the photographs, his chest rose and fell on a shuddering breath. His fingers shook as they hovered inches away from the protective glass covering the portrait of the original Miranda's.

The blend of nostalgia and longing stamping his jowled face

looked similar to the throat-clogging, chest-tightening ache Alejandro had always felt, but rarely admitted, in those rare moments over the years when he had allowed himself to think about home, his familia. Anamaría.

"What you have done here, hijo. These pieces of us," his father said. "Of nuestra historía."

Our history.

Not *my*, but *ours*.

Hope sprouted a tiny bud in a dark corner of Alejandro's soul.

"And here. The way you honor those of us whose parents sent us with little more than faith and dreams and determination." His papi ambled over to the images of Pedro Pan children, all now adults. He pointed at the photograph of Alejandro's uncle, his father's older brother, tall palms and verdant bushes surrounding him in his backyard in Miami. Tío Juan clutched an old yellowed photograph of the two brothers taken moments after they had landed in Miami. Scared. Uncertain. Already missing their parents and abuelos.

"When did you visit your tío Juan?" his father asked. "Él no me dijo nada."

"He didn't say anything to you because we both felt you didn't care to know," Alejandro answered truthfully. Though the words hurt him to admit. "I mean, my work, even a passion project like this one, has never been of much interest to you."

His father's broad shoulders sagged on a heavy exhalation. He hung his head, reaching up to rub at his nape as if the same tension gripping Alejandro held him in its clutches, too. "I have not made it easy for you, hijo."

The gruff admission was a gross understatement. And yet Alejandro had to accept his own fault in their rift. Guilt weighed on him as he hobbled closer to his father. "I gave you good reason to be angry . . . worse, disappointed . . . in me."

"You were—"

"Immature. Full of youthful ego and ignorance." A mistake he had recently come to realize would only be rectified if he stopped acting like a child, blaming others and taking the easy route by running away. Never turning around to follow that route home.

"Bueno, I will not argue that." His papi turned to face him, his expression inscrutable under the muted gallery lighting. "But your work. In your own way, hijo, you honor us, our familia. The legacy my papi wanted for us."

That tiny bud of hope grew bigger, gaining strength in the sunlight of his father's praise.

Gripping his shoulder, his father pulled Alejandro closer, wrapping him in a tight bear hug.

"Gracias, hijo. Your work brings my papi and what we left behind to life in a way I never expected. Me da tanto orgullo," his father rasped.

Stunned by his father's admission of pride in his work, it took Alejandro a moment to return the unexpected, long-awaited paternal embrace. Relief flooded him, elation dragging pent-up words from his lips as he hugged his father.

"Perdóname, papá," he apologized. "I didn't mean it. I've only ever wanted to make you proud, in my own way."

"Lo sé. I know that now." His large hand pounded on Alejandro's back, a reassuring weight that knocked away the guilt and self-reproach. "I should have tried to understand, instead of pushing you away. But you are home now, hijo, where you belong."

Tears pricked Alejandro's eyes, and he squeezed them shut, overwhelmed with gratitude.

A shocked gasp had him and his father turning to find Alejandro's mother standing in the curtained entry. Señora Navarro stood at her side, an equally astounded expression on her lightly lined face.

Tears pooled in his mami's eyes, spilling down her round cheeks. She hurried into the small space, her low heels tapping against the faux-hardwood flooring. Arms wide, she wrapped her husband and son in a hug as a sob tore from her lips.

They held each other for several moments. Then his mother cupped her husband's face, rising up on her toes as he bent to brush his lips against hers. They murmured apologies and shared another soft kiss while Alejandro looked on with relief.

She spun to Alejandro, cupping his face like she'd done with her husband, whispering prayers of thanks as she pressed her cheek to his.

When she finally released him, Alejandro couldn't help but peer past her toward the entrance, searching for the one person who would understand better than anyone else what this moment meant to him.

Disappointment soured his mouth when Anamaría didn't appear behind her mother, who still hovered near the curtain.

As if she read his intent, Señora Navarro shook her head with a sad frown.

"She hasn't come back yet?" he asked, having touched base with Señora Navarro earlier while skirting the crowd looking for her daughter.

"No, mijo, I'm sorry."

He dug his phone out of his pants pocket. A growl of frustration rumbled up his throat at the blank screen. No text message replies. No returned phone calls.

"Enrique?" he asked.

His best friend's mother shook her head again.

"¡Coño! I don't understand what happened?" Frustrated, Alejandro drove his fingers through his hair. "I have no idea why she left or where she went. Or how to find her."

"I do." A hand on her elbow, Señor Navarro guided his wife into the now-crowded viewing area. "Elena, saca tu teléfono, por favor."

His wife unzipped the black purse hanging at her left hip. Dipping her hand inside, she extracted her phone as he had requested.

"I am assuming you still make the kids share their location, ha?" the Navarro patriarch asked.

Both mamis exchanged knowing grins.

Understanding dawned in Alejandro like the bright orange sun peeking over the Atlantic horizon at Higgs Beach.

Impatience clawed at him while Señora Navarro tapped at her cell screen. Her red nail skimmed over the surface before she tapped one final time. Her head slowly rose, her gaze meeting his. Trust . . . and a clear warning . . . flashed in the hazel eyes her only daughter had inherited.

Straightening his shoulders, he faced Anamaría's parents— humble, hopeful, determined.

"La quiero," he said, going on to repeat the words he hadn't allowed himself to think, much less say out loud, in over a decade. "I love her. I've never stopped."

Her lips curving in a gracious smile, Señora Navarro handed her phone to him.

Chapter 20

Anamaría kicked the sandy playground dirt, grimacing when tiny grains dusted over the front of her sandaled stilettos, wedging uncomfortably between her toes.

She should have driven home after dropping Enrique off at his place like she had promised when he balked at her leaving in his car, alone and upset. The detour to Higgs Beach and Astro City Park had been unintentional.

Her mind . . . her memories . . . her heart had led her back to where it had all begun.

Where she and Alejandro had taken that first step. Dios, back then it had felt like such a huge leap. A heady, scary, titillating first kiss that moved them out of the friend zone.

Appropriately, it'd been July Fourth weekend, too.

Perhaps this was a natural place for her to snip the frayed threads of their relationship and begin anew.

Closing her eyes, she gripped the cool metal chains pressing against her shoulders and pushed off the sandy dirt. The flexible rubber seat swung back, then forward, her loose hair and the skirt of her chiffon dress fluttering in the breeze. Legs pumping, arms extended, she leaned backward, willing the swing's rhythmic motion to calm her roiling thoughts. Dull her misery. The ocean's familiar, salty-sulfur smell filled her lungs as she compelled herself to finally . . . finally . . . let go.

Of her adolescent dreams. Of her longing for a relationship with Alejandro that simply could not exist. Of the self-inflicted chains that shackled her dreams. Of him.

Sure, she'd have to face Alejandro again before she left for the fitness expo on Wednesday. She owed herself, and him, the chance to say a proper good-bye. Achieve the closure they had promised each other. It's what she needed to move on with her life, whether her heart agreed or not.

By the time she returned from her trip, Alejandro should be gone, back to Atlanta or wherever his agent booked for him, given his doctor's okay.

She and Brandon would be full steam ahead planning for their first Key West retreat, looking forward to the fall and scheduling another. With more AllFit events on her calendar and an uptick in online-training clients, she'd focus on all the new opportunities. No longer tied to the past.

Tire's squealed nearby and she glanced over her shoulder to see a gray sedan speeding around the curve between the Casa Marina and the public tennis courts. The car veered sharply toward the parking lot in front of Astro City, screeching to a halt at an odd angle that took up two spaces alongside Enrique's SUV.

She scowled at the darkened vehicle, annoyed by the driver's carelessness. Sure, the park was empty except for her. At 8:30 P.M., the families with young children were long gone and the teens who would hang out until the park and beach closed and the cops kicked them out hadn't finished their primping at home. Their arrival would be her cue to leave.

Now she hoped the reckless driver would take the cue that a single car in the parking lot probably meant its occupant wanted to be alone.

Instead, the driver's door opened. A dome light flickered on inside the vehicle, illuminating the occupant. Anamaría's hands tightened around the swing chains, the curved ridges digging into her palms, when she recognized Alejandro.

What was he doing here?

Momentum carried her swing forward and she stabbed at the ground with her feet to stop herself. Her right ankle twisted on a rock, and she winced at the sharp twinge. Hobbling to a stand, she tucked her hair behind her ears, then squared her shoulders to face him.

Alejandro exited the car and craned his neck over the sedan's roof to peer inside her brother's vehicle. He jabbed a hand through his hair and turned toward the park, spotting her immediately.

The air crackled between them. One of the streetlights flickered high above the sidewalk, its yellowish light trembling around them.

Even fifty or so feet away from him, the intensity of his gaze made Anamaría's stomach clench. Anger, disappointment, and resolve swirled inside her. She grasped on to the resolve, straightening her spine.

In the melding of the evening's darkness and the wavering streetlights she couldn't quite make out his expression, but she noticed that he had ditched his crutch and now wore the protective CAM boot over his left dress pants leg. He moved toward her, each step-limp matching her rapidly pounding pulse.

The park equipment and smattering of trees cast long shadows across the patches of grass and sandy dirt, falling over him when he came into their path. He had removed his jacket at some point, and now his white button-down, the sleeves pushed up to reveal his forearms, gleamed under the glow of garish light.

His mouth a thin line, his angular features hardened under a fierce frown, he drew closer.

Anamaría stayed put. Not allowing herself to meet him halfway despite her concern for his injured leg. He'd been the one to leave before. He was the one intent on leaving again. Let him come to her now.

Alejandro stopped several feet away, jaw clenched, his gaze

searching hers for answers to questions she more than likely didn't care to answer.

"You said you'd be back. What happened?" His tone straddled the line between worry and accusation.

"I figured you were busy." She hitched a shoulder, pretending it was no big deal. "Natalia was selling pieces like fresh coconut water on a hellish summer day. I needed some fresh air."

Hands deep in his pant pockets, he eyed her intently and took a step toward her. "What's going on? Talk to me, Princes—"

"Stop."

Alejandro flinched at her brusque command. His confused gaze bounced between the open palms she held out to ward him off and her eyes.

"You should go back to Bellísima. I'm sure your familia and friends . . . your fans . . . are wondering where you are."

"I don't care about them."

Exactly! That was the problem. All he seemed to care about were *his* goals. *His* dreams. No matter where they took him or whom he left behind.

Part of her knew she was being unfair. Their new relationship dynamic had been her idea. She was the one breaking the rules this time. But that didn't make it hurt any less, and she couldn't seem to stop herself from lashing out at him.

"You *should* care about them. And I should be home packing for my trip. This—" She gestured back and forth between them. "Our friends with benefits arrangement has been . . . I don't know, fun?" She nearly choked on the lie.

"Don't do that. Don't cheapen what we have."

"Ha!" she scoffed, air whooshing out of her in a harsh, disbelieving breath. "What we have? And what exactly is that? Other than something whose time has come to an end."

Despising the weakness inside her that ached for him to refute her words, Anamaría shifted to stare at the empty tennis courts across from the Casa Marina resort. Everywhere she looked held memories of them together. From the resort where they'd held their senior prom to the tennis courts' tiny darkened parking lot where they'd shared their first kiss under a firework-lit sky to their picnic spot on the darkened beach across the street. Ages and heartaches and dashed dreams ago.

She sensed him approaching, then caught his shadow spreading across the sandy ground beside hers. Doggedly she kept her gaze turned away from him, afraid he'd see the pain she wasn't sure she could hide.

"Our time together hasn't been some tawdry affair. Not to me," he said.

Her eyes fluttered closed, her head refusing to believe what her heart wanted to easily accept.

"Every moment we've shared this summer has been a thousand times better than any I've dreamed about over the past decade. And believe me, I've spent many restless nights dreaming about you. My subconscious is unable to deny how much you mean to me, even if I try."

"Yeah, well, maybe I didn't have that problem."

Liar.

"The selfish part of me hopes that's not true," he said, his voice a gravel rough. "But an even bigger part hates the thought of you having been as miserable as me."

His fingertips grazed her collarbone as he grasped a lock of her hair, running the pad of his thumb over the silky strands. Fissions of awareness skittered through her chest, across her breasts, and lower. Silently she cursed her body's reaction to simple touch.

"Look, we're both leaving soon," she said, gathering her hair at her nape, then twisting it and leaving it to drape over her opposite shoulder, out of his reach. "I figure, let's end on a high note, you know? Your success tonight mere days before my first big AllFit trip seems appropriate. No need to drag out a good-bye before going our separate ways, like we agreed."

The words were like shards of glass forced down her throat, leaving her raw and bleeding from the lie.

A humid breeze set her dress skirt fluttering around her knees and upper calves, and her traitorous mind recalled his soft kisses along her skin, his mischievous grin as he made his way up her legs, along her inner thigh, higher.

She swallowed, fighting the urge to forget about tomorrow and simply take what they could have tonight. But that wasn't enough anymore. She'd been foolish to ever think a few weeks would be enough.

"And what if I changed my mind?" he asked.

Her breath shuddered, then caught. He wouldn't be so cruel as to make a joke like that. Would he?

Alejandro's hand slipped around her waist to the small of her back. The slight pressure of his fingertips urged her to step closer, but he didn't push, leaving the decision up to her. Unable to resist, she leaned into him, tipping her chin to meet his gaze.

The earnestness in his dark eyes shone in the streetlight's glow, calling to the part of her that wasn't ready, might never be ready, to let him go.

Gently, he caressed her jaw, heightening her need for more of his touch. As if he read her thoughts, he cupped the juncture of her neck and shoulder, and she swore his palm seared her skin.

She knew she should step back, stop putting off the inevitable end. But his thumb swept over the line of her collarbone and her resolve threatened to ooze out of her like guava jelly seeping from the flakey crust of a pastel de guayaba.

"What if I don't want us to go our separate ways?" he asked. "What if I don't want 'closure' like we talked about?"

"You're not making any sense. We both know this isn't where you want to be. It's like you told Marcelo when you turned down his job offer tonight; there's so much opportunity out there. You can't stay here."

"Yes, I— Wait, you overheard us?" Guilt flashed in his eyes, confirming her original conclusion. "Let me explain—"

"There's no need." Shaking her head, she stepped out of his arms and quickly moved behind her swing. As if the flimsy chains and rubber seat were a barrier suitable for keeping them apart.

"Everything's clear to me now. It's not that you can't stay in Key West and pursue photography. It's that you won't."

"That's not entirely the truth."

"Did you turn down a job with Marcelo that would have kept you here for . . . what was it you said . . . six months?"

"Yes, but—"

"Right. Because you can't 'stick around here.'" Her fingers bent in air quotes around the hurtful reason he'd given Marcelo for turning down the gallery owner's offer. "Because what we have isn't enough."

"That's not—"

"Because *I'm* not enough!" The torturous words were ripped from her wounded soul.

An agonized expression scrunched Alejandro's handsome features as he stumbled forward, his CAM boot dragging through the sandy dirt. He grabbed on to the swing chains, his large hands covering hers. "You're wrong. It's me. I've always known you could do better than a man whose own father is ashamed of him."

His raw, gut-wrenching admission shocked her into silence. Stark pain deepened the grooves on his forehead, carving what should have been laugh not sorrow lines on the sides of his mouth.

"I fucked up before," he went on, the words spilling from him like a torrent that rained down on her. "We were both too young, and I was like a greedy kid needing you to pick me. Choose me over everything, hell, *everyone* else."

He flung an arm out in a wide circle as if indicating the world around them. The swing chain swayed with his jerky motion and he teetered sideways on his good leg. She grabbed on to his shirt to keep him from falling.

"You okay?" she asked softly, once he'd grasped the chain with both hands again and had regained his balance.

He wiped the sweat off his brow with his sleeve, then nodded, his expression solemn. "I know that my expectations of you were selfish and unfair. Worse, I blamed you for my mistakes and my papi's harsh dismissal. If I could go back . . . if I could change things . . ."

His throat worked as he shook his head, a visible loss for words.

She longed to cup his cheek, comfort the young man who'd been hurt and disillusioned by a father who had probably felt the same way. Both unable to communicate with the other.

"I was scared," she admitted, surprising herself by sharing the truth she had never told anyone. Not even her cousin Vanessa. "Even back then, you were larger than life. Confident and daring. Doing everything you set out to do, despite your dad. But I wasn't sure how I could fit in to all of that without losing myself. Before I could even know who or what I was meant to be. I needed to find my place and how I could do my own good in this crazy world."

"You have." His hands softly squeezed hers around the swing chains. "Do you know how many people I've run into here, not to mention your on-line clients and followers I've never met, all of whom can attest to how you've helped them live healthier lives?"

His compliment was a spirit-lifting gift.

"And you've brought awareness to cultures, people, and causes everywhere. Educating others in a beautifully artistic way," she told him, proud of his work, even though it inevitably took him away from her.

Alejandro's lips curved with the ghost of a smile, but sadness lingered in his dark eyes. "I'd say, we've done good."

"Yes, we have. Apart." The last word stung, but she refused to lie to herself anymore.

Alejandro's hesitant smile disappeared.

Across the street, a rowdy group of people emerged from Salute! On the Beach, drawing Anamaría's attention. Their laughter and calls good night carried on the humid breeze, and she watched as they climbed behind the wheels of their cars, waving out their windows as they drove away. Unaware of the bittersweet conversation taking place in the shadowy park.

"My father came to my show tonight."

Alejandro's barely heard whisper was so unexpected, several thudding heartbeats passed before it registered in Anamaría's shocked brain.

"Your father didn't have an emergency at the fire station," Alejandro continued. "He went to Miranda's, where he convinced Papi to, in his own words, 'get his head out of his ass' and come to Bellísima."

"No wonder he wasn't answering his phone," she murmured. She had called him several times during the drive to Enrique's apartment, but their father never picked up. "I can't imagine your dad accepting that ultimatum without a fight."

"Me either. But then again, your dad isn't one to mess with. But . . . when my papi and I stood in the Mi Cuba collection together . . . God, Anamaría, I wish you could have seen him." His face lit up with pure joy, and she nearly flung her arms around him in a congratulations hug.

"He was so moved," Alejandro said, his voice raspy with awe. "He actually thanked me. And he said he was . . . he was . . ."

"Proud," she finished, absolutely thrilled for him, and his father.

Alejandro grinned. An endearing version of his sexy smirk that still managed to make her toes curl.

"What did your mom say? She was pretty pissed at him when I left."

"Thankfully they made up tonight. I mean, I've been pretty worried about them. She's barely said a word to him the past two weeks." Alejandro gazed at her, remorse shadowing his eyes. "I should have told you, but I was ashamed. That's why I didn't think I should stay. Because I couldn't be the wedge that drove my parents apart. I'd never forgive myself. But that didn't mean I was ready to give up on us."

Anamaría ducked her head, afraid to consider the possibility that they could still be an "us" with him unwilling to stay and her unwilling to leave her familia for good. Dejected, she poked at a tuft of grass with her toe. "That's wonderful about your parents, Ale. And I'm really happy for you and your dad."

"Yes, it was a wonderful evening. Only, it wasn't perfect because while my parents made up, and my papi and I finally found some common ground, there was something missing."

She glanced up at him when he stopped, leaving her to guess what he referred to.

An expectant expression stamped his face. He tugged on the swing chains, and Anamaría shuffled a baby step closer. "Some-*one* missing."

Hope flared like a July Fourth sparkler waving in her chest at the love shining in his dark eyes.

"There's only ever been you for me, Princesa. You've always owned my heart. And if you'll forgive me for taking so damn long to make things right between us, to be the man you deserve, I'll spend the rest of my life proving how much I love and treasure you."

Tears burned in her eyes. Love for him swelled within her, stealing her breath. Robbing her of the ability to form coherent words.

Alejandro must have taken her silence as doubt, because he released his hold on her hands, then reached in between the chains to wrap her in his embrace. His woodsy, patchouli scent enveloped her, and she breathed it in like an aphrodisiac.

"I know your business is taking off, and mine leads me all over the place. But we can make this work. Travel together when we can. Returning here, to each other." He pulled back, his hands moving to cradle her jaw. His right thumb traced the edge of her lower lip as his gaze strayed to her mouth, then up to meet hers. "Go on your trip this week. Be your incredible self. And I'll be here, at home, waiting for you. If you'll have me—"

Anamaría lifted on her toes to cover his mouth with hers.

He groaned, tightening his arms around her and deepening their kiss. His tongue glided across her lips and she opened for him, savoring the taste of Prosecco and mint. Of him.

Needing to be closer, she slid her arms around his waist, flinching when the swing's rubber seat bit into her lower thigh.

They broke apart long enough for her to shove the swing aside, then step into his open arms where she belonged. His sexy smile greeted her before he stooped to drop a kiss on her forehead, her nose, her—

"Te quiero," she murmured as his lips feathered over hers.

His grin widened and her soul sang. "I love you more."

The loud bang of a firework sounded from several streets over. Heads pressed together, they craned their necks to stare up at the pink squiggly lines worming their way out from a tiny center point to create a poofy ball across the inky black sky.

Another shot blasted through the quiet streets, followed by the flash of bright orange lights twinkling and crackling high above.

Content, Anamaría snuggled against Alejandro's chest. They'd come full circle, the two of them. One Fourth of July ages ago, they'd taken that first tentative step as adolescents bitten by young love. Tonight, they took a confident, new first step as adults, committing to each other as well as their individual and shared goals.

"No matter where our jobs take us, as long as our hearts remain anchored together, I'd say we're all good. Right?" She gazed up at him, no longer afraid to let her love for him blaze in her eyes.

"More than good. I'd say, perfect."

She smiled with delight, and Alejandro dipped his head to seal their promise with another heady kiss.

Acknowledgements

A good chunk of the first draft of this manuscript, plus revisions and copyedits, were completed during a difficult yet important year—a pandemic, social distancing, separation from those we care about most, marches and movements demanding racial and social justice and reform. In the midst of it all, technology helped us stay close with loved ones and make new connections, while allowing our voices to be heard!

More than ever, during this emotional time, I relied on many to help keep me sane and motivated. Mil gracias to all who encouraged, supported, cheered, threatened with a chancla, or in some way helped Anamaría's and Alejandro's book become a reality.

Here are some key individuals who made this book possible:

To the firefighters in Key West and Monroe County who put their lives on the line every shift, and especially to those who let me hang out and pick their brains while researching my Keys to Love series, especially the Sellers brothers and Daniela, who brought Anamaría to life in remarkable ways . . . any discrepancies in this book are all my own.

To Hector, whose photography skills are divine and whose patience during a looooong phone call with me helped form the foundation for Alejandro's passion for his craft. ¡Gracias, mi amigo, te lo agradezco!

To author sister-friends who via text, DM, PM, Facetime, Zoom, Google Hangout, critiques/feedback, and more helped me keep on keeping on in the midst of the insanity and doubts . . . Farrah, Kwana, Sonali, Falguni, Jamie, Barbara, Sally, Virginia, Tracy, Amy, Tracey, Tif, Michele, and Nina . . . I can't wait until we can retreat in person and brainstorm over drinks together!

Para mis amigas-hermanas en la comunidad de autoras Latinx-Rom, especialmente Mia, Alexis y Sabrina . . . from 4ChicasChat to a retreat house with more, I'm exceedingly blessed to know, love, and learn from you all! May our numbers continue to grow, and our stories continue to be shared and appreciated. Mil gracias for the sisterhood! Abrazos.

To my agent and editor team—Rebecca, Esi, and Norma—thank you for being such an integral part of bringing my island home and the Navarro familia to life. I'm exceedingly thankful to work with you.

Para mi familia . . . Mami y Papi, my sister and main brainstormer-beta reader, Jackie, my three girls, Alexa, Gabby, and Belle . . . when I'm pulling all-nighters, needing "get off social media" reminders or a partner to bounce an idea or scenario around with, or when it's time to pop a bottle of bubbly to celebrate good news or submitting a manuscript, one or all of you are always there. Life can be hard at times. Life definitely throws us wicked curves. Life (and a pandemic) may keep us apart. But through it all this remains true . . . my love for you all and my thanks for the blessing of our familia is boundless. ¡Los quiero mucho!

And of course, to you, dear reader, for choosing to escape to Key West with my beloved Navarro familia for a second, or maybe the first, time, with *Anchored Hearts*. My hope is that you dive into the books in my Keys to Love series and feel as if you've traveled to Key West, made some new friends, came to appreciate island life and the Cuban-Latinx culture, and were able to forget about life's stresses for a while. I wish you and your loved ones much joy, good health, laughter, and love.

Abrazos/hugs,
Priscilla

Don't miss the first romantic escape

in the Keys to Love series,

Island Affair,

available now

wherever books are sold.

Connect with Us

Visit us online at
KensingtonBooks.com
to read more from your favorite authors, see books
by series, view reading group guides, and more.

Join us on social media

for sneak peeks, chances to win books and prize packs,
and to share your thoughts with other readers.

facebook.com/kensingtonpublishing
twitter.com/kensingtonbooks

Tell us what you think!

To share your thoughts, submit a review,
or sign up for our eNewsletters, please visit:
KensingtonBooks.com/TellUs.